Raves for
THE ASSASSIN

"Selena McCaffrey [is] sure to give J. D. Robb's Eve Dallas a run for the money in this rapid-fire first novel...Butler delivers a taut tale with clever twists and turns, lots of well-drawn characters and an unexpected ending....A fine read that will surely bring suspense and crime drama fans back for the next book in the series."

—*Publishers Weekly*

"Butler has created an unforgettable new heroine whose future adventures promise to be just as riveting."

—*Romantic Times,* Top Pick!

"*The Assassin* delivers the goods: fast action, surprise twists, and a heroine who's positively killer with a gun!"

—Lisa Gardner

"Wow! Fast-paced, sexy suspense: *The Assassin* is a thrill ride I didn't want to end."

—Karen Robards

"Compulsively r⋯⋯⋯⋯"
⋯⋯⋯zine

"Gritty and sex⋯⋯⋯⋯iller
are a dynamite ⋯⋯

⋯Kane

Deep Cover

RACHEL BUTLER

A Dell Book

DEEP COVER
A Dell Book / December 2005

Published by Bantam Dell
A Division of Random House, Inc.
New York, New York

ISBN-13: 978-0-440-24121-8
ISBN-10: 0-440-24121-9

Printed in the United States of America
Published simultaneously in Canada

www.bantamdell.com

OPM 10 9 8 7 6 5 4 3 2 1

Deep
Cover

1

Selena McCaffrey had had one hell of a day.

A .45 gripped loosely in both hands, she sighted on a paper silhouette target seventy-five feet away. She'd emptied the previous magazine center mass in the target's chest. This one was going into the head.

She double-tapped the target—fired two shots in rapid succession—then did it again. The ground around her was littered with brass. In the time since the owner of the shooting range had left her alone to relieve her frustration, the sun had set and the flood lamps had come on, but she didn't feel much better.

The day hadn't started badly. She'd gone for a run that morning and then put in a good six hours at the easel. Then she'd opened her door to find Special Agent King of the FBI on her stoop, and everything had gone to hell.

It sounded so reasonable the way the FBI put it. She had a fourteen-year pseudo–father-daughter relationship with Henry Daniels, better known to her as William Davis, head of an extensive drug operation. He had always intended for her to take over the business someday, and now that he was out of commission, the FBI was pressuring her to fulfill his wish—and in the process, help them shut down the operation once and for all. If she cooperated, they would be willing to forget their list of charges against her. If she didn't...

Sweat trickling down her spine, she fired the last of the

bullets in the magazine, set the pistol on the table beside her, pulled off the ear protectors, and combed her fingers through her hair. Summer nights in Oklahoma weren't much different from back home in Key West—hot and muggy—though she missed the ocean breezes. In Tulsa the best they could offer was the Arkansas River, sluggish and brown, and the scents of the oil refinery on the west bank. But that was all right. She hadn't come for the weather, and she wasn't staying for it, either.

Clenching her jaw against the curses she wanted to shout into the night, she reached for the box of bullets. A puff of dust rose from the concrete only inches from her hand and she stared at it—and the small neat hole left behind—for an instant. The same instant it took another bullet to glance off the cement and ricochet into the night. Instinctively she dove to the ground, taking cover behind the nearest half wall. From her position she could see her gun on the table—and fewer than ten rounds of ammo in the box beside it. She hadn't had a chance to reload, and the shooter probably knew that.

He couldn't have picked a better place for an attack. The neighborhood was largely industrial, and the people who worked nearby were accustomed to gunfire. Even if anyone was around that late, they wouldn't think to call the police.

Another shot splintered the concrete above her head, showering fragments and dust on her skin. She flinched, and the switchblade in her waistband dug into her skin. With the blade and her extensive martial arts training, she'd always felt confident in any situation, but neither was of any use against an attacker secreted in the darkness. He could kill her, then disappear with no one the wiser.

Damned if she was going to die without a fight.

She shimmied on her belly along the length of the cinder-block wall, stirring up dust. When she reached the far end, she drew a deep breath, murmured a prayer, then eased to a crouch. There was no sound—no heavy breathing, no fumbled reloading, no sirens racing to her assistance. Nothing but the thudding of her own heart.

One, two, three, she counted, then launched herself around the corner toward the table where her weapon lay. Bullets followed, biting into the ground, the cement, the wood posts that supported the overhanging roof. She hit the ground with a thud, rolling, reaching up to grab the pistol and the box of bullets. Relief rushed over her when her blind groping found both. She rolled again, came up on her feet in one fluid movement, then dove once more for the cover of the cinder-block wall.

Her hands were steady as she fed the bullets into the clip. Once the final round was in place, she shoved it into the butt of the pistol, chambered a round, and pushed the remaining ammo into her pocket as she rose onto her knees.

The angle of the shots indicated they'd come from the same location, the wooded hill to the south of the range. Presumably that meant there was only one shooter, and he had a bird's-eye view of the entire area. He knew she was alone, knew her odds of making it to the squat building that fronted the range or to her car in the parking lot beyond were minimal. He could pick her off like a sitting duck.

She was forty feet from the door, and the wall that currently shielded her was the last cover available. The door opened into a hallway that ran the length of the building. On the right at the back was the indoor range, used during the worst of Oklahoma's inhospitable summers and icy winters. At the front was the office and the armory, both heavily secured. She was a fast runner, but not fast enough, not with the shooter's vantage point and the flood lamps that turned darkness into day.

Unless he couldn't see her.

She quickly sighted on the nearest light and fired. The bulb exploded with a pop. She hit a second one, and a third, even as the shooter opened up on her protective cover with a hail of automatic weapon fire.

The instant the last lamp went out, she surged to her feet and made a furious dash for the door. Clods of dirt exploded around her and something hit her arm with enough force to send her staggering against the building. Biting her lip against the pain, she jerked the door open and raced down the dark hall. Wherever the assassin was parked, she had no doubt she could reach her Thunderbird before he made his way down the hill. Seconds were all she needed...unless he had an accomplice waiting outside.

She refused to let the thought slow her. Gripping the pistol in one hand, she dug in her pocket for her keys with the other. As she burst outside, she unlocked the car with the remote, yanked the door open, and threw herself inside. The engine roared to life, and the tires squealed wildly as she backed up, then accelerated out of the empty parking lot, barely making the turn onto the street before stomping the gas pedal to the floor.

She'd gone two miles, the speedometer pushing eighty, before the adrenaline rush deserted her. Her foot eased up on the pedal. The throbbing in her left arm was growing too strong to ignore. When she reached back with her right hand, her fingers came away sticky with blood.

In the last seconds her breathing had gone beyond rapid to nothing less than a pant, and her entire body was starting to shake. She turned off the street into a shopping center that was closed for the night, drove around one end to the back, and parked in a loading zone, where tall walls shielded her on three sides. Pressing a tissue to the wound in her arm, she closed her eyes and forced herself to breathe, calmness and control in, fear and pain out. When the trembling had stopped, when her heart rate had returned to some semblance of normal, she reached for her cell phone and dialed one of only two numbers stored in it.

"Tony, this is Selena," she said when he answered, surprised by how calm she sounded. "I was wondering if you could come meet me. I think I've been shot."

2

The street was quiet when Scott Fleming pulled into his driveway, inching along as the garage door slid up to reveal his wife's SUV. It seemed he always got home late—for him, at least, working for the FBI had never been a forty-hour-a-week job—but this night it was several hours later than usual. No doubt the kids were already tucked into bed. Jen was probably in bed, too, watching *Frasier* or *Cheers* on the tube.

He parked his GOV—government-owned vehicle—beside the Lexus, watched the garage door close in the rearview mirror, then climbed out, gathering his briefcase and suit coat. Holding them in one hand, he loosened his tie with the other as he went into the house, where he paused to set the security alarm for the night.

A few dim lights shone downstairs. He walked through the house, turning them off and admiring everything along the way—the leather furniture, the giant-screen television and home theater system, the gourmet kitchen, though Jen was anything but a gourmet cook. He listened to the sound of his footsteps on the imported marble tile and drew his fingertips across the textured surface of the faux-painted wall, then followed his nightly ritual of turning the dimmer switch on the chandelier in the entry, a one-of-a-kind blown-glass thing, until the lights went dark. Then he started up the curving staircase.

The house was a showplace—four thousand square feet of class, taste, and refinement...not bad for a man who'd grown up on the wrong side of Memphis, who'd gone hungry through most of his youth, worn ill-fitting hand-me-downs, and been harassed and bullied every single day of his life. It was much more than a home to him. It was a symbol of how far he'd come, of how much he'd achieved.

A symbol, a sly voice whispered in his head, that was slowly crushing him under its weight.

There were four bedrooms on the second floor, along with a game room for the kids, stocked with everything they could possibly need to be entertained. He stopped in Brianne's doorway and watched her sleep for a moment, then did the same across the hall at Brad's room before continuing to the master suite at the end of the corridor.

He never walked into the bedroom without marveling that it was bigger than the entire house where he'd grown up with his parents and two sisters. There was a sitting area with a fireplace, a whirlpool tub in the bathroom big enough for two, a bed big enough for four. His closet was the size of a normal bedroom, and Jen's was even bigger. It was luxurious.

Wasteful, the voice whispered again. *Indecent.*

He'd been right about Jen. She was curled up on her side in bed, her blond hair falling forward over her face. Like the house, she was a symbol, too—the youngest daughter of an old Oklahoma family that had made its fortune in the oil boom days and secured it with diversified investments. She'd had the kind of upbringing he had never even dreamed about—nannies, private schools, chauffeurs, debutante balls. She'd had her choice of rich, powerful, socially elite suitors, but she'd married *him.*

Damned if he would give her reason to regret it.

When he shut off the television, she stirred, her blue eyes

fluttering open, her smile sleepy. "You're late." She fanned the air with one elegant hand when he sat down next to her. "And a bit ripe, too. What have you been doing?"

"I had a flat."

"And ruined your shirt." She fingered a rip in the white fabric before yawning. "You should have called someone."

"Hey, I can change a flat. And it's just a shirt. I'll get a new one." That was one of the benefits of success—no more hand-me-downs, no patching or making do. When he needed something, he bought it. More importantly, when he *wanted* something, he bought it. "You go back to sleep, babe. I'm going to take a shower."

She made a kissy-face at him, then snuggled into the covers once more.

He went into the bathroom that was all marble, chrome, and glass, and stripped naked, tossing his shirt in the wastebasket, the rest of his clothes in a pile on the floor. His gold-and-diamond cuff links went into a dish on the counter along with his watch and wedding band, then he stepped into the shower. As the water beat down on him from four separate heads, he thought about the real reason he'd been late getting home. He never told Jen anything she didn't want to know, and he was pretty sure she wouldn't want to know *this*.

Truth was, they were in deep trouble. He was swimming in debt and about to go under. That night, right or wrong, he'd done something about it.

Sonny Yates's primary place of business was a bar so shabby that it couldn't in fairness be called a *dive*. It sat in a clearing on the outskirts of Savannah, cypress and weathered shingles sheltered by tall sugar pines, just yards from the banks of a sluggish stream that flowed past the city to join the Savannah

River and, so on enough, the Atlantic. There was no sign out-side. Customers parked their pickups on sandy dirt littered with crushed shells and pine straw, and they drank away their cares inside the unadorned walls. Anyone looking for food, fancy drinks, or friendly conversation looked else-where, and anyone not interested in minding his own busi-ness damn sure went somewhere else.

Normally Sonny conducted business from a table in the darkest corner of the bar, his back to the wall, a cell phone on the table in front of him, and a Glock tucked into his belt. Not so that night.

The midnight air hung low and heavy. It was ripe with smells of the mill upriver, the sweet fragrance of pine, the salty tang of distant ocean, the damp and decay of the marsh. Water lapped against the shore, and an occasional fish broke the surface before submerging again.

Four men stood in front of him, shoulder to shoulder. Their breathing was ragged, raspy, and in spite of the rich scents surrounding them, he could smell their fear. Good. They *should* be afraid.

Sonny stood in the shadows, unmoving. So did J.T., off to his left. Devlin and LeRoy, flanking the four guests, were more restless, swiping at no-see-'ems, tiny little gnats that could eat a man alive, and drying sweat from their faces. Their constant movement emphasized his own lack of it, giv-ing his stillness a more ominous air. Not that much could be more ominous than what he had planned.

Under ordinary circumstances, he would have discussed the situation with Mr. Davis before taking this kind of action, but his calls to Damon Long, Davis's go-between, had gone unanswered, as had his calls to Davis himself. Besides, while he might work for Davis—for the time being—he was still his own boss. He didn't need the old man's permission to deal with thieving employees.

He stepped into the thin light cast by the moon and stopped a half dozen feet in front of the man on the left.

He lifted one hand slowly, and a shot rang out as J.T. put a bullet dead center in the man's forehead. The impact knocked the man into the water, where his body bobbed a few yards downstream before sinking.

Sonny shifted his attention to the second man in line. He was already shaking, and a sour odor indicated he'd pissed himself.

"Where's my dope?"

"I—I don't know. I s-swear I don't."

"Pat, isn't it?" Sonny shook his head. "I'm giving you a chance to make things right, Pat. Tell me what you did with the shipment, and we'll work something out."

Number four in line, captain of the fishing boat whose catch had gone missing, snorted loudly, but Sonny ignored him. He would get to him soon enough.

"I—I don't know nothin', Mr. Y-Yates," Pat stammered. "It was all the c-captain's doin'. We didn't know nothin' un-until it was too late." To his left, the third crew member nodded anxiously.

Pat was probably telling the truth. None of these guys was particularly bright. They knew boats, knew the ocean, and didn't care whether their haul wound up on some yahoo's dinner plate or up his nose as long as they were paid fairly. It was very possible the captain hadn't told them about the double cross until it came time to transfer the load to another boat and scuttle the first. They might not have had any choice at the time, but they'd had choices once they'd reached shore. They could have come to Sonny at any time and confessed. He would have let them live. Probably.

Sonny signaled to J.T. The report cracked, and Pat dropped to the ground, half-in, half-out of the water.

The third man began to cry and grabbed Sonny's arm. "Please, you can't do this—I got a wife, k-kids— The captain's got the stuff, he's the one that took it. We ain't seen it s-since we got back to Savannah."

Sonny gently unpeeled the man's fingers from his arm, then stepped back, leaving a clear shot for J.T. The faint echo of the man's blubbering had faded by the time the water's surface was calm again.

"Anything you want to say, Eddie?" Sonny turned toward the boat's captain.

Fast Eddie, they called him, because he never got boarded, never had to dump a load, because he was slick and sly and clever. This time he'd been too clever for his own good.

Eddie wasn't shaking or crying...yet. He stood there, shoulders back, gaze insolent. He knew he was going to die, but he was arrogant enough to think he was taking his secret to his grave. If he couldn't have the quarter of a million dollars' worth of cocaine, neither could they. Sonny intended to prove him wrong.

"Go to hell."

"I imagine I will, when it's my time." Sonny took a pack of cigarettes from his pocket, lit one, and drew deeply on it before exhaling. The smoke hung there, a thin, curling wisp, dissipating slowly into the thick air. "Where are my drugs?"

"Where you'll never find them."

"Don't be a fool, Eddie. Tell me where you—"

"You gonna make a deal with me if I do? You gonna work something out? Let me walk away?"

"No," Sonny stated calmly. "You're dead either way. We have to make an example of you."

"So why should I tell you?"

"Because there's all kinds of ways to die. We can make it quick and easy, like your crew, or so slow and hard that you'll beg to end it. It's your choice."

Eddie's gaze shifted from Sonny to J.T., from Devlin to LeRoy. Calculating the odds for escape? The only place he could go was into the creek, where the water was deep enough that, with his hands tied behind him, he wouldn't make it far.

"Last chance," Sonny said. "You gonna take it?"

Eddie stared at him, tight-lipped.

After one last drag, Sonny dropped the cigarette and ground it into the dirt. "Give him what he wants," he said, then turned and walked through the bar's back door. A scream ripped through the night as he closed the door behind him.

The April afternoon was balmy, the streets busy with locals and tourists alike. No one noticed the girl standing in a doorway in the middle of the block. Her long curls were tangled, her clothes too small, and her canvas shoes were torn, exposing her little toes. She wore a backpack, as tattered and dirty as she was, and she watched the comings and goings with a practiced eye. She'd made a good lunch of the fruit and pastries she'd stolen three streets over. Now it was time to go to work.

She chose her target, a tall, slender man with a camera that would be worth at least fifty dollars, to say nothing of the cash he must have in his pocket. It was impossible to say for sure, but it seemed that she was his target as well. He pointed the camera in her direction and snapped off pictures so regularly that she imagined she heard the whir of the film winding. One of those pictures, she knew, would end up fastened to a page in William's journal. What would happen to the rest?

She blinked, and the scene shifted. She was behind the camera now, and in front of it, as well. She watched herself through the viewfinder and wondered why William wanted the photo. He hadn't yet met her—that wouldn't happen for another six months. She knew nothing about him, and he should know nothing about her, but obviously he did. The answer must be in the journal . . .

The fourteen-year-old girl in the viewfinder flattened into a one-dimensional image, a moment caught in time. Startled, Selena reached for it, intending to take the picture from the journal, to claim it for her own, but a sound behind her stilled her. Then everything went black. Dear God, she was trapped in William's vault. Claustrophobia tightened her chest and knotted her throat so the only sound she could produce was a frightened whimper. Her lungs were burning, her chest tightening so only the thinnest breath got through . . . until familiar voices penetrated the panic.

Tony. And William. No, not William. His real name was Henry. Selena tried to move toward the door, but arms clamped around her, squeezing her against something solid and warm. She tried to speak, but a hand locked across her mouth. She'd forgotten she wasn't alone. Damon Long held her, and for a moment she was grateful. It was only his presence that kept her from shattering into a million pieces. But he was imprisoning her, not protecting her. He and Henry intended to kill her, and if she died, Tony would die, too, and the girl in the photo would never know—

With a strangled gasp, Selena jerked awake. Her skin was damp, her pulse racing, her mind so thoroughly dulled that it took her a moment to regain her senses. She wasn't in Henry's vault, but in Tony's bed, and Damon Long wasn't holding her prisoner once more; it was the covers tangled around her body that kept her from moving. She wasn't going to die, Tony wasn't going to die, and the girl in the photo...

She worked free of the sheet and blanket. The girl in the photo was *her*, taken fourteen years ago on an Ocho Rios street. But she hadn't seen the photographer who'd snapped that picture, hadn't even heard of Henry Daniels or his alias, William Davis, at the time, had been unaware of the very existence of the photo until that day two weeks ago when Tony shot him in his study.

Even then, all she'd gotten was a glimpse—long enough to recognize herself, long enough to note the date and the inconsistency with her history with Henry as she knew it. With everything that had followed, she hadn't gotten the chance to return to the journal, to learn the secrets of her life that she was sure it contained. By the time she'd remembered, it and all the other journals had been taken into FBI custody, evidence in their case, impossibly out of her reach.

She tried to comb her fingers through her hair, but the muscles and nerves in her left arm protested. Instead, she used her good arm to stuff pillows behind her back, then took note of the empty half of the bed—empty of human life, at least. Tony's dog, Mutt, lay curled at the foot of the bed. When she looked at him, he shifted to her side and rested his head on her stomach, waiting patiently for a scratch.

She listened for some sound of Tony moving about, but heard none. A glance at the clock showed that it was past time for him to report to the Detective Division, though she doubted he'd left yet. Not without checking on her. Not without saying good-bye. Not without worrying about her.

He had worried the night before—on the drive to the hospital, while the staff had examined and treated her, when he'd taken her home. He'd undressed her, put her to bed, and tried to coax her into taking the pain medication the doctor had prescribed. When she'd refused, he'd lain down with her and held her, and she'd felt the tension in his body. *I'll keep you safe,* he'd murmured.

No one had ever truly cared about her safety before. Even Henry had merely been protecting his property, for that was how he'd thought of her. He'd believed that in saving her life, he'd won her heart and bought her soul.

He'd been uncomfortably close to right. She had actually considered killing for him, just as he had once killed for her. In the end, he had intended to kill *her*. Only Tony had stopped him.

Now some stranger out there wanted to finish the job for Henry.

What was she going to do? She couldn't live in fear, couldn't allow Henry to make her a prisoner again. He'd controlled every aspect of her life since she was fourteen—had told her how to dress, talk, and act, where to go to school and what to study, what to think, what to want, what to do. She should be free of him now that he lay in a coma, but she wasn't. As long as people who worked for him were willing to kill her, as long as the FBI used her association with him to threaten her, as long as much of her own history was still secret even from her . . .

Henry's ultimate goal had been to place control of his business in her hands. He had chosen her as his heir and expected her to obediently follow his bidding. Could she do it? Could she accept the FBI's offer, step into Henry's shoes, and run his business . . . right into the ground? It seemed that only then, with his legacy in ruins and the FBI's cases resolved, would she be truly safe.

And she would learn the truth about her past along the way.

Outside the bedroom door, the stairs creaked, making her nerves go taut. Her gaze shifted to the nightstand, where both her pistol and switchblade sat in easy reach. She took a deep breath, then exhaled slowly. Mutt wasn't the greatest watchdog, but only around her and Tony did he get so relaxed. The sound of a feline hiss in the hallway confirmed that it was Tony on the stairs. The fat black cat he'd taken in months ago when his neighbor died greeted every sight of him with a hiss and the swipe of a paw.

An instant later Tony stepped into the room, dressed in his usual white shirt, dark suit, and dark tie. He'd already started combing his fingers through his hair, making him look adorably boyish. The grin when he saw that she was awake completed the picture. "How do you feel?"

She smiled ruefully. "Like someone took a few shots at me."

"Seventy-two, to be precise. That's how many shell casings they found on the hillside above the range."

While she'd been examined by the emergency room doctor, Tony had reported the ambush. Police officers had been sent to the range, along with the crime-scene unit, and one young detective had come to the hospital to interview her. She'd had little enough to tell the officer. She hadn't seen the shooter, hadn't seen his vehicle, didn't know anything that would help identify him.

Selena shifted into a sitting position without disturbing Mutt. "Why aren't you at work?"

"I told them I'd be in late. That I might get lucky and get to help you shower."

"I think I can handle it. But offer again sometime when I'm *not* sore." Aware of his gaze, she eased from the bed, then gingerly tested her arm. The movement was painful, but she'd endured worse. The wound wouldn't put her out of commission.

Steadier, she raised her good arm and combed through her hair, dislodging bits of debris. A glance at the bed showed more dust and splinters on the pillowcase. A shower sounded wonderful, with or without Tony's help. Too bad what she was planning after the shower wasn't a fraction as appealing.

"What's on your schedule for today?" Tony asked, moving to lean against the dresser. "Besides resting, of course."

She wished she could lie to him and swear that was the only thing on her agenda, but she couldn't. She'd told so many lies before the whole ugly truth had finally come out. She didn't intend ever to lie to him again.

Warily she approached the dresser. Her purse lay a few feet to his right, and inside was the business card she needed. Her fingers folded over it as she forced herself to meet his gaze. "I need directions to an address."

"A follow-up visit for your arm?"

If only she could say yes. . . . She unclenched her fingers and laid the card in his outstretched hand. He needed no more than the briefest of glances to recognize the FBI badge embossed there, and his gaze turned dark. "You're not working with them, Selena."

"I have no choice."

"The hell you don't! They'll get you killed!"

She shook her head. "They're my only way out."

"They'll paint a damn target on your back!"

"The target's already there! Remember last night? Someone tried to kill me. Damon Long told you that Henry made no secret of the fact that he intended to turn the business over to me, and that it wasn't a popular decision."

"And you're taking Long's word for it? A career criminal and a freakin' murderer?"

"So you think it was someone else shooting at me last night. Someone with no connection to Henry." She raised one brow. "Just how many enemies do you think I have that are willing to resort to murder?"

"It could have been a random shooting."

She wished she could believe that the ambush had been nothing more than a senseless attack, but she couldn't. And she could see in Tony's eyes that he didn't believe it himself. "Somebody—most likely one of Henry's people—wants me out of the way, and he'll try again...unless I help the FBI stop him—stop all of them."

He stared at her, frustration and anger stamped on his features. Resolutely she stared back, resisting the urge to shrink away under the weight of his censure. She didn't want him angry with her, didn't want to upset or disappoint him, to jeopardize their relationship in any way.

But if the relationship wasn't strong enough to survive, better that they find out right away, while *she* could still survive.

Dragging his fingers through his hair, he pushed past her and paced to the window, then back. "This is stupid, Selena. I thought we'd agreed to take our chances in court. The feds are bluffing. They don't have a case against you—everyone knows that but you. They can't tie you to Henry's business. They can't connect you to any of the vigilante murders, not when the lead detective on every one of them testifies that you weren't involved. The worst they can do is deport you, and even that's not going to happen. Hell, you were born in Puerto Rico! You're an American citizen!"

"I can't *prove* that!" She'd once used the same defense with Henry when he'd threatened her. *Prove it,* he had taunted. *You have no birth certificate, no records of any kind, no way of proving you've ever been to Puerto Rico. However, there is proof that you lived in Jamaica. The birth certificate you do have shows you were born in Ocho Rios. Immigration records show that you entered the US from Jamaica.* He'd finished with an elegant shrug. *You could, of course, take your chances with the courts.*

She stood very still, reluctant to give voice to the words rising inside her but unable to stop them. "It's not *our* chances, Tony. *I'm* the one who will stand trial. *I'm* the one who faces deportation or life in prison or worse. *I'm* the one who got shot at last night. From where I stand, it's *my* problem and *my* decision."

That stopped him midpace. He turned to face her, one brow raised, the frustration and anger joined by hurt. After a moment, his expression turned blank. "I see. I thought this couple thing meant we were in this together—you know, I love you, you love me, we deal with things as a team. Apparently, I was wrong."

She reached out to him, but he took an awkward step back, avoiding her touch. Feeling some of his hurt, she let her hand fall to her side again. "I love you, Tony, more than I can say . . . but I have to do this."

"They'll sacrifice you if it suits their purposes. They'll get you killed."

Once more she shook her head. "They'll give me a chance to live."

"This is crazy. Your lawyer—"

"—can't protect me from the people who want me dead. The FBI can."

When the hurt in his dark eyes deepened, too late she remembered his words from the night before. *I'll keep you safe.* She knew he would die to protect her, but that wasn't enough. And if he got hurt because of her, if, God forbid, he died because of her . . .

"So that's it." His voice was flat, empty. "You get to make the decisions, and the hell with what I think. You're going to let the FBI set you up as a target for every bastard who works for Henry, to put your life on the line just because those assholes from the Bureau are making empty threats, and I have no say in the matter."

She didn't say anything. Couldn't.

He rubbed the center of his forehead—amazing how quickly she'd sent him from a boyish grin to a headache—then exhaled loudly. "I'd better get to work." He walked past her, far enough away that they couldn't accidentally touch, then turned back when he reached the door. For a moment he looked blankly at the business card crumpled in his hand, then he tossed it on the dresser. "The office is on Sixty-fifth, just west of Memorial. You can't miss it."

When he turned away again, she quickly spoke. "Tony? I love you." Any other time the pleading in her tone would have embarrassed her, but not then. She would beg him to believe her if that was what he wanted.

He was still for a breath or two, then he murmured, "Yeah. I love you, too."

And that was it. No kiss, no gentle hug. No, "Take your pain pills," or "Take it easy." No, "I'll see you tonight." He could have been walking away from a stranger. Fair enough, since he was probably thinking that he'd fallen in love with someone he didn't know at all.

Selena stayed where she was a long time, barely able to breathe for the tightness in her chest, until Mutt jumped off the bed, rubbed against her, then positioned his head under her limp hand for a scratch. She obliged him, then dropped to her knees and hugged him. "You're easy, Mutt," she whispered. "I scratch you, I feed you, and you love me. People are so much more complicated."

And so very rewarding. She would prove to Tony that she'd made the right choice. Once the threats were gone, she would be truly free for the first time in her life—free to chase after every dream she'd ever had. If only she could know he would be waiting for her ...

He was the one, he'd promised, who would never leave, and she had believed him. For the past few weeks, they'd pretended they were a normal couple involved in a normal relationship, and she wanted that for forever. But the truth was, she couldn't have it, not with someone trying to kill her. Maybe not ever.

Just one more thing to blame Henry for. One more reason to destroy his life's work.

Releasing the dog, she locked up and went to her own house next door. Henry had chosen it for its proximity to Tony's house—had paid cash for it and put everything in her name. That way, when the police officer next door turned up dead, the trail would lead only to her. She also liked it for its proximity to Tony, though she spent little enough time there.

Showered, dressed, and armed with the switchblade and the compact .22 in her handbag, Selena studied herself in the bedroom mirror. She didn't look dangerous. More importantly, she didn't look fearful. She knew better than to show any weaknesses to the enemy.

She was halfway down the stairs when the doorbell rang. Visible through the sidelight, a familiar figure stood, hands in his pockets, rocking back on his heels. She opened the door, then folded her arms across her middle. "Special Agent King. What a surprise seeing you here."

Her sarcasm wasn't lost on him. "I thought we could continue the conversation from yesterday."

"I thought we finished the conversation yesterday."

"It won't be finished until we get what we want."

"We can't always get what we want."

"But sometimes we get what we deserve." A cool smile

accompanied his words. "Now...do you deserve to go to prison for the rest of your life, maybe even face the death penalty? Probably not. But you don't deserve to walk away free, either. You committed crimes, Ms. McCaffrey. You have to pay."

Illegal weapons. Document fraud. Illegal entry into the country. Crimes, yes, but minor compared to taking a man's life. "I had nothing to do with Henry's drug business or those murders."

"So you say. But it seems to me that an innocent person would want to do whatever she could to put the guilty people in jail. A person who refuses to send criminals to jail must not be so innocent."

She hugged herself a little tighter. "Or maybe she just wants to live a normal life."

"You should have thought of that before you got involved with Daniels and Damon Long." His expression hardened. "You've got two choices, Ms. McCaffrey. You can risk jail or deportation...or you can help us. Turn me down, and I will do my best to put you away for the rest of your life."

Selena opened her mouth, then closed it again. She hated giving in, surrendering what little control she had. She hated that the FBI—and, to some extent, Henry—were getting what they wanted. But she would get what she wanted, as well.

She laid her purse on the hall table a few feet away, gestured for him to step inside, took a breath, and asked, "Exactly what are the terms of your offer, Mr. King?"

Surprise flashed through his eyes, then disappeared. "Complete immunity in exchange for your cooperation in shutting down Daniels's business. We'll forget that Selena McCaffrey exists—or, rather, that she *doesn't* exist." Speaking deliberately, he said, "We won't charge you with any crime of any sort or attempt to remove you from the country. Ever."

"And what would you expect of me in return?"

"To all outward appearances, you'll be running Daniels's business while providing us information that will assist us in making cases against his associates."

He had a talent for making the difficult seem simple. Run the business . . . exactly what she'd been fighting against for six years. She hadn't wanted to be involved with drugs, not for power, not for wealth beyond imagining. But she would do it for freedom, for Tony, for a future. She would do it to destroy what Henry had loved far more than he'd ever loved her.

She nodded once. "Would I be working with you?"

"No. You don't meet the undercover agents until you're on board. It's safer that way."

His distrust made her smile faintly. She suspected he saw her as the best of a bad situation. The feeling was mutual.

He waited a moment before asking, "Are you coming on board?"

She shrugged. "I have a condition of my own. Henry kept journals. At least one of them had information about me. I want to see it."

His immediate response was to shake his head. "The journals are evidence in a criminal trial."

She remained motionless.

"They're being examined by our documents experts right now."

Still she waited.

Finally, King made an impatient gesture. "It'll take some time, but . . . all right. So . . . ?"

Once again Selena folded her arms across her chest—to hold the trembling inside. "As soon as you put it in writing and my attorney signs off on it . . . we'll have a deal, Mr. King."

3

Kathryn Daniels Hamilton sat in the reception area of the FBI office, idly paging through a magazine in between glances at her watch. When Mr. King had called to set up this appointment, he had offered to meet with her at the hospital or at the family's Riverside Drive estate, but she'd politely refused. She didn't want a stranger coming to Henry's hospital room, and she certainly didn't want to invite the FBI into his home. That was reserved for family and friends, not glorified police officers.

As a police officer himself, her brother didn't appreciate her opinion that policemen ranked with the hired help. One paid their salaries and benefited from their particular skills when necessary, but one didn't socialize with them. After all, they were called public servants for a reason.

She'd always thought Henry had undercut his own potential significantly by choosing a career in law enforcement, no matter that he'd risen through the ranks to become chief of police. Business and politics—that was where the real money, power, and prestige lay. If he'd gone into either, he wouldn't be lying in a coma, wasting away before her very eyes.

Footsteps drew her out of her thoughts, and she watched as the receptionist to whom she'd spoken earlier approached. "Mrs. Hamilton? Special Agent King will see you now. If you'll come this way..."

Ninety minutes later, moving as if on automatic pilot, Kathryn nodded politely to the uniformed guards at the main gate of the estate, drove around to the back of the house, then went inside. Sonja, the Daniels family housekeeper since Kathryn was a girl, was at the stove, and her husband, Cecil, the butler, sat at the nearby table, the newspaper open in front of him. Kathryn greeted them both, brushed off Sonja's offer of coffee, and passed through into the house proper.

She'd always loved the house—a beautiful white gem plunked down in the middle of a vast lawn, filled with beautiful things and, her grandmother had liked to say, beautiful people. Definitely privileged people, for all the good it had done them. Her father had grown up there, his every whim fulfilled, but it hadn't stopped him from dying of cancer before his forty-fifth birthday. She and Henry had been raised there as well, spoiled as well, but nothing they'd been given— not wealth, not attention—could raise him from the hospital bed, where he lay dying before her very eyes.

She wandered through the rooms—the very formal living room called the white room, because everything in it was: the library filled with leather-bound first editions; the gentlemen's drawing room, where her grandfather had played poker with his cronies, betting oil wells and real estate; the ladies' drawing room where Grandmama had entertained their wives; the formal dining room that could seat thirty; the informal dining room that seated only ten. Every piece of furniture was antique, every slab of marble imported, every painting and knickknack and lamp worth a small fortune.

Kathryn had taken it all for granted when she was a child. All her friends had lived in beautiful homes, though none so beautiful as her own. She'd been the only one to have a Monet hanging on her bedroom wall, but there had been a great master in every room; she'd paid them little attention. She had been in college before she'd realized that not everyone lived that way. A sorority house was as close as she'd ever come to seeing how the other half lived, and that had been more than enough for her.

Trailing her hand along the banister, she climbed the grand staircase to the second floor. Her meeting with the FBI had been far more unpleasant than she'd expected. She had thought they would talk about the men who'd harmed her brother, offer their sympathy, and leave her to visit the hospital.

Instead, they'd told her a fantastic tale . . . and had proof to support it. About how Henry, loving brother and highly regarded chief of police, was a drug dealer. How he'd suffered his injuries while trying to kill one of his own detectives and the young woman he'd referred to as his niece. How he'd lived a secret life, complete with a different identity, for twenty years. How the FBI wanted to use his family home to destroy the business he'd worked so hard to build.

She hadn't been able to decide which part of the story stunned her most. In the time since, she'd figured it out: the niece.

Henry living a secret life as a drug dealer . . . it should shame her, but she could see that. He'd always looked for thrills and challenges; that was why he'd become a police officer in the first place. He'd been a master game player all his life. He loved competition, strategy, outsmarting and outlasting everyone else. He loved pitting his skills against all comers, and he especially loved winning.

And he had proven himself quite capable of looking the other way when a crime was committed. She'd seen that for herself.

But the niece . . . the FBI agent had called her by various

names—Rosa Jimenez, Gabriela Sanchez, Selena McCaffrey. Henry had apparently met her when she was fourteen and claimed her for his own. He'd treated her like family— dressed her in the finest clothes, sent her to the best schools, filled her every need.

No matter how Kathryn tried, she simply couldn't imagine Henry's taking someone else's child to raise. He'd been uncompromising when she'd told him she and Grant were adopting a child, and he'd never shown the least interest in Jefferson once the boy had joined the family. A simple legal process couldn't make a stranger family, he'd insisted. Blood mattered.

But then *he'd* taken in a stranger, and a fourteen-year-old girl at that. At least Jefferson had been a mere five years old when they'd adopted him. By fourteen, the damage caused by their upbringing was done; they were rebellious, troublesome, and not the least appealing. The only reasons she could think of for a man to take in a stranger's teenage daughter were too perverse to give voice to.

At the top of the stairs, she turned to the right and went to the one room she'd avoided since returning home—Henry's study. That was where the events of that Sunday had taken place. The police had removed what they considered evidence, and Sonja had cleaned the room, then closed the door, and it had remained closed. Now, her hand trembling, Kathryn turned the knob to go inside.

It had been raining that day in Greenhill, Alabama, when Kathryn received the call from a distraught Sonja saying that Henry had been gravely injured. Kathryn had hastily packed while Grant arranged the use of a friend's jet for the trip to Tulsa. One of the deputy chiefs had picked her up at the airport and delivered her to the hospital, and he'd filled her in on what had happened.

A daytime burglary. The estate was encircled by a six-foot iron fence; there was an elaborate alarm system with panic buttons in every room; armed guards patrolled the grounds; and still the thugs had managed to find their way inside. It had been no secret that Henry was making a public appearance with the mayor that day—some sort of fund-raiser— but he'd left early and surprised the burglars in the act. One of them had shot him, and the impact had knocked him through the window behind his desk. He'd fallen headfirst onto the parapet four feet below and been in a coma ever since.

That was the *official* version of events—what she'd been told by the deputy chief, read in the paper, heard on the news.

Now the FBI was saying, no, sorry, it didn't happen that way at all.

The hand-knotted rug Grandpapa had brought back from Turkey was gone, leaving bare marble. There were dark spots on the wall near the vault door, and a large splatter at the far end of the room. *Blood,* her mind supplied, even though she didn't want to know. No one had died in the room, but not for lack of trying. Though one of the thugs had only bruises and contusions, another had been shot, and the third had suffered a concussion and a broken nose along with a stab wound. The young detective credited in the media with saving Henry's life had, in fact, been the one to shoot him, and he'd been shot himself by Henry's other target that day. Selena, the girl he called niece.

Actually, someone *had* died that day, she thought as she forced herself to approach the windows and gaze down onto the narrow parapet. Sonja had brought in a crew to clean away the broken glass and blood, but it was still far too easy for Kathryn to imagine Henry lying there, dying. Machines kept his body functioning, but his spirit, his essence, was gone.

As a chill rushed over her, she swept from the room, shutting the door firmly behind her. She'd told Mr. King that she needed time to consider his request, to take in everything he'd told her, and he'd agreed none too graciously. He'd made it clear, though, that asking her permission was no more than a courtesy. He'd mentioned words like criminal enterprise, seizure, and forfeiture, and asked her to please give him an answer within the next day or so.

At the end of the corridor, she entered Henry's bedroom. Sonja continued to dust it every day, as if he was merely away on a trip and might return home at any moment. His toiletries still filled the bathroom, his clothes the closet. Kathryn pressed her face into a jacket, inhaling the familiar scent of him, and her breath caught on a sob. "Oh, Henry, you fool! Any man in the world would have been satisfied with what you had, but not you. No, you wanted more—more money, more power, more challenge, more excitement. And look where it got you."

As she stepped back from the closet, she stopped in front of the portrait that hung in the sitting area between two love seats. Grandmama and Grandpapa were seated in the middle, Mother and Father stood behind them, and she and Henry flanked them. They'd been a beautiful family. Now they were all gone, or as good as.

On a small table beneath the painting stood two dozen or more framed photographs. Henry graduating from the academy. When he'd been promoted to detective. His first job as deputy chief. Receiving awards and commendations. It was his equivalent of what Jefferson called an "I love me" wall—photo after photo of himself in the highlights of his law enforcement career.

"What about your other career?" she murmured as she studied his handsome, smiling face. "Nothing to commemorate earning your first million in drug money? No photograph marking your move from just another dealer to the big time? Nothing to remind you of the first murder you committed in the name of the almighty dollar?"

She was about to turn away when a small frame caught her eye. It measured barely three inches tall and was easily overlooked among the larger, more ornate ones. Her hand trembled when she reached for it—and with good reason, she soon realized.

The girl in the photo must be Henry's "niece," the woman who called herself Selena—the only woman who figured prominently enough in his life to be included among these photos. She was in her teens in the picture, and she wore a school uniform along with an uneasy smile. Her skin was a creamy light brown, her hair black, and her features bore the obvious stamp of her African-American heritage . . . along with a familiarity that made Kathryn's heart clutch.

The frame fell from her unsteady grip, landing faceup on the floor. One hand clapped over her mouth, Kathryn stared at it—at the lovely young girl she hadn't seen in twenty-eight years. The girl who had haunted her all those years. The girl she'd believed was dead.

She sank to her knees and covered her face with both hands. "Damn you, Henry! Dear God, *what* have you done?"

"Murder is our business, and business is good."

The solemn voice came from Tony's left, along with the crashing of footsteps, but he didn't turn. He'd heard his occasional partner, Frank Simmons, shout his name a couple times, then start his climb up the hill. Hell, a dead man could have heard his approach.

"Business is *too* good for you to be doing someone else's job for him. What're you doin' up here? CSU's already been over this area with a fine-tooth comb."

Tony knew that. Marla Johnson, a crime-scene tech and an ex-girlfriend, had filled him in on what they knew so far. She'd also reported that she'd gotten a call from the FBI, wanting the same info. If the hit had come *after* Selena had accepted their offer, the feds could have taken over the investigation, but as it was, they had no jurisdiction—a fact that never sat well with them.

"I'm just looking." Tony was crouched in the weeds in the shade cast by a gnarled post oak. Sumac bushes grew to one side, and wild honeysuckle tangled around everything on the other side. The only clear view was ahead, a perfect downward angle to the firing range.

Though it had been less than twenty-four hours, the damage from the attack on Selena had already been repaired—flood lamps replaced, a new cinder-block support for a new concrete slab, the debris cleaned up. No doubt, the owner had thought it bad for business to advertise the fact that someone had ambushed one of his customers right on the range.

"You talk to the lab?" Simmons asked as he leaned back against the tree trunk and wiped the sweat from his face.

"Yeah. The ground's too rocky to get any footprints. They collected seventy-two shell casings from an AK. No prints on the casings. They also found a black fiber on the brambles over there. A synthetic blend. Could have come from any of a million garments. That's it."

"Who knew Selena would be here?"

"Me." He'd gone to spend the evening with his father

while his mother went to her first support group meeting for the caregivers of Alzheimer's patients. Anna had really needed the break, and the meeting, and he'd needed to feel as if he was helping.

"Anyone else?"

"She doesn't *know* anyone else."

"Anyone could have been watching her. She tends to stand out in a crowd."

Grunting in agreement, Tony stared down at the range, but his mind's eye saw it the way it would have been when Selena was there—the night dark, the flood lamps lit, the place empty but for her. She'd emptied her magazine, set her gun down where the new table was, and the first bullet had hit a few inches away.

Why? The shooter couldn't have asked for a better vantage point. He'd had a perfect shot at her from the waist up— an easy head shot, an easier center mass shot. But he'd missed. Seventy-two times. *Thank God.*

"Guy must have been one hell of a bad shot," Simmons commented. "Couldn't have been a pro."

All of Henry's pros in the area were locked up—at least, the ones they knew about. "Maybe he wasn't trying to hit her."

"Then why ... To scare her?"

"Or send a warning."

"To stay out of Daniels's business." Simmons pushed away from the tree and moved closer as Tony straightened. "Seventy-two shots is one hell of an ineffective warning. More likely, the guy panicked. He thought it'd be easy to pick her off, and when it wasn't, he freaked and blew the hell out of the place, hoping that at least one of the bullets would hit her."

"Maybe," Tony muttered. Henry had had plenty of shooters working for him, but there had been other employees whose jobs didn't routinely involve murder. It was easy enough to imagine one of them attempting to remove Selena from the picture. After all, according to Long, Henry had made no secret of his plans for Selena. It seemed a common misconception that she knew more about the business than she really did.

Simmons tugged at his collar. "Come on, man, let's go. It's damn hot out here."

Tony gave him a sour look. He'd had a really shitty day, thanks to Selena, and he didn't need Frankie's pissing and moaning on top of it. "Hey, no one asked you to come."

"I got used to tagging along behind you, working Daniels's homicides. It's a hard habit to break."

Tony moved, but only far enough to clear the sumacs. There he stopped to look around. The area was industrial, perfect for late-night visitors to the range. Unfortunately, no one around to complain about the shooting also meant no one around to see any suspicious persons or cars. Some of the buildings might have security cameras, but the odds of finding one that recorded activity outside its immediate vicinity were slim.

"She was parked right down there," he said, more to himself than to Simmons, "and she left that way and didn't see any cars. So the guy must have parked on the other side of the hill."

"Why don't we drive around and look?" Simmons suggested. He muttered a curse as Tony headed in the opposite direction, but he followed.

There was no trail on the other side of the hill, so they made their own, coming out on a dead-end street. There was a chain-link fence on the other side, but no buildings, no streetlights, no security cameras, no nothing. The street was paved, so there wasn't even the possibility of finding tire tracks. It was literally a dead end.

His face gleaming red, Simmons loosened his tie, then undid the top two buttons on his shirt. "Come on, son, it's fuckin' hot out here, and it's quitting time besides. Let's you and me find a dark bar and a cold beer—or a cold bar and a dark beer—and put this day behind us."

It was an invitation he made often, but one Tony hadn't accepted in a long time—not since meeting Selena. Removing his sunglasses, he blotted the sweat from his forehead, then slid the glasses back into place. "Yeah, okay."

They returned to their cars and settled on a midtown bar. After locking his weapon in his trunk, Tony met Simmons at the door.

They were halfway through the first round when Frankie finally broke the silence. "What's up with you, Chee? All day you been actin' like a man that ain't gettin' any, but you're damn near livin' with Island Girl, so that can't be the case. Tell Uncle Frankie all about it."

Tony wasn't the sort to confide his problems in coworkers—and since this problem dealt not only with his love life but an undercover FBI operation, that should go double. But he trusted Simmons. The guy was a putz; but he was Tony's putz, and he knew when to keep his mouth shut.

Still, it took Tony the second half of the beer to reply. "She took their deal."

"Who took—? Selena? And the feebs? Holy shit, son. The cop and the drug lord . . . that's gonna put a crimp in the romance department, ain't it? You're gonna be just like us married fools and not gettin' any."

Tony scowled. Sex was the least of his worries. "They've got her convinced that if she doesn't help them, she'll either spend the rest of her life in prison or get deported. I told her that's bullshit, but she..." Didn't believe him. Didn't trust him over the goddamn feds. Didn't value his opinion. Didn't think he was even entitled to an opinion. After all, it was *her* life, *her* choice, all about *her*, and the hell with him.

Simmons signaled the waitress for two more beers. "Maybe this is the right choice for her. If it gets the FBI off her back and guarantees they'll stay off..."

"They'll get her fucking killed," Tony said, each word clipped.

"Maybe not," Simmons said. "Stranger things have happened. But someone's looking to kill her anyway, Chee. At least this way, she'll have some protection."

"*My* way, she wouldn't *need* protection."

"Yeah? What would happen the next time someone comes around with an AK?"

Tony wanted to insist there wouldn't be a next time. When no orders came down the line from Selena, Henry's people would realize the rumors weren't true. It had been two weeks since he and Long went incommunicado. A few more weeks at most, maybe even just a few more days, and the rest of the bastards would be divvying up the spoils among themselves. They would forget Selena even existed.

But until they forgot, she was in danger.

She believed the FBI could protect her.

And she believed Tony couldn't.

He finished the second beer, turned down a third, and headed home. His senses zeroed in on Selena the instant she came into sight, standing at the easel on her patio as if the temperature weren't a hundred sizzling degrees. She wore denim shorts that rode low on her hips and left her long legs bare. Her tank top was one of his favorites, fitting like a second skin and bearing the message, I MAKE GROWN MEN CRY. Her hair was pulled back in a ponytail, she held a paintbrush in her right hand, and the fingers of her left hand were tucked into the belt loop of her shorts, providing support for her injured arm.

She looked damned amazing.

He parked his Impala, got out and hefted his attaché case, then walked to the mailbox at the end of his driveway. All the way back, he looked at her, and she looked back. He felt guilty that he hadn't called her once during the day to ask how she was, but he'd been so angry, so convinced that she was making the worst mistake of their lives—yes, damn it, *their* lives. Everything that affected her affected him. Didn't she understand that?

Or did she just not care?

His steps slowed to a stop behind the Impala. If he was going to cut across the yard and join her on the patio, this was the place to angle off to the right. Forty feet, and he'd be there...to say what? Do what?

Damned if he knew.

He turned to the left instead, went inside the house, and slowly locked the door behind him.

When Selena arrived at the FBI offices on Wednesday morning, the receptionist showed her to a conference room, offered her coffee, then left her alone to wait. With a sigh, she walked to the windows and gazed out, but hardly noticed the surroundings.

After Tony had arrived home from work the night before—and given her that long, unfathomable look—he'd disappeared inside his house and she'd spent the night in hers. Funny how quickly she'd gotten accustomed to sharing his bed. If, as she feared, their relationship was too new and fragile to survive the demands she'd placed on it, she might never share it again. That was too bleak a future to contemplate.

When the door behind her opened, she didn't immediately turn. Three faint reflections in the glass showed that she'd been joined by Special Agent King and two other men. She slowly turned to face them.

"Ms. McCaffrey. Sorry we're late," King said. "This is Adam Robinette"—he gestured toward the man with reddish-blond hair—"and Brian Jamieson. They'll be working with you. I'll leave you to get started."

"Have a seat," Robinette said, tossing a manila folder on the table.

She leaned against the windowsill instead and studied the two men. Robinette was a tall, lanky man with bad posture and a piercing gaze that never wavered. He lacked Jamieson's polish and easy manner, as well as his taste in clothes, but compensated for it with an extra dose of suspicion and distrust.

Thanks to Henry, her life was filled with people who routinely used multiple names, and no doubt, Robinette and Jamieson were merely the latest. Even if she were a trusted member of their team, they wouldn't share their true identities with her, no more than Damon Long had, no more than Henry had. After all, they had real lives with wives, girlfriends, children, and extended families to protect. Information she didn't have was information she couldn't pass on to the wrong people.

Almost as if he'd heard her mental reference to Henry, Robinette said, "First thing . . . for convenience, we won't use Henry Daniels's name. His people will be more comfortable with William Davis since that's how they knew him."

Truthfully, the name was *all* his associates had known about him—that, and that he was a man to fear. No one but

Damon had ever met him face-to-face. No one but Damon had ever visited his house, or even known exactly where he lived—including, during the years she was growing up, *her*. Being socially prominent because of his money and politically prominent because of his law enforcement career, he'd had far too much to lose by being identifiable, so he'd put Damon out front and remained a mystery even to his oldest associates.

"Second . . . you'll be moving into Davis's house. If you're going to play the heir to a multimillion-dollar enterprise, you've got to live the part. Your little house just doesn't cut it. Besides, the estate's better for security."

Selena's breath caught in her chest. Move into William's house. Once, the idea would have thrilled her. Until two years ago, she had never been allowed to visit him at home; when he had finally invited her, he'd sequestered her in the guesthouse and declared the main house off-limits. She had been inside only twice—once when she'd broken in, and once when Damon Long had escorted her at gunpoint. And now they wanted her to live there. Eat there. Sleep there. She wasn't sure she could.

But what choice did she have?

"Everybody in town knows that house belongs to the former chief of police," she pointed out.

"Doesn't matter," Robinette replied. "You're going to tell Davis's cohorts the truth about him—that he was the chief of police and he's in a coma and, as his chosen heir, you're taking over."

Just as he'd wanted. How reluctant would they be to take orders from a woman they knew nothing about? How long would it take them to start thinking about removing her and claiming their share of the business for their own?

Someone had already thought about removing her, a twinge in her arm reminded her. That was why she was there.

She nodded once to signal agreement, not that Robinette seemed to care. Why should he? He knew her options were limited.

"Third . . . you'll be working with Damon Long."

Grateful for the solid sill supporting her weight, she concentrated on controlling her breathing, on keeping her voice steady and hiding the shock that chilled her. "Damon Long and I have what some would call an adversarial relationship. He tried to kill me. I thought I *had* killed him. To say I don't think we would work well together would be an understatement."

"We know he's dangerous."

Selena walked to the nearest chair, sliding into it as if her knees hadn't gone totally weak. "He's facing nine murder charges in a state that carries out executions in a timely manner."

Robinette shrugged. "Long knows more about Davis's business than anyone else alive. He knows the people. He knows the details."

"Then why don't you make a deal with him and forget about me?"

Color seeped into Robinette's cheeks. "We'd rather deal with you."

She looked from Robinette to Jamieson, who was toying with a pen, his eyes averted. "You tried, didn't you? And he turned you down. That's why Mr. King was pressuring me— because Long refused."

"Actually," Robinette said at last, "headquarters refused. Damon Long is guilty of more crimes than we'll ever know. They won't let him walk away from this."

Which made her their next best choice. Through her, they

could get Long's help but still punish him when they were through. "So you want me to pretend to Long that I'm really taking over. That I'm getting him out of jail and it will be business as usual, except he'll be reporting to me instead of William."

Robinette shrugged. "Consider it the first test of your skills. If you can convince Long, you can convince anyone."

True enough. And if she couldn't convince Long, she wouldn't have to worry about convincing anyone else.

"Security won't be a problem. We can control him. We'll have the judge order an electronic bracelet, and one of us will be with him twenty-four/seven. He'll be as much a prisoner at the estate as he currently is in jail."

Except he wouldn't *be* in jail, and she would be a prisoner right alongside him.

Certainly, she understood Long's value to the FBI. He knew enough about William's business to put away everyone involved for a very long time. It would take the FBI years to gather even a fraction of that information. And, truthfully, that fact strengthened her position with them. They needed him, but they needed *her* to get to him.

Jamieson spoke for the first time. "The only realistic way to bring down a criminal enterprise of this magnitude is with the help of criminals. Long's not going to straighten up and fly right. He's not going to repent or reform, and he's not going to help us shut down what he's spent more than half his life building. He's got a hell of a lot more to lose by working with us than he could ever gain. But working for you . . ."

He would resent every minute of it, but he would realize that the benefits—freedom from jail, the possibility of escape, the chance to be in power once again—outweighed the drawbacks.

Her stomach knotted. Robinette claimed they could control Long. Was she willing to risk her life on his say-so? *They'll sacrifice you if it suits their purposes,* Tony had warned. She understood his dislike for the FBI, but they *were* the FBI. She didn't believe they would deliberately let harm come to her. Was that reasonable? Or incredibly naive?

She quashed the faint smile conjured by the thought. She hadn't been naive since her mother's husband had beaten the innocence from her with his fists. Adam Robinette was a federal agent charged with upholding the law. He might not like her, he definitely didn't trust her, but he *would* protect her. After all, where was his case without her?

And she would protect herself. She'd been doing it a long time.

Opening the folder in front of him, Robinette fingered the pages on top of the stack inside. They were a copy of the papers she'd signed in her lawyer's office the afternoon before, detailing her agreement with the FBI. What she would give them. What she would get in return. What would happen if she failed to uphold her end of the bargain. Too bad she hadn't known about Damon Long before she signed them.

Though it wouldn't have changed anything. She would have signed them anyway to avoid prosecution or deportation. To learn more about her past—to have a future with Tony—she would have made a deal with the devil himself.

Looking at Robinette's thinly veiled smugness, she thought perhaps she *had* made a deal with the devil.

"Fine. But I won't live in the same house with him."

There was a hint of relief in his eyes. "Of course not. He and I will stay at the guesthouse, along with one of the agents tasked with security. You'll be in the main house, with Jamieson and a female agent."

Selena nodded grimly.

When William had offered her a new life fourteen years ago, she had been so young and so grateful to him. If she'd known then what she'd learned in the last few weeks, would she have run in the opposite direction? Would she have avoided the pressures, the constant striving to please, the blackmail, the coercion, the threats, and stayed in Jamaica?

Probably not. Clean clothes, all the food she could eat, and a bed to sleep in were powerful temptations to a half-starved street rat whose future held nothing more than prostitution and early death. The promise of affection, when she'd been denied even a hint of it her entire life, had been even more powerful.

With all its problems, this life was far better than the one she'd left behind. Once her work for the feds was over, it would be even better.

If she survived.

"So what now?" she asked flatly.

"You convince Long that you're taking over and you need his help. Once he agrees, you'll get him out of jail."

"And how am I supposed to convince Long that I can get a judge to let a suspect in multiple homicides out on bail?"

"No one knows better than Long how many corrupt people hold positions of authority in this country. He's paid off more than his share over the years. If your act is believable, he'll believe."

If she delivered the right words with the right attitude. "And then?"

"He'll be released in the morning. That'll give us today and tonight to get settled in the Davis house, just as soon as Mrs. Hamilton gets her stuff out."

Selena paused in rising. "Mrs. Hamilton?"

"Davis's sister. Kathryn Hamilton. Lives in Alabama."

The pretty blonde in the photograph Selena had found

while snooping through William's closet a few weeks earlier. In fourteen years he'd never admitted to having any family besides Selena. In the aftermath of his injuries, she'd learned of Kathryn's existence, had even known she was in Tulsa; but she'd given the woman little thought.

"Is she returning to Alabama?" she asked, her tone level, uninterested.

"No, she's staying in town a while longer. Stay away from her."

She graced Robinette with a sardonic smile. "I'll have enough to keep me busy just talking to Long."

"We'll clear your visit through the jail. Meet us at Davis's house—your new house—around one."

She thought of the imposing white mansion on Riverside Drive with all its treasures...and all its memories. If it was really hers, she would burn it to the ground, then leave the place to grow wild. She wouldn't voluntarily set foot inside. But it wasn't hers, and neither was the choice. "I'll be there," she replied. Then she walked out of the room before the shudders rippled through her.

4

The correctional center, located downtown, served as jail for both the Tulsa Police Department and the Tulsa County Sheriff's Office. Selena had never been there before, though she'd been threatened with it a time or two in recent weeks. As she sat in the parking lot, gazing at the fence, the high walls, and the small windows, another shudder washed over her. Because the jail reminded her of those desperate hours she'd spent years ago, locked in a cramped, dark cabinet, pleading with her mother's husband until she was hoarse, clawing at the door until her hands bled? Or because Damon Long awaited her inside?

If she'd had a love/hate relationship with William, her feelings for Long had been simpler: Distrust. Suspicion. Revulsion. He'd beaten her in his futile attempt to rape her two years ago, and more recently had been party to William's plan to kill her. Was she really going to walk inside the jail and offer him the freedom to make good on that plan?

The obvious answer made her laugh, though there was nothing humorous about it. She tucked her weapons under the seat, drew a warm, heavy breath, and got out of the car. Inside the correctional center, the guard she spoke to tried to turn her away, insisting that visitation days for the prisoners in Long's pod had already passed, that she would have to come back some other time. But after a whispered conversation with a second guard, he escorted her to an interview room to wait.

The space was small enough to trigger her claustrophobia, and the idea of being locked in it alone with Damon Long didn't calm her nerves any. She would rather be a hundred other places, facing a million other people. Someday, she reminded herself, she would have that freedom.

The door opened and Long walked in, unshaven and surly. Surprise flashed across his face when he saw her, covered instantly by the smile that had once charmed her and that now reminded her of a snake at its most dangerous. "Well, well," he said, shuffling forward and sliding into the chair opposite her. "This is my lucky day."

Pain twinged in her arm when her fingers tightened.

"What do you think of the nose job you gave me?"

Tilting her head to one side, she studied him. He'd always been something of a pretty boy, whether his hair was brown or blond, long, or short and spiked. Even at that moment, looking every bit as disreputable as she knew him to be, there was a certain appeal to him that the crook in his once-straight nose couldn't diminish. "It adds character," she said at last.

He laughed. "Which I sorely need?" His handcuffs clanked as he rested his hands on the tabletop. "So what brings you to jail? I'd figure getting even this close to the cells would give you the heebie-jeebies."

"Would you also figure that you're the last person I'd want to see?"

"Actually, I'd think next-to-last. Ol' William's probably got me beat there."

Not by much. William existed in a vegetative state. He couldn't hurt her. Long could.

"So . . ." That quickly, his entire persona changed. Gone

was the friendly, smiling rogue, and in his place was the cold-eyed killer. The shift was so sudden, so complete, that it made Selena's skin crawl. "What do you want?"

"I have a deal to offer you, Mr. Long." She hesitated an instant over his name. She couldn't call him by his first name. It was too friendly, too intimate. While she couldn't keep her distance from him physically, she could keep him at arm's length emotionally. Additionally, the formality would serve as a regular reminder that she was now his boss.

"What kind of deal?"

"You give me what I want, and I'll get you out of here."

For a time the room was utterly silent as he stared at her. There was nothing to read on his face or in his blue eyes—literally nothing. No hint of hope, skepticism, suspicion. Just icy blankness. Finally, he shifted, his chair creaking. "I'm listening."

"It's very simple. You have information I want. If you give it to me, I'll get you released into my custody."

"The court has already denied bond."

"I can change the judge's mind."

"How?"

She shrugged. "William had a fondness for blackmail. He kept excellent records on people in authority. Of course, bribery is an option, as well."

He showed no surprise, no disbelief. When you grew up working for the most powerful drug dealer in four states, who also happened to be one of the most powerful police officials in those states, the idea of a judge for sale was easy to accept.

"You get me released, and for that, I tell you . . . what?"

"Everything you know about the business."

He considered that a moment before asking the question she'd been waiting for. "Why?"

Either he would believe her or he wouldn't, but either way, he would accept her offer. With freedom came hope, and his situation was too tenuous to turn that down.

Selena smiled coolly. "Because I plan to run it."

Damon had always figured his death would come quickly—a hit gone wrong, betrayal by an associate, revenge carried out by some fuckup who worked for him. He'd never imagined himself strapped to a table in the state prison with a goddamn needle in his arm, but lately that had become a distinct possibility.

He'd been sitting in jail for two weeks, minus the couple days he'd spent in the hospital, and other than the lawyer he was paying out the ass for, he hadn't had any visitors that mattered. No local cops assigned to the case, none of the feds now also working it, no one from the DA's Office. Nobody gave a shit that he was sitting in a cell going stir-crazy, not even the goddamn lawyer. Nobody wanted to make a deal. Nobody wanted to give him a chance to save his hide.

Except Selena, sitting there all prissy and calm and feeding him a line of pure bullshit. She and William had fought for years about her getting involved in the business. No freakin' way was he going to believe she'd done a complete one-eighty simply because the old man was out of the picture.

Sitting back in his chair, he rested one ankle on the opposite knee. "What happened to, 'Thank you, Uncle, but I'm not interested'?"

"Do you believe everything people say?"

Her implication that he was gullible made him bristle. "I believe *that*. For six freakin' years you told him no. It was the only thing he wanted from you, and you refused to let him have it."

"For fourteen years, I gave him *everything* he wanted. I talked the way he wanted me to talk. I dressed the way he wanted me to dress. I acted the way he wanted me to act. He controlled every aspect of my life—where I went to school, where I spent vacations, what subjects I studied, what grades I made. I lived and breathed for him, and all I wanted in return was his love. But he refused to give it. So I refused to give him the one thing he truly wanted."

Her smile was elegant, similar enough to William's to give Damon a chill. If he managed to overlook it, she really was a beautiful woman, though damaged, as the old man had liked to point out. Damon didn't trust any woman—fuck, any man either—but he trusted Selena less than most.

"Now William's out of the picture," she continued, "and I fully intend to take control of the business that was so damned important to him. He groomed me for it, and I want it."

Was it possible all her refusals had merely been for spite—one small rebellion, a way to get back at the old man for withholding his affection? William had been good at making people resent the hell out of him. He'd done pretty much the same for Damon that he had for Selena—taken him off the streets, given him a home, clothes, money, an education, though of a vastly different nature. He'd been Damon's mentor, his father figure, the most important and influential man in his life...but given the chance, Damon would have killed him without so much as a qualm.

"I want the Cézannes and the Monets. I want the house, and the money, and the power. Most of all, I want the satisfaction of knowing that what I denied him in life, I'm now enjoying in his death."

"He isn't dead yet," Damon pointed out.

Another elegant smile. "He might as well be."

Damon shifted in his chair with the clink of chains. "So it was all a game, and now that you think you've won, you want your prize."

"Come now, Damon," she said chidingly. "You would have killed him and taken over yourself if you'd had the chance . . . and the nerve."

Annoyance tingled along his spine. He *had* wanted William dead. But it wasn't lack of nerve that had kept him from taking action. The time had never been right. But now that William was as good as dead, *someone* was going to take over. *Someone* was going to gain control of those millions. If not he and Selena, then someone else who'd worked for the old man. At least *he'd* earned it. He'd busted his balls for the bastard for twenty fucking years.

And he could get rid of Selena far easier than William.

"What about Detective Ceola?"

Something flashed in her eyes, gone too quickly for him to identify. Guilt? Regret? "What about him?"

"Having an honest cop boyfriend will interfere with running an international drug operation."

"Detective Ceola isn't a concern any longer."

Did that mean he was out of the picture? Ceola *was* honest. He would never forgive his godfather for wanting him dead. He wasn't likely to forgive Selena for attempting to carry out William's plan, however unwilling she'd been.

And just how unwilling had she really been? Had her reluctance to carry out the hit merely been another way to spite William?

He wasn't sure he believed a word that had come out of her mouth, but that meant nothing. All that mattered was that she could get him out of jail. Once he was free, he could take care of a few things—add some cash to the three mil stashed away in the Caymans. Retrieve his backup documentation from the safety-deposit box in Dallas to be consistent. Ensure that William's network stayed intact long enough for him to set up in his new location with his new identity and get back to business as usual.

Rising from the chair, he walked to the door and signaled to the guard, then faced her once again. He gave her his big ol' shit-eating grin, then winked. "Contact the judge and you've got yourself a deal, boss."

At least, until he found an opportunity to kill her.

Kathryn Hamilton took up residence at a bed-and-breakfast a few miles away from her family estate. The house was an old oil estate, built of massive stone blocks, with tile floors, elaborate moldings, and an unfortunate trend toward what some decorator had likely dubbed Oklahoma chic: table bases made of antlers, shelves supported by steers' horns, cowboy prints framed in weathered barn boards, curtain tiebacks fashioned of rusted barbed wire. It was overwhelmingly tacky, and exactly the sort of thing Grandpapa would have put in his house if Grandmama hadn't refused.

Kathryn finished unpacking in the master suite, then took her lunch—black coffee, a salad, and fresh fruit—onto the tiny patio, along with her cell phone. She'd already tried to call her son, Jefferson, but got only his voice mail. Work and an active social life kept him busy, though he made an effort to call her at least once a week. Sometimes she nagged—gently—for more of his attention, but usually she was grateful for what she got. After all, God and nature had conspired to keep her childless. She had looked on Jefferson as a blessing when he'd come into her life all those years ago, and still did.

Now it was time for her regular call home. It would be like all the other calls: The housekeeper would answer the phone and locate Grant in his office, where he spent the bulk of his time. He would come on the line, clearly distracted, and they would have an excruciatingly polite conversation before saying good-bye.

To be fair, Grant had been distracted most of the thirty-four years of their marriage. In the beginning, it had seemed sweet, the fact that when he concentrated on something, the rest of the world slipped past unnoticed. In the beginning, though, *she* had been the thing he'd concentrated on. Then one day she'd become the rest of the world. Unnoticed.

Unwanted.

Making an effort not to grind her teeth, she pressed the SEND button and listened to the telephone ring. On the second ring, Nell answered. She spent a few moments on chitchat—*How are you? How is Mr. Henry? I'll get Mr. Grant*—then put Kathryn on hold.

Since discovering that photograph in Henry's bedroom, she felt as if she'd been living on hold. She didn't know what to do, what to say, what to think. For twenty-eight years—half her life—she'd believed a lie. She didn't know how to accept the truth, or how to make things right.

It was all Henry's fault, damn his soul.

Grant came on the line, sounding distant. She could close her eyes and see him at the partner's desk that had belonged to his great-great-grandfather, his computer looking out of place on the gleaming antique, files spread around him. She'd married a lawyer who, in the tradition of Southern lawyers, had done very well for himself. They lived in the Hamilton antebellum mansion, they still owned the thousands of acres that had made Greenhill one of Alabama's most profitable plantations, they were among the South's social elite, and yet they were as estranged as two people living the same life could be.

All Henry's fault.

"Hello, darlin'," she greeted as if she had every right. Having been married to him thirty-four years, didn't she? "How are things at home?"

"Oh, they're fine."

She restrained a snort. The house could fall down around him, and he wouldn't notice as long as the four walls of that damned office remained intact. He didn't care about the two-hundred-year-old mansion, or the thousands of acres, or the Hamilton legacy. These days he didn't care about much of anything.

"How is Henry?" he asked, only because it was expected. In the beginning, he'd tried to impress Henry, because after all, he was courting Henry's only sister. Because they'd had things in common—their upbringing, their intelligence, their interest in law—she'd expected them to become friends. It hadn't happened.

"The same. I go to the hospital every day, hold his hand, talk to him. The nurses say he can probably hear me, so I remind him of better times." What a shame that she had to go back decades in their lives to find those better times. Not that she believed the nurses, anyway. She thought they were being overly optimistic. Everything that had made her brother who he had been was gone. The body in the hospital bed was just the shell that remained. "The doctors tell me it's time to consider transferring him to a long-term-care facility. They say there's not much more they can do for him."

"Hm. Well, that's good."

No, she wanted to scream. *That's* not *good. Listen to me, damn it. Don't shut me out.* But she didn't. She'd quit trying to get through to him twenty-eight years ago.

"Have you seen any old friends?"

She poked a hundred holes in the slice of cantaloupe on her fruit plate before setting the fork aside. "A few. There have been the obligatory dinners, a few lunches . . . But so much time has passed. So much has changed." She was an entirely different person than she'd been when she'd lived in Tulsa. Back then, she'd been excited, ambitious, full of life and hope, and happy. She'd thought she could have anything, everything. Time, and Grant, and Henry, had proven her wrong.

"Well, I'm glad you're having a good time. I'd better get back to work now."

Kathryn's mouth tightened until she had to force the words out. "You do that, darlin'. And if you talk to Jefferson, tell him to call his mama. Love you. Bye-bye." She always said good-bye like that, in a rush—*loveyoubyebye*—to avoid the awkward pause when he had nothing to offer in return. She couldn't remember the last time he'd said *I love you*, but she damn well remembered the only time he'd said *I don't love you*. Those four words had changed her life and his, as well as the lives of everyone close to them. Little words to hold such power, to wreak such destruction.

As she began dialing Jefferson's number again, her frown eased. Her husband might not give a good damn about her, but her son loved her—always had, he'd told her since he was six, and always would. He was the best thing that had ever happened to her, the only thing that made life bearable.

For an instant when she heard his voice, she thought she'd been lucky enough to reach him, but then she realized it was his voice mail again. "This is Jefferson," he said in his easygoing Southern drawl. "I can't take your call, but leave a message and I'll get back to you soon as I can."

Just the sound of his prerecorded voice made her smile. When he'd come to live with them, he'd been a small, tow-headed, solemn little boy who'd called her ma'am for the first six months. Eventually he had eased his way into Mother, then Mom, before finally getting to Mama. That was the magic word. If she hadn't already loved him, she would have fallen in love with him the first time that name came from his mouth.

She waited for the beep, then said, "Hey, baby, it's just your mama again. Yes, it's only been twenty minutes since my last call. What can I say? I miss you. I wish you would take a few days to come to Tulsa and see your uncle Henry. I know, I know—he's in a coma and doesn't have a clue who comes to see him and who doesn't, and he hasn't been the greatest uncle in the world, but he *is* your only uncle on the Daniels side, and it would mean a whole lot to your mother if you'd be the bigger man this once."

She drew a breath, then quickly continued. "Anyway, I just wanted to hear your voice. I love you, Jeffer—" The voice mail beeped, cutting off her message. She flipped her phone shut, then laid it on the table and gave a heavy sigh. "Always have. Always will."

Until that day she'd thought she could say the same about her brother. She'd idolized Henry growing up, had turned to him whenever she'd needed advice, comfort, help. Even his refusal to accept Jefferson as a member of the family hadn't lessened her love for him...but her discoveries had. Learning about his "niece," finding the photo of the girl, recognizing her all-too-familiar features...

Of course she still loved Henry. He was her brother; how could she not love him? But at that moment she hated him every bit as much as she loved him. God help her. God forgive her.

Selena laid aside the skirt she'd been folding and went to the bedroom window to watch as Tony pulled his department-issue Impala into his driveway. He climbed out, in shirt-sleeves as usual, the cuffs turned back a few times in deference to the heat, then leaned into the backseat to get his briefcase and suit coat. Out of habit, he went to the mailbox, then stood there, day's mail in hand, and gazed at her house.

She raised her hand to tap on the glass, then silently flattened her palm against it instead. If he wanted to come over and see her, he would. Trying to influence his decision wasn't fair.

When he finally started in her direction, she realized she'd been holding her breath. If he'd gone inside his own house, as he'd done the night before, she would have . . .

Faintly she smiled. She didn't know what she would have done. Being in a relationship was new to her, and being in love was totally outside her experience. In truth, she probably would have gone back to her packing, while pretending that she wasn't slowly dying inside.

The doorbell rang as she started down the stairs. She wished she had the nerve to open the doors, wrap her arms around Tony, and give him one of those deep, hungry, hard kisses she was craving. If she was sure he would welcome it, she would, but that was a big *if*.

He looked hot and tired, his hair disheveled and a faint shadow of beard darkening his jaw. He looked as if he hadn't slept well the night before. That was fair. Neither had she. When he saw her, a smile slowly curved his mouth, as if he couldn't help it. "Hey."

"Hi." She wasn't sure what to do with her hands, so she kept one on the doorknob, the other folded behind her back.

He dragged his fingers through his hair, glanced around awkwardly, then gestured. "How's your arm?"

"It's fine." She'd coated the wound with antibiotic cream and dispensed with the bandage, and found that the pain had diminished to nothing more than a dull throb unless she overstressed it. She wasn't back to her fighting best yet, but she would be soon.

"When do you see the doctor again?"

"A couple days." Though she doubted she would bother. She had more important things to worry about. Staying alive. Not losing Tony.

Funny, that she'd lied to him, betrayed him, and shot him, and he'd forgiven her, but he was having such a tough time with her working as a confidential informant for the FBI.

He wasn't likely to be pleased about her working with Damon Long.

The central air-conditioning unit rumbled softly as it came on, and the nearest vent released cold air over her, making her more aware of the heat radiating through the open door. "Want to come in?"

Tony hesitated, then stepped across the threshold. When she faced him again after closing the door, she found him gazing at the boxes of painting supplies and canvases sitting inside the living room doorway. Hugging herself tightly, she said, "They want me to move into Henry's house."

A stillness spread over him. She felt the distance between them growing, and she didn't have any idea how to close it again. He didn't even look at her as he asked, "When?"

"Tonight." She forced a weak smile. "Want to help me?"

Slowly, he turned his head. He wanted to say no. She could see it as easily as she could see his eyes were brown and his mouth was flattened. He struggled with it before dragging in a breath. "Sure." Another hesitation, another mental struggle. "Do you have time for dinner first?"

Warm relief rushed over her, easing the tightness of her muscles and unclenching the knot in her stomach. "Sure. Want to go out or cook here?"

"Let's go out." He set his briefcase next to the boxes, then draped his jacket over the top. "But not yet. Not for a few hours."

The warmth turned to heat as he took a step toward her. He slid his arm around her waist and pulled her hard against his body, then lifted one hand to tenderly cup her face. "I've missed you," he murmured, his mouth brushing hers.

"I've missed you, too," she whispered an instant before his mouth closed over hers, his tongue thrusting inside. She slid her hands into his hair before wrapping her arms tightly around him and rubbing against him like a cat. She wasn't sure, but she might have started purring, too, a deep, contented *Ummm* that went on forever.

They made it only as far as the stairs, shedding necessary clothes on the way. As he bent to suckle her nipple, she gave a vague thought to the condoms upstairs in the nightstand, then took him inside her anyway.

It was fast and hard, over in moments, then they completed the short trip to her bedroom. He moved the suitcases while she swept up the unpacked clothes and dropped them aside, then they met in the middle of the bed and started all over again.

When they'd both come several times, when their bodies were slick with sweat and their breathing had settled from frantic to merely ragged, she turned onto her side to face him. "I love you."

He looked as solemn as she sounded. He didn't smile, not

even a little, but lifted her hand, pressed a gentle kiss to the palm, then clasped it to his chest. "I know. I love you."

His heart rate was slowing, but strong and reassuring. Just beyond the tips of her fingers was the puckered scar from where she'd shot him, still purplish red, an obscene reminder of what William had done to them.

"I have to do this," she whispered. Not just for her own safety, not just for their future. She had to settle scores with William. Had to pay him back for all he'd cost her. Had to avenge herself, and Tony.

Amazingly, she didn't have to explain it to him. He understood, even though he shook his head in grim disagreement. "He'll never know that he lost." He whispered, too, as if the subject was too important for normal voices.

"I'll know."

His expression turned sad and worried, and tugged at her heart. "But at what cost, Selena? You could lose your life."

Or her reason for living. "I won't let that happen," she said fiercely, laying her head on his shoulder so he could hug her tightly.

Because if William cost her the one thing that mattered most in her life, then he really would have won, and that was one thing she couldn't survive.

Jen Fleming sat on the edge of the bed, her delicate little features screwed up in a pout as she watched Scott pack. "You keep that up, your face will freeze that way," he warned.

That made her laugh. "Marcella used to tell me that when I was little."

Marcella, nanny to Jen and her brothers, had been the most influential person in her life as a kid, but she'd been adamantly against hiring a nanny for Brianne and Bradley.

He'd given in to her on the matter, though he'd privately liked the idea of *his* kids having a nanny. Wouldn't that have given the people he'd grown up with something to talk about?

Jen drew her feet onto the bed and rested her chin on her knees. "If this case is here in town, I don't understand why you can't come home at night."

"Because we don't want the bad guys finding out who I really am."

"Big, bad FBI agent," she teased. "What is this case that you can't wear your wedding ring?"

"I can't wear the ring because no one's supposed to know I'm married."

"What name are you using?"

"Can't tell you."

"Where will you be staying?"

He couldn't blame her for all the questions. He'd never worked undercover before, so this was her first experience with it, as well. It was hard for her to imagine that he had a fake name and all the documentation to go with it—driver's license, address, credit history, job history, even an arrest record. The Bureau was nothing if not thorough.

He added the last of the clothes to the suitcase, then closed it. "Ask me no questions, and I'll tell you no lies."

She laughed again. "Marcella used to tell me that, too." Rising onto her knees, she twined her arms around his neck. "Of course, you would *never* lie to the light of your life, would you?"

"Never." Guilt flickered through him, because even that was a lie. To cover it, he bent his head to kiss her, and felt his body's instantaneous response. Nine years they'd been married, and it was always the same. Looking at her, touching her, kissing her—everything that involved her turned him on. Nine years, and he still had trouble believing she was his.

He was doing everything in his power to make sure that didn't change.

Regretfully he pulled away from her. "I've got to go, honey. I'll see you when I can."

She didn't offer to go downstairs with him, but lay back in bed, her blue silk robe draped over her perfect body. With her hair mussed and her face flushed from the lovemaking before he'd returned to his packing, she looked wicked and wanton and incredibly beautiful. When he glanced back from the doorway, she blew him a kiss.

He'd rather stay with her than carry through what he'd started. But the price of not carrying it through was steep— losing her. Losing everything. Damned if he would let that happen.

He drove across town to the Daniels estate and let himself in through the back door. Robinette sat at the kitchen table, the newspaper spread open. Across from him was a slender redhead—Beth Gentry, who'd been brought in from the Seattle office.

Robinette had come from San Francisco, the agents providing security from various other field offices. It was safer that way, lessening the chances that anyone in Davis's local operation could recognize any of them. Scott—

He gave himself a mental shake. Now that he was officially on the job, he had to get in the habit of thinking of himself as Brian Jamieson. He was the exception, and it had taken a lot of hard bargaining with the SAC to get a place on the team. Since his field of expertise was computer crimes, and he kept a fairly low profile even in his social life, it wasn't likely anyone in the drug business had ever seen or heard of him. Plus, being local had given him a bit of a head start—he had been the agent on duty the day the shootings happened, making him the first in the Bureau to know about Henry Daniels's dual lives. By the time the SAC had decided to step in on the case, Brian had already done the initial background investigations, had already begun uncovering bits and pieces about William Davis's business.

So he was in. This case was going to make his career... and save his life.

He left his luggage near the door leading to the servants' quarters, introduced himself to Gentry, then surveyed the dinner on the table—a box of Krispy Kreme doughnuts, paper-wrapped deli sandwiches, and a jar of instant coffee. "Jeez, I didn't know we were going to be roughing it," he groused as he helped himself to a sandwich.

Robinette didn't glance up. "Gentry doesn't cook. Doesn't make coffee. Doesn't make food runs."

The redhead gave him a smug smile.

"Hell, *I* make coffee. What's so hard about it?" The coffeemaker sat on the counter; a quick look in the cabinets located a box of filters and a can of coffee. He got a pot started, then sat down to wait. "What's the plan for today?"

"Get unpacked. Settle in." Robinette unwrapped a sandwich, checked its contents, then took a bite. "Long goes to court in the morning, then he'll get fitted with an electronic ankle bracelet. Once that's done, you'll spring him from jail and bring him back here."

"By myself?" Long was desperate and dangerous, two qualities Brian tried never to underestimate. But then, he wasn't just a computer geek himself. He had the same training as the other agents involved.

"You can't very well show up with an entire squad, can you? But don't worry. You'll have escorts. You may not recognize them, but they'll know you."

Well trained or not, Brian didn't like the idea of being alone with Long right off the bat. The guy was cagey, one hell of a criminal mind. What if he saw through Brian's act? What if Brian blew the whole operation before it had hardly even begun?

But he wouldn't blow it. He would never give Long any reason to suspect that Brian might be more—or less—than he pretended. He *couldn't* make Long suspicious because, like it or not, whatever success they achieved depended, in part, on Long.

And failure could be blamed on him as well. That fact might come in real handy.

After Tony and Selena showered and dressed, they drove to south Tulsa for sushi before returning to load boxes and suitcases into both their cars. When Selena had locked up her house for the last time, Tony wrapped his arms around her. "It's not too late to change your mind."

She smiled, though she'd never felt less like doing so. "It's not too late for you to change yours."

Regretfully, he shook his head. "I'm sorry. I can't."

"I can't, either."

For a moment he simply held her close. She rested her head against his chest, listening to the soft thud of his heart, the even tempo of his breathing, and wished she could stay there forever. Too soon, though, he let go and stepped away. "I'll follow you."

It was only a few miles to the estate on Riverside Drive. When Selena had stayed there as a guest two years earlier, she'd been restricted to using the back gate, reserved for servants and deliveries. When she'd broken in a few weeks ago, she'd gone over the fence once and slipped through the back gate the other time. For the first time in her life, she drove up to the front gate and the undercover FBI agent on duty smiled politely and waved her through.

The estate was more secure than her small house, Robinette had said, and since Monday's incident at the shooting range, Selena was all in favor of security. With the expansive grounds cleared for two hundred yards in every direction from the house, the tall fence, the alarms, and the security cameras, getting inside the property required an extreme level of determination. It wasn't impossible—she'd demonstrated that—but the average thug wasn't likely to succeed.

When they reached the front door, Brian Jamieson greeted them. Selena walked ten feet into the entry, then stopped, setting her two bags on the marble floor.

Her first time entering the house through the main gate and the front door, as if she had a right to be there, rather than slinking in through the back like a shameful secret. Somehow she had expected something more from the experience, but it was oddly empty.

A young woman came down the hall that led into the kitchen, dismissed Tony with a look, and apparently wished she could do the same with Selena. Instead, she said, "You've met Jamieson. I'm Beth Gentry."

Gentry was probably a few years older than Selena, several inches shorter, and spoke with an indefinable accent. With short, sleek red hair, a golden hue to her skin, and green eyes, she was pretty enough, but there was a toughness about her that had nothing to do with the .45 holstered on her belt. Did that come from being a woman in a predominantly male profession? Or was she ensuring that Selena knew up front where they stood with each other?

"This is Tony Ceola," Selena said. Of course, the agents already knew. No doubt, they knew as much about her life as she did—certainly enough to control her. Disliking the feeling intensely, she issued a small demand to shift the balance of power. "The rest of my things are in our cars. Get them, please, and take them upstairs." Without waiting for a response, she turned away, picked up the bags she'd brought in, and started up the grand staircase.

On her previous visits, she'd regretted not taking a tour of the whole house. The artist in her had wanted nothing more than to spend endless hours studying each and every masterpiece, but she'd had other things in mind, such as staying alive. Now her gaze flitted from painting to sculpture to architectural detail. The night she'd broken in, she'd searched each of the five bedrooms on the second floor. She turned to the right and into the room that looked as if it was ready and waiting for a visit from a beloved niece.

Not that she was so very beloved anymore. But then, she'd never been a niece, either, so what did it matter?

Tony set his load down at the foot of the bed, then glanced around. "Was it as satisfying as you'd thought it would be?"

The question startled her, a nice accompaniment to the cool prickling at her nape that had started when she'd reached the landing. She tried to erase the discomfort with a smile. "How did you—?"

"I know you."

"No, it wasn't," she admitted.

"Because Henry wasn't here to witness it?"

She shrugged.

"He won't be here to witness it when you bring his empire crashing down."

Stifling an impatient sigh, she went to slide her arms around his waist. "No, he won't. But for the first time in my life, I'll be so totally free that I won't care. Free to do what I want, to please whom I want. Free to live my own life. To have . . . things." Love. Marriage. Friends. Family.

He nuzzled her hair back from her ear. "You already please me. Isn't that enough?"

His question called to mind a line from an old song. *Sometimes love just ain't enough.* She'd never imagined that. She'd always thought that loving someone, and being loved in return, could overcome anything. Was she idealistic or just plain uninformed? After all, she'd never felt this kind of normal, whole, healthy love until Tony. What did she know about it?

Instead of answering his question, she kissed him, breaking away only when Gentry and Jamieson entered the room. They left the bags they carried at the foot of the bed, then Gentry said, "We'll be around if you need anything. Use the intercom." She gestured toward the panel next to the door before following Jamieson from the room.

Though she longed to return to Tony's embrace, Selena began unpacking. Her movements felt stiff, forced, as she carried an armload of clothes to the closet, as she emptied a bag full of shoes. She didn't want to be in this place, didn't want to let its darkness embrace her. But living there temporarily was the only way she could go back to Tony's cozy little house on Princeton Court. It was a price worth paying.

As she placed a stack of underwear in a dresser drawer, she glanced at his reflection in the mirror. "You can spend the night if you'd like."

He looked around again, then his gaze drifted to the doorway. Across the hall was William's study, where he'd spent so many hours visiting with his godfather. Where Selena had shot Tony. Where he had shot William. "No," he said quietly. "I can't."

She understood. He had choices, and she couldn't blame

him for taking the one she would make, given the opportunity. "Well..."

Forcing a smile, he caught hold of her hand and pulled her out into the hall. Their footsteps echoed on the bare stone as they descended the stairs, then walked out onto the porch. There he held her close once more. "Call me."

"I will," she promised. "You call me, too."

He nodded. "I, uh, I'll see you when I can." A hard squeeze, a quick kiss, and he was heading toward the steps.

"Tony?" She tried, but couldn't hold back the plea. "Don't stop loving me."

On the top step, he stopped and, amazingly, laughed. "Oh, yeah, right. As if I could. I'll see you soon, babe."

5

The mansion, Selena had discovered after an extensive tour, was more of a museum, or mausoleum. Filled with great antiques and priceless art, it was cold, lifeless—not the sort of place she wanted to call home, not even temporarily. But her second-floor bedroom was comfortable enough, and the ballroom that encompassed the third floor offered tremendous possibilities. It seemed a world apart from the stiff formality below—a world apart from William. She could easily envision him in the rooms downstairs, could *feel* his presence in every object, in every shadow, but she felt no such presence in the ballroom. The floor-to-ceiling windows that let in an astonishing amount of light, the expansive wood floor, and the extravagantly high ceilings made it the perfect place to paint, to work out, just to breathe...or to plot an undercover operation that would, she hoped, result in a lot of arrests and few, if any, deaths. Especially not her own.

By ten Thursday morning, she had turned a corner of the massive room into a gym. Mats covered the gleaming wood, and the lines and pulleys of a home gym cast shadows on the pale blue walls. The FBI had turned another section into a conference area, bringing up a cherrywood table from the library, along with a set of matching chairs.

It was the first argument she'd won with Robinette. He'd suggested using the second-floor study, and she'd refused.

The brief times she'd spent there were filled with more bad memories than she could handle. She'd suffered such disappointment and heartache within those walls. She didn't think she could set foot inside again.

Robinette hadn't made the suggestion out of spite. He was analytical by nature, cynical by experience. Emotion, she suspected, held no place in his life, and certainly not in his job. He wouldn't feel guilty if anything happened to her, but he would do his damnedest to make sure nothing did. It was a matter of pride for him, of doing his job efficiently.

She had lost their next argument. He'd prohibited her from running along the river that morning, so she'd made endless laps instead, back and forth along the rear fence, with Gentry following at ten paces and the guards stationed at the back gate watching. It had given her the opportunity to note the recently installed motion sensors, as well as the greatly extended surveillance system. William had been overly confident with his security setup, which had allowed her to break in twice. The FBI, she'd been pleased to see, were doing serious upgrades.

"You know how to spar?" she asked Jamieson as she finished up on the home gym and dried the sweat from her face.

"Sure."

"Come on." Rising from the bench, she picked up two sets of sparring gear and offered one to him.

He gave her a dubious look. "I don't fight girls."

"Afraid she'll kick your ass?" Robinette asked from his seat at the head of the table.

Jamieson tilted William's antique chair back on its rear legs. "My mother would kick my ass if I even thought about hitting a girl—"

Selena gave the back of the chair a shove. His arms swung

wildly as he tried to catch himself, then he crashed to the floor with a grunt. "Hey! That was a sucker move!"

"You're right. Sorry. Let me help you up." She offered her hand, and he grudgingly took it. As he pushed away from the floor with his other hand, she pulled, taking advantage of his forward momentum to execute a flip. The ballroom echoed with the slap of his body against the wood. He lay there, his mouth working but lacking the air to produce sound.

"Another sucker move, huh? Sorry again." She turned... and walked into a punch that sent her reeling. Regaining her balance an instant before stumbling into the gym equipment, she shook her head, then focused on Gentry.

The woman stood, weight evenly balanced, a faint smile curving her mouth. "Sorry," she said, her apology no more sincere than Selena's had been.

Selena worked her jaw side to side, decided it was all right, then tossed the sparring gear at Gentry before donning her own. All her past sparring partners had been men—at the gym in Key West where she'd trained, at the Tulsa gym where she'd worked out—and her only real fights had been against men, as well. She figured she could more than hold her own against the smaller woman.

Gentry struck first with a kick that sliced through the air mere centimeters from Selena's head. Selena's responding kick connected low on Gentry's back and sent her sprawling. She regained her feet an instant after hitting the mat and tried a heel-palm strike. Selena blocked it, but the other woman grabbed her wrist and twisted it hard.

"Okay." Robinette set aside the file he'd been studying and glanced around the room. "Can you listen while you do that?"

"Sure," Selena responded, as Gentry forced her to the floor. A knee to the back knocked her flat on the mat, and an instant later, the full brunt of Gentry's weight held her there. The woman was trying to maneuver her arm around Selena's throat, but she resisted, tucking her chin tightly to her chest, until an opportunity presented itself.

When she'd bitten Damon Long the night he'd broken into her bedroom, he'd bellowed in pain and smacked her across the face. Gentry merely grunted and eased her grip long enough for Selena to wriggle onto her back, then dislodge the woman with an upward heave.

"Davis kept a lot of records," Robinette said. "Unfortunately, most of them are encrypted. Even the parts of his journals that deal with the business are written in some kind of code that we haven't figured out yet. We've learned a little there, and we've conducted extensive interviews with the people arrested after the incident. We're also working with local law enforcement in Boston, Savannah, and Philadelphia to determine which drug operations in those areas might be Davis's. Long can help us with that, though he can lie to us, too. We'll take his word when we have to. We'll try to verify everything else. Jamieson did a preliminary check of Davis's family. He's got a sister, and she's got a husband and a son. Husband's a lawyer in Alabama, the son's a stockbroker in Florida. They're all clean—no arrests, names have never come up involved in anything illegal, they're not on any known associates list. Nothing to suggest that they even knew about Davis's business, much less participated."

Gentry was circling, and Selena kept pace with her, her gaze shifting constantly from face to hands to feet. Gentry was good, though; she didn't telegraph her intentions, but came in with a jab to the abdomen that Selena blocked, and a chop to the upper right arm that she didn't. Though Gentry had pulled the punch—if she hadn't, Selena's arm would be broken—intense pain radiated from the blow.

Selena took a step back and massaged the spot. When she lowered her hand, Gentry mouthed something around the mouth guard that might have been, "I'm sorry," but just as easily could have been, "Fuck you."

Then she struck in the same place again.

For the first time since Monday's ambush, Selena's left arm provided the least of her pain. Sweat dripped off her, and her right arm was rapidly swelling. So far, she'd gotten the worst of this workout, a position she wasn't accustomed to. She'd walked away from many a sparring match bruised and battered, but able to say she'd given as good as she got. This one wasn't going to be any different.

She stripped off the red vinyl-covered mitts, loosened the strap that secured the headgear, then approached Gentry, her hand extended. Warily Gentry offered her own hand for a shake, drawing back at the last instant but too late to save herself. Gripping the woman's hand, Selena took her to the floor with a sweep kick, then swiftly flipped her onto her stomach. Keeping her there with her knee centered in her back, Selena pinned her wrists together and raised them high between the shoulder blades. With her free hand, she pulled out the mouth guard and said, "You're not bad."

"Not bad, my ass. I'm damn good. You're taller and heavier, and I still inflicted the only real damage." Gentry didn't waste any energy trying to free herself but waited until Selena let go and got to her feet. Then she stood as well and moved both shoulders in an exaggerated shrug to ease their strain.

"If you two are done, can we get back to work?" Robinette asked impatiently. "Jamieson's got to leave to pick up Long, and we need to be ready."

Drying her face with a towel, Selena took two bottled waters from the small stainless-steel fridge against one wall, tossed one to Gentry, then drank deeply from the other. "I'm listening."

"When Long gets here, you introduce us to him. You have our backgrounds."

She nodded. He'd given her the typed information the night before—a little bedtime reading, he'd said with what passed for a smile. Their assumed identities came with assumed criminal backgrounds, much of which she'd committed to memory as she'd tried to distract herself from where she was . . . and who she wasn't with.

"Lay out the rules for him right up front—no weapons, no access to a phone, no going anywhere on his own. Give him whatever story you want—it's the terms of his release, you don't trust him, whatever. Start off strong with him. Otherwise, since he has all the knowledge, he'll think he's also got all the power."

Pretend that she had power. Why not? She was pretending about everything else.

"What does he know about Ceola?"

She shrugged. "I told him Tony was no longer a concern."

"Then maybe he shouldn't come around here anymore."

Selena's chest tightened. If she wasn't allowed to go anywhere, and Tony wasn't allowed to come to the estate . . . The operation would take weeks, probably months. With no contact with Tony? "We'll have to negotiate that," she said, aiming for that strength Robinette had recommended moments earlier. When he opened his mouth, she raised one hand. "Tony isn't a threat to me, and as large as this estate is, there should be no problem with keeping Long from knowing when he's here."

"Ceola's a cop, and you're a drug dealer."

"He's a cop with a legitimate investigative interest in this house and in me. If that interest requires an occasional visit..." She shrugged. Even bona fide criminals had occasional contact with law enforcement. She'd been involved in a major homicide case that had been wrapped up in that very house, and no one—not William's associates, not any hit men waiting out there for her, not even Long—would be surprised if the lead detective showed up a time or two.

"We'll see," Robinette said dismissively. "Tell Long you want the quick course on who's who in your organization. Concentrate on the big names, the ones responsible for each of the East Coast operations. Find out the status of operations at the time of Davis's shooting. Get names, contact information, details."

Selena nodded. Pretend to be strong and in control while acknowledging that she knew nothing about the business. Piece of cake.

But at least Long *knew* she knew nothing. It was the others, those responsible for the operations, that she had to fool.

"Okay." Robinette glanced at his watch. "Jamieson, you'd better get going. You two"—he nodded at Selena and Gentry in turn—"need to hit the showers. Meet back here as soon as Jamieson's back with Long."

Selena trailed Gentry to the door, then turned. "In the meantime, Mr. Robinette, why don't you see about the lunch?"

His grumble followed her down the stairs. "See about lunch? What does she think I am? Her goddamn personal assistant?"

With the unfamiliar discomfort of the electronic bracelet chafing his ankle, Damon followed the corrections officer through a doorway and into the reception area. Outprocessing hadn't taken as long as he'd expected. A few more yards, and he would be outside and free...more or less.

The guard stopped in front of a man waiting near the door. "This is Damon Long," he announced uninterestedly before leaving them alone.

"Nice to meet you." The stranger offered his hand.

Damon ignored the hand and instead looked him over head to toe. His jacket was expensive and well cut, but didn't quite disguise the shoulder holster underneath. His watch was pricey, as well. He looked like a banker or an accountant—book-smart, soft, harmless. "Who the hell are you?"

"Brian Jamieson."

"Yeah. Who the hell are you?"

"I work for Ms. McCaffrey. Same as you."

Selena hadn't said a damn thing to him about bringing in strangers. Personnel had always been his responsibility—hiring them, firing them, and, except on rare occasions when William's temper got the better of him, killing them.

Restraining a snort, Damon pushed the door open and stepped outside. Hell, he'd decided, would bear a strong resemblance to summertime in Oklahoma, but it was a damn sight better outdoors than it had been inside. The air smelled better, things looked clearer, and life had possibilities. It had restrictions, too, he acknowledged, as the bracelet shifted with his movement, but that was all right. He was experienced at escaping restrictions.

Jamieson gestured to a car in the nearest parking space—William's Cadillac. "Where are we going?" Damon asked as he opened the passenger door.

"Mr. Davis's estate."

So one of Selena's old wishes had finally come true—she was living in William's house. He would have figured she'd want to stay hell and gone from there, considering the bad memories the place must hold for her. Then again, maybe all those memories hadn't been so bad after all. Maybe neither he nor William had known her nearly as well as they'd thought.

"When did she hire you?"

Jamieson fastened his seat belt, looked over both shoulders, then backed out of the space. Before pulling out of the lot, he repeated the double look. Afraid someone might be waiting to spring Damon from his custody? Or just cautious by nature? "Recently," he finally replied.

"Huh. How'd she find you?" When Jamieson glanced at him, Damon shrugged. "You didn't work for the old man. She damn sure didn't run an ad in the Tulsa paper. She didn't ask me for recommendations, and she doesn't know anyone to turn to for help of this sort."

"You'd have to ask her that."

Gazing out the side window as they turned onto Riverside Drive, Damon asked, "Exactly what is your job?"

"I do what Ms. McCaffrey tells me to do."

Ms. McCaffrey. Not Damon. So Selena wanted him to teach her everything, wanted to work together, but she'd gone out and hired someone—multiple someones?—to help protect her interests. Interesting.

Definitely *multiple someones,* he saw when they turned into the estate drive a few minutes later. None of the guards at the gate were familiar. Neither was the man fixing a cup of coffee when they entered the kitchen through the back door, nor the woman sitting at a table, impatiently tapping a pen against a pad, in the third-floor ballroom. He wouldn't mind the chance to get to know her better, though. He'd always had a weakness for redheads.

He did recognize Selena at the easel a few yards away, brush in hand. "Damn, Selena," he said with a wolfish grin as he strolled toward her. "All this new help might make a man feel you don't trust him."

Her smile was cold-blooded as a snake. "I don't trust you, Mr. Long. Why pretend otherwise?"

He grinned again. "But you need me."

"I do. Just as you need me."

"For the time being," he acknowledged.

"Yes." She cleaned the brush, then laid it aside and picked up another before meeting his gaze. "For the time being."

He picked up the brush, flicking the damp bristles across his finger. Imitating William's most scathing look, she pulled it away and returned it to its place.

Long gave her a smug smile and shoved both hands into his hip pockets. "Does William's sister know you've made yourself at home here?"

"It's really none of her business."

"I don't know . . . the family home . . ."

She dabbed a few strokes of green paint on the canvas, then blended white over it with the same brush. "William was so certain that he could persuade me to join him that he put his estate under my control should anything happen to him. Mrs. Hamilton might not be happy about it, but I'm enjoying my inheritance."

The old man *had* been goddamn sure of himself, Damon acknowledged. He'd never seriously considered defeat, not even that day downstairs when Selena had turned her gun on him.

He wasn't considering defeat, either. "I don't like you hiring new people without consulting me first."

"These people work for me. So do you."

"No. I'm working *with* you. Big difference."

"William left the business to *me*. The extent of your role, the freedom I allow you, is up to me."

The freedom *she* allowed . . . bitch. It was going to be such a pleasure to give her what she deserved.

With a jerk of his head, he indicated the others. "How did you find these clowns?"

Head tilted to one side, she studied him a moment before smiling thinly. "I know you like to think you were privy to everything William did, but that wasn't the case. Even though I was an unwilling student, he gave me lessons anyway."

Damon wanted to call her a liar, to insist that he *had* known everything the old man did, said, or even thought. But she was right. William's conversations with her had been private. For all Damon knew, they could have talked about nothing... or everything. Certainly William had been arrogant enough to assume she would take over the business as he wanted. Certainly he could have begun her education even while she refused.

Sullenly, he gestured toward the hired help. "Who are they?"

She gave the painting, one of her usual tropical beach scenes, a last look before starting across the room. "You met Mr. Jamieson. This is Beth Gentry, and that's Adam Robinette."

"That doesn't tell me shit."

She raised one slender hand in the blond's direction. "Mr. Robinette used to work for a gentleman in Miami by the name of Gonzalez. I assume you've heard of him."

Damon snorted. Hector Gonzalez was to south Florida what William had been elsewhere. William had tried to broker a merger with the man a couple of times, but Hector hadn't been interested. If he had, he might not have been executed in a bloody coup a few months previously.

"Mr. Jamieson is Mr. Robinette's computer expert," she went on.

Book-smart, soft, harmless. "And Ms. Gentry?"

Gentry rose from her chair to get a bottle of water from

the refrigerator. Definitely not harmless. She was pretty, all lean muscle, feminine but also tough—as different from the last woman he'd been with as night from day. After twisting the cap off, she raised the bottle in a salute. "Uncle Sol sends his regards."

Sol Vitelli from Detroit. William hadn't tried to take over *his* business. Vitelli would have chewed him up, spit him out, then pissed on what was left. "You don't look like a Vitelli."

She smiled. "It's an honorary title."

Damon studied the three. Was this really just a job to them, or did they have an agenda? Maybe Robinette and Jamieson had been satisfied working as flunkies to ol' Hector. Maybe they weren't interested in moving up, taking control. Maybe Gentry was just taking a break from Michigan, or maybe she was there to give Sol an in. The old man had never expressed any interest in expanding south and east, but then, a good businessman wouldn't.

Either way, the three would bear watching.

Selena moved to the chair at the head of the table. It was elaborately carved, a souvenir of one of William's trips to Germany. It looked like a goddamn throne, and she looked right at home in it. Imperious. Just like the fuckin' old man. She waited until everyone else was seated—the two men on one side, Gentry on the other, and Damon at the far end—then said, "First, Mr. Long... I take it they explained the conditions of your release."

He propped his left foot on the table and pulled his jeans leg up to show the monitoring bracelet. "The latest in high-tech jewelry. Tells 'em where I am within three feet. I can't even take a piss without 'em knowing."

She nodded once in acknowledgment. "You'll be staying here, in the guesthouse. You won't have access to weapons of any kind, and you won't be going anywhere without one of us accompanying you. For all practical purposes, you're still in jail, Mr. Long, albeit a more comfortable one."

Now, there's a fucking surprise, he thought dryly. But he didn't need a weapon to be dangerous, and babysitters were easy to get rid of.

Her smug piece finished, she folded her hands together on the tabletop and said, "Let's get down to business. Tell me what you know, Mr. Long."

"About what?"

Once again, she smiled that cool, William-like smile that made him want to wrap his hands around her throat and choke it right out of her, along with her life, and she replied in that cool, William-like voice.

"My business, of course."

Long's voice was even, his manner exaggeratedly patient, as he explained the basics. There were three major areas of operation. Vernell Munroe was based in Boston and controlled New England. Sonny Yates worked out of Savannah and had the Southern region, and Barnard Taylor ran everything in between from Philadelphia. Munroe and Taylor had been with William for nineteen and eighteen years, respectively. Yates was the newcomer, with only ten years on the job.

Selena kept her hands folded loosely in her lap and half wished she'd allowed William to teach her at least a little about his business. It was definitely to Long's advantage to lie. The FBI would try to verify everything he passed on, but there would no doubt be much they couldn't prove or disprove until it was too late.

But if she'd let William teach her the business, she wouldn't be posing as a drug dealer. She would *be* one. More dangerous or not, she preferred the pretense.

"How did Yates come to be in charge of the Southern region with so few years experience?"

Long grinned. "How did you come to be in charge of the whole damn game with no experience whatsoever?"

She fixed her gaze on him. "I had an in with the boss. Are you saying Yates did, as well?"

"Nope. Just like the others, Yates never met William. But the number of years you've been doing the job doesn't have anything to do with how good you are at it. Sonny was the right-hand man to the previous boss. When he disappeared, Sonny was ready to step into his shoes. He keeps his employees happy and makes a good profit, and that kept William happy."

"What happened to the previous boss?" Robinette asked.

Long's gaze narrowed when he directed his attention to the other man. He resented the newcomers—because he suspected they might usurp his authority? Selena wondered. Or because they were a barrier he would have to go through to get to her? "Sonny happened. He was ambitious. He didn't want to be number two forever. The old man taught Sonny everything he needed to take over, so naturally, he did."

Naturally, Selena silently echoed. Just as Long would take over from her given the chance. "What do you know about Yates?"

"Not much. Born in Atlanta. Has lived in Savannah for years. Never been arrested. Closest he's ever come was a speeding ticket ten or twelve years ago. Doesn't have any family. Very good at keeping a low profile. Cops there in Savannah have never even heard of him."

"And what about Mr. Taylor and Mr. Munroe?"

"Cops in Philadelphia and Boston know all about them. They've been trying to put them both away permanently for as long as they've been in business—some forty years. They've done a few stints here and there, but nothing since they went to work for William."

"Helped to have a highly respected police officer running interference for them, didn't it?" Selena asked dryly. "You said none of them ever met William. Is that true? They never saw him face-to-face? Never knew his true identity?"

With a scrape of wood on wood, Long pushed his chair back, then propped his feet on the gleaming cherry table. "Did William strike you as the sort to set himself up as a target for blackmail? His safety came first—before the money, before the power, before everything. Besides, that's what he had me for. To be the face man."

William had been good at that—rescuing young people in desperate need so he could manipulate them into fulfilling whatever role he had in mind for them. Long had accepted his role willingly. How differently would things have been if Selena had, as well? She would have been better off dead on the streets of Ocho Rios.

"So they never dealt directly with him. They were never guests in his home."

"God, no." His grin was sly. "He was picky about who he allowed in his house."

She refused to show that the barb had found its target. "How did he form these relationships?"

When he heaved a sigh, she stared at him. "Are you bored, Mr. Long?"

"Pretty much."

"Get over it, because we'll continue this until *I'm* bored." Her words crackled with ice. "Let's try again. How did he form these relationships?"

The conversation dragged on, until Selena's head was so full of information that she felt stuffy with it. Boiled down, Vernell Munroe had been a small-time dealer in Boston during William's stint there with the police department. After having much of Munroe's competition executed, William had sent Long to the man with a deal too good to refuse. He repeated the process when he hired on with the Philadelphia Police Department, and again when he'd taken over as chief in Savannah. Whatever curiosity the men had about their mysterious boss was inconsequential; millions of dollars in profits could excuse any eccentricities in their boss, could silence any number of questions.

In need of fresh air, Selena called for a break. Taking a bottle of water, she went onto the balcony that ran along the back of the house, overlooking the pool and the guesthouse, and stood there a moment, eyes closed, breathing deeply.

"He was wrong about one thing."

She'd heard the faint creak of the door an instant before Robinette spoke, so his voice didn't startle her. Nor did his words surprise her.

"Sonny Yates's name has come up with the authorities in Savannah. They don't know much about him, but they know he's into something dirty." The agent leaned against the stone balustrade, grimaced at the heat, and swiped his shirtsleeve across his forehead.

She liked the heat, would like it more if she could feel the sun on her skin, chasing away the chill brought on by the house, Long, the afternoon's discussion. But the house blocked the sun, leaving only its heat and the still, muggy air.

"In fact, Yates came up in a missing persons case. A fishing boat and its crew disappeared. The wife of one of the crewmen said her husband worked for Mr. Yates."

According to Long, William had enough boats to fish the Atlantic dry, along with a fleet of planes, trucks, and automobiles. Until recently, when she'd thought of a drug dealer, she'd thought of individuals smuggling a few pounds here or there, or standing on a street corner selling small packets for ten or twenty dollars each. She hadn't realized how very like a legitimate business it was—but she was learning. "I assume the boat's catch disappeared as well."

"Presumably. These people don't take kindly to being robbed." He exhaled heavily, then pushed away from the warm stone. "Let's look into it. We'll meet with Mr. Yates first. Reward him. Invite him here."

Meet with him. Let him come into her home. Show him that while she was running William's business, she was doing it her way.

He waited for her nod, then walked to the door. When he turned back, she thought for a moment it might be to offer a compliment, or even just a comment, on her performance so far. It wasn't. "Don't stay out here too long. Long's still got to provide introductions to Munroe, Taylor, and Yates for you."

Once more, she nodded. After the door closed behind him, she gazed into the woods that backed the iron fence. On the other side of the trees, running where railroad tracks once had, was the River Parks trail. She'd jogged it every day since coming to Tulsa until that week. If she could reach it, she could run far and fast . . . but between the armed guards, the surveillance cameras, and the motion detectors, the odds of reaching the trail were somewhere between slim and none.

Besides, she acknowledged with a faint smile, the only place she would want to run was to Tony—the first place they would check.

After finishing the water, she returned to the ballroom. Jamieson had moved to a separate table, a delicate little Queen Anne piece, and was typing away on his laptop. Gentry was flipping through a magazine, looking totally absorbed by it but, underneath, totally alert. Robinette was setting up a telephone, and Long was sprawled in his chair, head tilted back, eyes closed, looking lazy. Attractive. Sexy. The first time they'd met, he'd charmed her right into William's blackmail scheme. A few weeks earlier, he'd charmed Tony's younger sister, Lucia, right into his bed.

In the end, both efforts had cost him. Selena had cracked his skull open with a marble statue, and Lucia had given Tony the lead he'd needed to knot all his loose ends around William and Long.

Apparently aware of her study, Long slowly opened his eyes and stared back at her with such cold regard that she had to stifle a shiver. He could appear so normal—handsome, friendly, outgoing—but it was all an act. Deep inside, she suspected, he didn't really feel much of anything. He didn't care about anything except himself.

Breaking away from his gaze, she sat down, then gestured to the phone. "Call Mr. Munroe for me," she said politely. "Introduce us."

His feet hit the floor with a thud, and he grudgingly came to her end of the table, sliding into the chair to her right. He dialed the number from memory, then settled back in his seat. "Hey, DeShaun, this is Damon. How's it going? . . . Yeah, things have been kind of busy here. Listen, put Mr. Munroe on the phone, would you? The boss wants to talk to him."

The boss. Selena had never been anyone's boss, not even her own. Could she really convince these career criminals that she was in control? She had to. Her life depended on it.

A distant greeting echoed from the receiver. "Vernell, how are you? . . . Yeah, I know we've been out of touch. A lot's been going on here. Bad news is . . . William got shot. He's in the hospital, in a coma, and the doctors don't think he'll ever wake up. That means his niece is taking over sooner than anyone expected. She wants to talk to you about that."

Selena's hands had turned clammy. Surreptitiously, she

dried them on her skirt, then accepted the receiver from Long. She swallowed hard, but it didn't clear the tightness from her throat. "Mr. Munroe. I'm Selena McCaffrey. Uncle William has told me a lot about you. I'm looking forward to working with you, though I wish the circumstances were better."

"I'm sorry for your loss." Munroe's accent was New England, his voice raspy. "Who shot him?"

"It was one of his own men."

"One of ours?" He sounded disbelieving.

She glanced at Robinette, half-surprised he hadn't gone off somewhere to listen in. But the call was likely being recorded—they didn't trust her, and a wiretap seemed logical—so he could listen to the tapes later. "No," she replied. "It's a long, complicated story, but . . . around here, Uncle William was better known as Henry Daniels, chief of police. He was shot by one of his officers, who'd discovered his other identity . . ."

"Chief of police," Barnard Taylor repeated. "I'll be damned. Well, that explains a lot."

Selena acknowledged that with a small sound. "At the present time, Mr. Taylor, I see no reason why we shouldn't continue with business as usual."

"The local cops aren't trying to shut it down?"

"As far as they're aware, they *have* shut it down. They think it's a local organization, and they've arrested most of those involved. Those arrested have little enough information to share. I've escaped the authorities' notice, and I've persuaded the judge to release Mr. Long into my custody. We'll have to give up our share of the business here for now, but we'll take it back when the time is right. So . . . once things are a bit more settled here, I'd like to meet with everyone and discuss any changes that might be necessary."

"Meet," Taylor parroted again. "You know, I never met Mr. Davis. Now I understand why. I take it you don't have a secret life to protect."

"No, Mr. Taylor. With me, what you see is what you get."

To her right, Long snorted.

"You *are* keeping Damon on, aren't you?"

She turned a cold stare on him. "Oh, absolutely. I couldn't possibly run this business without Mr. Long."

"Fuck you," Damon mouthed . . .

"I doubt anyone could, not even Davis." Sonny Yates chuckled. "Or Daniels. Christ, he was chief of police here in Savannah, too. No wonder he used Damon as his front guy."

"Did you ever meet him when he was chief in Savannah?"

"Nah. I make it a point not to hang out with cops. They tend to be pretty narrow-minded about this right-and-wrong business." He chuckled again. "Though, obviously, there are exceptions to the rule."

Thank God, Tony wasn't one of the exceptions, Selena thought, sparing just a moment to miss him. On a normal day, he would get off work soon, go home, and show up at her doorstep shortly after. This not being a normal day, she had no clue when she would see him again. "How is business in Savannah?"

"The usual. A few problems. Nothing we can't handle."

"What kind of problems?"

"Nothing much. We had a boat go missing a few weeks ago. We handled it, though, and got the cargo back."

He spoke so casually, as if he'd done nothing more than fire the crew. A shiver crept through Selena. She knew other people's lives meant nothing to William and Long, and apparently, Yates, but the ease with which they could kill still made her blood run cold.

"That's good. Very good." Her voice sounded shaky, so she drew a breath and hurried on. "I'd like to meet with you, Mr. Yates. You have the honor of being the first person I'm inviting to my home."

"I *am* honored," he said, and sounded it. "But I can't leave Savannah right now."

"Why not?"

"It would be bad for business to get called in to see the boss right now." When she remained silent, he patiently continued. "When your own employees start stealing from you, you have to make an example of them, and you have to look damned strong while doing it. If word gets out that the boss has demanded my presence right after something like this, people are going to start thinking I'm in trouble, and it won't matter that I'm not. It'll undermine my authority." His voice softened and turned steely at the same time. "I don't let anything undermine my authority. If you want to see me anytime soon, you'll have to come here."

Selena glanced at Robinette, fairly certain he wouldn't like what she was about to say, but that didn't deter her. "All right. We'll be in touch with the details, Mr. Yates. Until then."

After hanging up, she clasped her hands in her lap. "Pack your bags, gentlemen, Ms. Gentry. It appears we're going to Savannah."

Gentry and Jamieson exchanged glances before they both looked at Robinette. He was very still, almost managing an unaffected look . . . but not quite. She might as well make it easy for him to say what he needed to say. She shifted her gaze to the others. "Mr. Jamieson, why don't you get Mr. Long settled in the guesthouse? Ms. Gentry can help."

"Uh...yeah...sure." Jamieson scraped back his chair and got to his feet. The others left without a word.

Hands still folded, Selena listened to their footsteps receding. A moment later, she thought she heard the kitchen door close, though more likely, two floors away, it was just her imagination.

Finally, Robinette pushed away from the wall where he'd leaned. He shoved his hands in his pockets and strolled to the far end of the table, pushing in Jamieson's chair, closing Gentry's magazine, straightening Long's chair. "Go to Savannah. You think it's that easy?"

"People travel there every day."

"One of the reasons we're using this house is because it's relatively easy to secure. We have our people inside and out. We have surveillance. We have backup just a phone call away. If we go to Savannah, we'll have to stay in a hotel. There will be civilians around. We'll be on Yates's turf. Security will be a problem."

She smiled tightly. "Handling problems is your job, isn't it?"

Color flared in his cheeks. "Making decisions is my job, too."

"Yates refused to leave Savannah. Was I supposed to ask him to hold on while I asked my employees what I should do? That would certainly convince him that I'm capable of running this organization, wouldn't it?" She held his gaze, but naturally he didn't reply. "Assuming we all go, that's five people. Not a big deal."

"Five...have you not noticed the three shifts of guards working the gates? This is a major investigation. There are plenty of people besides us involved. It's not a simple matter of getting on a plane. I'll have to arrange private transportation. I'll have to clear it for Long to make the trip. I'll have to find a place for us to stay and set up security and surveillance at that end. You're not going to be nearly as safe there as you are here. We'll have to account for that, as well."

She stood up, fingertips resting on the tabletop. "So arrange. Clear it. Account for it."

The color spread from his cheeks to flush his entire face. "Look, Ms. McCaffrey, regardless of what the bad guys think, *you* work for *me*—"

"I'm working *with* you," she disagreed, parroting Long. "And what the bad guys think is all that really matters, isn't it? You tell me to act as if I'm a drug lord, as if I'm now truly running this venture. Well, Mr. Robinette, I have to have the leeway to make some decisions myself, or no one's ever going to believe that I'm in charge."

He looked as if he wanted to argue, but how could he? She was right, and he knew it.

She waited a moment. When he said nothing, she did. "I told Yates we would get back to him with the details. You set up the trip, and I'll let him know."

6

It was almost quitting time when Tony settled in at his desk with a stack of folders. With Henry in the hospital and Damon Long in jail, his workload had dropped off significantly. His current cases consisted of three gang-related drive-bys and a bank-robbery homicide, plus some old cases that he hadn't yet given up on.

And an attempted homicide that he wasn't assigned to but had a personal stake in. The lab hadn't found anything to help them—no fingerprints on the shell casings, nothing remarkable about the fiber. The shooter must have been lucky or well instructed, since Tony was convinced he wasn't a pro. There was just no way a pro would have missed his target under those circumstances.

Sending in an amateur certainly limited the suspect list. If a hit had been put out by any of the top men who worked under Henry, the job would have been given to someone with experience. Had a lesser employee taken it upon himself to kill Selena in an attempt to save himself? Or had the person who'd sent him been faced with limited options?

Damon Long had limited options—sitting in jail, facing a certain conviction and the death penalty. Every visitor he had was logged in, every phone number he called duly noted. And he had plenty of reasons to want Selena dead.

Standing up, Tony pulled his suit coat on. "I'm going over to the jail," he announced to no one in particular.

Darnell Garry, on the computer, nodded absently. Simmons stood up from his own desk. "Lucky you," he said sourly. "I get to question the dearly bereaved of that little smart-ass that got shot in the bar fight the other night. Wanna trade?"

"When you have such a knack for interrogating the victim's loved ones?" Tony joked.

"More like pissing 'em off," Garry put in.

"Is it my fault these people insist on pretending that their kids were perfect little angels? Besides"—Simmons grinned broadly—"I get along just fine with the victims themselves."

"What does that say about you, Frankie, when the only people who can stand being around you for long are dead?" Garry asked.

Tony left them squabbling and took the stairs to the parking garage. It was only a few blocks to the correctional center. He parked and went inside, stowed his weapons in a lockbox just off the lobby, and went to find the information he was after.

"Phone calls made by Damon Long," a corrections officer named Johannes repeated as he checked the records. "We have three—two to the same number the first couple days he was here, then another a week later."

Tony wrote down the numbers, then checked through his notes that filled half the legal pad. The first two calls were to Long's lawyer, as he'd thought. He would have to run the second number through telephone security to find out who it belonged to. "What about visitors?"

"Lawyer, lawyer, lawyer . . . here's one—Carl Heinz. Was here last Friday and again yesterday. The only other one was a Selena McCaf—" At Tony's choked curse, the officer broke off. "You know her?"

Tony's fingers curled so tightly around his pen that it cut

off circulation. He wished it was Selena's neck he was squeezing, wished a good strangling would shake some sense into her. Goddamn it to hell, what was she doing visiting Long? How stupid could she be?

"Yeah, I know her." He unclenched his fingers and flexed them to get the blood flowing again. "I want to talk to him. Can you get us an interview room?"

Johannes checked the computer again, then shook his head. "You're a couple hours too late. He was released this morning."

Panic building inside, Tony shook his own head. "He was denied bail."

"Judge reconsidered and granted it."

"Why would he do that? The man killed at least nine people! He's committed more crimes than all your inmates here combined. Why in hell would the judge release him?"

Johannes shrugged. "I don't have any idea. But Selena McCaffrey might. He was released into her custody. You know where to find her?"

Ice spread through Tony, making his movements and his voice stiff and unyielding. "Yeah, I know." *Goddamn!*

It took less than ten minutes to reach the Daniels estate, where he was stopped at the gate by armed guards. He showed his badge as he said, "I want to see Selena McCaffrey."

"Ms. McCaffrey isn't seeing visitors at this time."

"She'll make an exception for me." She'd damn well better. If she turned him away...

The thought gave him pause. If she turned him away, it would mean a significant change in their relationship...as if they hadn't already faced a few of those. The difference was, so far they were surviving. But one more disagreement—one more disillusionment—just might be one too many.

The guard stepped a few yards away and made a call on his cell phone. While he waited, Tony drummed his fingers on the steering wheel, feeling the knot of tension in his gut growing.

Finally, the guard got off the phone, opened the gate with a remote, then bent to look in the driver's window. "Park at the side there and use the main entrance."

Instead of pulling onto the parking apron on the north side of the drive, he stopped at the foot of the steps to the porch, took them two at a time, then jabbed the doorbell. Before its chime was half-through, the door swung inward. "What the hell do you think you're doing?"

Instead of one of the feds, it was Selena who stood there, wearing her usual sexy, tropical clothes, looking her usual sexy self except for the wariness in her eyes. She ignored his question and took a step back. "Come in."

He glanced past her to the tall man with reddish-blond hair, watching from a few feet back. "Why don't you come out?" His voice was sharp, clipped. "I'd rather not have an audience."

She glanced at the man—for permission?—then stepped out onto the porch, closed the door behind her, and strolled to the south end, where she leaned against a fat round pillar and folded her arms over her middle. A stranger would have thought she was perfectly at ease, but he wasn't a stranger. She knew she had something to fear from him.

"What the fuck is going on, Selena?"

She opened her mouth—to offer a lie? to pretend ignorance?—then closed it again. After a moment, she sighed. "You know about Long."

"Hell, yes, I know. Did you think I was too stupid to notice that some idiot had gotten the prime suspect in nine of my homicide cases out of jail? How long did you think you could hide it?"

Her only immediate response was a hard swallow. Her fingers tightened where they clasped her arms, leaving pale spots on her skin. His gaze moved automatically from those to the wound healing on her upper left arm, then to the bruise darkening her upper right arm, ugly and purple in color. He wouldn't let himself ask what had happened, wouldn't let himself care.

"I wasn't trying . . . It wasn't my idea."

He dragged his fingers through his hair. "Christ, well, that's a relief. You got this multiple murderer out of jail—this man who physically assaulted you on several occasions, who would have helped Henry kill you and me both, who would still kill you if he got the chance—but it wasn't your idea. I feel so goddamn much better now."

Her eyes, already the color of rich chocolate, turned nearly black and her shoulders stiffened as she pushed away from the column. "I had already signed the FBI's agreement when they told me I would be working with Long. I had no choice in the matter—"

He interrupted, his voice harsh. "This argument's getting old, Selena. You had every choice. You could have backed out. You could have come to your senses."

"And risk going to jail or getting deported?"

"Fuck that! Why is everyone in the world smart enough to see that they're bluffing except you?"

For a long moment, she stared at him, her expression too blank to read a damn thing. Then she started toward the door. "You're right, Tony. This argument is getting old. I'm not having it with you again."

He let her get a half dozen feet away before he spoke. "Don't walk away from me, Selena, not now. If you do . . ."

Her steps slowed until she was motionless, but she didn't turn around. Not right away.

He squeezed his eyes shut and rubbed the ache between them before he found the courage to finish. "If you do, it's over."

Finally, she turned, and this time there was emotion on her face. Her eyes were huge with shock, hurt. The hand she reached out trembled, and her jaw worked a few times before she found her voice. "You don't . . . you can't . . ." Abruptly, she filled her lungs, as if she'd just realized she'd stopped breathing, and she came back a few steps, touching her icy fingers to his. "I know you're worried, Tony. Damon Long is more dangerous than William dreamed of being. But I *don't* have a choice in this. The FBI is right. He knows everything. We need him."

" 'We,' " he echoed. His experience with the FBI had always been of a more adversarial nature, even when they were working toward the same goal—an "us" versus "them" situation. And Selena had aligned herself with "them." She was falling for their threats, taking their advice, trusting their judgment with her very life.

A faint flush pinked her cheeks. "You know what I mean. If I'm going to do this, I need to have the best information possible . . . and Long has it. Without him, I'd be walking in blind."

If she'd taken *his* advice, she wouldn't be walking in at all, he thought bitterly. The emotion came through in his voice when he shook her hand away. "How can you even consider trusting him? He wants you *dead*."

Once again she folded her arms across her middle, and once again became cool and distant. "I'm not trusting him. He's wearing an electronic bracelet. An FBI agent is with him at all times. He's under constant watch. He's a threat, but he's a controlled threat. He has less freedom here than he did in jail."

"How much freedom does he need to snap your neck?"

"In front of my three hired thugs?"

Tony stared at her. She looked so damn arrogant, so damn much like Henry, that it was scary. She was actually pretending that this was a rational move. If anyone could thwart an electronic bracelet and constant surveillance, it was Long. Didn't any of these bastards realize how easily, how quickly, he could kill her? He had nothing ahead of him but the death penalty. Why not die for ten murders instead of nine?

If he still faced the death penalty. "What kind of deal did they make with him?" he asked suspiciously.

"The deal is with me, not the FBI. I told him I could get him out of jail, that I would make it worth his while to teach me William's business. He has no idea the FBI is even involved."

"So he thinks these guys are..." *Hired thugs,* she'd called them. "Christ." Tony walked to the next pillar, resting one hand against it and staring out across the lawn to the River Parks trail on the opposite side of the street. It didn't seem to matter to the fishermen, joggers, and cyclists that the heat index was hovering somewhere around 110 degrees, or that the air quality had been deemed unhealthy. Proved the idiots inside the house weren't the only ones in town.

Selena edged around the pillar to face him, a bright splash of color against the blinding white paint in his peripheral vision. He couldn't bring himself to look directly at her. "You're playing games with a man who kills for fun and profit. Do you have some death wish I know nothing about?"

"I have a life wish, Tony. This is the only way my life will ever be my own. Yes, Damon Long is a threat, but he's a *con-*

trolled threat. He's a danger whether he's here with us or locked up in jail. At least here, we know what he's doing."

"Do you know Carl Heinz?" Tony asked grimly. When she shook her head, he went on. "He went to see Long on Friday, and again yesterday."

"Do you think he might have been the one shooting at me?"

He shrugged. "I'm going to check him out. What if he was? What if Long put him up to it? Would it make you rethink this?"

For a time she stood still as a statue. Finally, though, she gave a small shake of her head.

A hollow formed in Tony's chest, and he rubbed it absently. "Okay. So I shouldn't bother checking out Heinz. If you don't care who's trying to kill you, why should I?" He pushed away from the pillar and started toward the steps. Halfway there, he heard the scuff of footsteps on brick as she caught up with him.

"Tony, I'm sorry. I should have told you about Long, but...I knew you wouldn't approve, and I knew that wouldn't change anything. I just...I guess I was hoping you would trust me to know what I'm doing."

He looked at her as he took the steps, but didn't slow. "So it's my problem because I don't trust you. How the hell can I, when I *know* you don't know what you're doing?"

She stopped short at the bottom of the steps. "Oh, that's right. I'm the idiot who got your suspect out of jail."

"If the description fits..." He jerked open the car door, then glared at her over it. "You're putting your life on the line—putting *us* on the line—for nothing. You think bringing down Henry's organization will make a difference in the larger scheme of things? You think there aren't a hundred guys out there ready and willing to take over their drug markets once they're out of the way? You think you'll actually accomplish something *if* you succeed, *if* you're not killed in the process? I've got news for you, honey—people might go to jail, drug supplies might be disrupted for a few days, maybe even a few weeks, and then life will go on as usual... except maybe for you and me."

The color drained from her face, even as heat flushed his own. The air between them turned too thick to breathe; his chest grew tight from lack of oxygen.

She backed up one step, then another. When she reached the top, she stopped. "Just for the record, so you don't accuse me of keeping things from you, I'll be going to Savannah soon. I have no idea how long we'll be there. If you'd like, I'll let you know when we return." She waited, and he swore he could hear the seconds ticking past, stretching into minutes. Then she nodded once, crossed the porch, and disappeared inside the house.

He stood there awhile before prying his fingers loose from the car door and sliding inside. He hadn't lied to her the night before, when she said, *Don't stop loving me.* He couldn't. Couldn't even imagine it. He'd promised he would always be there for her, and he meant it.

He just hadn't realized he'd meant within limits.

He damn sure hadn't realized some things about living with her could be worse than living without her.

Barnard Taylor—Barney to his wife, Mr. Taylor to everyone else—was a creature of habit. Up at six every morning, work out at the gym, run three miles, then home to shower and have breakfast with the aforementioned wife. While she shopped and lunched, he took care of business from a spacious office in the detached garage behind their house, then it was dinner at seven, a little tube, then bed.

Habits weren't good, the people who handled his security told him. Vary the routine, make it harder to become a target, they said. Hell, he'd lived to the ripe age of fifty-nine without taking their whiny-assed advice, and he wasn't about to change. It wasn't routine that got people killed. It was carelessness, and he was never fucking careless. He doubted everything, suspected everyone, and figured it was better to kill an innocent person than to let a guilty one continue to breathe.

That Thursday evening, he was where he always was—in the one room of the fuckin' house that Connie had let him have for his own. He'd paid a fortune for seventeen rooms filled with antiques that weren't much to look at and for damn sure weren't much for sitting on. For art that was just plain ugly, and trinkets like vases too valuable to stick flowers in. But room number eighteen—that was *his* room. Paneled walls, with red drapes at the windows, a big-screen TV, comfortable leather recliners, and cigar smoke perfuming everything. Connie wouldn't set even one expensively shod foot over the threshold, which suited Barnard just fine.

A fine Cohiba was burning in an ashtray—cheap, clear glass, filched from his favorite hole-in-the-wall bar—and a glass of whiskey sat on the table beside it. His chair was reclined, his socked feet were propped up on the footrest, and *CSI: Crime Scene Investigation* was on the big screen. It was, hands down, the best way he could think of to spend an evening.

When the cell phone on the end table rang, he glanced at it, debating letting it go to voice mail. But it was his business number, so he muted the TV, picked up the phone, and said a gruff hello.

"Hello, Mr. Taylor. I hope I'm not disturbing you." The voice was unfamiliar, male, lacking an identifiable accent.

"Who is this?"

There was a pause at the other end, then, "Let's just say a friend."

"I ain't got no friends."

"Then you can use one. How's business?"

"My business is none of your fuckin' business," Barnard growled. He'd been in that sort of mood ever since the phone call with Selena McCaffrey a few hours earlier. It was a given that someday Davis would be forced to turn over the business to someone else, but everyone had figured it would happen sometime down the road, in five, ten, fifteen years, when old age or death caught up with him. Given how paranoid and cautious Davis was, it had never crossed anyone's mind that he'd get caught. Christ, he'd kept his real identity hidden from his oldest and closest associates for twenty years. They'd thought he was bulletproof.

"Getting used to the idea of working for Mr. Davis's niece?"

Barnard scowled at the pretty blonde on the silent TV screen. He hadn't been wild about working for anyone even before this afternoon—had already been thinking it might be time for him to branch out on his own. Davis had been good to him, true, but he'd been damned good right back. He'd made himself a rich man and Davis an even richer one, and it was about time that he began keeping more of the fruits of his labor for himself. He wasn't getting any younger, and Connie was pestering him to think about retiring. If he was his own boss, he could turn things over to a few trusted people, work when he wanted, and continue to rake in the money. That was better than retirement any day.

"Are you there, Mr. Taylor?" Mystery Man prompted.

"Yeah, I'm here."

"Have you met Ms. McCaffrey yet?" After a brief pause, the guy went on. "Nah, she's probably been too busy. She's going to Savannah tomorrow to meet with Sonny Yates. She'll probably find time for you after that."

Once things were settled, she'd said, she wanted to meet. But things were already settled enough for her to travel to goddamn Savannah to see that snot-nosed punk, Yates? What the hell kind of deal was that?

Apparently the same thought had occurred to Mystery Man. "How long have you been with Mr. Davis? Eighteen years? And how long has Mr. Munroe up in Boston been with him? Even longer. And Sonny Yates has worked for him for ten years. But who does she go to meet first? The senior partners in this venture? No. The new guy. Why do you think that is?"

Why, indeed? It didn't matter whether Yates's operation showed more profit—a possibility that Barnard found impossible to believe. It was just common courtesy for her to meet with the senior partners first. Simple respect to men who'd been with her uncle from the beginning, men old enough to be her father. Instead, she was snubbing them in favor of a kid who hadn't even been alive as long as they'd been in business.

Barnard took a calming breath. "Yeah, well..." She was new to the life. She was bound to fuck up from time to time. When he did see her, he would set her straight. If he liked her and she was amenable to his guidance, maybe they would work something out. If he didn't like her...

But damned if that was any of this asshole's business. Hell, for all he knew, the guy could be calling on her orders, testing Barnard's loyalty. "As long as she continues to do business as usual—"

"Which she has no intention of," Mystery Man interrupted. "Word is that she plans to make some big changes. That while Uncle William might have been satisfied with a bunch of old men working for him, she wants to clean house and bring in people closer to her own age—closer in age to the majority of her customers. You know, ol' Sonny's only four or five years older than her. And you're what? More than twice her age."

Culling the old to make room for the young. It wasn't a big surprise. Legitimate businesses did it all the time. Why keep around some geezer who was close to retirement when you could replace him with a kid just out of school and save all that pension money? Hell, it even happened in the fucking animal kingdom—young males killing old ones so they could take over their territory.

Well, he might be old, but damned if he'd let some little bitch-girl come in and take away the business he'd started building while she was still playing with her fucking dolls.

"What do you think, Mr. Taylor?"

What he thought was his own fucking business, but instead of telling him that, Barnard asked testily, "What is it you want?"

"I just wanted to touch base—give you a heads up about what's going on."

"Give," Barnard repeated skeptically. "And to show my gratitude, I'm supposed to . . . what? Give you some cash?"

"Isn't that how it usually works?"

"How much cash?"

There was a moment's silence on the other end—no television, no voices, no background noises at all. Barnard wondered who the guy was, where he was calling from, whether he was being set up. He wondered if he should call the bitch-girl as soon as he hung up and tell her about Mystery Man. If she was testing him, she would know he'd passed. But if she wasn't, if this was a genuine opportunity to deal with a problem before she became a bigger problem . . .

"Have you considered the full extent of what I'm offering you, Mr. Taylor? If you take care of Ms. McCaffrey, and do it in Savannah, Sonny Yates will be the prime suspect. With him out of the way, you can move right in—natural, what with you being the closest. And once you've solidified your control of his region, in addition to your own, you take the rest of it. You'll be the big boss, Mr. Taylor. You'll be raking in the millions Davis was taking in, only you'll be sharing a lot less of it and keeping more for yourself."

"How much you want?"

"How about two hundred thou?"

Barnard snorted. "And what are you gonna *give* me that's worth that?"

"The information necessary to remove the only obstacle that's standing between you and Mr. Davis's empire."

Barnard tapped the ash from the cigar but didn't lift it to his mouth. Instead he held it where the smoke curled, sweet and thick, around his head, filling his nostrils, stinging his eyes. "What'd she ever do to you to deserve this?"

"I've got my reasons."

Probably money. Young people today were like that. They'd shoot a stranger on the street for a pair of tennis shoes. They didn't know a goddamn thing about loyalty or honor or self-respect. Everything was *me, me, me* to them.

Barnard was from another generation. William Davis had earned his loyalty; he'd conducted his business with honor, with his head held high, and he'd never done a thing he couldn't live with. But Davis was out of the picture. Now Barnard's loyalty was to himself and the people who worked for him.

"Mr. Taylor?"

"I need some time to think about it," he said gruffly. "Call me tomorrow—7:00 A.M. I'll give you an answer then."

Before Mystery Man could say anything to that, Barnard disconnected, looked regretfully at the television, then pressed the POWER button, shutting it off. He dialed a number, waited for a curt hello, then said, "Get your guys and meet me at the office. We've got business to take care of."

Years ago, when William was working in Savannah, Selena had dreamed of visiting the city. Be careful what you wish for, the old adage said, for you just might get it. She'd certainly never dreamed of going under these circumstances— posing as a drug boss, meeting a dealer who placed as little value on life as William and Damon Long did, who likely wanted her dead.

She wasn't hoping for a pleasant trip, she thought as she traded her window seat on the private jet for the right-rear passenger seat of an SUV. But it should be memorable.

Her last conversation with Tony had been so memorable that she couldn't stop it from replaying in her mind. She'd known the instant she'd seen him that he was angry, but hadn't realized just how angry until the profanity had slipped from his mouth. Joe Ceola didn't tolerate vulgarity around women from his sons, and Tony generally succeeded at keeping it to nothing more than a mild *hell* or *damn*. But not when she'd last seen him.

It's over. She hadn't known two words could hurt so deeply. Tony didn't threaten lightly. He never issued ultimatums he wasn't fully prepared to follow through. He was that angry with her, that convinced she was needlessly endangering her life. Could he be right?

She honestly didn't know. But she did know one thing: This charade might frighten her, but it didn't hold near the terror that jail did. Thanks to her mother's husband, she didn't do well in small places. She might survive a prison cell physically, but emotionally... She couldn't risk it. Better to face drug dealers and killers than her worst nightmares.

And better to feel that she was *doing* something. For only the second time in her life, she was actively rebelling against William. Instead of spinelessly following the path he'd set her on, politely, passively refusing his job offers, and letting him manipulate her, she was taking steps to destroy his legacy. Granted, she was allowing herself to be manipulated by others in the process, but that was only temporary. Soon she would be *free*.

For all his compassion and empathy, Tony couldn't understand how important that was to her.

On the opposite side of the seat, Long leaned forward to see past Jamieson, who was seated in the middle. In spite of the cramped space, he managed to extend his foot so the ankle bracelet came into view. "How'd you manage this—me leaving town without all the alarms going off?"

In the front seat, Robinette made no secret of the fact he was listening.

Selena raised her voice to make it easier for him. "I told you Mr. Jamieson is a computer expert. He's very good at bypassing alarms." In truth, it had taken nothing more than one phone call from Robinette to someone in the local FBI office. They'd taken care of the rest. She hesitated, then asked, "What do you know about Carl Heinz?"

There was a flash in Long's eyes—surprise?—that disappeared as he gave a shrug that was a bit too careless. "He's a little weasel that worked for William. What do *you* know about him?"

"That he visited you in jail...twice. How did he escape arrest?"

Another shrug. "Just lucky, I suppose."

"What kind of work did he do?"

"He's an accountant and computer wiz."

"No more active roles? No enforcement, no surveillance, no shooting?"

Long's expression remained bland. "Like I said, he's a weasel. Couldn't hit the broad side of a barn."

Or a lone woman 150 yards away? "Considering that I already have Mr. Jamieson, would it be worth bringing Heinz back on the job?"

"You'd have to find him first. That might prove a little difficult. Cowards like him go to ground when things get hot."

Tony would try to find him, even though he'd said he shouldn't bother. Would he tell her if he had any luck? Sure, if he found any evidence to suggest that Heinz was the one who had tried to kill her Monday. Especially if he found evidence that Long had been behind it.

And even if he did find such evidence, she would still have to work with Long, and Tony would...Make good on his threat? Walk away from her?

In an effort to ignore the cold emptiness that tightened her chest, she asked, "What do I need to know about Sonny Yates?"

"Just one thing." Long grinned. "Watch your back."

Unneeded advice. That was her rule with everyone. Everyone wanted something from her—her business, her life, her freedom. Even Tony wanted some measure of control over her.

She continued to watch him, and after a moment, he shrugged. "Sonny's got an ego. He's ambitious. He's liable to resent you coming in and taking over. William always figured at some point, he'd want to take control of his region for himself." He paused for effect. "William wouldn't have allowed that to happen."

"Would he have allowed you to take over any part of the business for yourself?"

"No. That's why I intended to kill him." His expression was utterly emotionless. "To take what's rightfully mine."

And how long before he tried to kill *her*?

"Should I attempt to mollify Mr. Yates? Should I offer him a reward for handling the matter of the missing boat?"

"Give him a reward for doing his job?" Long snorted. "The old man would sit up in his hospital bed. More likely he'd threaten Sonny with losing a few body parts for the boat going missing in the first place. Of course, cutting off body parts isn't quite your style, is it?"

She let her gaze drop to his denim-clad thigh, where she'd once sunk her switchblade to the hilt. "If I'd cut you a few inches higher, you might be missing the most vital of your body parts," she pointed out mildly.

He shifted uncomfortably in the seat. So did Jamieson.

Long settled back with enough force to rock the seat. "You give Sonny anything besides hell for losing that boat, he's gonna think you're easy pickin's. You may as well go ahead and kill him tonight, because if you don't, he'll come after you. And I don't think these guys"—he gestured around the vehicle—"can stop him."

Selena turned her attention to the window and watched the outskirts of Savannah rush by. From there, it was a short flight or a long day's drive home to Key West, and for an instant she wanted that additional trip so badly she ached. But the FBI could find her there, and so could William's associates.

And Tony probably wouldn't want to.

She was staring absently at the passing scenery when the sound of a powerful engine broke into her thoughts, followed by a curse from Gentry. "Stupid son of a bitch doesn't understand what 'no passing' means," the woman muttered as a silver Hummer sped past in the opposite lane.

To the accompaniment of squealing brakes and blaring horns, the driver swerved into the right lane only seconds before a head-on collision would have been inevitable. An instant later, he slammed on his brakes.

"Don't stop," Robinette ordered, and Gentry obeyed. She jerked the wheel hard into the oncoming traffic lane and gunned the engine.

As they passed the vehicle, it was impossible to tell through the nearly black windows how many occupants the truck carried, but Selena thought four men, along with a complete arsenal, seemed likely.

Ignoring the honks and obscene gestures from drivers forced onto the shoulder, Gentry pressed the accelerator to the floor, pulled ahead of the Hummer, then veered back into the right lane. The speedometer was inching past seventy in a forty-five-mile-per-hour zone, and up ahead, as they drew nearer to town, traffic grew heavier. There were no turnoffs, nothing but pine forests ... and a narrow bridge over a sluggish river.

Selena didn't need to look to know the Hummer was rapidly overtaking them; the roar of the engine, the horn blasts, and the constant shifting of Gentry's gaze from the road ahead to the rearview mirror made it clear.

The Hummer drew even with them again, but this time both passenger windows were down. Selena had a quick impression of two men with short brown hair, dark glasses, and a pair of high-powered rifles, and then the first shots rang out, shattering the cargo-area windows as Gentry quickly pulled away.

The Hummer came abreast again, and Selena flinched in anticipation of the next round of gunfire, but suddenly both men laughed and lowered their weapons instead. An instant later the Hummer slammed into the side of the SUV, metal grinding, tires squealing. Gentry hit the brakes, but the other driver slowed with her, relentlessly keeping the pressure on, forcing the smaller vehicle to the right.

Selena held tightly to the armrest as the right wheels left the roadway and the ride turned bumpy, jerking her against the seat belt. Next to her, Jamieson was holding on, as well, while in the front seat, Robinette looked relatively unaffected... until he noticed the bridge. They were approaching the concrete abutment at an alarming speed; even if Gentry tried to stop, she couldn't. Their only hope was to escape the Hummer and get back in the lane, or get off the road entirely. Escaping the Hummer wasn't an option, so at the last instant, Gentry jerked the wheel hard to the right.

The sudden turn smacked Selena's head against the side of the door as they crashed down an embankment. Her vision dim from the blow to the head, she fumbled for the button and lowered the window as the SUV sailed across the remaining few feet of earth, then plummeted into the middle of the river like a three-ton rock.

Water flooded the passenger compartment, pouring through the open windows. Robinette, already freed, was fumbling with Gentry's seat belt; her body was limp, and a gash darkened her forehead. Looking dazed, Long unclasped his seat belt as Selena took care of her own. Between them, Jamieson sagged, unconscious. As the water came up over the SUV's roof, she eased out the window, only to duck back in when gunfire started again. Their attackers had stopped on the bridge with the intention of picking them off as they surfaced.

The water was murky, tinged green, but she had no problem undoing Jamieson's seat belt. As the river closed over the top of the vehicle, she pulled him free, over the seat and into the cargo bay, then out the shattered window. She swam straight ahead, towing him with her, in the direction of the bridge and the cover it offered. When the water darkened thanks to the shade of the bridge, she swam a few more feet, then dragged him halfway onto the shore. Taking his pistol from its holster, she sliced back into the river, swam into the sunlight, then surfaced and fired three rapid shots at the figures on the bridge. Immediately she ducked under and swam to another location before surfacing and firing again. This time she was rewarded with a howl of pain followed by the splash of a .223 in the water a few feet away.

"Let's get outta here!" The shout was punctuated by slamming doors and a savage acceleration. An instant later, amidst the squeal of brakes, a stranger shouted, "Hey, are you okay down there? The police are on their way!"

Selena tucked the .45 in her waistband, drew a deep breath, dove under again, and returned to the truck. The vehicle had settled at an angle on the river bottom, tilting precariously to the right side. Long was wriggling through the passenger window, but the angle was awkward, the going slow. With his shirt collar in one fist, she began kicking to the surface, feeling the burden ease when he was free of the SUV.

Leaving him to find his way to shore, she went under once more. Robinette was still struggling with Gentry's seat belt; apparently, the locking mechanism had jammed. Selena pulled herself back through the window, drew her switchblade, and sliced through both the shoulder and lap belts.

This time when she surfaced, Robinette and Gentry were

right behind her. Long was waiting on the shore with a half dozen passersby; a few other Good Samaritans were helping a groggy Jamieson out of the river and onto solid ground. Sirens wailed in the distance. As she treaded water, Robinette gave her one of those smiles that brought absolutely no warmth to his face, and said, "Welcome to Savannah, Ms. McCaffrey."

7

Despite the heat, Selena stood at the side of the road, a blanket around her shoulders, and gazed down at the divers and the wrecker preparing to tow the SUV from the water. Gentry came to stand beside her, a gauze bandage covering the gash on her forehead but leaving plenty of the resulting bruise uncovered.

"Robinette tells me I owe you my thanks."

Selena glanced at her but didn't speak.

"He also told me to confiscate that knife." Gentry watched as the rear of the SUV broke the water's surface before glancing Selena's way. "I don't think it's always fair to send a witness into a dangerous situation unarmed. So if he asks, I took the switchblade, right? Right."

Selena watched her walk away. It hadn't escaped her notice that Gentry had failed to thank her for helping save her life, but getting to keep the knife more than made up for that. Still, she wouldn't mention the .22 packed in her suitcase inside the SUV.

After everyone had provided the investigating officers with identification, Robinette did most of the talking, telling a story verified by the witnesses—some crazy people had taken shots at them and run them off the road. No, no one had gotten a description or a tag number; no, they had no idea why they'd been singled out. In the meantime, the tow truck left with the SUV and two men from the rental agency, looking more than a little stunned, delivered another and helped to load their sopping luggage.

Once they were finally allowed to leave, they completed the short drive into the heart of Savannah. They passed lovely old houses, statues and fountains, locals and tourists, other vehicles and horse-drawn carriages, before turning into the drive of a three-story house. The place had come recommended by the local FBI office, Robinette had told her on the plane, better for security than a hotel filled with strangers and numerous ways in and out. They had it to themselves for the duration of their stay; the owners had been persuaded—there had been a glint in his eyes when he said the word—to go away for a few days.

Selena climbed out of the SUV and looked around. High stucco walls surrounded the property on three sides, with an elaborate wrought-iron fence and gate enclosing the front. The house wasn't impenetrable, but what was—besides, perhaps, a prison? For their purposes, it should be fine... provided nothing else went wrong.

Grateful for the waterproof bags that held her toiletries—and the .22—Selena gathered them and retreated to her room for a shower. The river muck was gone and she was sitting on the bed, wrapped in a towel and applying coconut-scented lotion to her skin, when a knock sounded at the door, then Gentry walked in, shopping bags in hand.

"One of the agents from the local office got us clothes for tonight. Jamieson will get the laundry done tonight, and the rest has been sent to the cleaners, so we can have our own stuff tomorrow." From one bag, Gentry removed a dress in turquoise linen, along with a bra, panties, hose, and strappy, heeled sandals. From another she took out a roll of tape and a jumble of wires and a transmitter. "Put the underwear on, then I'll get you hooked up before you put the dress on."

Selena did as instructed, then stood motionless as Gentry taped the microphone between her breasts, ran the wire along the band of the bra, then taped the transmitter to her middle in back. The dress came with a wide leather belt that would camouflage the small lump. When Gentry stepped away, she slid the dress on, fastening the buttons, securing the belt, then turning slowly for inspection.

"Good. Can't see a thing. Now Robinette wants to talk to you."

With a shrug, Selena sat down at the old-fashioned dressing table and spread out the contents of her cosmetics bag. The .22 had already been transferred to a small beaded handbag resting on the marble tabletop. She doubted Robinette would give the bag a second look—hoped he wouldn't. As Gentry had said, it wasn't fair sending a witness into a dangerous situation unarmed.

A moment after Gentry left, the door opened again and Robinette came in. He walked to the lace-curtained windows and gazed out before glancing her way. "Nervous?"

She finished smoothing moisturizer over her face before reaching for the foundation. *I'm having dinner in a strange city with a man who's already tried to kill me and another who probably just tried to kill me. Of course I'm nervous.* "Should I be?"

"We'll have people around."

"What people? Where?"

"They know who you are. You don't need to know who they are." He leaned against the windowsill and crossed his ankles. "Jamieson will be your driver tonight. I'll be in the surveillance van outside the restaurant. Gentry will be keeping watch here while we're gone, and Long will be with you."

Lucky me. "Is his ankle bracelet really deactivated?"

"No. We're monitoring it. But he doesn't need to know that."

"Then, in his mind, this would be a good time to try to escape—alone in a restaurant with just me to watch him. He could go to the men's room and never come back."

"He could try. He wouldn't get far. Our surveillance team knows you. They know him."

She wiped her fingers on a washcloth, then selected two pots of eye shadow and a brush. "Any advice for tonight?"

He looked uncomfortable, as if he didn't like what he was about to say. "You want to make decisions—this is where you get to. Use whatever tactic works best with Yates—intimidation, friendliness, seduction."

A chill slid down her spine. Once, William had ordered her to use sex to get the information he wanted from Tony. She wasn't anyone's whore. If seduction was what worked best with Yates, the FBI might as well lock her up now.

"You're trusting my judgment?" she asked coolly.

Not in the least, his smile said, though his words suggested otherwise. "You'll be there. I won't. Feel him out about the boat that disappeared, and any other aspect of the business he's willing to discuss, but don't expect too much. You may be his boss, but you're a stranger. It'll take some time to earn his trust."

"How much time do we have for this?" How long was her life going to be on hold, her freedom curtailed, her relationship in limbo?

He walked to the door, then turned back, wearing that thin smile again. "As long as it takes."

Long after the door had closed, she continued to gaze at the spot where he'd stood. Shaking her head she reached for a fat brush and a container of powder and dusted it across her face. *As long as it takes.* Now, there was a depressing thought.

Once she was properly made up, adorned, and perfumed, she picked up the beaded bag, drew a breath for courage, then went downstairs to join Jamieson and Long in the gleaming silver Mercedes they'd rented for the occasion.

Their destination, a restaurant by the name of Pawley's, was located in the middle of a downtown block. Built of aged red brick softened to a rosy hue in the setting sun, it looked as if it had occupied that square of earth forever. Jamieson parked in front and jumped out to open the rear door, like a good chauffeur. Ignoring the curious looks of passersby, Selena climbed out and casually glanced around while waiting for Long to join her. There were several vans parked on the street, with nothing to give away which one hid Robinette's surveillance team.

When Long came to stand beside her, she started across the sidewalk toward the restaurant door, held open by a smiling young man in shirtsleeves. Before they were close enough for him to hear, she murmured, "You try anything tonight, Mr. Long, and I'll shoot you."

She was rewarded with a scowl as the young man greeted them. "Welcome to Pawley's. Enjoy your meal."

With Long at her side, and Yates awaiting her inside, the meal, she thought grimly, was the least of her concerns.

By Friday evening, Tony had discovered that the only number Damon Long had called from the jail besides his lawyer's came back to Carl Heinz at a midtown business address. The storefront office specialized in small-business bookkeeping, accounting, and tax services, according to the sign in the window. It was closed, and had been for most of the week, the woman at the tailor shop next door told him.

Heinz's residential address was in a Brookside neighborhood of small lots and neat houses. The mailbox was crammed with junk mail and a handful of bills—electric, water, gas. A narrow trail worn through the overgrown yard led to the house. There was no car in the driveway, no answer to Tony's knock, and nothing to see through the living room windows but cheap furniture.

Luckily, there was a talkative neighbor who'd told Tony everything she knew about the man—that he was quiet, kept to himself, didn't have loud parties or any company at all. He'd been polite but not overly friendly, and had taken care of his house just like everyone else on the block, though he had slacked off on the mowing in the last few weeks.

Maybe because he'd known he wouldn't be staying much longer. Just long enough to try to kill Selena.

Heinz had left town Wednesday afternoon, the old lady said—had come home, loaded up his car, given her the keys to return to the landlord, and driven away. He hadn't mentioned where he was going.

But before disappearing, he had spoken to Long, had visited him in jail. He must have found out that Henry was in the hospital and that Selena was in part responsible. Had he been on that hillside Monday night or had he passed the job on to someone else? Had he taken it on himself or been following orders—and, if so, whose?

And where was he now? He could have gone anywhere in the country—hell, in the world. Or he could have holed up in a motel down the street, awaiting further instructions. He could be on his way to Savannah, or already there, waiting.

Tony didn't know anyone on the Savannah PD, but he could call, chat up a detective, ask him to do whatever he could to keep an eye on Selena...and risk blowing the feds' cover or, worse, giving them away to a dirty cop. After all, he knew for a fact that the former chief of police there had been corrupt as hell.

Or he could send them Heinz's driver's license photo, tell them he had reason to believe Heinz was in their jurisdiction and that he was a person of interest in a multiple homicide, and ask them to keep an eye out for him. It wasn't much, but it was the best—and safest—option he could come up with.

He detoured to the station downtown, sent the request, then left again. He sat at a stoplight, drumming his fingers on the wheel. Home was a few miles to the left, but he didn't want to go there. The house seemed so damned empty—or maybe *he* was the one feeling empty. At least at work, he had people to deal with and cases to concentrate on. At home, all his distractions reminded him of Selena. There was her house—pretty hard to ignore—and Mutt moping around because she wasn't there to spoil him. Even the cats seemed to be hiding out less and aggravating Tony more.

When the light changed, instead of turning left, he switched lanes and headed south. He drove automatically, trying not to think too much about anything, until he recognized LaFortune Park. He was going home, he thought with a rueful smile. Just as he'd done when he was a kid and something had gone wrong.

He parked in the driveway behind his mother's car, then rang the doorbell. For years Anna had left the door unlocked during the day, but Joe's Alzheimer's made that impossible now.

Anna opened the door, her face flushed, an apron tied around her waist. She gave Tony a hug and a kiss, then stepped back and took stock. "No bruises, no black eyes, no bullet holes. Good."

"How are you?"

"I'm fine," she said, though she didn't look it. Lines bracketed her mouth, and her eyes wore a layer of worry.

"How's Dad?"

She shrugged. "He's on a Henry kick. He's asked me fifty times this afternoon where Henry is, why he hasn't come for a visit, is he mad at us, why doesn't he call."

She'd told Joe part of the truth about Henry—that he'd been shot, but not why and certainly not by whom—but Joe forgot more often than he remembered. Anna thought that was a blessing, but Tony wasn't so sure. Was it better to think that the friend you loved like a brother had abandoned you than to know that he lay comatose in the hospital?

"How are you?" Anna asked, cupping her palm to his cheek.

"I'm okay."

"Where's Selena?"

Who knew? He'd driven past Henry's estate that afternoon, but it had been impossible to tell whether she had left for Savannah yet. Everything looked the same as always— guards on duty at the gate, the house quiet, the grounds undisturbed.

Anna studied him a moment longer, then asked suspiciously, "Did you two have a fight?"

"Gee, you should be a detective, Mom," he said dryly. "And it wasn't exactly a fight." All he'd done was doubt Selena's abilities and call her an idiot. But getting Long out of jail *was* incredibly idiotic. Didn't truth count for anything?

"Was it your fault?"

"No." No matter how Selena argued, there was nothing rational or reasonable about what she was doing. It was dangerous, plain and simple.

"Not even a little?"

"No." Though he wasn't proud of the way he'd let the

conversation end the day before. She'd made a conciliatory effort—*If you'd like, I'll let you know when we return*—but he'd said nothing. It had been petty, but he couldn't have forced an answer to save his life.

Anna gave him a chiding look. "It takes two to argue."

Not necessarily. One person could simply tell the other what an idiot she was being. It was her response that determined whether an argument would ensue.

"Even if it wasn't your fault, apologize and make up."

"Why?"

"Because you love her."

See? A simple statement of fact. He could argue it, but there was no point because it was true.

Convinced she'd made her point, Anna headed back to the kitchen, and Tony followed. The aroma of fresh-baked cookies filled the air. Her peanut butter–oatmeal–chocolate chip specials were cooling on a rack, and another batch baked in the oven. Joe stood at the sink, gazing out the window and absently munching on one.

"Hey, Dad."

"Son. Did you just get off work?"

"Yeah, a while ago."

"Did you see Henry today?"

"No, I didn't."

Petulance twisted both Joe's expression and his voice. "He hasn't been over in a long time, and when I call, he never calls back. Do you think he's mad at me? Did I do something?"

"No, Dad, not at all. I think he's just probably . . ." Unsure what lie to tell, Tony couldn't finish, but his mother did.

"He's busy, Joe. Remember?"

"Too busy for his best friend?" Joe shook his head as if he found the idea incomprehensible. How much more so would the whole truth be?

Taking two cookies from the nearest rack, Joe slipped one to Tony with a wink before he went into the family room. A moment later the sounds of the evening news filtered out.

"Have you seen Henry at all since...?" Anna finished with a shrug. No one in the family liked to finish that sentence.

Since Selena shot you. Sometimes he could say the words without flinching. Other times they sounded unbelievable. The woman he loved had pointed a gun at him, cold as ice, and pulled the trigger. Logically, he knew she'd probably saved his life. Realistically, he didn't know how she could have done it—didn't know, if the situation were reversed, if he could have risked killing her to save her.

"No," he answered at last.

"Do you want to?"

This time it was Tony who shrugged. "I can't ask him how he got so greedy, how he managed to fool us all, why he did the things he did. What would be the point?"

"It's so hard to understand. And poor Joe..."

Joe wouldn't have understood even before the Alzheimer's. He was black-and-white, by the book. Right was right and wrong was wrong, period. He would have been furious and heartbroken, and he never would have understood.

"We never suspected a thing," Anna continued, her voice soft with regret.

"No one did. He hid it well."

After a moment of gazing into the distance, she gave herself a shake. "Want to stay for dinner? Then you can take some of these cookies home to Selena. No one can stay mad long with peanut butter–oatmeal–chocolate chip cookies around."

A few hours later, Tony steered the Impala onto Princeton Court, a bag of cookies and enough leftovers to feed him through the weekend on the seat beside him. An unfamiliar car was parked at the curb in front of Selena's house, and the driver was talking to Dina Franklin, who lived in the third of the four houses on the block. Tony parked in his own driveway, then walked over to join them. "Hey, Dina, what's going on?"

"This man was asking some questions about our new neighbor." She handed over a business card. "I told him you know her better than us. I've seen her a few times, but we've never actually spoken."

Tony glanced at the business card—plain white, the Tulsa Police Department seal, the Detective Division's phone number. That glance was all he needed to know the card was a fake. It looked official enough, but the seal was printed instead of embossed, the paper was lesser quality, and the edges were microperfed. He shifted his gaze from the card to the man claiming to be Detective Jerry Baldwin—six feet tall, rough-edged in spite of his suit, certainly an impostor. The Detective Division wasn't so large that Tony didn't have at least a passing acquaintance with everyone in it.

"What can I help you with?" he asked calmly.

"We're just looking for information about Ms. McCaffrey."

"What kind of information?"

"Any kind you have." The man grinned. "You never know what's important until you try to put all the pieces together."

Tony looked him over again. He wasn't wearing a badge clipped to his belt, as most detectives did, but odds were, that bit of black leather barely visible inside his coat was a holster. "I know Selena pretty well," he said at last. "Why don't we go to my house and talk there? See you, Dina."

He kept up a running conversation as they walked— about the weather, what a season the Drillers were having, the arena football team. As soon as they got inside, he invited the guy to have a seat in the living room while he remained standing in the doorway. "What's your interest in Selena?"

The man shrugged. "Purely business. How long has she been living here?"

"Four, maybe six weeks."

"What kind of neighbor is she?"

"Quiet. She keeps to herself. Doesn't have loud parties or any company at all." Tony's description echoed the neighbor's description of Carl Heinz.

"What about a boyfriend?"

You're talking to him. Tony leaned one shoulder against the jamb. "You know, you didn't show me a badge. But that's okay. I'll be happy to show you mine." He held his badge up in his left hand and, as the man started to rise from the sofa, drew his gun with his right. "Take your gun out of the holster and toss it into that chair."

Looking grim, the guy obeyed.

"You have any other weapons on you?" When he shook his head, Tony backed into the hall, then gestured for him to stand. "Get your hands up and walk over here slowly, then put your hands against the wall and spread your feet."

When the man had done as directed, Tony reached for the handcuff case on the back of his belt. He'd secured the guy's left wrist when the door suddenly burst open, knocking him off-balance. Stumbling, he hit the floor hard enough to send his gun sliding across the polished wood.

"Hey, Ton—" His brother Matt's greeting ended in a grunt as the man shoved away from the wall, plowed through both Matt and Dom, and bolted out the door. Lunging to his feet, Tony grabbed his pistol and dashed after him, taking the steps in one leap. By the time he reached the mailbox, the guy was already in his car, revving the engine. Tires squealing, he turned the wheel hard to the left, bumping over the curb and into the grass, then back onto the street.

Halfway down the block, Tony skidded to a stop, took aim at the back end of the car, then eased his finger off the trigger as the car fishtailed around the corner and out of sight. For a few seconds the roar of a powerful engine lingered on the air, then faded.

"Goddammit!" Standing in the middle of the street, he jerked his cell phone from his pocket, dialed 911, and gave a description of the man, the car, and the tag number, then asked the dispatcher to send an officer to pick up the weapon for processing.

He returned to the house, absently rubbing the ache where his shoulder had hit the hardwood floor. He loved his younger brothers, who were both standing on the stoop watching his approach, but the perpetual delinquents of the Ceola family were more than he could handle at the moment. His shoulder hurt like a son of a bitch, the bastard poking around about Selena was likely gone for good—the car already ditched, his escape from Tulsa well under way—and Tony had lost a good shot at finding out who was after her.

Dom and Matt each stepped to one side as Tony climbed the steps. He walked through the open door, then blocked their way when they would have followed. "Don't ever come into my house again without knocking," he said, pretty calmly considering he'd like to thump them both. Before he closed and locked the door in their faces, he added, "You owe me a pair of handcuffs."

The evening was suffocatingly hot as Kathryn set out for St. John Medical Center. She'd spent most of the morning and afternoon at Henry's side, and truly, the last thing she needed was more time in that depressing room, where the only signs of life were the beeps and whooshes of the machines, but something drew her back. Worry, perhaps, or anger. Frustration. The bone-deep need for answers that her brother couldn't give.

Traffic on Twenty-first Street was fairly light, and the hospital parking spaces that were at a premium during the day were plentiful. She parked her rental, hurried inside to the cool, sterile environment, and took the elevator to Henry's floor.

Outside his room, she pasted on a smile—habit, since Henry certainly never noticed. She swept into the dimly lit room and bent to brush a kiss to his cool, dry cheek. "I'm back again," she announced cheerily. "You just can't keep me away. You don't know how lucky you are to be inside. It is unbearably hot out there. I'd forgotten how bad July in Oklahoma can be, and August will be even worse. But maybe we'll be home before then."

At least, *she* would. Henry would go from there to a long-term-care facility, the doctors' fancy way of saying nursing home, where he would die, quickly if he was lucky. Perhaps she would find a place near Greenhill, so she could visit him regularly. Though what did that matter? He was as dead to her as their mother and father, long in their graves. His body just hadn't acknowledged it yet.

"Did I tell you I'm staying at a bed-and-breakfast in what used to be the Rogers estate? You remember Grandmama and Grandpapa taking us over there when they visited Mr. and Mrs. Rogers." The cheer in her voice was starting to wobble, but she kept up the pretense. She was good at it; she did it every day for Grant. "It was wonderful being back in the family home for those few days. So many memories—the parties, the celebrations, the holidays, the family times. I saw your special memories in your room—all those photographs commemorating the highlights of your career..."

Her voice broke, tears dampened her eyes, and her next words came out rough, accusing. "And *her*. I saw that picture of her. For God's sake, Henry, why didn't you tell me? All these years I thought... I believed... Do you have any idea how much I hate you for not telling me about her?"

He lay there, unresponsive, untouched. Even if he were awake and well, he would remain untouched. He wouldn't care what damage his twenty-eight years of lies had done. If he cared, if he'd ever cared, he never would have kept his little secret.

"She's striking. Beautiful, really. At least, in that picture. I imagine she's even more impressive all grown up. She looks so much like—" A sob choked off the sentence. Even after twenty-eight years, she couldn't say the name without dredging up old hurts and betrayals.

"When the FBI told me that you had this—this niece, do you know my first thought was that you were a pervert? That you needed a little girl to find satisfaction. After all, you never acknowledged Jefferson because none of your precious Daniels blood was running through his veins, so it was logical that there was something sick about your relationship with this girl." She tried to laugh, but it was closer to choking. "Under the circumstances, your being a pervert would be infinitely better than... than..."

Spinning away from the bed, she paced to the window and opened the blinds. The sun, low on the horizon, was turning the sky shades of pink and purple. Pressing a tissue to her mouth, she whispered, "I'm going to find Selena McCaffrey, Henry. I'm going to find out everything you've done, every lie you've told, everything she knows. I'm going to find out just how big a threat she is. And then..."

She didn't finish the sentence out loud. It was too personal, too frightening. But that didn't stop it from echoing inside her head with all the rage and betrayal and hatred she was feeling.

And then you'll pay.

Selena followed Damon Long and the maître d' through the dining room at Pawley's. The walls were hung with paintings of old Savannah, the tables covered with linen cloths, the subdued lighting enhanced by candles. A row of French doors along the east wall opened onto an enclosed courtyard, made cozy by the splash of a fountain and the riotous colors of flowers spilling down the brick. Every table both inside and out was occupied, and she scanned them, wondering which of the diners were there to keep an eye on her. She couldn't begin to guess.

The maître d' led them through a broad arch into a semiprivate room that held two tables. The one on the left was set for three, with two places already occupied. The one on the right held two settings, and the man there waited patiently.

"Sonny boy." Long extended his hand as Yates stood, pumped it, then slapped him on the back as if they were old friends.

"Damon. How was life behind bars?"

"Let's say I like it better outside than in. How's business here?"

"Can't complain."

"I bet the crew members of that missing boat can't complain either, can they?"

Yates grinned. "Hey, fishing is a risky business. Accidents happen. Storms blow in."

"Bodies drift out." Long stepped to one side, giving Selena

a better view of the man. "Sonny, this is Selena McCaffrey, William's niece and our new boss."

Yates studied her for a time, his expression mixed. She was accustomed to the male appreciation; she'd been on the receiving end of that, thanks to genetics, most of her life. She was also accustomed to the not-quite-concealed surprise. This Georgia good ol' boy hadn't expected her to be half-black. Not William's niece. Not his new boss.

Slowly he held out his hand. "Selena. Welcome to Savannah."

"Thank you." Her breathing carefully controlled, she extended her own hand, grateful it didn't shake, then let go as quickly as she could. When he would have moved around to hold her chair for her, she waved him off and slid into the seat, setting her bag nearby. As Long settled in at the other table, she fixed her gaze on Yates. "We had a little excitement on the way into town. Have you heard about it?"

"No. What happened?"

"Someone took a few shots at us before running us off the road and into the river." She watched him for some fleeting hint of guilt, but his expression remained bland, his manner vaguely concerned.

"Was anyone hurt?"

"One of my people got a few bumps. One of theirs got shot. You're sure you don't know anything about it?"

He leaned forward, resting both arms on the table. "I'm not stupid, Selena. I wouldn't try to kill you in my own hometown."

Maybe not. Or maybe that made a good defense. "Then, since it *is* your hometown, perhaps you can find out who did try."

"I'll put my people on it tonight." He gestured toward the men seated with Long as the waiter came in to fill their glasses. A second waiter delivered appetizers of crab cakes in a delicate sauce, then disappeared once more.

Selena took advantage of the food to study Yates. He was probably in his midthirties, auburn-haired and fair-skinned, with a sprinkling of freckles. His eyes were hazel, his smile practiced, and his chin weak. He didn't look like a drug dealer, but rather an up-and-coming lawyer/banker/stock-broker who drove a BMW, played racquetball, and dated the daughters of genteel Southern families.

"I'm sorry about William. How the hell did that happen?"

After ensuring her hand wasn't trembling, she lifted her glass and sipped the wine, then set it down again before shrugging. "One of his detectives tied him to the business and to a string of murders in Tulsa. Apparently, he got care-less."

"Arrogant is more like it. He was the damn chief of police. Didn't he keep track of what his people were doing? Didn't he realize this detective was a threat to him?"

"He was aware. He'd made arrangements to deal with him, but . . . they failed." She gazed at her appetizer a moment before looking at him. "*I* failed."

Sonny's brows rose. "You were supposed to take out the cop?"

She nodded. "I shot him, but . . . he still managed to shoot William."

"Christ." Then a speculative look entered his eyes. "You blew your job, and now you're in control. Some might think that's convenient."

"I never wanted to hurt William," she said defensively. It wasn't a lie. She would have killed him if he'd left her no choice, but she'd never *wanted* to harm him. "He was my un-cle. He was the only father figure I've ever had. He taught me everything I know. He was still teaching me, preparing me to take over the business. It wasn't time."

"You would have killed the cop?"

She hesitated. It was a simple question with a simple answer, but it took more strength than she would have guessed to give it. "That was my intent." *God forgive me.*

"So why weren't you arrested? Why did everyone go to jail except you?"

Her smile was so cool, so careless, that it hurt. "I told them a story about how mistreated, manipulated, and abused I'd been. I told them I'd been coerced, blackmailed, but in the end, I risked my life to save Detective Ceola's. With him supporting my version, the police believed me."

"Detective Ceola wouldn't happen to be young, single, and susceptible to a beautiful woman's charms, would he?"

Her smile widened even as her chest went taut. "He would. He believed my claim that I'd merely intended to wound him. Even the best detective can be gullible at times."

Yates finished his wine, then refilled the glass. "So what does this gullible detective think of your new job?"

Her shrug made the knotted muscles in her neck and shoulders protest. "Relationships can be so difficult to sustain, you know, and we had so much more to deal with than most couples. I shot him, he put my uncle in a coma, our jobs don't exactly mesh . . ."

"So once he supported your tale and kept you out of jail, you broke it off with him."

It's over. Selena didn't believe Tony would end it, couldn't believe it . . . her throat tightened, but she still managed to smile. "Once he'd served his purpose, what was the point of keeping him around?"

"Cops have other purposes. We all take advantage of them when we can."

So William wasn't the only dirty cop in the organization. She hadn't been naive enough to think he was—nor was she naive enough to try to get more information from Yates just yet. "Not this one. Detective Ceola believes in the law. He can't be bought. Don't you think William would have gone that route if it was an option? Killing a police officer can create more problems than it solves."

He acknowledged that with a nod. "So you broke his heart, and that's that."

Desperate for a change of subject, Selena folded her hands together. "Tell me about this fishing boat."

Sonny waited as the two waiters returned bearing salads and baskets of bread. Apparently, he'd taken the liberty of ordering for both of them, not that she cared. What she ate was her last concern.

"The boat supposedly went down in a tropical storm a few weeks ago with both the load and the crew."

"But you didn't believe it did?"

He shook his head. "Captain Rollins had been with me a long time. He was one of the best. He would have stayed hell and gone from that storm. Either he wanted to die, or to make us think he was dead. There was no indication that he wanted to die, and two hundred fifty thousand reasons for him to want us to think he was dead."

Apparently William wasn't the only arrogant one around, Selena thought as she took a bite of salad and swallowed without tasting it. Rollins had surely known what kind of man Sonny Yates was, and yet he'd stolen from him anyway, believing he could fake his death and sail off with a small fortune. "You located him and the crew?"

"I did. We got the product back, the crew have been dealt with, and no one's gonna think about ripping us off again for a very long time." Yates removed a roll from the bread basket, tore it, and buttered one half. "So...you've got something for me?"

Her hand stilled as she forked another bite of salad. "I don't know what you mean."

Annoyance flashed across Yates's face, quickly disappearing behind that bland expression. "Odd. Seems like the finer details of the business would have been one of the first things William would have explained to you."

She swallowed hard, her fingers tightening around the fork, her lungs reluctantly expanding with the breath she forced in. "Uncle William explained things in his own way in his own time. Since he apparently overlooked this, why don't you tell me?"

His gaze pinned her, steady, cold, speculative, until abruptly he looked away. "It's no big deal. William and I had an agreement. I do something above and beyond, and I *get* something above and beyond. A bonus. A reward."

She glanced at Long, clearly listening in spite of the conversation at his own table. He raised both brows in a parody of surprise, and mouthed, "Oops."

Bastard. The smile on her face wanted to sink to her toes, along with her stomach, but she fixed it in place and hoped her voice remained half as steady. "Now, there's a thought—rewarding an employee for doing his job. No wonder Uncle William didn't want to tell me he worked that way."

"He did. I still do."

Selena delayed, cutting through a tomato slice, delicately stabbing it and a mouthful of greens with her fork, raising it to her mouth. She chewed deliberately, this time noticing the flavor of the dressing, the freshness of the vegetables, as she wondered how to respond. Clearly Yates expected money, and he wouldn't be satisfied with the fifty bucks in her purse.

How much did he expect? How much would Robinette agree to pay? How long would it take him to get the cash?

You want to make decisions, this is where you get to, Robinette had said. Straightening her spine, figuratively if not literally, she faced Yates again. "How about this? We do away with the reward system, and I'll increase your share of the profits."

He looked suspicious, but too curious—too greedy—to turn her down without hearing her out. "How big an increase?"

"I'll know that after I've gone over the books."

"William never asked to see the books."

On the surface, that statement was probably true, but the impression was misleading. William probably *hadn't* seen the books, because he had employed people to do that for him. The request would have come from Long, and very well might have bypassed Yates completely, but it *had* come.

"You and I both know, Mr. Yates, that there's no way Uncle William operated the financial aspect of his business on faith," she said mildly. "Besides, I'm not William. Our methods of conducting business might not be the same, but you'll benefit from the differences. Trust me."

The final words seemed a foreign language to him. Understandable. She wouldn't trust him, either.

She'd already made that mistake with Long—not a big deal this time. But the next time it could be fatal.

8

Selena McCaffrey had a sense of humor, Sonny thought. *Trust me.* No more than he could breathe underwater.

He sipped his wine as he gazed through the archway into the main dining room and wondered which of those innocent diners was there to protect her. No one had shown excessive interest in her, but a good bodyguard wouldn't. She was too new, her position too precarious, to travel with no one but Damon. Hell, he wouldn't lift a finger to help her unless his own hide was on the line. After all, if something happened to her, Damon was the next in line to take over, and *his* position wouldn't be precarious. He already commanded respect from everyone who knew him, while Selena still had to earn it.

In ways, she was exactly what Sonny had expected. William had always had a taste for beauty, for elegance, sophistication, and all things exotic, and she fit in every way. But her race had taken this born-and-bred Southerner aback. Being part black wasn't necessarily a strike against her. Just a surprise.

He didn't like surprises.

"You said earlier that William was still teaching you. Just how prepared are you to take over this business?"

She was an expert at those cool, aloof smiles. "I admit, there are some gaps in my education, but I'm a big believer in on-the-job training. Mr. Long is helping me, and truthfully, I'm counting on you, Mr. Taylor, and Mr. Munroe to help as well."

"Damon's more likely to help himself." Then, in a moment of candidness, he went on. "We all are."

"I know. Unless I make it worthwhile for you to continue doing business with me."

"And how do you plan to do that?"

"That's part of what I'm here to find out. What would it take to ensure that you, Mr. Taylor, and Mr. Munroe continue with business as usual?"

"I can't speak for the others."

"But for you?"

"A bigger cut is a good start."

"And a start I'm willing to make once I've examined the books. When and where can I do that?"

Sonny didn't like anyone looking over his shoulder. It made him feel like a kid. But if she really was willing to give him a larger share—possibly the only thing that would keep him working with her . . . "How's tomorrow morning? Nine o'clock?"

She nodded regally, as if she was granting him some great favor. "Where?"

"Bar outside town. Clancy's. Damon knows how to find it."

Another nod, this one accompanied by that damn smile. "We'll be there."

Sitting back in his chair, Sonny signaled the waiter outside the arch, and he quickly came in to clear the salads from the table. He frequented a number of restaurants in town, but he liked Pawley's best. He never failed to dine there without remembering his early days in Atlanta, when he went hungry more often than not. If he had even set foot inside such a place then, he would have been tossed right back out. Now everyone at Pawley's knew him by name and catered to his every wish.

Including the owner.

As the waiter returned, balancing platters of filet and shrimp, crusty baked potatoes, and steamed asparagus from the chef's private garden, Charlize Pawley glided into the room. She rested her hand on the back of his chair and greeted him like an old acquaintance—warm, friendly, but with a bit of reserve. "How is everything so far?"

"Outstanding, as usual. Selena, this is Charlize Pawley. She owns this lovely establishment. Charlize, Selena McCaffrey, a . . . business associate from out of town."

He watched the two women size each other up. They were about the same age, both beautiful, but where Selena was dark, Charlize was blond and fair, her pale skin looking as if it had never been exposed to the Georgia sun. Selena's hair curled wildly down her back, while Charlize's was pulled back in a severe style that emphasized the delicate lines of her face. Selena's turquoise dress shouted for attention, while Charlize's was simple, the color so pale that naming it was difficult. But they were both elegant, cool, moneyed, and privileged.

Both important to Sonny.

"Where are you visiting from?" Charlize drawled, all honey and softness.

"Oklahoma."

"Really. I confess, I don't know much about your state, except that there seems to be a preponderance of cowboys, oil, and football."

If Selena took offense at the stereotypes, she didn't show it. "It's a lovely place. You should visit sometime."

"I'd like that." Charlize turned her attention back to

Sonny, moving her hand to his shoulder in an intimate touch. "Sonny, it's always a pleasure."

"For me, as well." *Every damn time.*

He watched her walk away, stopping to greet this diner, to question that one. When she was out of sight, he realized that Selena was watching him.

"She's a lovely woman."

If he had had less self-control, he might have flushed. Instead, he knew he showed nothing he didn't want seen. "Yes, she is. Her family has been in Georgia for generations. Her great-granddaddy was right-hand man to the governor, and she's got ties all the way up to Pawley's Island in the Carolinas. I swear, if you pricked her, she would bleed blue."

"Does she know what you do?"

"What I do?" he repeated innocently. "I provide steady support for her business. Pawley's is my favorite restaurant in the city. I recommend it to everyone, and she's well aware of it. As for anything else . . . my business is my business."

And Selena's. Though who knew for how long?

Sliding away a dish filled with remnants of peach cobbler and melted ice cream, Damon shifted in his chair to look out across the restaurant. It felt strange being there. The place had been William's favorite during his time in Savannah—hell, it was the favorite of all the socially prominent in Savannah, as well as the wannabes—but Damon had gone there only on rare occasions, and never with the old man.

It hadn't changed at all, but then, that kind of enduring tradition held a lot of appeal to old-money Southerners. Every house William had lived in had been a historic old mansion, with only small changes like central air to make life more comfortable, and he wouldn't have had it any other way.

Damon liked change. The hell with tradition—he'd take new and improved anytime. His only concern with history was that it didn't repeat itself, not where he was concerned. He wasn't going to live the next twenty years answering to someone else, and he damned sure wasn't going to spend them rotting in jail.

He drained the last of his wine, then slid his chair back. "Man, I've gotta take a leak. Where's the john?"

"Past the bar, turn right," LeRoy replied.

Selena's gaze jerked his way as he got to his feet. She was pissed at him about the reward thing, but that was okay. It had taught her a valuable lesson—don't believe everything you're told and don't assume you're being told everything.

Leaving his chair pushed back, he faced her, both hands lifted from his sides. "Hey, I've got to piss."

"Jeez, Damon," Sonny muttered.

She stared at him. Willing him to remember her threat on the sidewalk? Wondering whether she could trust him to do his business, then return? She couldn't. But she couldn't ask Sonny to send Devlin or LeRoy with him, either, not without rousing his suspicion, and the last thing she wanted from Sonny was more suspicion.

"Be back," Damon said with a grin and a wink, then he walked out of the room and into the main dining room. The bar was ahead on the right, set in its own alcove, dimly lit and paneled. William had often had drinks there after an honest day's work at the police department, before moving out into the courtyard to dine next to the fountain. Damon couldn't count how many times the old man had gotten his picture in the paper with this influential person or that. Savannah society had loved William, making it even more important that no one in the business discover his real identity.

And now Selena had told them flat out. If the old man was in a grave, he'd be spinning.

Damon really did go to the bathroom, unzipping and relieving himself. If the scene had been a book or a movie, there would have been a window opening into a back alley, and he could have slipped out and been long gone before anyone noticed he was missing. But there wasn't a window, just the door he'd come through. He walked back out and stopped in the shadows near the end of the bar. To the left, just out of sight, sat Selena and Sonny. To the right, down a short hall and through a crowded foyer, was the main entrance.

He didn't have any money. No clothes besides what he wore. But money, he'd learned before he was ten, was easy to come by. And all he needed was enough to get to Dallas. There he had a new identity waiting to be taken on, along with an old fortune ready to be accessed. He could disappear, and Selena and Ceola and the fucking FBI would never find him again . . . until he showed up to destroy her. All he had to do was turn right. Walk out.

That was what he did, so casually that no one gave him a second look. Five feet, ten, twenty, and he was pushing the door open, stepping out into the muggy night, really free for the first time in weeks, to do what—

"Going somewhere?" Brian Jamieson leaned against the Mercedes, parked directly in front of the door. His ankles were crossed, his hands pushed in his pockets, looking as relaxed and bored as a driver could get. But the way his jacket was pushed back ensured Damon saw the butt of the pistol in the shoulder holster. He waited a moment, then straightened and stepped away from the car and toward Damon.

Fuck. Only Selena would choose a goddamn computer wiz who knew which end of a pistol was dangerous. Heinz was a weasel, and Sonny's guy was afraid of his own shadow, but not Jamieson. He looked like shooting Damon wouldn't bother him in the least.

Damon glanced one way down the street, then the other. Traffic wasn't bad, but there were plenty of people out, wandering through the park across the street, window-shopping, waiting outside restaurants. One-on-one, with nobody around, he could take Jamieson without breaking a sweat, but not in front of witnesses. Not when he needed to make it out of town and halfway across the country to be safe.

He shoved his hands into his pants pockets and rocked back on his heels. "Just getting some fresh air. Thought maybe I'd bum a cigarette."

Jamieson patted his coat pockets, including the breast pocket that brought his hand in contact with the pistol. "Sorry. I don't smoke. But then, neither do you." After a pause to let that sink in, he went on. "Maybe you'd better go back to your table. And Long? Don't try going out through the kitchen."

Fucking Robinette was probably hanging out back there. And Damon *knew* that cold bastard wouldn't think twice about shooting him.

Scowling, he took Jamieson's advice—as if he had a freakin' choice—and went back inside. Okay, so he'd tried, and failed. Another chance would come. He would be ready.

When he got back to the table, the dishes had been cleared and the check had arrived. The men looked bored, but Selena was pretty edgy. The glance she shot him could have cut ice.

"Jeez, we thought maybe you fell in," Devlin joked. "We were just arguing over who had to go check on you."

Shaking his head, Damon sprawled in his chair but didn't scoot it back up to the table. "Hey, when nature calls . . ."

Before he'd had a chance to get settled, Selena laid her napkin aside and stood. "It was a lovely dinner, Mr. Yates. We'll see you in the morning."

Sonny finished scrawling his name on the credit card slip, then, like the gentleman he was pretending to be, he stood, too. Following his lead, Devlin and LeRoy lumbered to their feet. "Some people don't do well bright and early"—he gestured, and Damon grinned his shit-eating grin in response—"so feel free to leave him at home. Clancy's is my territory. It's secure."

It is that, Damon thought. Secure. Isolated. An excellent spot for killing people.

All Selena did was nod and smile, then she made a gesture of her own, a simple lifting of her hand, a wave of slender fingers, that meant Damon was supposed to lead the way out. It was so much like William that it was goddamn freaky.

She waited until they were in the backseat of the Mercedes to turn that icy look on him again. "You lied to me."

"About?" He drew the word out, accompanying it with the best innocence he could muster. "Oh, the bonus. I didn't lie."

"You said William would never give Yates a reward for merely doing his job."

"Yeah, well, reward, bonus—they're not quite the same things. You've got to be specific, Selena. In this business, it's the little details that matter."

She sat rigidly, hands clenched in her lap, probably wishing they were around his throat instead. "Pay attention to this little detail, Mr. Long. That was your first screwup. One more, and you're going back to jail."

"Fuck you."

"You tried once, and got a concussion for your effort. Remember?" She let the reminder hang between them, looking so goddamn smug, making him hate her so god-damn much.

"You're cutting the business up into so damn many pieces that there won't be enough to make anyone happy. You promised me more, you promised Sonny, you're talking about giving Munroe and Taylor more. Where do you think all that extra's gonna come from? Not my share."

"I didn't promise Sonny anything. I suggested I might be willing to increase his share. After I see the books, of course. After I decide whether to continue doing business with him at all."

"I guess that's only fair," Damon said as he rested his head against the seat. "Because right now he's deciding whether *he* wants to do business with *you*... or get rid of you like he did that boat's crew."

And Damon didn't give a shit either way.

As long as he didn't get caught in the cross fire.

"Well, you survived. What'd you think of Yates?"

Selena glanced up from unbuttoning her dress as Gentry came into the bedroom. She was looking forward to crawling into bed and putting the day behind her, but first she had to get rid of the microphone and wire. "He looks like a mild-mannered accountant."

Gentry snorted. "It's the guys who don't *look* dangerous who are the deadliest of all. Like Davis. Handsome, charming, well-bred, respectable... and not one shred of remorse for all the lives he took."

Hers would have been one of those lives if Tony hadn't stopped him. Would her death have been different? Would William have regretted killing her? Perhaps. After all, for fourteen years he'd considered her his property, to do with as he would. Then again, perhaps not. Killing her had been his choice to make, just as saving her had been.

"Robinette wants to talk to you downstairs," Gentry said as she removed the last piece of tape. She dropped the equipment into a shopping bag, walked to the door, then turned back. "You probably won't hear it from him, but... you're doing a good job."

Surprised by the compliment, Selena paused while sliding back into her dress. "Thank you."

With an abrupt nod, as if Gentry regretted that Selena had heard it from *her,* the woman walked out.

After she was dressed again, Selena gazed out the window, absently removing her jewelry. In the years he'd lived in Savannah, William had driven the same streets, seen the same sights, had no doubt passed this house at least a time or two. He might have lived in one of the old mansions whose lights shone softly through the trees, or perhaps in one on the next square over, and had likely met the owners of this house at one event or another.

And he'd done it all while keeping his secrets. His other identity. His drug business. *Her.* He'd gone to such lengths to keep her out of both parts of his life. He'd refused to acknowledge her when he could, and now that he couldn't, the best she could do was accept it and move on. It was just so hard when she had so many questions.

Like why her? Why had he saved, then threatened, her life? Why had he maneuvered to meet her? Why had he chosen her as his heir? For years she'd told herself he'd taken her in out of kindness and generosity, that eventually affection and even love had come into play... but William hadn't been known for his kindness, and his generosity had always had strings attached. In her case, the strings had been the business—he'd rescued her, raised her, educated her, and in return, she would go to work for him, obey him, be controlled by him.

But why her?

If she could have the answer to that question, she could live with the rest of it. She could be satisfied.

Shaking her head as if it would disperse her melancholy, she drew a deep breath, left her belt dangling from the dressing table's marble countertop, kicked off her shoes, then finally left the room in search of Robinette.

Long and Gentry were in the living room. The dining room was empty, and so was the kitchen, but the door opening into the utility room was open, the washing machine was running, and the hushed murmur of voices came from there. She stopped in the doorway, smiling faintly at the sight of Jamieson sorting lacy undergarments and briefs, silks and denims and cottons.

Robinette was the first to notice her. He beckoned her in with a nod. "What do you think?"

That I'd rather be home. She leaned against a cabinet whose top served as a folding table and clasped her arms across her middle. "Yates is a good businessman. If staying with us is the smart choice, that's what he'll do."

"And offering him more money can make it the smart choice."

She nodded. That was as close as he was going to come to admitting she'd thought well on her feet.

"Why did you agree to meet at that bar? Our people checked it out—followed Yates there, in fact. It's in the middle of nowhere, with no cover. The surveillance team can't get close."

Almost a compliment, followed by criticism—it reminded her of William. Instead of reminding Robinette that he'd told her to make her own decisions, that she'd known nothing about the bar to base that decision on, she maintained a cool, level calm. "What do you want me to do? Tell him I've changed my mind? Ask him to meet here?"

"No, not here. If he doesn't know where you're staying, there's no reason to tell him."

"Maybe we could meet at Pawley's. He's a regular there, and he has a relationship of some sort with the owner. I don't think she'd mind letting him in before the place opens."

Robinette considered it a moment, then nodded. Pulling a cell phone from his pocket, he called up a number in the phone book, pressed SEND, then handed the phone to her.

Selena didn't realize she was holding her breath until Yates's voice mail picked up. "Mr. Yates, this is Selena McCaffrey. I need to reschedule our appointment for tomorrow morning. Instead of Clancy's, I'd like to meet at the restaurant. I'm sure Ms. Pawley wouldn't mind, and of course, I'd be happy to compensate her for any inconvenience. If this is a problem, call me at—" Robinette mouthed the number, and she repeated it. "Otherwise, I'll see you at Pawley's at nine o'clock."

After handing the phone back, she said, "Long lied to me about the bonuses."

"And he tried to escape," Jamieson put in. "I caught him coming out the front door."

"I heard. I saw." Robinette fixed his gaze on her. "Do you think he bought your threat?"

"I hope so. He's walked away the loser every time we've faced off."

"A concussion, a broken nose, a knife wound...you've been hard on the guy."

"Not hard enough. He's still breathing," she said dryly. "How are you going to keep him from disappearing after you've gone to sleep tonight?"

He flashed a rare smile, not an encouraging sight. "Hand-cuffing him to the bed should work nicely."

She would like to think he was serious, but no such luck.

"I'm a light sleeper. We've installed motion sensors at the tops of both staircases, so we'll be alerted if anyone tries to leave the second floor during the night. All the outside doors and windows are wired into the alarm system, and we'll have a team outside keeping a close watch on the house."

Short of handcuffing Long to the bed or barricading him in a windowless closet, that was the best they could offer, Selena acknowledged. If it was anyone but him, she would have been comfortable with the precautions. But it *was* Long.

Changing the course of her thoughts, she said, "I'm assuming Mr. Jamieson will go with me tomorrow."

Both men nodded. Selena was quite capable of handling her own finances, but William's were infinitely more complicated. Everything about William was more complicated, and that made her life more so.

Delicately she cleared her throat. "There's something I want to discuss."

In the silence that followed, Jamieson looked from Robinette to her, then said, "I, uh, I'll just go . . ." He left, closing the door behind him.

"Well?" Robinette prompted.

"William kept some journals in the vault at his house. It's part of my agreement with Mr. King that I can see them."

He didn't even pretend to think about it. "No."

She reined in her rising impatience. "This has already been discussed and settled."

"If King didn't tell you they're evidence in a major case and, as such, are off-limits, he should have."

And they could provide evidence of her life. Obviously that wasn't important to him, but it meant a lot to her. "I don't care about the evidence. Black it out. I just want to read what he says about me."

"What makes you think he says anything about you?"

"That day..." She paused. There had been plenty of momentous days in her life, and she hoped there were plenty still to come. But no matter what happened, *that day* would always refer to one hot July Sunday when life as she knew it had ended. "I looked at the journal for the year William took me in. There was a photograph of me dated April of that year. I didn't meet him until November."

Robinette made a brush-off gesture. "So he mislabeled the photo. So what? Everybody makes mistakes."

"Not William. Not that kind of mistake."

There was more, though she intended to keep it to herself for the moment. That same day William had said, *I should have left you in Jamaica to die. If I hadn't returned for you when I did...* Not *If I hadn't saved you* or *If I hadn't taken you with me,* but *If I hadn't returned for you.* Their November meeting hadn't been as innocent as it seemed. He'd been watching her—a forty-some-year-old man stalking a fourteen-year-old girl. Why?

And there was the man she'd robbed in Ocho Rios. He wasn't a local, but he'd known better than to wander around in that part of town flashing that kind of money. Even American tourists knew better. And if he'd been as drunk as he'd pretended, he never would have realized she'd lifted his money, much less been able to catch her and threaten her.

William had happened along at just the right moment to save her. Had he set up the whole incident to gain her trust? Had he been cold enough—sick enough—to pay a man to attack a child just so he could rescue her, then ensure his accomplice's silence by killing him?

Absolutely, yes.

Robinette started toward the door. "Take this up with King when we get back to Tulsa."

She sidestepped to block his path. "I've already taken it up with him. I expect that journal to be waiting when we get back, or my role in this game is over."

Color flared in his cheeks, but belying the apparent heat, his manner turned colder. "Let me remind you, Ms. McCaffrey, you're not in a position to be making threats."

"I'm not making threats, Mr. Robinette. I'm stating the facts. That journal will be waiting for me when we get back to Tulsa. Understand?" She waited a moment, not expecting a response, then turned on her heel and walked out of the room.

Jamieson was standing near the island, looking awkward, as if he'd eavesdropped or was afraid she would think he had. She gave him a cool nod. "I'll be ready to leave in the morning at a quarter of nine."

"Yeah. Sure. So will I. Good night."

Not from her point of view, but she quietly repeated the words all the same. "Good night."

Growing up an only child with a father he'd never known and a mother who was gone more often than not, Vernell Munroe had always wanted a large family. It had taken two wives and thirty years, but he'd gotten it—six children and seventeen grandchildren, with three more on the way, and every one of them living close enough to visit their old man every weekend and in between.

On this beautiful Saturday morning, he was sitting on the patio behind his house, a cup of coffee and a platter of fruit on the table in front of him. The coffee was decaf, the fruit low-calorie, low-sodium, low-cholesterol, low-everything.

Since his second wife had passed three years ago, his oldest daughter had taken to fussing over him. She'd taken away his cigarettes cold turkey, he hadn't had a piece of bacon or a biscuit drowning in gravy in longer than he could remember, and she had him walking the yippy little dog she'd bought him for companionship three times a day. He couldn't complain, though. He was healthier than he'd been in years.

When the cell phone rang, he looked at the caller ID and gave a sigh. Private call. He'd received only one call lately that had come in as private, and it was someone he didn't want to talk to that morning, not with his grandkids playing nearby.

"Want me to take it?" DeShaun offered.

Vernell shook his head. DeShaun was a good boy—practically family, except that no one in Vernell's family was allowed anywhere near his business. He'd promised that to his first wife before the cancer took her all those years ago, and he'd never wavered.

He picked up the phone and said "Hello," and the immediate response was a chuckle. "If yesterday is an example of the best you can do, it's a wonder you could hold on to your territory for a month, much less twenty years."

His new best friend. The man had called out of the blue, offering information, wanting money. Vernell had heard him out, had even made a first installment, but he didn't like the whole setup for fear that was exactly what it was—a setup. Anonymous strangers calling on the phone, suggesting a hit . . . the whole thing stunk. But there was a lot about this business that stunk.

"I don't know what you're talking about," he said. *Deny everything and admit nothing.* That was the first piece of advice he'd gotten from the old man who'd given him his start in the business, and it had proven good for nearly forty years.

"Yeah, right, so it's just coincidence that after I gave you the information on Selena McCaffrey's trip to Savannah, someone tried to kill her as soon as she got there."

"Must have been someone else you *gave* that information to." If he'd tried to take out the new boss, he wouldn't tell this guy, and if he hadn't tried, he wouldn't tell him. Theirs was a very narrow deal—the man gave him facts, and Vernell paid him for them. What he did after that was his business.

"Lucky for you, you get another chance," the man went on. "She's meeting with Yates this morning. You want the details?"

Vernell gazed across the lawn, where three of his grand-daughters were fiddling with each other's hair. Four-year-old Anjanae was pushing that yappy dog in a baby carriage, ignoring the boys' shouts when she strolled across their makeshift baseball field. Did he want the details? Not particularly. He'd rather be playing pitcher to his grandsons' All-Stars. Would he take them? Of course, because business was business, and Vernell always gave it the attention it deserved. That was how he'd risen to the top, and that was how he stayed there.

Gesturing to DeShaun for a pen, he said, "Go ahead." He wrote down the time and location of the meeting, handed the note to DeShaun, then watched him leave the table before he asked, "How did you come by this information?"

"What does it matter as long as it's good?"

"People in this business don't just pass their schedules around to strangers. Either you work for Yates, or you work for her."

"Like I said, what does it matter? It's good, I'm getting paid for it, and you'll be rewarded, too, if you use it— hopefully a little more efficiently than yesterday." There was another chuckle. "It's nice doing business with you, Mr. Munroe. You'll hear from me again."

Vernell didn't doubt that for a minute. Trouble always kept coming back around. Did Yates or McCaffrey have a clue that one of them had a traitor working for them? Hard to guess. There was a time when loyalty counted for a lot. But it was a different world today. Everything was for sale—loyalty, honor, a woman's life. It wasn't a world he particularly liked . . . but one he had to live in.

"DeShaun," he called. "Let's talk."

9

The smell of fresh-brewed coffee lured Selena downstairs Saturday morning. She found Robinette sitting at the kitchen table, a newspaper and a half-eaten doughnut in front of him. With a grunt in greeting, he pushed a bakery box toward her. She chose a bagel, popped it in the toaster while she fixed her coffee, then sat down opposite him.

Her clothes had been waiting, cleaned and folded, in a basket just inside the bedroom door when she'd finished her shower. She'd chosen the outfit that offered the most concealability for the wire—a sleeveless top and capris in ivory linen—removed the dry cleaners' tag, and quickly dressed, all the while concentrating on the appointment ahead. Not home. Not Tony. Not the lazy Saturday mornings she'd become accustomed to.

It was astonishing how important Tony had become to her, and how quickly. Six weeks ago, she hadn't even known he existed. Now she couldn't imagine living without him. If she had to, if William cost her the most important person in her life...

She let the thought trail off. If the worst happened, there was nothing she could do but accept it. Just as she'd always done.

She was tired of accepting.

She turned to Robinette. "What did you find out about Charlize Pawley?" She had no doubt he'd begun checking out the woman, probably within moments of her stopping by their table the night before. In the ten hours or so since, he'd likely learned everything there was to know about her.

"She's thirty-five. Has owned the restaurant for twelve years. Owns a hundred-fifty-year-old house on waterfront property, also for twelve years. Paid cash for both, with money from an inheritance, supposedly. She's never been arrested, never gotten a traffic citation. She votes in every election, donates money to the right charities, socializes with the right people. She drives a nice car, wears nice clothes, has some nice jewelry, but she also invests prudently—has a tidy little sum in a retirement account."

He left the table to refill his coffee, stirred in an extraordinary amount of sugar and cream, then sat down again. "Funny thing about her, though—her driver's license only goes back twelve years, too. Ditto for her social security number, her credit record, and her name. As far as we can tell, she sprang to life full-grown, with a lot of money and no history. Sound like anyone you know?"

Selena gave him a dry look. "I've earned my money legitimately, and I didn't pay cash for my house. I have twenty-eight years to go on a thirty-year mortgage." Then . . . "Do you think she's part of Yates's business?"

"Hard to say. She could be laundering money through the restaurant. It's certainly profitable enough." He paused, then met her gaze. "It was Davis's favorite place when he lived here. He was a regular, three, four times a week."

And where William had gone, his friends had followed. Charlize probably owed a good deal of her success to him. Clearly, she'd been aware of him as Henry Daniels. Had she also known him as William Davis?

"The stuff Yates told you about her great-granddaddy and Pawley's Island . . . that's the public version of her past.

Whether he believes it like everyone else is hard to say. It'll take some luck to find out the truth about her. Unless she's in the system, finding out who she was before she became Ms. Pawley is gonna be tough."

"And how do you find out if she's in the system? Finger-prints?"

His shrug was jerky, awkward. "That would be a good start. Any smooth surface she handles..."

She envisioned herself trying to sneak a wineglass into her minuscule handbag and smiled faintly. Fortunately, she was more resourceful than that.

"Jamieson knows everything there is to know about money, offshore accounts, laundering, hiding assets. He can learn a lot just looking at Yates's records, but he's gonna need a copy to study in depth. Yates will probably balk at letting you have it."

"I'll deal with it."

"Those two guys with him last night—Devlin and LeRoy... They both have a string of felony assaults on their records, and LeRoy's done time for manslaughter. Likely they're the ones who do most of Yates's dirty work for him... not that he isn't fully capable of doing it himself."

And enjoying it, Selena thought with a shiver.

"It'd be interesting to hear what they discuss with Long. To that end..." He pulled a compact cell phone from his pocket and laid it on the table between them. "This can pick up conversations at close range, but it's also fully functional as a phone. We'll be able to pick up every word he says to any-one, and if he makes a phone call, we'll pick that up, too, both the number and the conversation. Give it to him before the meeting."

With a nod, Selena picked up the phone and pushed away from the table. It would be to their advantage to know who

Long would call in his current situation. And Devlin and LeRoy *were* likelier to talk freely with their old buddy than Yates was with his new boss.

As she exited the room, she passed Gentry in the doorway, murmured a greeting, and headed down the hall.

A glimpse of Long in the living room, his hair standing on end, his sleepy gaze on the television, stopped her in her tracks. She couldn't think of a single believable reason for suddenly giving Long a phone. He knew she didn't trust him, and, after last night, had even better reasons for keeping him on a short leash. He would know something was up if she gave him a cell phone.

But if he acquired it on his own . . .

She flipped the phone open and punched in one of only two numbers she knew by heart—her gallery in Key West. The instant it began to ring, she disconnected, but kept the phone to her ear. One arm folded across her middle, she paced past the living room doorway, and muttered, "Oh, come on. Answer the phone. I know you're there."

She pretended not to notice the lowering of the television volume, or that he watched her until she'd pivoted and retraced her steps. As if she'd abruptly felt his gaze, she scowled at him, slammed the phone shut, and set it with a thud on the hall table next to her. "Don't say a word," she warned, then spun around and climbed the stairs in a huff.

Damon listened to the closing of an upstairs door—even angry, Selena didn't slam doors—then shifted his gaze to the table, barely visible around the door frame. The cell phone sat there, a marvel of technology—powerful enough to talk around the world, small enough to misplace on a regular basis. He listened, but beyond the distant voices in the kitchen, there were no other sounds. No footsteps, no Selena coming to reclaim the phone.

He eased from the couch and crossed to the doorway, looked up the stairs and down the hall, then palmed the phone. Flipping it open, he checked the CALLS MADE screen and recognized Selena's own Key West number. She'd been away from her gallery for weeks. Maybe there was trouble in paradise.

But the days when the stupid gallery was her primary source of support were gone. She had bigger things to worry about. Like Sonny. Like him.

After a round of fruitless phone calls to cell-phone providers, looking for an account belonging to Carl Heinz, Tony gave up and left his office at the police station. If it was a matter of life and death, he could find out anything anytime, but Saturday mornings were a bad time to make routine requests for information. He'd known that, but figured it couldn't hurt to try. After all, what else did he have to do?

One thing he did have access to, no matter the day or time, was property records. He'd tracked down the names, addresses, and phone numbers of Heinz's landlords, and now that the time had finally crept past eight, he was on his way to talk to them.

The woman who owned Heinz's house was about eighty years old, hard of hearing, and knew as little about the man as Tony did. He was a good tenant—nice, quiet, didn't complain, and paid his rent on time. He'd come with references, but she couldn't put her hands on them at the moment. She'd taken Tony's card and promised to call him once she found them, but since her filing system consisted of overflowing piles everywhere, he wasn't hopeful. She did finally locate the key, though, and gave him permission to check the house.

He was waiting at the door when Marla Johnson pulled into the driveway behind his Impala. She wasn't on call—evidenced by her shorts and snug-fitting tank top—but she'd agreed to come in. She liked him and, more importantly, liked Selena, and was happy to do whatever she could to help find the man who'd tried to kill her.

"You're lucky I was available on such short notice," she said as she climbed the steps to stand beside him. She set her case down on the stoop, then removed two pairs of latex gloves and the necessary powders, brushes, tapes, and mounting cards to print the doorknob.

"I appreciate you coming. How's Dickless?"

"Still basking in the posthoneymoon glow." She'd recently married a captain out of Uniform Division Southwest. Tony hoped they were happy. He wanted the best for her even though he hadn't been able to give it to her. "How's Selena?"

He opened his mouth, then closed it again. Frankie was the only one who knew the whole story about Selena and Long and the damned FBI. Much as he trusted Marla, he couldn't confide in her. "She's fine. Still a bit shaken up."

"I imagine someone trying to kill you will do that."

Actually, he'd been referring to their last argument, but the murder attempt made for just as good an explanation.

Once she'd printed the door, they went inside. The house was small—living room, eat-in kitchen, two bedrooms, one bath—and looked as if nothing had been changed since it had been built some sixty years ago. The paint was faded, the wallpaper peeling, and the linoleum in the kitchen had worn through to black in places. The appliances were bona fide antiques, the curtains bleached of color. Had Heinz noticed the dreariness of the place? Had he cared?

While Marla lifted prints from the surfaces Heinz likely would have touched, Tony looked around. The house had been rented furnished, according to the landlady, with a mismatched collection of castoffs all that was left. There were no magazines, books, or photos, no mail forgotten in a drawer. There wasn't even any trash to sort through.

"He's had experience at clearing out in a hurry," Marla remarked.

"Yeah." People in Selena's world did seem to have that expertise. Even she, at one time, had been packed up and ready to go on a moment's notice, with fake ID and cash to make a new life. *He* wouldn't even have a clue where to start. He was too rooted.

"I got prints from the faucets, the refrigerator, the switch plates, the knobs, and the medicine cabinet door in the bathroom. What's next?"

He peeled off the gloves. "His office. His landlord's going to meet us there."

It was a short drive to the run-down strip center. Tony had asked the man to wait outside the office, and he'd obeyed, leaning against a planter filled with the dried carcasses of what had once been flowers. After the man handed the keys to Marla, Tony asked, "What do you know about Carl Heinz?"

"His references checked out." The landlord handed over a copy of a rental application. "He paid his rent six months in advance. He didn't tear things up. He was here almost two years and never called me once."

"No notice that he was leaving?"

The man shook his head. "He dropped the key off next door on Wednesday and said to keep the rent he's already paid in lieu of notice. For three months' rent, I don't care about notice."

"So you didn't talk to him often—didn't get to know him?"

"Nah. I doubt I'd recognize him if he walked up right now."

"You have any idea how good business was?"

The man shook his head. "You can ask next door. They'd've seen whether people were coming and going. But like I said, he paid his rent six months at a time. He must've been doing all right."

No doubt Heinz had made good money, Tony acknowledged. Apparently, Henry had paid everyone well.

"Listen, my kid's got a T-ball game in twenty minutes. Do I need to stick around?"

"No, go ahead. Thanks for your help."

"Just lock up and leave the key next door," the man called as he climbed into his pickup, then backed out.

The office was about as shabby as the house had been, and the only thing useful Tony learned next door was that Heinz's walk-in business had been virtually nonexistent. No doubt, his official books suggested otherwise, but the bottom line was the business was a front for his real job as the accountant for Henry's illegal drug operation.

Christ, no one in this business was what he appeared to be.

Including Selena.

Jamieson pulled up in front of Pawley's a few minutes before nine. The nearest empty parking space was half a block away. He let Selena and Damon out, and they waited at the restaurant door while he parked, then walked back.

The door was unlocked, the foyer and hallway into the

dining room cool and dimly lit. Near the bar, Selena stopped and called into the empty room. "Hello?"

Almost immediately footsteps tip-tapped in their direction, and a moment later, Charlize Pawley appeared around a corner, elegantly dressed even so early. "Hello. Mr. Yates is waiting for you in one of our private dining rooms. If you'll come this way…"

They followed her past the arched room where they'd eaten the night before and through a doorway. The room was small, dominated by a gleaming mahogany table that seated twelve and a matching buffet at one end. The chandelier overhead reflected in the wood and off the silver that lined the buffet, and the smell of lemon-scented polish drifted on the air, faint beneath the fragrance of fresh flowers on demilune tables against one wall.

Private was the key word. The walls were thick, there were no windows, and the wood door was solid. *Power* was the next word that came to Selena's mind. No doubt, plenty of powerful people had met in this room in the past, negotiating agreements, brokering deals, determining the courses of people's lives. If she'd asked Ms. Pawley whether Police Chief Daniels had sat at that very table during his reign in Savannah, she was sure the answer would have been yes, numerous times.

Sonny Yates was seated at the near end, his trousers starched and pressed, his shirt looking as if it had come straight from the tailor. The shirt was tucked in, leaving no place on his person to conceal a weapon, but she had no doubt he had one somewhere, perhaps in the briefcase that leaned against his chair leg. Certainly on his two felon pals, Devlin and LeRoy, seated at the far end of the table.

A fourth man—slender, bespectacled, furtive—sat in

front of a notebook computer in the middle. Yates's accountant, looking every bit the part.

"There's coffee here on the buffet," Charlize said, as comfortably as if she played hostess to secretive business meetings on a regular basis. Who knew? With William as a onetime steady customer, maybe she did. "I also have bottled water on ice and a selection of pastries. I'll be in the kitchen preparing for opening, so if you need anything at all, just call."

She closed the door on her way out, and Selena moved farther into the room. "Gentlemen. This is Brian Jamieson. He'll be examining the records for me."

Yates acknowledged him with a nod, then eyed the notebook Jamieson was removing from its carrying case next to the accountant. "What's with the computer?"

"We just need copies of the accounts," Jamieson said, his manner easy.

"I don't—"

"—think it'll be a problem at all, will it?" Selena finished for him as she pulled a bottle of water from the bucket and dried it with a napkin. "After all, an in-depth accounting could take days, and I'm sure you and I have better things to do with our time. And besides . . . it *is* my business."

His smile tight, Yates exchanged looks with his accountant, then shrugged.

Business is business, William had often told her when trying to persuade her to join him. Looking over Jamieson's shoulder at the data on the computer screen brought that home. Regardless of the fact that Yates's was a criminal enterprise, it required the same extensive bookkeeping as any other multimillion-dollar business. There were many of the same expenses . . . and many that were totally different.

It didn't take long for Selena's mind to glaze over.

Numbers weren't her strong suit; she'd rather be painting, running, fighting . . . or kicking back with Tony, Mutt, and the cats. Jamieson, though, was like a kid at Christmas. His eyes had lit up at the sight of the first spreadsheet, and he was still engrossed well into the second hour.

After a time, Selena moved to sit at the end of the table. Yates joined her. "What do you think?"

"Everything appears to be in order." She waited, watched for the faint signs of relief, then added, "So far."

"Everything *is* in order," he said testily. "I take my business seriously. So . . . I can expect the profit-sharing balance to tip in my favor."

"Unless Jamieson uncovers something untoward on closer inspection."

Apparently confident that wouldn't happen, Yates relaxed in his chair. "Why would you do that—pay me more money?"

"Because you're valuable to me."

"I was valuable to William, too, but he didn't offer me a raise."

"Uncle William built the business from scratch. He wasn't doing all the work, by any means, but it was *his,* and he felt that entitled him to the bulk of the profits. I don't have twenty years invested in this enterprise. I don't have his attachment to it, or his need for the money. I'd rather be partners with you and the others, make less money, and have more peace of mind than be the top boss who always has to watch her back."

For a time he studied her. Trying to understand that sentiment? She would bet he did have William's attachment to the business, as well as William's need for money—not financial need, but an emotional one, to gather as much of it as he could, because it was a tangible symbol of his power, his success.

She didn't care if he understood her. As long as he was willing to take more money for doing the same work . . .

"What will happen to him?"

The question caught her off guard. "To William? I suppose eventually he'll be moved to some sort of long-term-care facility, where he'll . . ."

"Eventually die," Yates supplied.

William dead. Selena closed her eyes briefly. She had been prepared to kill him that day at the estate, but she'd never really thought that through to its logical conclusion. If she killed him, he would be dead. Gone forever. No longer there to advise her, control her, pressure her . . . or make her feel as if she belonged somewhere and to someone. He'd given her that—that sense of belonging. Not always in a good way, but there had been times. Her own mother hadn't wanted her, her father had never bothered even to meet her, the surrogate parents who'd taken her in had cared so little that they'd sold or traded her away. But William had wanted her. He'd been her family. When he died, a part of her life would end, too. A part of *her* would die.

"When you told me he was a cop . . . Jesus." Yates shook his head.

"Would you have worked for him if you'd known?"

"I don't know. There's something more than a little ugly about a dirty cop."

"You steal, lie, cheat, deal drugs, kill. But William's worse for doing the same things because he was a police officer?"

"Hey, I never swore to uphold the law. I didn't take a salary or wear a badge or arrest other people for doing the same things I'm doing."

"But you have no problem paying people like William to

make your job easier." She gestured toward Jamieson and the accountant. "Your 'public relations' expenditures."

"Yeah, some of that money goes to cops. A DA or two. A judge here or there. People on the take are going to help somebody. It might as well be us. After all, I don't have to like them to do business with them. If that was a requirement, we'd all be in trouble, wouldn't we?"

The ominous little comment made Selena's blood run cold. She hid it, though, as she toyed with her bottle of water. "What happens if they suffer an attack of conscience?"

He gave her a chastising look. "Did William?"

"Not once in his life." Not about using her. Not about ordering his godson's death. Not about intending to order *her* death. How cold had he been, that he could invest so much time and money in her, and so many years of affection in Tony, then have them killed?

"If my people had a conscience, they wouldn't be my people to start with. But if I thought they were tempted to make things right, I'd take care of them, like you were supposed to take care of William's detective. Except for one big difference—I would succeed."

Stiffening her spine, she gave him a haughty look. "I would have succeeded if one of William's thugs hadn't gotten in the way. I shot him, too, but unfortunately, he survived."

"Yeah, well, the only cop I ever shot didn't." Yates glanced at his watch, then grimaced. "This is taking a long time. I have another appointment."

She smiled coolly though everything inside her was coiled tightly enough to explode. "You don't need to stick around. Just leave us your accountant and go."

He subjected her to another of those long studies, then strode to the other end of the table, talked to his men there a moment, and headed for the door.

"Mr. Yates, I almost forgot...have you learned anything about the men who attacked us yesterday?"

A muscle in his jaw tightened. "We know it's nobody local—at least, no one professional."

"I assumed that. If they were professionals, they would have done a better job."

"I've got people out beating the bushes. If there's anything to find, we will."

"I hope so. It would be a shame to have someone in your territory taking shots at your boss *and* able to hide from you. It wouldn't look good for your command of the situation."

At that, his entire jaw worked spasmodically, and the color flared in his face, but he gritted his teeth instead of saying whatever was trying to get out. After a moment, he took an obvious breath, then smiled. It looked more like a grimace. "We'll find them, and when we do, J.T. and I will take care of them."

She gestured negligibly. "When you do, you'll bring them to me. Profit-sharing aside, there will be a bonus in it for you."

With a nod, he left, closing the door with a little more force than necessary.

Sonny walked out the restaurant's rear door into the narrow cobbled alley and stopped short. There, leaning against his spotless pewter-gray Porsche, was Charlize. Hair up, delicate arms exposed, she looked incredible enough that all he wanted to do was stand there and look at her. Not speak. Not even touch. Just look. Admire. Want.

As if she knew that, she remained motionless for a time, watching him with the tiniest of smiles playing over her lips. Finally, though, she straightened and maneuvered her high heels with ease over the uneven cobbles. Stopping close, in his personal space but not touching, she prompted, "Well?"

"She wanted a copy of my books."

"And you agreed?"

He shrugged. He'd wanted to say hell, no, but for one small matter: She *was*—for the moment, at least—the boss. The records were more hers than his. Besides, he had nothing to hide . . . and that little mouse of an accountant would have given them to her anyway. The man had never tried to disguise the fact that his loyalty was to William. The only reason Sonny kept him on was he was good, and he *was* loyal to the old man.

"What do you think of Selena?"

Charlize tilted her head to one side. "I've spoken to her for all of five minutes, if that."

"But you have excellent instincts. I trust them more than my own. She says she wants to continue with business as usual, except with a twist—she wants to work as partners instead of boss and peon."

"You don't believe her?"

Sonny shrugged. "Why would a woman volunteer to pay more money to her employees? Why take a cut in her own income and increase ours without increasing our responsibilities?"

With a soft, sensual laugh, Charlize smoothed a nonexistent wrinkle from his shirt. "Not everyone gauges success by money. For some of us, there is such a thing as 'enough.'"

They'd had this discussion before—enough to pay bills, enough to buy groceries, enough to provide security and maybe a little bit of luxury. Sonny thought it was all a crock. Over dinner the night before, Damon had told LeRoy and Devlin a little about Selena—that she'd been discarded by three sets of parents, that she'd begged and stolen to fill her belly. He'd done that himself, and knew there would never be "enough" to make him forget the experience. "But why *offer* to pay more? If she had no choice, that would be one thing, but to just say, 'Here, let me give you a raise' without even being asked? It doesn't make sense."

"Did you ask her why?"

"She said she'd rather be partners than to have to watch her back all the time."

Charlize's shrug was softer, more expressive, than his had been. "So there you go. Consider it a kind of life insurance."

Interesting concept—she paid them enough money, and they agreed not to kill her. "Do you think I should trust her?"

Charlize's gaze grew distant. He hated it when she went away like that, and he automatically did what he always did—touched her to remind her he was there, to bring her back. She looked at him with a faint smile. "You know my motto—never trust anyone."

"Except me." He said it as fact, but truth was, he was never really sure. He'd known her for ten years, had been sleeping with her for eight and in love with her about that many, but he always had this suspicion that he didn't really know her at all. She was so aloof, quiet and private. She said she loved him, said she trusted him, and her actions pretty much bore that out. Still, sometimes he wondered . . .

Her smile banishing the distance completely, she laid one pale, elegant hand on his. "Of course I trust you, Sonny."

The words came easily to her, but he knew the feelings didn't. She never talked about her life before him, but he knew it hadn't been good. Sometimes he caught glimpses of the way she must have once been—open, carefree, tranquil—but then the aloofness reclaimed her, burying that innocence under a protective shell. Someone had hurt her badly, and all these years later she was still paying the price. He wanted to help her, wanted to heal her, but didn't know how. Didn't know if a healed Charlize would want him the way the wounded Charlize did.

He wasn't proud of it, but he would rather have her wounded than not at all.

"Where are you off to?" she asked.

"I have a meeting at Clancy's." Just like any businessman, he had shipments coming in that required receipt, quality control, payments, distribution. "If you get a chance to talk to Ms. McCaffrey"—he gave her name a scornful twist—"I'd like to hear your impressions."

"Will do," she said with one of her phony smiles, bright and warm. She started toward the restaurant door, but stopped halfway. "Be careful."

"Always." He watched until the door closed behind her, and even after. They might disagree on how much money or power was enough, but in every other aspect of his life, he knew exactly what was enough: Charlize. With him.

For a lifetime.

Selena shifted her gaze to Long. "Who is J.T.?"

"William's hitter for this area."

Such an innocuous nickname for a killer. But then, "Damon" wasn't exactly a name to put you in mind of a cold-blooded killer, either. "Have you met him?"

Long shook his head. "Hitters don't tend to be real sociable folks. All I know is he's been with William a long time, and he keeps a very low profile."

She looked at the other two men. "Have you met him?"

They exchanged glances—surprised that she'd spoken to them? Unsure whether to answer truthfully or even at all? After a moment, they both shook their heads.

Swiveling in her seat, she faced Jamieson. "What do you think about the records?"

His expression was distracted when he looked up from the computer, his mouth quirking as if he'd rather not be bothered while he was playing with his numbers. "Mr. Yates runs an efficient organization, minimizing risks and maximizing profits."

"Though books can be made to say whatever a person wants them to say, can't they?" she asked.

Yates's accountant blustered in his seat. "I've worked for Mr. Davis for more than half your life. He never accused me of showing him phony books."

"I'm not accusing you, either," she said with a placating smile. "I was just making a comment. Of course, you're smart enough to realize that if there were any irregularities in the records, Mr. Jamieson would eventually uncover them. Besides, if Uncle William kept you on all those years, he must have had great faith in you." *Or someone keeping an eye on you,* Selena thought.

She stood up, slid the chair in, then started toward the door.

"Where are you—" Jamieson broke off abruptly, apparently realizing that an accountant shouldn't question his boss.

She gave him a wry look. "I'm going to the ladies' room. I'll be back."

A glance at her watch showed it was nearly eleven. The lights had been turned up in the dining room and hallways, a woman in a crisp white shirt and burgundy bow tie was setting up behind the bar, and the waitstaff were readying for the first diners. None of them appeared the least bit curious about her.

She was on her way back to the private room when

Charlize came out of the kitchen, two plates in hand. The woman smiled serenely when she saw Selena. "There you are. Since Mr. Yates had to leave, I was hoping I could tempt you out of the meeting long enough to share our chef's latest creation with me."

"I really should get back inside." Though Jamieson, no doubt, had things under control, and Long's cell phone was providing a record of any ongoing conversation for Robinette's people.

"Oh, come on. The spirit must be nourished, and it won't take long." Charlize lifted one of the plates closer, and a tantalizing aroma drifted into the air.

The dish held a salad—torn greens providing a bed for vegetables and seafood, drizzled with a lemongrass dressing. Her bagel suddenly seemed a long time ago. Selena smiled. "Let me tell my companions."

That task took all of sixty seconds, then she settled at a corner table with Charlize. The restaurant was officially open and the staff was seating early diners, keeping them far from Charlize and Selena's table.

Charlize took a delicate bite before speaking. "So you and Mr. Yates are . . . friends?"

Was that hesitation merely searching for the right word or jealousy? Selena wondered as she chewed a bite of squid, shrimp, and pickled carrot. "This is delicious," she said, then casually added, "We're business associates, actually."

"Really? And what kind of business are you in?"

"Customer satisfaction. We see a need, we satisfy it."

"That describes all business, doesn't it?"

"I suppose so." Without giving her a chance to go on, Selena asked, "How long have you been in the restaurant business?"

"Twelve years. We started out serving only lunch in about

half the space. As the profits grew, so did the restaurant. Now we're so well established that our customers can hardly remember a time when we weren't a part of their lives."

"Mr. Yates is certainly a fan."

Charlize's smile was reserved. "Oh, yes, he's one of our best customers."

"I understand Uncle William was also one of your best customers."

"Uncle William?"

"You probably knew him better as Henry Daniels."

"Of course I knew Chief Daniels. Everyone in town did. I didn't realize he was your uncle." One brow arched up. "I had no idea he used a different name."

"One for family, one for others," Selena said with a careless shrug. The curious repeating of his name, the surprise evidenced by the brow lift, seemed sincere, but there had been something more. The slightest hesitation, no more than an instant, before the curiosity, the casual surprise that felt a shade too casual.

"Yes, Chief Daniels was a regular here. He's an impressive man—intelligent, capable, compassionate... and, of course, he has exquisite taste in restaurants." Charlize shrugged to excuse her immodesty. "I have a photograph of the two of us together. Let me get it." She crossed to the bar with long strides, removed a frame from the wall, then returned. "We call that our wall of fame, featuring all our local celebrities. This was taken... oh, we were celebrating the restaurant's expansion, so it must have been about seven years ago."

Selena accepted the photograph, taking note of the courtyard scene, the sparkling fountain, the luxe linens covering the tables, the women's jewel-toned dresses, the men's summer suits, before she let herself focus on the two people at the photo's heart. Charlize, in a vivid-hued dress, looking beautiful, elegant, and cool, and William.

Her heart tightened at the sight of him—a few years younger, always handsome, smiling that broad, encompassing, charming smile. All his life people had loved him, admired him, looked up to him, and he'd accepted it as nothing less than his due. Such arrogance, and such confidence that no one could hold the arrogance against him. He *had* been an impressive man.

Except for the twisted, ugly nature of his soul.

She studied the photograph a moment more—the way Charlize smiled at her guest, the way his arm rested proprietarily around her waist. William had been proprietary about everything. The world had revolved around him, everything in it there for his use, his amusement, his satisfaction, his gain.

Subdued, she handed the photo back to Charlize, who gave it a fond glance before setting it aside. She signaled to the bartender, who brought over two glasses of wine, then leaned forward cozily. "So . . . tell me about your art career."

The mention of her other life startled Selena, though she was certain she hid it. "How do you know about that?" Surely William hadn't told her, not when he'd pretended she didn't exist. Perhaps Yates had checked her out. After all, William had. So had the FBI.

"Actually, I own several of your paintings. I've had them for years. I have to admit, I didn't pay much attention to the artist's name when I bought them—I just fell in love with them—but when I met you last night, your name sounded familiar, so I checked."

"I'm very flattered."

"You have a great talent. Something to fall back on if the family business doesn't suit you."

The comment sounded innocent enough, but it sent apprehension creeping down Selena's spine. If any other business didn't *suit*, the solution was easy—quit. Find another job. Walk away. But how many people walked away from *this* business?

However few the number, she intended to be one of them.

The conversation turned to polite chitchat about the weather, tourist sites, museums. Their salads were done, their wine gone, when Charlize gave a delicate sigh. "I suppose I should return to work and let you get back to your meeting."

Thinking back to the morning's conversation with Robinette, Selena opened the small purse she wore bandolier style and removed a silver compact. Out of sight under the table, she gave it a quick polish with her napkin, then, holding it by its edges, she held it out. "You have something at the corner of your eye."

With a chuckle, Charlize accepted it. "I pay a fortune for makeup that promises not to smear, but I always seem to manage." She flipped the compact open, raised it so she could see her eye, then made an expression of surprise. "Except this time."

"Sorry. It must have been the lighting."

"Better safe than sorry." She closed the mirror as she rose, then offered it back. "Thank you for the company, Selena. I hope to see you again before you return to Oklahoma."

Careful once more to hold the compact by its edges, Selena slid it back into her purse. "That would be nice," she said. Lied. When all this was over, she never wanted to see any of these people again.

10

It was past noon when Jamieson and the accountant completed the transfer of files from one computer to another. Selena thanked the mousy little man, and she, Jamieson, and Long walked through the now-busy restaurant to the entrance. The others, like the rodents they were, slunk into the kitchen and, presumably, out the rear door.

At the entrance, Jamieson paused. "Why don't you wait here, and I'll go get the car."

It was the middle of a busy, sunny day, the car was only a half block away, and Robinette and Gentry were somewhere out there on the street with the surveillance team. The risks in walking that half block were minimal. If someone was set up outside to shoot her, he could easily do it in the ten feet from the door to the curb, and walking to the car eliminated the need to be alone, even for a few minutes, with Long. But she nodded and chose a spot against the wall to wait.

Long stood near the window, alternating quick glances out and more thorough studies of a group of women waiting to be seated. Two of the three were returning the attention. At one time Selena had been foolish enough to fall for his charm, but the price for those few hours' flirtation had been dear.

So had the reward. If not for Long, William never could have blackmailed her into going to Tulsa, and she never would have met Tony.

"There he is." Opening the door, Long mockingly gestured for her to precede him.

With a thin smile, she stepped outside. The sun was radiating all its summer intensity, bringing an immediate sheen of moisture to her skin, warming her from the outside in. If she were home on a day like this, she would set up her easel outside and simply luxuriate in the heat and light. Shaking off the longing the mere thought of home and painting stirred, she looked to the right, saw nothing out of place, then checked to the left.

The Mercedes was a few car lengths away, caught in the traffic that jammed the narrow street. Gentry stood in front of a store a few doors down from the restaurant, looking like a tourist in denim shorts and a T-shirt bearing the city's name in neon colors. Her gaze flickered over Selena and Long without the slightest hint of recognition as she strolled along to the next shop, where she paused to look at the window display.

Tires squealed on the hot pavement at the end of the block. Selena turned and watched as a brown panel van accelerated toward the stalled traffic, the driver showing no intention of stopping. At the last instant before crashing into Jamieson became inevitable, the van jerked to the right, slamming into the rear of a car parked next to the Mercedes. To the accompaniment of tearing metal, the car bumped over the curb and skidded toward Selena and Damon, pushed along by the van's ongoing acceleration.

"Fuck this!" Long muttered, sliding over the trunk of another car, then darting into the street.

Before Selena could think about following him, a hand grabbed her from behind. "Let's get the hell out of here!" Gentry ordered.

Hoping Jamieson went after Long, Selena followed Gentry,

dodging frightened pedestrians. With a grind and squeal, the battered car came to a stop against a storefront, leaving the van no place to go. An instant later, car doors slammed and, a breath after that, gunshots exploded into the air. They threw themselves around the corner to safety but didn't slow their steps. Arms pumping, feet pounding, they headed for the next intersection.

"Goddamn sons of bitches," Gentry said, her breathing hardly labored. "They couldn't have waited until the sun went down? It's too fucking hot for this. Turn down that alley."

The alley was narrow and stank from the Dumpsters that lined it.

"Damn! When you make enemies, you do it good, don't you?" Gentry was still keeping pace with Selena, though she was shorter and less accustomed to the heat and humidity. The will to live was a great equalizer. "We've gotta find a place to hide, only please, God, not the Dumpsters."

They were practically to the end of the alley when Selena noticed a door ajar on the right side. Jerking Gentry up short, she shoved her inside, then followed. They were in the dimly lit storeroom of an Asian restaurant, judging from the smells. Juggling boxes marked FORTUNE COOKIES, they took cover in the darkest corner.

"Can you hear anything?" Gentry whispered.

"Just my heart." Selena strained to listen, to distinguish sounds of an ambush from the everyday noise of the restaurant. There—footsteps pounding against pavement, angry Southern voices. They continued down the alley, grew faint, but still Selena waited, listening. Moments later, the men came back, moving slower this time, cursing.

"Fucking bitches," one of them said, then banged his fist against the restaurant door. It swung open, then bounced back, and both Selena and Gentry stopped breathing. The silence was heavy, broken at last by the creak of a shoe sole as someone eased inside the door. Through a slit between boxes, Selena could see the intruder was over six feet tall, had a Marine Corps globe-and-anchor tattoo extending under one short sleeve, and held a Glock in his left hand. Behind him was the shadow of his partner.

How long until the tattoo shoved the boxes aside? How many seconds would she and Gentry have to act before he shot them? One? Half of one?

Her muscles were tensing as she gauged the distance between the man and their cover. If she acted first, if she leapt from her hiding place and kicked the gun from his hand—

A scream split the air, followed by shrieks in Chinese, as a round little woman stopped short inside the storeroom door and grabbed a broom. Her shouts brought everyone else piling in from the kitchen, yelling angrily at the men, forcing them out the door again. While several young women comforted the woman who'd screamed, a man slammed the door and locked it, then shepherded the others back into the kitchen.

Selena exhaled in a quiet whoosh as she sank against the wall. Next to her, Gentry did the same, then murmured, "Confucius say you are one lucky cookie."

Lucky. She'd nearly been run down, then chased through downtown Savannah by men with guns who wanted to kill her. Her heart was thudding, her knees were shaking, and she'd broken out in a cold sweat. She didn't feel lucky.

But she was alive. And if that didn't make her lucky, she didn't know what did.

Pulling out her cell phone, Gentry punched in a number. Even from several feet away, Selena heard the adrenaline in

Robinette's voice when he answered. "Gentry, tell me you have our CW with you and she's alive."

"She's alive. Did you get Long?"

"We're tracking him. Where are you?"

"In the storeroom of a Chinese restaurant a few streets away." She started to recount the route they'd run, until Selena turned one of the boxes they'd hidden behind so she could see the shipping label. She read off the name and address, told him to come to the alley, then disconnected.

Seconds ticked past as they huddled there. Ordinary sounds drifted from the restaurant kitchen, along with the distant rumble of traffic—average sounds, normal, made surreal by the fact that someone had just tried again to kill them. If the Chinese woman hadn't come in when she had...

"I think we could have taken 'em," Gentry said, her tone aiming for boastful but not quite there. "Once you'd dropkicked the big guy..."

Selena gave her an appraising look. "Why couldn't you have taken the big guy?"

"Did you see that big gun? Besides, you were poised to strike. I didn't want to disappoint you by stepping in." Gentry lifted her hand, saw that it trembled, and gave a laugh that verged on hysterical. "Does this sort of thing happen to you often?"

"More every day. What about you?"

"Even with all the training we do, the first rule is to avert danger if we can. So, no, not often. In fact, in my twelve-year career, today was only the second time anyone ever shot at me."

"And yesterday was the first?"

The redhead nodded. "I've never fired my gun at a person, never had a serious physical confrontation with anyone."

"That'll probably change before this case is over."

"Looks like." Gentry tilted her head to one side to study Selena. "You're damn calm."

Selena's answering smile was weary. "That's shock, not calm." The last time her mother's husband, Rodrigo, had beaten her had been as scary as the first. The time Long had tried to rape her had been as traumatizing as when the man in the Ocho Rios alley had tried. Getting chased through the streets today made her feel as vulnerable as getting run off the road yesterday. She would never get used to people wanting to hurt or kill her.

A low buzz came from Gentry's pocket, and she pulled out the cell phone. The conversation lasted mere seconds, then she pushed away from the wall. "Come on. Robinette and Jamieson are outside."

When Gentry cautiously eased open the door, the Mercedes was parked a few feet away and Robinette stood next to the open rear door. Jamieson was settling in the front passenger seat, his laptop open and running. "Get in," Robinette commanded, one hand extended to Selena. "Gentry, you drive. Jamieson will tell you where to go to pick up Long."

As Gentry headed toward the street, Selena removed the compact from her purse and offered it to Robinette. He looked questioningly without making a move to take it.

"Charlize Pawley," she said. "'Any smooth surface...' You'll find my prints around the rim. The rest are hers."

Understanding dawning, he accepted the compact, careful to touch it only on the rim. The possibility of discovering Charlize's true identity clearly tantalized him—she could see it in his eyes—but he didn't offer thanks or a *good job*. She didn't think he was capable. But she hadn't done it for his gratitude or respect.

"We'll get these checked out, just as soon as we pick up

your boy. Then we're going to get packed and head back to Tulsa."

The words startled Selena, and she paused in closing her bag. "Why?"

Robinette gave her an impatient look. "Someone's trying to kill you."

"I expected that. Surely you did, too."

"We figured they'd try," he admitted.

"So why run away because they lived up to your expectations?"

"It's called caution, Ms. McCaffrey."

"Mr. Yates might call it fear."

"Are you so eager to get shot at again?"

She gazed out the window, her sad smile reflected in the glass. She could happily live the rest of her life without being someone's target. But since she *was* a target, better to find out whose and stop him than hide in fear. Better to stop them all. And the sooner that was done, the sooner she could have her life back. "No, of course not. But we're here, Mr. Robinette, and Yates is cooperating with us, however grudgingly. We've got his financial records, but that's not all you want, is it? Personnel records, suppliers, distributors, the identity of his hit man . . . Why give him an opportunity to rethink his cooperation?" She paused, but he offered no response. "When we leave, it should be because it's *our* choice, not theirs."

They drove a block or so before Robinette broke his silence. "Have you ever heard the saying, 'The third time's the charm'? You might not be so lucky next time."

She smiled again. She never should have survived Rodrigo's endless beatings, all those years on the streets, that day in William's study, that night at the shooting range. She had been incredibly lucky. "Now it's time to make Mr. Yates feel unlucky."

After jogging a zigzag route through most of downtown, Damon slowed to a walk, wiped the sweat from his face, then turned a corner onto a busy waterfront street. He'd caught a glimpse of Jamieson getting out of the car, but given a choice between coming after *him* and protecting his boss, without a doubt he'd protect the boss. After all, she was his current meal ticket, and was proving to be a damn generous one. By the time any of them realized that Damon was missing, it would be too fucking late to do anything about it.

The first thing he had to do was get his hands on some money. That was why he'd chosen that street. It was filled with trendy, touristy shops and restaurants—a target-rich environment. Next, he knew an old boy outside town who was handy with all kinds of tools, who would be happy to remove Damon's ankle jewelry for the price of a bottle of booze.

He studied possible marks as he walked, settling on a middle-aged couple. The man wore knee-length shorts and a bright Hawaiian shirt, and she wore a summer dress in colors so loud that they hurt to look at. It exposed her soft, fleshy arms and clung to the rolls that made up her body.

He lengthened his stride, then fell into step directly behind them as they reached the end of the block. When they stepped off the curb and into the street, Damon deliberately stumbled against the man, knocking him forward and smoothly sliding the wallet from his hip pocket. "I'm so sorry!" he exclaimed, putting on a drawl, helping the man regain his balance. "I just slipped off that curb there like I didn't even see it. Are you all right? I didn't hurt you, did I?"

"No, no harm," the man said, straightening his shirt. "Don't worry about it."

Still murmuring apologies, Damon crossed the street

with them, but when they went straight, he turned right. In the middle of the block, he turned down an alley, retrieved the wallet from the pocket where he'd stashed it, removed the money, and tossed the rest into a Dumpster. Whistling softly, he continued down the alley, turned another corner, and came to an abrupt stop.

Robinette and Jamieson stood three feet in front of him, looking none too happy. Parked in the street, motor running, passenger doors open, was the Mercedes, with Gentry behind the wheel and Selena in the backseat.

Well, hell.

Damon stood there, weighing his options . . . as if he had any. He could flee, but Selena's two goons would be right on his heels, and Gentry would probably as soon run him down as look at him. Besides, they'd tracked him once already, and it would be just as easy to do again. He should have gotten the goddamn bracelet off first and worried about money later. He could have persuaded his old buddy to do it, even if it had meant beating the shit out of him.

Scowling, Robinette jerked his head toward the car, and Damon reluctantly headed in that direction. He was taking his sweet time about sliding into the backseat when Robinette shoved him and damn near sent him tumbling into Selena's lap. As he settled in the center of the seat, he gave her a chastising look. "This ankle bracelet isn't deactivated at all, is it?"

She shook her head.

"You fucking lied to me."

"You lied to me first. I'm just returning the favor."

Robinette got in beside him, and Jamieson took the front seat, lifting his laptop off the console, clicking out of some kind of electronic tracking program. Resting his head against the back of the seat, Damon frowned straight ahead. He'd been suckered—had believed he really had a chance at getting away that weekend, when nothing had really changed, except which fucking asshole was monitoring him.

"You know, I'm starting to think I can't trust you," he said mildly.

"You never trusted me."

"And you don't trust me, which makes our working together kind of pointless. Once you make your deal with Sonny boy, why don't you pay me off and let me go on my way?"

"I spent a lot of money getting you out of jail, and I took on a lot of responsibility. I don't intend to get nothing for the money, and I don't intend to take the blame if you fail to show up in court."

"I'm not going to trial."

She gave him a long, steady look, then a speculative light came into her eyes. "Prove your worth to me, and you might not have to."

He returned the look, searching her face, but there was nothing else to see. "What do you mean?"

"Exactly what I said. Quit lying, quit trying to escape, quit setting me up to fail, and when it comes time to go to trial, Damon Long might have ceased to exist." She gestured toward the front seat. "Mr. Jamieson *can* deactivate the ankle bracelet, and Mr. Robinette has helped previous employers relocate with new identities when situations got too sticky. We can help you, if you give me reason. Or..." Her voice chilled. "You can keep screwing around with us, and Damon Long really might cease to exist. It's your choice."

He would rather see her dead than alive. But more than that, he'd rather be alive himself, and that wasn't likely to last long if he went to trial on a whole shitload of murder charges in a state where executions were a regular thing. If the price of saving his neck was letting her live... Living was better than dying, winning better than losing. In the long run, getting out of the situation with his skin intact was the only thing that counted. A new name, a new start, and a fortune to make that start—what more could a man ask for?

"Okay," he said, hands raised in surrender. "No more misdirection and no more escapes on my part, and I don't set one foot in court. Deal?"

Selena nodded coolly. "Now prove it. How should I deal with this latest attack?"

"You gotta have a come-to-Jesus meeting with Sonny—threaten him if he doesn't find the people responsible. No nice little chitchat. You've got to scare him. Make him think he's gonna die."

She nodded again, then opened her purse. Damon caught a glimpse of a sweet little Beretta inside before she snapped it shut again, then patted her waist and pockets. "Damn. My cell phone..."

Damon shifted on the seat, too aware of the phone making the smallest of bulges in his pocket. "You must have dropped it when you took off like that. It's better to surprise him, anyway."

"I suppose so."

He dropped his hands to his lap, his arms effectively concealing the phone, and gazed ahead. The deal he'd just made with her hadn't really changed anything. It wasn't as if reneging on it would affect his honor, because he didn't have any. She knew that—knew better than to take his word for anything. And if he got a chance for a little payback... well, hell, a man had to keep his options open.

Just as she was likely keeping *her* options open.

• • •

Clancy's Bar was located a half mile out of town, an unremarkable building in an unremarkable location. There wasn't so much as a neon sign to identify it, but people who frequented places like Clancy's didn't need a sign. Rodrigo had had such a place in Puerto Rico, where he drank away money that could have been used for food and came home too drunk to hurt her when he tried.

Long's advice had dovetailed nicely with their own plan, formulated while they'd followed the bracelet's electronic signal. The local FBI agents had followed Yates to the bar when he'd left Pawley's. Devlin and LeRoy had gone straight there, as well, and there had been several visitors in the meantime, presumably Yates's other appointment. Selena's task was to put the fear of God into the man. It shouldn't be difficult, considering she was still shaken herself.

An expanse of pines stretched out on either side and a creek out back isolated the bar from its nearest neighbors. No one to complain about loud music, rowdy customers...or gunshots. There were only two vehicles parked out front—a beat-up pickup, blue and white except for a primer-gray fender, and an older SUV that looked as if it had seen its share of off-road use. The tail end of a third car, a silver convertible, was just visible around the back corner of the building.

Gentry parked near the door and shut off the engine. For a moment, the silence was unnerving. Selena could feel anticipation radiating from Robinette, in direct opposition to the dread building in her stomach. Make Yates think he was going to die, Long had advised—in Robinette's more polite terms, hold him responsible. Give him an ultimatum to find the hit men or suffer the consequences.

She was suffering the consequences. She was looking over her shoulder, feeling like a little yellow duck in a shooting gallery. How unfair was it that to be safe in the future, she had to make a target of herself in the present?

As she opened the door, Jamieson handed something from his laptop case to Robinette, then stowed the computer under the seat. It was two heavy-duty cable ties, she saw, their purpose to ensure Long didn't make another escape attempt. Leaning forward, Robinette secured the tie around Long's ankle and to the steel undersupport for the front passenger seat.

"Hey, what the fuck— Get this thing off!"

"You wait here," Selena said politely as she climbed out. Ducking to eye level, she smiled. "We won't be long."

"Goddamn son of a bitch!" He jerked his leg, but succeeded only in shaking the seat.

They approached the building en masse. Selena twisted the doorknob and found it locked. When Jamieson motioned her back, she shook her head, then executed a side kick next to the lock. The impact vibrated up her foot into her leg as the door swung open, rattling on its hinges. Without taking even a second to shake off the blow, she strode inside, and the others followed.

"What the hell—" Sonny Yates rose from the table in the back corner, his hand going automatically to the holster on his belt. LeRoy and Devlin, seated at the bar, got to their feet, as well, and, along with the bartender, were in the act of drawing their weapons when Yates raised one hand to stop them. "Well, shit, Selena, if you'd only knocked, we would have been happy to unlock the door for you," he said, sitting again.

As Devlin sank back onto his stool, she brushed close to him, drew his weapon before he realized what she was doing, then crossed to Yates's table in two strides and raised the pistol mere inches from his hazel eyes.

"Goddamn, Selena, what are you doing?" His tone was mild, but there was a hint of fear in his eyes. He sat motionless, hands splayed on the tabletop.

"Tell the others to hand their guns over to Mr. Robinette."

He nodded once in the direction of the bar without ever taking his gaze from her. She listened to footsteps on the wooden floor, the rustle of clothing, steel rubbing against leather, then the footsteps returning.

"You may notice that I'm not looking my best this afternoon. We got a surprise as we were leaving Pawley's. A man tried to run us down, and when that didn't work, he and his accomplice opened fire on us. We had to flee on foot through the streets of Savannah, and we barely escaped unharmed. Who was it?"

It took a moment for her words to sink in. She searched his face for some reaction—surprise, dread, a heavier, thicker fear. There was a hint of surprise, and a hint of anger in the tightening of his mouth, but no fear. "You think I sent someone to kill you and you're still walking around? I'm insulted, Selena. William always said I had the best hitter in the organization. My man wouldn't have failed."

Her movements slow and deliberate, she thumbed back the hammer on the pistol. "You keep telling me it's not you, but this is your territory—*your* home turf. If you're not behind these attempts on my life, then you've got some outsider acting as if he never heard of Sonny Yates and damn sure isn't afraid of him. Either way, that worries me, Mr. Yates. If you can't control one small area like Savannah, how can I possibly believe you can handle the entire Southeast region?"

With every word, Yates's color turned paler and his manner grew stiffer. "It *isn't* me," he denied through clenched jaws.

"So you say. And yet you can't seem to find out who it is."

"We're working on that."

"And while you're working—and *failing*—people continue trying to kill me right here in the heart of your city. That causes me grave concern, Mr. Yates."

His gaze shifted around the room, from her men to his own, then back to her. "I'm not stupid, Selena. If I wanted to kill you, do you think I'd do it right here in town where the obvious trail would lead back to me?"

"Maybe that would be your alibi—that everyone knows you aren't stupid." She shrugged, and the movement made the .45's barrel shift from his left eye to the right before centering again. "Using your reasoning, if *I* wanted to kill *you*, I should do it someplace other than Tulsa so the obvious trail wouldn't lead back to me. Someplace like . . . here."

There it was—that heavier, thicker fear she'd been looking for earlier. Yates knew she could kill him for no reason other than her suspicions, knew none of his men would intervene or even care, knew the only disadvantage to her would be replacing him.

Abruptly, she eased her elbow, drawing the pistol back from Yates's face, lowering it to her side. The relief that rushed over him was apparent despite his efforts to camouflage it. It was short-lived, though, because she brought the pistol back up and gestured. "Let's take a walk, Mr. Yates."

"A-a walk?"

"Just a short one. Let's go out back."

He paled even more and needed a second effort to rise from his chair, needed a third effort to appear unflustered by her suggestion. "I have to warn you, out by the creek on a warm day like today, the mosquitoes are liable to carry us off."

"In the greater scheme of things, mosquitoes are minor

nuisances. I've dealt with nuisances before." She stepped back and motioned for him to lead the way, then stopped him with one arm extended. "Lay your gun on the table, please."

He wanted to refuse, of course, and not just for the obvious reason. For someone who always carried a weapon, going anywhere without it was like going out without clothing.

Yates reluctantly pulled the pistol from its holster and laid it atop the papers spread across the table. She hefted it in one hand, comfortable with the size and weight of it, then handed Devlin's gun to Robinette. If Yates thought he was walking outside to his death, then let him think he would die by his own gun.

Gentry stayed inside to watch Yates's men. Robinette and Jamieson followed Selena and Yates around the bar, into a dingy storeroom, then out the back door. After the dimness inside, the midday sun seemed doubly bright, the light painfully sharp and clear.

The door opened into a clearing. Pine needles carpeted the ground, surrendering only here and there to the plants determined to take up residence. The creek was larger than the word suggested—at least twenty-five feet across. The current was lazy, meandering slowly toward the river that would carry it out to sea.

She made a show of looking around. It was private, sheltered on all sides, isolated despite its proximity to the city. "Is this where you took care of that little problem with the missing boat's crew?"

Yates shrugged.

"What did you do? Line them up on the bank? Save Devlin and LeRoy the hassle of having to drag them over and throw them into the water?"

He just looked at her, his expression empty now even of fear.

"You questioned the crew, then killed them while the captain watched." It would have happened at night. Her imagination could easily replace the sun overhead with the pale, thin light of the moon, deepening shadows, mysterious rustles in the dark. What seemed a perfectly peaceful place by day could be menacing by night. Particularly when you knew it was the last place you would ever see.

"Where were they?" Selena walked to the edge of the bank, gazed into the water, then turned to face Yates. "About here?"

Again he remained silent.

"Were they standing or on their knees?" After a heavy pause, she went on. "Standing, I think. That way the impact of the bullet would knock each of them into the water. Am I right?"

This time, when he didn't respond, she drew back the hammer on the pistol and pressed the barrel into the soft underside of his jaw. "Am I right?"

His words came out grudgingly. "Yes. They were standing. Right there."

They knew they were going to die—had probably known it from the time they'd disappeared with William's cocaine. Was it better knowing, having time to regret, to repent, or to be caught by surprise? Six months ago she would have said it didn't matter; dead was dead. Now that she had someone and something to lose, surely surprise must count for something.

They stood so close that she could hear his breathing, shallow but steady, over the hum of insects and the lapping of water. Perspiration glistened across his forehead, and emotion radiated from him. Not fear so much—he'd accepted that—but anger, hatred, and something akin to respect.

"Captain Rollins watched his crew die, then you turned

your attention to him. How did you get him to tell you where the coke was?"

Once again he swallowed hard, then shrugged. "That was Devlin and LeRoy's job. Whatever happened"—another hard swallow suggested he knew that *whatever happened* had been torture—"it was his own fault. All he had to do was answer the questions, but he refused."

Inwardly Selena shuddered. This benign up-and-coming lawyer look-alike had ordered a man tortured before mercifully killing him, and he could stand there and put the blame on the victim. Just as William had, a few weeks ago, blamed her for her own impending death. If only she'd been more grateful, more malleable, more accepting...

A wave of nausea swept through her, bringing with it the real or imagined smells of blood, fear, death. She wanted to leave that place, to forget these people, these things. She wanted...but what she wanted didn't matter.

Taking a few steps away, she pointed the Glock at the ground, eased the hammer down, put the safety on, and offered it grips first to Robinette. Then she smiled at Yates. "Uncle William liked you, Mr. Yates. More importantly, *I* like you. I'll like you more when you find out who's trying to kill me and clear your name. Make it your number one priority."

Once again relief swept over him, but it turned into something else almost immediately—determination, resentment, and grudging acceptance. "I'll have an answer for you within forty-eight hours."

She nodded, then started toward the building. But he stopped her before she'd gone far.

"A friendly word of advice, Selena," he said, though there was nothing the least bit friendly about him. "Don't ever pull a gun on me again unless you intend to use it."

She looked at him a long time before allowing her mouth

to curve upward in a full smile. "Absolutely," she agreed. "I'll remember that."

Jamieson went to his room after dinner. While the laptop booted, he dialed his home number, switching the phone from one ear to the other as he shucked his jacket, then his shoulder holster and tie. By the time Jen picked up, he was in his shirtsleeves, shoes kicked off, and leaning back in the chair at the tiny writing desk.

"Fleming residence."

"Jeez, you sound so formal. Is that how the butler answers at your folks' house?"

Her throaty laugh echoed in his ear. "We didn't have a butler, silly—at least, not since I was a kid. Can I ask where you are?"

"You can ask—"

She chimed in with him on the rest. "'But I can't tell.' How are you?"

"Missing you so much it hurts." Just how much he could miss her still took him by surprise at times. Growing up, he'd been so driven, so determined to be more, have more, than anyone else in his family. His commitment to his studies, then to his career, had been 110 percent. And then he'd met her, and all that had changed. "Tell me what you and the kids have been up to since the last time we talked."

She laughed again. "It's been all of twenty-four hours. Let's see . . . we slept all night, got up this morning . . ."

They talked longer than he'd intended, but not as long as he wanted. Finally, though, the kids were demanding their mother's attention, so he said a reluctant good-bye, then turned to the computer.

Most agents he knew hated financial crimes. They were

complex investigations that required patience, diligence, an ability to follow a dozen paths that tangled in two dozen directions, an understanding of and appreciation for the finer details of banking, accounting, and computing, and a sheer love of numbers. He'd worked other areas over the years—wasn't interested in counterterrorism, did okay with cyber crimes, didn't care about civil rights, violent crimes, or sex crimes. But he excelled at financial crimes.

That was what had gotten him on this team—his love for the complexity of the issues and his enthusiasm for making sense of them.

Both fueled by his need for taking advantage of them.

This particular job gave him access to accounts all over the world—first Davis's, now Yates's. Accounts set up for the sole purpose of secreting ill-gotten gains. Accounts that held millions of dollars. As far as the Bureau knew, no one besides Davis's money man and Davis himself had had access to his accounts, or had known how much was there. Yates's accountant had confirmed the same was true of Yates.

Now it was Jamieson's job to figure out those accounts. He'd spent every free moment deciphering Davis's information, following electronic trails through twists, turns, and dead ends. Now it was time to benefit from all that work. This was the reason he'd asked for this case—the reason he'd wheedled, coaxed, and damn near pleaded his way onto the team.

Five thousand dollars—enough to matter to him, but nothing in the big picture. He would take it from one of Davis's Cayman Islands accounts and route it electronically from one sham account to another, using one name after another, before finally securing it in his own secret account. He was about ninety-nine percent sure that he'd covered his tracks thoroughly, though he was prepared with a cover story if time proved him wrong: It was well-known that Davis wasn't a trusting man; but obviously, he'd shared his financial information with someone else, someone who was currently testing the waters to see how easily he or she could make off with Davis's fortune.

He felt a twinge of guilt, but, hell, he'd been living with guilt for a long time. But the money was dirty, paid for with human lives and suffering. Davis didn't need it anymore. Eventually, the government would take it and disperse it among various agencies. They wouldn't miss a little here or there, and it would make a world of difference for him. It could save him from losing Jen and the kids.

He clicked through screen after screen, typing in passwords, codes, routing numbers. Finally, all that was left was the single mouse click that would set the transfer in motion.

It could damn him to hell.

Or it could save his life.

Or maybe even both.

The message on the screen seemed to pulsate. *Transfer? Yes. No.* His breathing shallow, he guided the mouse arrow to the YES button...and the bedroom door swung open. His finger twitched, clicking the button, and the message disappeared from the screen, replaced with one that read *Processing transfer.*

Shoving the screen down, he jumped to his feet and turned to find Damon Long standing in the doorway. "Oops. Wrong room," he said without any hint of sincerity. His gaze shifted to the computer, then back to Jamieson, speculation obvious in its chill. "Checking out a few porn sites?"

"Wh-what—*No.*"

Long remained very still, very suspicious. "People usually only jump like that when they're doing something they shouldn't."

Sweat popped out on Jamieson's forehead. "I was talking to someone."

"Yeah. Talking." Long glanced over his shoulder into the hallway, and a moment later Jamieson heard footsteps. "Sorry I interrupted the conversation." He pushed away from the door frame and went down the hall. An instant after his door closed, Gentry passed on the way to her room.

Jamieson dragged in a deep breath, then bolted from his position to close the door. His hand trembled when he twisted the lock, and again when he raised the lid on the laptop. Another message awaited him. *Transfer complete.*

He forced in another breath. No matter what Long had seen, it hadn't been enough. He couldn't possibly have known what he was looking at, couldn't have a clue what Jamieson had been doing.

What he had done. The money was on its way. Jamieson's hard work was starting to pay off. Disaster had been averted for another day.

Shaky with relief, he sank into the chair and shut down the computer.

11

By Saturday night, Tony knew nothing new about Carl Heinz, except for the certainty that wasn't the man's real name. He'd had better luck, though, with the bastard posing as a detective. Both the weapon he'd confiscated and the man's car were registered to a private investigator by the name of Kevin Stark, with an office over on Admiral. Stark wasn't answering his phone, and there had been no sign of him or his vehicle all day. The SOB knew he was screwed, but he would show up eventually. With three ex-wives and four kids living in Tulsa, as well as elderly parents nearby, Tony figured he wasn't a good bet for relocating. Likely, Stark would be willing to deal with him.

After spending part of the afternoon and early evening staked out outside Stark's house, Tony was set down across the street from the office. The 'Vette was backed up next to a burger place that had gone out of business, the car's top down in deference to the heat.

Stark's office was a grimy storefront, the name across the glass in flaking paint, the walls battered paneling, the furniture secondhand. It didn't give a great first impression, but when you were hiring a sleaze to spy on someone, who cared what the office looked like?

He'd been sitting there two hours, head tilted back, gun tucked between his thighs, watching traffic, and thinking too much about Selena. Three times he'd reached for the cell

phone, wanting to hear her voice, needing to tell her...
What? That he was sorry? He was, but it wouldn't make any
difference. He still hated what she was doing, thought it was
reckless and dangerous and pointless and stupid. That he
loved her? He did, but at the moment that didn't seem to
make a whole hell of a lot of difference, either.

Sometimes he found that as hard to believe as the fact
that she'd shot him. Loving someone was supposed to solve
everything. It was supposed to make everything easier, like in
the fairy tales his sisters and nieces had so dearly loved—*And
they lived happily ever after.* Was he naive? Too influenced by
his parents', brothers', and sister's marriages?

Falling in love with Selena was the easiest thing he'd ever
done. Being in love with her...that was turning out to be
pretty damn tough. But if they could survive all this, everything that followed would be simple.

It was shortly after nine o'clock when a familiar car pulled
into the parking lot across the street. Stark parked right in
front of the door and hustled inside, flipping on the lights,
then closing the blinds, leaving Tony with a view of nothing
but the carpet and paneling just inside the door. He waited
five minutes to see if anyone else was coming, then started
the engine, drove across the street, and parked directly behind the shit-box Chevy, blocking it in.

The office door was unlocked. Pistol held loosely at his
side, Tony pushed it open, stepped inside, and watched
silently as Stark dug through files in the corner cabinet.
Coming up empty-handed, he turned and stopped short
when he saw Tony. "Goddamn."

Tony let the door swing shut behind him. It was cooler in
the office, though not much. "Jerry Baldwin. Kevin Stark.
What other names do you use?"

Stark didn't appear disturbed that he'd gotten caught. "I

have a whole shitload of 'em. A whole shitload of occupations, too—cop, doctor, lawyer, insurance adjuster, reporter. Buy some business card stock at Wal-Mart, print up my own cards . . . You'd be amazed how many people believe that little piece of paper means you are who it says you are." He moved to the battered desk, opened the center drawer, and removed a set of handcuffs, letting them dangle by one cuff before dropping them with a clatter on the desk. "I believe those belong to you."

Tony slid the cuffs into his hip pocket while Stark waited expectantly. When he didn't say anything, the other man finally did. "Well? Don't you have something that belongs to me?"

"I turned your weapon over to the lab guys. You'll have to talk to someone downtown about getting it back. But don't hold your breath. You know it's a crime to impersonate a police officer?" *Or doctor or lawyer, and it should be illegal to impersonate a human being.*

"Yeah, well, there's crimes, and then there's crimes." Stark sat down, the chair squeaking under his weight, and leaned back, folding his hands over his stomach. "Besides, how was I to know a real cop lived next door?"

Maybe by doing his homework. If Tony had been checking out Selena, he damn well would have learned whatever there was to learn about her neighbors. But then, as Stark had just pointed out, Tony was a *real* cop. "What's your interest in Selena McCaffrey?"

"That's between me and my client. Confidentiality, you know."

Tony took a seat in the only other chair in the room, a molded vinyl orange piece. "Aw, Kevin, don't be difficult. You're in a world of shit—arrest, possible jail time, losing your license for sure. Don't piss off the one person who can help you."

Stark studied him. "What kind of help you offering?"

"That depends on what you have to tell me."

"Huh-uh. I ain't telling you nothing without an agreement in place."

"You've made this kind of deal before, haven't you?" Tony asked dryly. "Okay. I won't pursue the personation charge, and you'll tell me everything you know about Selena McCaffrey, including who hired you and why."

Stark took a whole thirty seconds to think about it, then confidentiality flew out the window. "You got a deal." He pulled a manila folder from the bottom desk drawer and tossed it between them. "That's all I know."

The folder contained handwritten notes—name, address, descriptions of both Selena and her car, along with sketchy information on her art career and her gallery in Key West. There was no mention of him or Henry, of the gym where she worked out or the shooting range where she'd been ambushed, or of her fondness for running along the River Parks trails, or her fondness for *him*. It was just the basics, enough to get Stark started on the case. "Who hired you?"

"A lawyer." After rooting around in the middle drawer again, he held out a business card for a local lawyer. Judging by the address, the guy wasn't much more successful than Stark. They probably dealt with the same clients.

What were the odds that the lawyer, or his client, was a law-abiding citizen with a legitimate reason for wanting to investigate Selena? Somewhere between slim and none. For starters, there *was* no legitimate reason for anyone local to be snooping into her affairs. Secondly, law-abiding citizens tended to stay away from Stark and his kind.

Running the business card between his fingers, Tony asked, "What kind of information did your client want?"

"Anything. Routines, habits, friends. Where she goes, who she sees, where she spends the night. What she does, what she's like." He shrugged and repeated, "Anything."

"And what did he intend to do with it?"

"I don't ask questions like that."

"Worried you might not be able to live with the answer?" Tony asked.

"Hey, the guy's reasons for wanting to know about her aren't part of my job."

"Maybe not, but they could damn well be your problem. Someone tried to kill Selena a few nights ago."

There was a brief flash of something in Stark's eyes— panic, maybe—then he shook his head. "That's got nothing to do with me."

"How can you be sure?"

"I just got the case Friday, and I haven't talked to my client since then. Hell, I haven't even seen the girl yet. If somebody's after her, that's too bad, but it ain't connected to me."

Tony opened the folder again and scanned the notes. The first entry on the top page was, presumably, the date and time of the meeting or phone call with the lawyer. Friday, 10:40 A.M.

Who was most likely to show this kind of interest in Selena? Not Carl Heinz. He'd known enough about her without a private detective's help to make an attempt on her life last week, and he'd cleared out of town. Another of Henry's local people who'd escaped arrest? Maybe someone on his Savannah crew, who'd gotten curious when the new boss had come to town? Or someone on his Philadelphia or Boston crews who wanted to learn all they could about the new boss before deciding whether they wanted her dead?

Closing the folder once more, he rolled it into a tight tube as he stood. "String this guy along. Don't tell him you've been talking to me, and don't tell him anything about Selena. See if you can find out if his interest is personal or if he's asking on a client's behalf. I'll be in touch soon." He was halfway to the door when Stark spoke.

"Hey, what about my pistol? They'd be more likely to give it back with your say-so."

Tony gave him a warning look, then walked out, tapping the folder against his thigh.

Ten minutes later, he turned onto Princeton Court. The Franklin house was the only one with lights on. The Watson house was unoccupied, as usual; the retired couple spent most of their time on the road in their luxury RV. Selena's house was empty, as well. He wondered where she was staying in Savannah, how things were going, if she missed him.

He pulled into his driveway, checked the mail, then went inside, flipping on lights. The black cat hissed, and the calico darted up the stairs. At the back door, the coonhound was baying for entry and a shot at sniffing Tony all over. At least someone was happy to see him.

He let the dog in, gave him a good scratch, then grabbed a bottle of water from the refrigerator and went into the dining room that served as his office. As he signed online, he cradled the phone between his ear and shoulder, dialed, and leaned his head back, closing his eyes. He was tired and would like nothing more than to forget everything for a few hours' deep sleep. But he had just a few things to check, and plenty of time to sleep. Alone.

The modem stopped its squawk about the same time the phone's ringing ended. "Records, this is Carole," a crisp voice answered.

"Hey, Carole, it's Tony Ceola. How are you?" He paused

for her usual *Everything's great* response, then said, "I need some information."

"Of course you do. You know, they only pay you for forty hours a week, and I bet you had those in by Wednesday. Repeat after me: The weekend is for rest and relaxation."

"Yeah, so I've been told." He'd just never been told how to rest and relax when someone was trying to kill the woman he loved.

"You're a lost cause, Chee. Give me the name and I'll see what I can find."

"It's Dan Johnson, common spelling. First name might be Daniel or Danny. He's a lawyer."

"Oh, well, obviously he's scum. Hold on and let me see what I find."

Since Oklahoma State Bar information wasn't available online except to members and he didn't want to drive downtown to check the directory in the Detective Division, Tony logged onto the lawyer locator on the Martindale Web site while he waited. Dan Johnson had graduated from Northeastern State University thirty years ago, received his law degree from the University of Oklahoma six years later, and was admitted to the bar soon after. He was fifty-two years old, practiced alone, and did a little bit of everything—criminal law, civil law, estate planning.

"You still there, Chee?" Carole asked.

"Yep." No place else to be, nothing else to do.

"I ran the name, and there's nothing in file and no wants locally."

"Thanks, Carole."

"Quit working. Have some fun."

"Yeah, sure." He hung up, then Googled Johnson's name. So the guy might not be much of a lawyer, but at least he didn't have a criminal record. That didn't mean he wasn't dirty, but it gave some hope.

Google listed nearly a hundred thousand hits. After taking a swig of water, Tony began scanning the entries for any that might refer to his Dan Johnson. Ten down, ninety-nine-thousand-plus to go. It would take a while, but so what?

It wasn't as if he had anything else to do with his time.

When Selena went downstairs Sunday morning, she found Long, Gentry, and Jamieson in the living room and Robinette alone in the kitchen, wearing his usual scowl. She took a banana from the basket on the counter, chose water instead of coffee, and sat down across from him. On a cast-off section of newspaper, Charlize Pawley's name was scribbled into the margin, with a circle drawn over it and a line slashed through it.

"Charlize's fingerprints aren't in the system?" she asked.

He shook his head, clearly disappointed.

"Not everyone who changes names to start a new life is a criminal. Sometimes they're hiding from things other than the law." None of her own name changes had come about to escape the law. Even the last time, when she'd thought she had killed Damon Long, she hadn't become Selena McCaffrey to hide from the authorities.

No, she'd needed to become a woman unlikely to be any man's victim, to become strong and capable, to erase Gabriela Sanchez's weaknesses from her mind. She had quit her job, moved to Key West, bought a house, started the art gallery, and begun self-defense training in tae kwon do and fighting with knives. She'd gotten stronger physically, but more importantly, she'd become stronger mentally—had learned to take a punch without giving in, to ignore pain, to fight back no matter what.

Selena McCaffrey was tough, and Gabriela Sanchez became only a reminder of who she would never be again.

"So what now?"

"The Coast Guard's done periodic searches since the boat went down. They're going to broaden the area to include the creek behind Clancy's. They're also going to study the tides and currents there and refocus their search for the crew's bodies. The local police don't have any knowledge of anyone named J.T. Of course, he may not *be* local. A hitter can live anywhere. We've got people checking out the shooting of any police officer anywhere in this region in the last ten years to see if we can tie Yates to it."

Selena recalled the casual way Yates had discussed killing a police officer, and her blood ran cold—although in an entirely different way than his did.

"The van used in yesterday's assault was stolen from a shopping center up the coast in Beaufort," Robinette continued. "The police didn't find any prints inside besides the owner's and his employees'. There were three dozen witnesses, and three dozen versions of what happened. By the way, a tourist got his pocket picked a block and a half away from where we picked up Long. He says he lost about $500. You have any idea where Damon was headed?"

"To ground," Selena said dryly. She popped a bite of sweet fruit into her mouth and chewed, then shrugged. "I didn't know he existed until two years ago. William didn't want me to have contact with any of his people until *he* was ready. In Damon's case, he told me his name was Greg Marland when we met. He asked me out, charmed me all through dinner, then tried to rape me. I thought I'd killed him." That was the leverage William had used to get her to Tulsa, to lure her into this mess.

"Any chance you can get him to give up his real name?"

"I doubt he even remembers his real name." She snorted. "He's planned ahead. I'm sure he has money and new ID stashed away someplace under some name that no one would ever connect with him."

"You had money and a new ID stashed away, too."

She smiled thinly. "Yes, but you found mine. Not that I made an effort to hide it." One day a few weeks ago, she'd planned to use it—had packed a bag and made arrangements to escape the FBI's surveillance—but she'd dallied too long and Tony had stopped her. For the first time since he'd learned the truth about what William had brought her to Tulsa to do, he'd spoken to her, touched her. For the first time ever, he'd told her he loved her, and for that, for him, she'd stayed.

"What about your backup?" Robinette asked.

"I didn't have any backup."

"One escape plan that you made no effort to hide? Right."

He could distrust her all he wanted, but she was telling the truth. A backup plan hadn't been necessary. She knew where to go, how to disappear. Doing it without money or documentation was an added challenge, but it certainly wasn't impossible.

Robinette let the subject drop. He wasn't going to believe her, and she wasn't going to lie to make him happy. "Anyway, see if you can learn anything from Long. Now... Jamieson needs some time for a thorough examination of the books. We want the share you'll offer Yates to be generous, but not enough to rouse his suspicions."

Too late for that. Like William—like Robinette—Yates had apparently been born with his suspicions roused.

"To figure that out, we have to have a full understanding of—"

Footsteps sounded in the hallway, then Jamieson appeared in the doorway. "Yates just pulled up out front."

"Speak of the devil . . ." Robinette crumpled the newspaper he'd written on, then tossed it in the trash under the sink. "Invite him in, offer him coffee, then come back and get us."

With a nod, Jamieson left. The doorbell pealed once, the sound fading as it traveled through the old house. There were voices, greetings, the scuff of feet on wood, then Jamieson returned. At Robinette's gesture, Selena walked down the hall between the two men and into the living room.

LeRoy and Devlin waited near the doorway, out of place in the elegant room. Yates and a fourth man stood in front of the fireplace. The stranger—short, wiry, his face battered, and his right arm cradled to his chest—looked scared, while Yates's expression was nothing less than pure satisfaction.

She chose to lean against a delicate table, one ankle crossed over the other, her hands loosely clasped. Robinette and Jamieson stood to her left, Long a few yards to her right, and Gentry remained seated. "What can I do for you, Mr. Yates?"

"I told you I would find whoever was responsible for yesterday's ambush."

Her gaze flicked to the smaller man again. "Am I to assume this is he?" He didn't look capable of organizing a trip to the grocery store, but appearances were often deceiving.

"No. But he knows something about it." Yates gave the man a nudge. "Tell her."

The man looked as if he would bolt, given the chance. "Th—this guy I knew from up north, he asked me to help him find someone to—to do a job with him, carrying out a hit on this woman in town from Oklahoma. I—I told him I couldn't recommend anyone—I ain't into that stuff no more—and he said he'd find someone on his own."

"What stuff?" Selena asked.

"You know…" His gesture encompassed everyone in the room. "I come down here to retire. I'm outta the business. I got family here. I ain't bringin' this kind of trouble around them."

He certainly looked old enough to retire, though she suspected the quality of life he'd lived had more to do with the age on his face than the number of years.

"This guy," she repeated thoughtfully. "Does he have a name?"

"Tarver. I don't know his first name. W-we just call 'im Buddy."

"Where up north was he from?"

"Philadelphia. I used to live there, and me and him, sometimes we did jobs for the same guy."

Barnard Taylor's share of the business was headquartered in Philadelphia, and odds were, he was no happier about her sudden rise in the business than Yates was. Was he unhappy enough to try to kill her on his competitor's turf? Probably. Was Sonny devious enough to try to blame him regardless of guilt? Definitely.

"When did he ask you to do this?" Robinette asked.

"Uh, must've been Friday morning. Yeah. I'd just opened up the shop—I have a little bait shop and station down on the river—and he come by."

So it had taken fifteen, maybe eighteen, hours after they'd decided to visit Savannah for someone to order her death. Yates was the only one she'd told she was coming, but she had no doubt that news got around in this business just as in any other.

When Robinette didn't ask any further questions, Selena gestured toward the man's injured arm. "What happened?"

His gaze darted to Yates. "Oh, uh, nothin'. J-just a misunderstanding."

"Ms. Gentry, would you please take him to the kitchen and get some ice for that arm?" She turned her attention back to the man. "When we're done here, Mr. Yates will take you to the hospital and pick up the tab for your care."

"Th-thank you," he said, but there was more fear than gratitude in his expression as he followed Gentry from the room. Did he expect a bullet in the brain as payment for his information? Probably. And because that was a very real possibility, she decided, on second thought, to send Yates away when they were done and let one of Robinette's people transport the man to the hospital.

Once they were gone, Yates asked, "What are you going to do about Taylor?" When she merely looked at him, he rolled his eyes. "You know he operates in Philadelphia. The guy who set up the hit is from Philadelphia *and* used to work for Taylor and probably still does. You can put two and two together."

"I certainly can." And in this case, four was no likelier to be right than wrong. "What about the guy who set up the hit? Where is he?"

Yates's mouth opened, then closed.

"I asked you to find the person responsible. You brought me a man who knows a man who was hired to hire somebody else. Where is this mystery man? Who hired him? Who did he hire?"

His expression turned stony. "I don't know."

"But you're looking." She smiled condescendingly. "Always looking."

It was the smile, she thought, that made the color flare in his cheeks while the rest of his face went pale. "You think it's so goddamn easy to go out and find an amateur hitter, go ahead. See how far you get."

"I don't think it's easy at all, Mr. Yates. I just didn't think it would be this difficult for you."

"I told you forty-eight hours. I've still got more than thirty left. I'll bring him in."

Before Selena could respond, Long moved forward from where he'd been lounging next to a window. Bending until his mouth was just above her ear, he murmured, "Tell him he'll have to bring him to Tulsa."

Ignoring the goose bumps that formed on her arms, she glanced at him, wondering why, and with a grin, he leaned close again and gave the only answer that truly mattered. "Because you can."

Because I can. How many times had William uttered those words with that supremely smug smile she'd hated so? Why had he turned to a life of crime, why had he murdered and stolen, why had he used her, why had he ordered Tony's death...So many questions and only one cold answer. Because he could.

She'd hated that answer because of its arrogance, because of the power it implied. Yates would hate it for the same reasons.

Still grinning, Long stepped back, and she refocused on Yates. "You do have more than thirty hours left, Mr. Yates. But if you don't find this man in the next few hours, you'll have to bring him to Oklahoma, because I'm going home as soon as arrangements can be made."

Robinette was surprised. Yates was nothing less than hostile. "I told you, I can't leave—"

"We're not partners yet, Mr. Yates. I'm still your boss, and you'll do what I say." She held his gaze a long moment, watching as the clenched muscles in his jaw worked. "I'm returning to Tulsa, and I expect to see you there Tuesday. That's another forty-eight hours. I'll have a preliminary partnership proposal ready for you then, though, of course, what happens in the meantime will influence that."

Wearing that amused grin, Long stepped forward. "Clock's ticking, Sonny boy, and you've been dismissed. Better get going."

The room was utterly still as Yates looked around at each of them. When he abruptly took a breath, it was noisy. His hazel gaze reached Selena again, and he nodded, as if he didn't trust himself to speak, then left the room. Devlin and LeRoy followed.

No one moved until the click of the front door closing echoed in the foyer, then Robinette gestured for her to precede him from the room. She went into the kitchen, where Gentry waited with the stranger. "Have someone take him to the hospital," Robinette instructed.

With a nod, she followed the man from the room.

Selena leaned against the counter, hands curved over the edge. Robinette watched the door until it stopped swinging, then slowly turned to face her. She wasn't sure what to expect—annoyance, irritation—but his expression was blank. "That was a quick change of heart. What happened to getting personnel records, suppliers, distributors, the identity of his hit man?"

"It was Long's suggestion. I thought it was a good one. Enough time has passed since the last murder attempt that it won't look as if we're running scared, and forcing Yates to come to us will remind him who's in control."

"What if he refuses?"

"He'll suffer the consequences."

His expression turned sardonic. "What consequences? You can't kill him."

"No, we can't," she agreed, then smiled William's deadliest smile. "But we can make him *think* we're going to."

The ring of the doorbell was distant, easy to ignore, but not so Mutt's sudden frenzy of barking. The dog raced to the door, barked, then raced back, leaping onto Tony's stomach and making him grunt. "Okay, okay, I'm awake," he mumbled, shoving the dog to the floor and sitting up. His joints ached, and his vision was bleary—because he'd spent most of the night on the computer, he remembered as he eased to his feet, and the rest of it on the couch. And he hadn't learned a damn thing except that he preferred sleeping in his bed. With Selena.

He reached the door just as the bell rang again. Dragging his fingers through his hair, he shut off the alarm, then opened the door.

Marla's ready smile faded, and her pert little nose—a description she hated—wrinkled. "Eww. Tough night, huh?"

The bright light made him squint, and the morning's heat made him yawn. "Yeah." Combing his hair again, he took in her appearance—blue dress on the modest side, heels on the low side—and asked, "What're you all dressed up for?"

"We're on our way to church."

He followed her gesture to the car idling behind his in the driveway, where her husband scowled from behind the wheel. Tony lifted one hand in greeting, and he did the same, even managing to get all five fingers into the air instead of the one Tony was sure he would have preferred. "No, really," he said, turning back to Marla again. "What's the occasion?"

"I do go to church sometimes. It's important to Richard's mother."

"You in church...or caring what Dickless's mother thinks. Now, there's an image that won't form."

She slapped his arm playfully with a rolled-up file folder, and he self-consciously pulled back. Her husband was a captain in the department—though not in Tony's chain of command, thank God—and he was a jealous man. Marla liked giving him reason to be. Tony didn't. "A little church from time to time wouldn't hurt you. Here. This is for you."

He took the folder and flipped it open.

"We stopped by the lab this morning, and I found this response to the prints I submitted yesterday. Your boy Heinz used to work for the IRS until he got caught with his hand in the cookie jar. It's all in there." She smiled breezily. "You can thank me later, when Richard's not around." With a flirtatious wink, she touched his hand, then sashayed down the steps and to the car.

Tony watched her go, then turned to the folder as he shuffled back inside. Like the driver's license photo he'd sent to Savannah, this photograph showed the sort of person people routinely overlooked—thin, studious, a mousy little guy. Sweat gleamed on his forehead, but that wasn't unusual in a booking photo. His real name was Charles Hensley. He was in his early fifties and had worked as an auditor for the Internal Revenue Service assigned to the Philadelphia office.

Another connection to Selena's enemies. Henry had set up his second drug operation in Philadelphia—an operation still in business and in the FBI's sights. Who else had Hensley known there besides Henry and Long? What were the odds he'd gone back there to hide out?

Making a mental note to contact the Philadelphia PD in the morning, Tony scanned the rest of the information. Hensley's career with the IRS had been unremarkable until his sideline had come to light. In cases with particularly large tax liabilities, he had proven willing to guarantee the subject a favorable outcome, asking only for a little consideration of the cash kind. Ten percent here and fifteen percent there had added up to a small fortune over the years, until an unhappy client, nabbed on other charges, had given him up. He'd been arrested, charged, and faced certain conviction and years in prison . . . but then he'd disappeared.

To resurface in Tulsa with a new name and a new career, working for the venerable chief of police. Had Henry known he was a fugitive? Of course. Knowing things about people was his job, his passion. He'd known Tony couldn't just let the vigilante murders go, had known eventually the pieces would fall into place for him, had probably even known that he wouldn't be able to resist Selena. As if any living, breathing man could.

Damn his soul, Henry had known everything about everyone.

Except Selena. The one person he'd thought he knew best, and she'd surprised him.

Tony wasn't happy to find they had that in common.

He tossed the file on his desk, then took the stairs two at a time to shower and dress. He should go visit his parents, but he wasn't in the mood for mass and Anna and Joe never missed it. He wasn't sure what he *was* in the mood for as he left the house. Not when he drove past Utica Square. Not when he turned off Twenty-first into the St. John parking garage. Not even when he took the elevator to the intensive care unit, where Henry had been a patient for the past three weeks.

Just off the elevator, he stopped. He hadn't once considered visiting Henry—hadn't been tempted when he was a patient there himself, or when he'd brought Selena in for treatment, or any of the countless times he'd driven past. He hadn't cared whether Henry lived or died, hadn't wanted anything to do with him now that he knew the truth. Some things were unforgivable, and Henry's sins surely fell into that category.

But Henry had been Joe's best friend for more than forty years. Had been godfather to all seven Ceola kids. Had been Tony's mentor, advised him, and treated him fairly, affectionately, respectfully. Next to Joe and his brothers, Henry had been the most important man in Tony's life for thirty-four years. Didn't all that count for something?

Something...but not much. They couldn't balance the wrongs Henry had committed.

He was about to turn back to the elevator when a woman approached. "Are you—You're Detective Ceola, aren't you?" Well dressed, Southern accent, probably in her late fifties. There was something familiar about her, but he couldn't place her until...He glanced down the hall in the direction from which she'd come—the direction of Henry's room— and remembered old portraits in the Daniels estate, casual mentions of a sister in Alabama.

She knew his name, somehow knew his face. Did she also know he was the one who'd shot her brother?

Uncomfortably he shifted his weight from one foot to the other. "Yes, ma'am, I am."

"I thought so. I've met your father a number of times, and you look just like him when he was your age." She extended her hand, diamonds glittering on her fingers. "I'm Kathryn Hamilton. Henry is my brother."

He didn't want to take her hand, didn't want to touch her, talk to her, or even acknowledge that she existed, but his mother had raised him too well. Unwillingly he offered his own hand, and he didn't even flinch when she took it. "I, uh...I'm sorry..."

Her smile was weary and added years to her face. "Aren't we all?" She gave his hand a maternal pat before releasing it and folding both arms across her middle. "Henry often spoke of you and your father. I've been hoping for the chance to see one of you, to talk, but I didn't want to intrude."

Talk. About Henry. In those first few days, Tony had talked about the man until he was sick—to the deputy chiefs, the chief of detectives, the shooting review board, the FBI. To his family, to Simmons and their fellow detectives. He didn't want to talk about him anymore, and he damn sure didn't want to talk about him to his sister. He didn't want to know what she believed, whether she blamed him, how she grieved.

But he couldn't walk away.

"Could we go someplace private?"

His gaze jerked down the hall again, toward Henry's room, and she smiled. "There's a family waiting room over there."

With a reluctant look at the elevator, Tony followed her into the room, closing the door as she seated herself on the couch. She was a lovely woman, about his mother's age, but where Anna was aging naturally, Kathryn had chosen the artificial approach. There wasn't a hint of gray in her hair or a line on her face. Even her hands, clasped around a tissue, looked as if they belonged to someone ten years younger.

"Henry talked about you Ceolas a lot. It meant a lot to him to be considered part of the family." Her unsteady smile slipped and discomfort crept into her expression. "Though, in the end, he had an odd way of showing it. What *happened* to him?"

That was the million-dollar question. What had turned straight-and-narrow Henry into a drug-dealing murderer? The best guess he could make was greed, not just for money but for power. But surely there was more to it than that. An honorable, respected cop didn't just wake up one day and say, *I think I'll turn my back on everything I've devoted my life to and become a killer.*

But the only one who could tell them was Henry, and he wasn't talking.

"I don't know, Mrs. Hamilton," he said awkwardly. "I didn't have a clue . . ."

Kathryn worried the tissue she clutched. "I always thought Henry and I were close. Oh, we didn't see each other as often as I would have liked, what with me living in Alabama and him moving from city to city, but . . . we had a connection. A bond. We talked regularly. He knew what was happening in my life, and I knew the same about him, or so I thought. Then the FBI tells me he's some sort of drug lord who's responsible for countless deaths, who tried to kill his godson, who'd built an entire life with this—this black girl, this *niece*, and I realized I knew nothing at all about my brother." Her gaze shifted from the cottony mess in her hands to him. "You know her? This girl?"

Tony nodded.

"Is it true what they told me? That he took her in when she was a child? That he treated her as his own child?"

"She was fourteen. He saved her life, brought her to the US, told people she was his niece." And took advantage of her gratitude, manipulated her, exploited her. If her survival instinct hadn't been so strong, he would have destroyed her. As long as she continued to play the FBI's games, he still might succeed.

"*Why?* He was never particularly interested in children. He always said you and your siblings satisfied whatever paternal urges he might have had." She said that last with a hint of bitterness. Did she have children of her own? Had she wanted Henry to take more interest in them than he had? Did she think that if he hadn't been godfather to the Ceolas and surrogate uncle to Selena, he would have been more involved in his *real* family's lives?

"I don't know why he became involved with Selena, Mrs. Hamilton." Probably because she'd been damaged, because she'd been easy to control, because he'd seen ways to use her once he'd finished molding and warping her.

"Do you think their relationship was..." Heat flushed her face, and her gaze dropped abruptly.

"Sexual?" he finished for her, and a shudder rippled through her. "No. Not at all."

"You're sure of that?"

"Absolutely."

"What can you tell me about her?"

Though he'd expected the question, it unsettled him. He walked to the window, but there was nothing to look at—just the unremarkable front of the physicians' building across the street. Finally, he turned back to face her. "She's a very talented artist. She owns a gallery in Key West. She's half–Puerto Rican, half-Jamaican, and grew up on both islands. She's smart, capable, competent, strong. She loved Henry and was grateful to him for all that he'd done, but..."

"She also hated him. For all that he'd done." She said the words quietly, as if she understood, and might even share, the sentiment.

Tony nodded.

"What about her family?"

"She never knew her father. Her stepfather sent her away when she was nine, and her mother let him."

"She was part of what changed Henry," she murmured.

He shook his head. "Henry was already in the business when he met Selena."

"But she must know... she must have some idea..." Slowly her gaze shifted to his, locking. "I'd like to talk to her.

I asked Special Agent King at the FBI how I could contact her, and he said he couldn't help me. I don't believe him. She was involved...a witness, a victim, a suspect. He must know where she is." She hesitated. "You must know. Surely you keep tabs on people who shoot you."

He touched his shoulder reflexively, remembering the ache that was mostly gone. "So far, she's the only one."

"But you know where she is."

At least the feds, in getting Kathryn's permission to use the estate, hadn't told her that Selena would be living there, taking part in their investigation. That was one thing he could credit them with doing right.

Tony doubted Selena could tell Kathryn anything that would ease her mind. But maybe Kathryn could answer a few questions—could give Selena some sense of who the man she'd loved like a father had once been.

"She's out of town right now."

"Do you know where? How to contact her?"

He shook his head. "I can talk to her when she gets back." It would be a good excuse to see her—and he needed to see her.

"Would you do that, please? I'm staying at a bed-and-breakfast in Maple Ridge." She got to her feet, drew a business card from the slim leather bag she carried, and offered it to him. "My cell phone number is on the back."

He glanced at the address on the front, a long-gone oil-man's mansion a few miles away, then slid it into his pocket. "I'll be in touch."

With a satisfied nod, she walked out into the hall with him. When he turned toward the elevator, she laid her hand on his arm. "You're not going to visit Henry?"

He glanced down the hall, then shook his head. "Not to-day." Maybe not ever.

12

"Your boyfriend called."

Selena was in the middle of packing when Robinette knocked at the open door. He came inside, closed the door behind him, and stood, hands on hips, watching her.

She stilled in the act of folding her robe, then immediately forced herself to continue as normal. "Really."

"Yeah. Got the SAC in the Tulsa office to give him my number. Said he had some info and wouldn't give it to anyone else."

That sounded like Tony—cautious. Stubborn.

She laid the robe in the suitcase, then pulled the turquoise linen dress from its hanger and concentrated on keeping her hands steady while she folded it. Her stomach was knotted and her chest so tight that dragging in a breath was difficult. She'd wanted to talk to Tony so many times since they'd arrived in Savannah, had wanted to hear the reassuring strength of his voice.

But now he'd called.

And he hadn't even asked to speak to her.

"He got an ID on that Heinz guy you and Long were talking about. Name's Charles Hensley, and he used to work for the IRS in Philly. He's wanted by the feds for various and sundry financial crimes." Robinette scowled. "Not that a name's much good when no one has a clue where the guy is."

"A name is more than you could come up with on Charlize Pawley."

He gave her a disgusted smirk. "He also said some jerk-wad lawyer hired some jerkwad PI in Tulsa to find out anything he could about you. Ceola talked to the PI last night, and he's going to see the lawyer in the morning. The guy's clean, no arrest record, and likely to claim attorney/client privilege to avoid answering any questions."

Breathe, she counseled herself. Slowly in, slowly out. "We knew Sonny would be gathering whatever information he could."

"Him, or maybe Barnard Taylor or Vernell Munroe. What can this guy find out in Tulsa?"

She tucked her cosmetics bag into a corner of the suitcase, then zipped it shut. "Nothing much. That I run along the river most days, I work out at a gym on Memorial, and I spend most of my time alone."

"That's not 'nothing.' He can learn your routine. He did learn that you lived on Princeton Court."

"But my routine's changed. And he didn't find out that I'm now living on Riverside Drive, did he?"

"No, not yet. Who did you tell you were moving in there?"

"Nobody but Tony."

"Who would he tell?"

She gave him a dry look. "He's a homicide detective. He doesn't want his girlfriend to become one of his cases. He didn't tell anyone." Except possibly Frank Simmons. Frankie was an odd one, but Tony trusted him with his life, so she would, too.

"He doesn't have to worry about that. Now that you're working for us, if anything happens to you, it's federal. Our jurisdiction."

"Thanks so much for the reassurance." She hefted the

suitcase off the bed and set it on the floor. "When are we leaving?"

"The pilot will call as soon as the plane's checked out. Be ready."

With an absent nod, she turned to gaze out the window, listening as he left the room. The garden that filled most of the yard was lovely, overflowing with flowers and a green so lush that it looked unnatural. Ordinarily, she would look at such a scene and yearn to paint it, but the only ache she felt at the moment was in her heart, not her empty fingers.

Tony hadn't even asked to speak to her. The hurt was sharp and raw. He didn't have it in him to be cruel, which meant he was still very angry with her, still unsure they could work things out. If they couldn't, she was going to be free to live her own life, but have no one to live it with.

It was late afternoon when Selena returned to William's estate with the FBI. Jamieson escorted Long across the lawn to the guesthouse, Gentry headed to the servants' quarters in the north wing, and, after carrying Selena's bag to the foot of the grand staircase, Robinette disappeared into the parlor. He returned carrying a fat manila folder, held shut with rubber bands, and offered it to her.

"What is that?" she asked, making no move to reach for it.

"Davis's journal for the year you met him, as requested. Everything you don't need to know was blacked out."

She stared at the folder. She'd asked for it, negotiated for it, but, even so, she was surprised. Surprised that her hand didn't tremble. Surprised that she could remove the rubber bands and open it. William's elegant handwriting filled the photocopied pages—at least, the ones she could read. Page after page was blacked out. *Everything you don't need to know.* She smiled faintly. She needed to know *everything.*

But what they'd allowed her would do for the moment.

After replacing the rubber bands, she cradled the folder in both arms. "Thank you, Mr. Robinette."

With an uncomfortable gesture, he headed for the kitchen and the back door. "We'll get something delivered for dinner," he called over his shoulder.

For a time she stood there, listening to the silence, wondering whether any of the answers she sought were inside the folder. When the grandfather clock in the parlor began to chime, she started, then picked up her bag. She'd climbed only a few steps when a chime of a different sort echoed through the foyer.

Who would be visiting, or even knew they were back in town, didn't concern her as she set the suitcase on the step and crossed to the door. Whoever was there had been cleared by the agents pulling guard duty.

She undid the locks, pulled open the door, and froze. Tony stood there, wearing denim shorts, running shoes, and a faded Tulsa Run T-shirt, and looking uneasy and wary and amazing. She was torn between wanting to fling herself into his arms and remembering his cruel words before she'd left for Savannah. She settled for folding her arms tightly around the folder and waiting silently.

He shifted his weight. "I, uh, heard you would be back sometime today, so I thought I'd check... How was Savannah?"

"Lovely. Hot. Humid."

"Not too different from here. Other than the lovely part."

"Tulsa's lovely enough."

He acknowledged that with a shrug that might have

meant agreement, or just the opposite, gazed out across the lawn, then back at her. "Can I come in, or can you come out?"

In response, she stepped back to allow him entry. After closing the door, she gestured toward the library on the right. "We can talk in here."

Before they'd gone more than a few steps, Gentry came into the foyer from the hall. When she saw them, she stopped short. "You know, *we're* supposed to answer the door. What if it was one of the bad guys?"

"Who'd taken out all the guards, gained access, and then was polite enough to ring the doorbell?" Selena countered.

"It could happen." Gentry shifted her gaze to Tony. "Why'd they let you in?"

"Because I asked nicely."

"What if Long sees you?"

His jaw tightened. "They told me to stay away from the back of the house, and they told whoever's with him to keep him in the guesthouse."

She looked unconvinced. "What if he still manages to see you? He thinks you're out of Selena's life."

Selena wouldn't have thought it possible, but his jaw tightened even more. She said a silent prayer that the agent wouldn't mention that she was telling people she'd truly intended to kill him, and still might if circumstances warranted it. "If he still manages to see me, then you've got a problem with your security."

The library was as cozy as a large room with twenty-foot ceilings could be. A fireplace took up a portion of one wall, leather chairs were placed in front of it, and a tall ladder leaned against the shelving to provide access to the upper reaches. Selena had explored it her first night in the house, examining the art that graced the walls and shelves, but hadn't returned. The books were rare, first editions, and hardly the stuff for a little light reading.

Now the truly interesting reading was in the file in her arms.

She seated herself in one of the chairs. "I understand you've been checking out this private investigator. Thank you." Her breath caught as she waited for his response. If he dismissed her with *It's my job,* she vowed she would hurt him.

He just shrugged and turned his attention to the collection of small bronzes on the fireplace mantel. Running his fingers over an Indian headdress, he remarked, "I plan to talk to the lawyer in the morning, though I doubt he'll tell me anything."

"Do you think his client is one of William's people?"

"Maybe. Maybe not. I don't know." Abandoning the bronzes, Tony turned to face her. "What's that?"

She laid both hands on the folder, her fingers curling around the edges. "It's a copy of William's journal. The one that had the photo of me in it. It was waiting for me when we got back."

He understood the significance at once. "Have you begun reading it?"

She shook her head. She was anxious to get to it . . . and more than a little reluctant. She might learn nothing at all, or more than she'd bargained for. The truth of her life as she knew it was tough enough. Who was to say it wouldn't turn out to be even tougher?

He hesitated, dragged his fingers through his hair, then asked, "Want me to read it?"

The offer eased a little of the chill inside her. He would do that for her, telling her everything she needed to know, leaving out anything she didn't. Part of her was tempted to accept, to give the folder to him so she could remain in the dark just a little longer, but the stronger part made her decline. "Thank you, but . . ." She shook her head. She needed to read it herself, needed to know what William had written in his own words.

He didn't mind her refusal, but merely shrugged, then drew an ottoman to sit a few feet in front of her. "I met Henry's sister this morning. You knew he had a sister?"

She nodded.

"She didn't know that he had a 'niece' until the FBI told her last week. She wants to meet you. She wants to know about your relationship with Henry."

"The FBI told me to stay away from her."

"They're good at telling people what to do." Then he shrugged again. "You don't have to meet her. It's just that she's grieving over her brother and she's overwhelmed by everything she's learned about him. You might be able to answer some of her questions, and she might be able to answer some of yours."

Selena resisted the urge to point out that if Kathryn hadn't known she existed until the past week, how could she possibly know anything of interest to her? But Kathryn had known William all her life. They'd grown up together. She knew him in ways Selena never could, and maybe, somehow, she could help Selena understand him.

She couldn't agree to meet her just yet, though. Not until she'd thought it through. Read the journal. Discussed it with Robinette.

Because she knew that last wouldn't sit well with Tony, she offered a noncommittal answer. "I'll think about it." Then . . . "Is that why you came here?"

His smile was faint, chagrined. "It was my excuse."

"What was the real reason?"

"I wanted to see you. I—I've missed you."

The tightness in her chest eased, making it easier to breathe, to feel, to smile tentatively in return. "You could have called. You could have asked to speak to me when you did call."

Color tinged his cheeks. "I wasn't sure you would talk to me after the way I behaved last week."

"I would have."

"So you could have called me, too."

"I didn't want to argue with you," she admitted. She had trained to handle physical danger; she always had options, strengths, solutions. But she didn't have a single idea how to handle emotional danger. Intimacy was still too new to her, too fragile.

She studied him—the hair that always needed a comb, the dark eyes, the stubborn line of his jaw—then drew a breath for courage, and said, "I've missed you, too, Tony."

"Took you long enough to admit it," he gently teased, uncurling her fingers from the folder, lifting her palm to his mouth, and pressing a kiss there. "This has been the hardest week since I met you."

"Harder than when you found out I came here to kill you?"

He grinned. "Harder than that."

"Someday," she murmured, "this will be over, and I'll be just a regular person again."

"Aw, you've never been just a regular person."

"Then I'll become one."

Suddenly serious, he tilted her chin up to gaze down at her. "I don't want you to become anything other than what you are. I love you, Selena."

The words should have brought her great pleasure, and they did. But it was tempered with the knowledge that it might not be enough. They could love each other with all their hearts, but without compromise, understanding, and acceptance, that meant... The word was silent in her head, too painful to give voice to even in her thoughts. *Nothing*. Their love just might mean nothing.

The thought sent a shiver of sorrow through her, and made her voice unsteady when she whispered, "I love you, too, Tony."

He didn't ask if she was cold or frightened. He just held her tighter, stroked her, and brushed gentle kisses to her hair, her forehead, her eyelids, her cheeks, finally reaching her mouth. It started as a sweet, claiming kiss, lazy, tasting, savoring, but before long it turned into something greedy, hot, and demanding, and she kissed him back in exactly the same way. The air around them was thick and steamy and practically sizzled, and her blood was thick and steamy and practically boiled. She thought about how much she'd missed him and how desperately she needed him, and she tried to remember if there was a lock on the library door; but her brain had turned to mush, too busy processing sensations to worry about little details like that.

Her lungs were threatening to burst, her skin was tingly, her muscles weak, when he ended the kiss and dragged in a breath. His voice was rough and hoarse as he asked, "Want to invite me upstairs with you?"

Unsteadily stroking his jaw, she managed a smile. "Want to go upstairs with me?"

"I thought you'd never ask." But he didn't head for the door. Instead, he cradled her face in his palms and stared intently into her face. He looked so serious that her heart clenched. "Whatever happens, Selena, know this: I'll always be here. I may get angry with you—hell, I'm sure I will—but that won't change anything. I'll always, always love you."

She wanted to believe him, and she did. For that moment, for the next however many moments they were together, and even after he was gone, she would believe him.

Until time, or fate, or the FBI and Sonny Yates proved him wrong.

The dream hadn't come in years. Though she was asleep, Kathryn was aware in some part of her brain that it *was* just a dream—familiar, frightening, but, in the end, powerless. All she had to do was wake up. Give herself a shake. Banish it back into the darkness where it belonged.

Easier said than done. Its hold was so strong. The muggy night, the scent of jasmine hanging in the air, the river smelling of mud and the mill upstream. Lightning had split the sky, and rain had begun falling before it was over. Tears, she thought. Even Nature had wept that night.

The smells were strong, the sounds magnified, the emotions overwhelming, but the voices were tinny, nearly lost in the reverberation of the thunder. She knew the words, though. They were burned into her soul. *My baby... what are you doing... noooo.* A wail of heartbreak that went on and on, filling the night, drowning out the beat of her heart, the thunder, the rain, the curses, the sirens...

That small part of her conscious mind caught. There had been no sirens that night, bringing help—or damnation. What the Danielses wanted, they got. More accurately, what Henry Daniels wanted, he got.

The siren continued, short bursts, insistent, pulling her back to wakefulness. As soon as she opened her eyes, the noise stopped. Breathing heavily, she stared at a ghastly contraption of antlers and lightbulbs before realizing where she was. The B&B, with its owners' mistaken belief that animal parts equaled decor. She had fallen asleep on the sofa, and the damn dream had returned.

As if that was a surprise.

The siren started again, making her jump. No, not a siren. Her cell phone. She located it on the coffee table beneath the information her lawyer had sent her on various long-term-care facilities and answered with a *hello* that sounded distant even to her.

"Well...considering all the messages you've left for me lately, I expected something a little more enthusiastic than that."

The voice was familiar and warm, its Southern accent far more pronounced than her own, flowing as lazily as molasses in winter. Nothing could ever be too bad as long as that voice, and its owner, were a part of her life. "Jefferson, baby, it's so good to hear from you. You know, if I was any less secure, I'd think you were avoiding your mama."

"No, Mama, I've just been busy with work."

She had wanted him to go into the law, like his daddy, but he'd had no interest in that. Instead, he'd gotten his degree in finance and, in spite of the turbulence of the stock market in recent years, made a handsome living in Orlando. And though it would have been nice to have another lawyer in the family, she really didn't care as long as he was happy.

"You know what they say—all work and no play makes Jefferson a dull boy."

He chuckled. "I find a little time to play."

"Have you found anyone you want to settle down with yet?"

"I'm too young for that, Mama."

"Maybe you are, but I have a terrible yearning to be a grandmother, and since you're my only child..." She thought of Selena McCaffrey, Henry's "niece," and her fingers clenched until her nails bit into her palm. Wishing for a stiff drink, she settled for a deep breath instead and forced her tone to remain light. "Did you just happen to find time to call, or did one of my seventeen messages pique your interest?"

He laughed again. He'd lived with them two months before he'd laughed for the first time. She'd thought it was the sweetest sound she'd ever heard, second only to his calling her Mama, and still did. "Seventeen? I thought I counted twenty-seven. But, yes, you could say they piqued my interest. So the high-and-mighty, straight-and-narrow, long-arm-of-the-law Henry Daniels was a drug dealer. Good God, Mama, there was more to the old bastard than I ever imagined."

"Jefferson," she admonished, but there was no weight behind it. Naturally she wanted her son to admire and respect her brother, but what had Henry ever done to deserve it? He'd made no effort to have any sort of relationship with his only nephew.

But he'd made plenty of effort for his "niece." Apparently, she'd been able to offer him so much more than Jefferson had.

"Well, it certainly makes the old man more intriguing," Jefferson continued. "A person runs across cops all the time, but a drug dealer who lied, cheated, stole, and murdered his way to the top—that's definitely different. Just think what my friends would say."

"Jefferson! You can't—" She broke off midshriek and laughed ruefully. "You're just playing games with me, aren't you? Of course you won't tell anyone about Henry. It wouldn't be good for the future Secretary of the Treasury if people knew his uncle was a major criminal."

"Secretary of the Treasury?" he repeated wryly. "And here I thought one day being CEO of my own investment firm would be enough to make you proud."

She closed her eyes briefly, and her throat grew tight. "Sweetheart, you don't have to do a damn thing to make me proud. I just about bust with pride every time I think of you. Just give me a grandbaby or two to spoil, and I'll be the happiest woman on the face of God's earth."

He was quiet for a moment, and when he did speak, his throat was tight, too. "Thank you, Mama. That means a lot. Grant might not give a damn, and Henry never did, but as long as I've got you, who cares about them?"

"Honey, your father—" Grimly Kathryn broke off. He was right. Grant hadn't accepted him as a member of the family any more than Henry had. Oh, he'd put on a better act—had tried to play the role even if he hadn't felt it in his heart—but his effort had been half-assed at best. One more thing to hold against Henry.

And Selena.

She smiled, well aware it was more of a grimace, and added a cajoling tone to her voice. "Any chance you'll come visit your uncle Henry?"

"Has hell frozen over?" he asked, feigning surprise. "Mama, my chances of visiting Henry are somewhere between slim and none. My chances of visiting *you*, though... I'll have to see when I can get away from work."

"That would be wonderful, Jefferson." She saw him at least a half dozen times a year—more often than some of her friends saw their grown children who lived right in the same state—but it wasn't enough. Sometimes, when she was weary of Grant's distraction, she fantasized about moving to Orlando, making a new home for herself, welcoming the wife Jefferson would surely take, doting on the grandchildren they would give her. Grant certainly wouldn't object. Heavens, he probably wouldn't even realize she was gone for at least a year or two.

And he wouldn't miss her. As far as she could tell, he never did, while she missed him every blessed day. The early years of their marriage had been so sweet, so damn near perfect... until the baby had come along and ruined everything.

The mere reminder was enough to rouse a surge of hatred for her brother.

"Let me check with my assistant tomorrow and see when I can manage a few days away, and then I'll get back to you. How does that sound?"

"That sounds perfect, which is only natural, considering that *you* are perfect. I'll hold my breath until I hear from you."

He laughed again. "Just make sure you're sitting down so you won't have far to fall when you turn blue and pass out. I'll call you tomorrow, Mama. For sure."

"All right. I love you, baby."

"Love you, too."

The line went dead, and she slowly lowered the phone from her ear. As she flipped it shut, she finished with her customary line, little more than a whisper in the silence of the suite. "Always have. Always will."

Selena and Tony sprawled across the bed, only their fingers touching, their breathing slowly returning to normal, the cool air drying the sweat that slicked their skin. Her hair tangled about her head, she turned to give him a lazy, satisfied smile. "Did I tell you I missed you?"

"In more ways than one." The rushing in his ears had subsided to nothing more than a dull whoosh, and his heart rate had edged out of heart-attack range. Turning onto his side, he stuffed a pillow under his head, lifted a handful of curls that were caught under the pillow, then settled his hand on her shoulder. "Tell me about Savannah."

Was it guilt that made her gaze flicker away, or reluctance to discuss something that, so far, had led only to arguments?

"We got in Friday afternoon," she said at last, "and I had dinner with Sonny Yates that evening. He's in charge of William's Southeastern operation."

She continued, her voice soft, her tone cautious, with what Tony was sure was the sanitized version. What she was describing sounded no more dangerous than any legitimate business trip . . . except legitimate business meetings weren't held with drug dealers and murderers.

Did he want to press for details? If the feds had put her in danger, did he want to know?

"So it was all fun and games. I worried all that time for nothing."

She tilted her head to study him. "Were you worried?"

"Jeez, Selena . . . every minute of every day. That's all."

"I don't want you to worry."

"Sorry, babe, but you don't get to control that. It's part of the whole love thing. You can't have one without the other." Under the circumstances, a whole hell of a lot of the other.

She was watching him wide-eyed, considering that, when the growling of her stomach broke the silence. Her cheeks turning pink, she laughed and laid her hand there as if to silence it.

"Sounds like someone's hungry," he teased. "What do you want for dinner?"

"To go out alone with you."

He would have liked that, too, dinner, then taking her home, where they could be normal, just two people making a life together. For a while.

Instead of offering comfort, though, he mimicked a

game-show buzzer as he got out of bed. "Ain't gonna happen, babe. But I can go out and bring something back, or we can call someone who delivers."

"Or I could insist Robinette send one of his people out to get something for us. Though he's posing as my assistant, it drives him crazy when I treat him as such."

"You've got a bit of a mean streak in you, don't you?" After buttoning his shorts, Tony fished under the bed for his shirt, then tugged it on. "You will put some clothes on first, won't you?"

"No one sees me naked but you."

"And I want to keep it that way."

She rose from the bed, lifted her suitcase to the mattress, then dug inside for an emerald silk robe. It was perfectly modest—sleeves falling past her elbows, the hem brushing her knees, the belt securing it so there wasn't even a chance of glimpsing anything intimate—but she still looked sexy as hell in it.

Of course, she looked sexy as hell in anything.

As she disappeared into the adjoining bathroom with an armful of clothing, his gaze fell to the suitcase. When he packed a bag, it looked as if a gang of monkeys had helped. Everything in this one was precisely placed—outfits here, bras there. Her makeup and toiletries were packed in matching bags, shoes in more matching bags, newspapers neatly stacked on the bottom out of the way . . .

Why had she brought newspapers back from Savannah? As souvenirs went, they were a pretty sorry choice.

She hadn't brought the entire papers, just one section each from the Saturday and Sunday editions. *Vehicle Forced Off Road,* read the Saturday headline, while the smaller text underneath announced, *Two Injured.*

Sunday's headline was shorter: *Gun Battle Downtown.*

He stared at the papers, trying to focus, until he realized that his hands were shaking. Dropping the papers on the bed, he paced to the window to stare out over the grounds. To the west, traffic on Riverside Drive was moving at its usual pace. People were jogging and walking in the park on the far side of the street, and fishermen were dropping lines from the pedestrian bridge. Everything looked so goddamn normal.

And he felt so goddamn cold. Angry. Afraid. Disappointed. She had lied to him—had lain there naked in bed with him and lied. *Fun and games, my ass!* They'd tried to kill her *twice*, and she hadn't thought it worth mentioning to him.

He forced air into his lungs and squeezed his eyes shut. He was trying to be more accepting, remember? Open-minded? He was trying to keep this relationship from falling apart, and getting pissed off was no way to accomplish that.

Behind him the bathroom door opened and bare feet crossed the wood floor to the rug. "Is this more to your . . ."

Her voice trailed off, and he turned from the window to see her staring at the newspapers. Yep, it had been guilt earlier, when he'd brought up Savannah, and it was definitely guilt there now. Her face was flushed, her throat working, and the arms she'd extended to show off the fact that she was dressed were trembling.

He folded his arms across his chest and leaned against the windowsill, needing its support more than he wanted to admit. "So . . . Savannah was lovely, hot, and humid. All fun and games." His voice was sharp, accusing, and remained that way despite his effort to tone it down. "Now tell me the fucking truth."

"Just how fucking incompetent are you?"

Barnard Taylor set his cigar aside and switched the phone

to his other hand. That damned lack of respect. There was a time when he would have shot any pup who dared speak to him in that tone. He might still be tempted, once he found out who the bastard was. There was no shortage of suspects—all the top people in Davis's organization had his private number—but the evidence pointed toward someone on Yates's payroll or Selena's. Hell, for all he knew, it could even be Damon Long. It would be just like that fucker to get someone else to kill his new boss so he could take over *and* get paid for the hit, too.

"Who the hell do you think you are, calling me at home and talking to me like this? Do you *know* who I am? Do you know what I could do to you?"

"You'd have to find me first, old man, and since your best men apparently trained with the Three Stooges, I'm not exactly sweating that."

"What men? What Three Stooges?"

"Playing dumb, huh?" Mystery Man chuckled. "One fuckup after another. Christ, maybe I should have taken my information elsewhere."

Yeah, right, Barnard mouthed. There wasn't a doubt in his mind that Mystery Man had sold the same info to Munroe, probably to Yates, and maybe even to half the competition out there. There were plenty of major players who would like to expand their territories. Trying had been a sure way to die when Mr. Davis was in charge, but with the bitch-girl, that had definitely changed. For all anyone knew, there could be a half dozen hitters out there stalking her.

"She's back in Tulsa now, living at her uncle's big, fancy estate. This time your guys won't get a clear shot at her on the street. They're gonna have to get past the fence, the guards, the alarm system. It's gonna be tough."

"You know what they say—'if you can see 'em, you can

kill 'em.' " Long-distance shots through a window, walking to the car, or sitting around the pool—that was what snipers were for. And every man in his line of work happened to know a damned good one. "You got the address of this fancy estate?"

"Yeah, I've got it. Though I have to think maybe I'm wasting my time giving it to you."

"Giving it? You moneygrubbing little shit, I've paid you plenty. You aren't *giving* me anything but grief."

Mystery Man snorted. "I've given you the opportunity of a lifetime. I set a target in front of you, and you've failed to take it out—*twice*."

"I haven't failed at anything, you little pissant. You try proving I was behind any attempted hit on the new boss. You won't find a goddamn shred of evidence leading to me."

"The man doing the hiring was from Philly."

"It's a big, big city."

"He used to work for you."

"I've employed hundreds of people over the years. Turnover's high in my line of work."

"So it's all coincidence, huh? And it's coincidence that he offered the job to someone else who used to work for you."

Barnard rubbed the ache between his eyes, then hauled himself out of his easy chair and went to the bar to fill a glass halfway with scotch. He tossed back half of it, grimaced, then set the glass down hard enough to slosh the rest over the rim. "Pure coincidence," he agreed. "Ain't it funny how that works? Now . . . you gonna give me that address or not?"

"You could find it yourself," Mystery Man said flatly. "Everybody in Tulsa knows the chief of police lived in that big, fancy house by the river. But I'll make it easy on you. Ready?" He rattled off the numbers and street, then added, "Try to get it right this time, will you?"

" 'Try to get it right this time,' " Barnard mimicked as he hung up. "Goddamn whiny-ass...I'll fucking get it right, and then I'm coming after *you*."

The boast felt good, not that there was much chance of making good on it. He didn't have a fucking clue who the guy was or how to find out.

Besides, he had other priorities.

13

Damon stood at the window in the guesthouse living room, gazing across the grass. It was the middle of the night, and except for the two guards pulling duty at the back gate and the three or more at the main gate, everyone was asleep.

He couldn't sleep. He had too much to think about.

Should he stay or should he go?

Staying held both advantages and disadvantages. There was Selena's promise of more money to look forward to, not that he'd seen a dime yet. The only money in his pocket was what he'd lifted off the tourist, cozied up next to the phone he'd lifted from Selena. At the moment, he didn't have a use for either. No place to spend the cash, no one to call on the phone. No one he trusted with his life . . . yet.

There was the possibility of getting rid of Selena and taking control of the business himself. He could use her own people against her—at least, one of them. He had caught only a glimpse of the computer screen last night before Jamieson had slammed it shut, but it damn sure hadn't looked like any e-mail or instant message screen he'd ever seen. Selena's mild-mannered accountant was up to something, and it was nowhere near as innocent as talking to someone on the Internet. Damon could use that to his advantage.

And the biggest disadvantage of all—there was the possibility of going to trial, to prison, to Death Row.

And if he left? Once he got rid of the damn bracelet, he would be free. He was only a few hundred miles from Dallas, where his new life awaited him. He would change his name, change his appearance, and disappear with his fortune. In a month, maybe two, he would resurface someplace new and use that fortune to build more fortunes.

Try as he might, he couldn't think of a downside to that option.

Once he got rid of the bracelet.

Once he got off the estate.

Once he created a big enough diversion to give him the head start he needed.

Eight or so dead bodies would be one hell of a diversion.

His feet made little noise on the wood floor as he prowled around the room, sliding open drawers, looking in cabinets, and finding nothing of use. No scissors, no knives, not even a fucking letter opener. No heavy skillets in the kitchen, no solid brass candlesticks or bronze castings. Even the bronze-and-marble statue that Selena had used to crack open his skull two years ago—that William had insisted not only on keeping but displaying—was gone from its place on the sofa table.

She had damn near killed him that night. After learning the truth about William a few weeks ago, she'd become convinced it had all been part of his plan to bend her to his will—that he had instructed Damon to get close to her, to assault her, to traumatize her.

He hadn't. Fucking with her had been Damon's idea—his way of getting back at William for all the insults, the disdain, the lack of regard. But damned if he would ever tell Selena that.

He stood between the living room and kitchen, hands in

his hip pockets. There wasn't a single fucking thing in the cottage that he could use as a weapon . . . but he didn't need a weapon. He'd killed with his bare hands before, including the very first time, and he found a visceral pleasure in it. It was the ultimate power—the ability to preserve life or to end it, right there in his hands.

The tick-tick of the clock underscored his shallow breathing. He'd been thinking about it since yesterday in an idle maybe-he-would-maybe-he-wouldn't sort of way. How would he kill them? How would he pit himself against eight or more and succeed? Where would he go? How would he remove the bracelet? How would he get to Dallas?

Killing them would be the easy part. Robinette was asleep down the hall. It didn't take much skill or strength to choke the life out of someone in his sleep. Leaving the cottage would set off alarms in the guard shack, and Damon would wait in the bushes outside to take out the guards who responded. It didn't matter whether it was one or five; he knew from experience that most security guards would hesitate to use deadly force. He wouldn't.

After killing any remaining guards at their posts, he would let himself into the main house. He knew alarms and had no doubt he could bypass the one on the mansion. He would kill Gentry first—between her and Jamieson, she was the more dangerous. After taking care of the computer wiz, he would take the prize—Selena. Just thinking about killing her was enough to warm the blood pumping through his veins.

Strangling would be his first choice of methods. Leaning over her, tightening his fingers around her throat, watching the fear in her eyes as she ran out of air, feeling the slowing beat of her heart beneath his hands, would be so sweetly intimate. But he knew from past run-ins that she wouldn't lie there compliantly while he killed her. No, she would fight like hell and would probably kick the shit out of him in the process.

It was less personal, less satisfying, but he would shoot her with the gun he would take from one of his first victims. She was too damn dangerous to fuck with, and in the long run, dead was dead, no matter how it was accomplished.

Then? William's cars were in the garage. A stop at a twenty-four-hour Wal-Mart for a set of heavy-duty bolt cutters, take his pick of cars from the surrounding neighborhood, and head south to Dallas.

It was a plan he could live with.

He moved silently down the hall to Robinette's room, turned the knob, then eased the door open. The room was similar to his own—large, one wall all windows, the furniture looking like something from the damned islands. William had spared no expense redecorating the place for Selena, but she'd refused to live there and refused the job offer that accompanied it.

Why? Because she could.

The only things different between this room and his own were the lump in the bed that was Robinette and the tiny green light that glowed on the nightstand—a cell phone in a charger. During the day, if he wasn't talking on it, it was clipped to his belt, as much a part of him as the pistol he wore in a shoulder holster. It was his contact with the world.

Considering that his world was now Selena's world, and Damon's, there weren't that many people he should be talking to.

Damon crossed the room, eased the phone from the charger, then retreated into the hall and to his own room. With the door closed and a chair wedged in front of it, he flipped open the phone and called up the OUTGOING CALLS screen. Highlighting the number that appeared most often, he pressed the SEND button. After two rings, it went to a recording that surprised him so damn much, he called back and listened to it again.

When he hung up the second time, he stood motionless, the phone gripped loosely, unsure whether to laugh or swear. Had he been suckered by Selena again? Had she been lying to him from the start? Did she have a clue what was going on, or was she the fool this time?

He didn't have any idea. But he did know one thing for sure: A lot of people would be damned interested to know what he'd just discovered.

Adam Robinette, advisor and flunky to the nation's newest drug lord, was making regular calls to the local office of the Federal Bureau of Investigation.

Robinette had just saved his own and everyone else's lives. Before Damon committed an act as final as murder, he needed to reevaluate with this new information in mind.

After all, if his reevaluation weighed out in favor of a big diversion and escape, he could always kill them another night.

Selena settled on her bed Monday morning, the folder holding William's journal on the spread in front of her. Tony had stayed late the night before, giving her a badly needed distraction from William, the case, and her life. Now, though, with her workout and breakfast out of the way and nothing else on her schedule for a while, she picked up the folder with unsteady hands and opened it.

The first entry of substance that hadn't been blacked out was dated January 14.

I'm back from my second trip to Puerto Rico and have had no luck at locating the Acostas. Of course, after taking my money all these years when they weren't taking care of the child, I have no doubt that they don't want to be found, certainly not by me. I'm not discouraged, though. It's simply a matter of offering the right price. Then someone will give them up. Someone always does.

January 29. *The right price was $5000 and a truck worth a tenth of that. It was Rodrigo's own sister who sold him out. Odd. I'm sure my sister would think I've sold her out ... if she knew. But she knows nothing about who I am, what I've done, and she never will. Tomorrow I'll visit Luisa and Rodrigo ... and perhaps take a pound of his worthless flesh for each year he took my money after sending the girl away.*

January 30. *Utterly worthless. The man actually tried to lie to me. He told me she had run away, that their hearts had been broken and still they searched for her. It was a lie, of course. Sending her to them was a mistake; I see that now. He's a lazy drunk who controls with his fists, and his fat wife is good for nothing but popping out more mouths they can't feed. Slovenly, slatternly trash. After some ... shall we say persuasion? ... he admitted that they'd sold the girl to a couple in Jamaica. Sold her!*

Ah, well ... after I finished with him, I seriously doubt he'll be getting any more brats on his fat, stupid wife. Thank God for small miracles.

February 1. *I'm in Ocho Rios and am planning an excursion to a small village named—*

Across the room, the intercom squawked, then Robinette's voice came through. "Sonny Yates is on the phone for you. Come on up to the ballroom."

Selena glanced at the intercom, then the journal, before reluctantly folding the corner of the page and closing the folder. She drew a deep breath before leaving the room and turning toward the stairs.

So William had known her—or, at least, known of her—years before they'd met. But how? Was his connection to Luisa, and if so, what was it? She couldn't think of a single circumstance in which elegant, wealthy, sophisticated William could have ever met—or noticed—poor, uneducated Luisa.

More likely, he'd somehow known Selena's father—though, *thank you, God,* he couldn't *be* her father. Luisa was Puerto Rican through and through, so Selena's black blood must have come from her father. Had he been Jamaican, as Luisa had told her? The drug trade had long been active in Jamaica. Perhaps he'd been one of William's partners in crime.

The possibility made Selena's stomach knot. She had always known the reality of her mother wasn't pretty—ignorant, downtrodden, too defeated by life even to care about her own child. But she'd had fantasies about her father. He was handsome, decent, honorable. He came from a large, loving family, and though his one night with Luisa had been an aberration, he would have welcomed Selena into his family if only he'd known of her existence. She'd been too black for her Latino family, but had persuaded herself all too easily that her black family wouldn't have cared about her Puerto Rican blood, if only they'd known.

But if he'd been one of William's associates, he was neither decent nor honorable.

And if he'd been one of William's associates, and William had been paying Luisa and Rodrigo to raise her, the most likely reason was that he was dead.

And his family hadn't wanted her.

No one had wanted her.

She was cold, empty inside, as she climbed the final steps to the ballroom. Everyone had gathered there—a scowling Gentry slathering lotion onto her hands, Long lounging in a comfortable chair with a motorcycle magazine, Jamieson off to one side, his laptop computer turned to give him some privacy. Robinette handed the phone to Selena, then pressed the button to connect the call.

"Mr. Yates."

"Don't you think you could call me Sonny once in a while?"

She smiled faintly. "I'll consider it. What do you need?"

"Just wanted to let you know that I'm on my way to Tulsa."

"Of course you are. Those *were* my orders."

The silence hummed with tension for a moment, then he continued as if she hadn't set him in his place. "I'll be there this afternoon. I booked a suite at the Renaissance. Perhaps you could invite me to William's legendary mansion for supper."

"Perhaps I could. What about the task I gave you?"

"I have news. I'll tell you when I see you."

"Call me when you arrive." She hung up without waiting for his agreement.

"Well?" Robinette prompted.

"He'll be in Tulsa in a few hours. He suggested I invite him here for dinner."

He considered it a moment, then shrugged. "That's not a bad idea. We know the place is secure, and if we need to put the fear of God into him, no one will interfere."

Selena glanced at Long for his opinion. William hadn't done business at home—not because it was sacred territory, but because his public life had been associated with the house. Anyone who knew William Davis lived there would have eventually discovered that Henry Daniels did, too, and that discovery could have meant ruin for William or death for the unfortunate one who figured it out.

It had almost meant *her* death.

But the only response Long offered was a shrug that mirrored Robinette's. "You don't have a public life to protect," he pointed out. "Nothing to hide."

"All right," she agreed. "Throw some money around and find a caterer who can handle a dinner party on such short notice."

Robinette's bristling was almost imperceptible—the slight tightening of his jaw, the narrowing of his eyes, the degree or two of frostiness in his voice when he spoke to his left without taking his gaze from her. "Take care of that."

Jamieson and Gentry exchanged glances. Since the odds of Gentry's taking on the job willingly were somewhere between nil and none, Jamieson gave a shake of his head. "I'll do it. Anything in particular for the menu?"

Selena shrugged. "Whatever they want. Tell them price is no object." The government would claim most of William's assets, as well as Yates's, Taylor's, and Munroe's, when they got to them. Let them spend some of it to support the charade. "Do we have an offer for Mr. Yates yet?"

Robinette looked at Jamieson, who paused in flipping through the Yellow Pages long enough to shake his head. "Soon," Robinette said. "If not by tonight, then in the morning."

Acknowledging him with a nod, she wandered across the room to the easel and painting supplies set up near the south wall. Under normal circumstances, if more than a few days passed without a brush in her hand, she was literally aching to get back to work, but that day she wasn't even tempted.

Who knew what might appear on the canvas if she tried? Surely something far removed from the idyllic views of paradise she was known for. Something dark and menacing, that might hurt to look at.

"What's up? You were white as a ghost when you came up here."

Selena fiddled with rearranging her worktable without looking at Gentry. "Considering that I'm half-black and half–Puerto Rican, I believe that would be a physical impossibility."

"You know what I mean. What's wrong?"

"Nothing." Or maybe everything. If William had known her father, why had he never told her about him? Easy answer: because he liked being in control. He had let her know what he wanted, and he'd hidden the rest. It would have suited him to keep that little secret, reserved for the time it could be best used to his advantage. Was there anything she would have refused if he'd offered everything he knew about her father in exchange?

She would like to think her scruples and honor weren't for sale, but she'd already proven they were. Hadn't she come to Tulsa to kill Tony to protect her own freedom? Hadn't she agreed to the FBI's scheme, again to protect that freedom? What would she have agreed to, to learn something—anything—about her father?

Looking as if she intended to pursue the subject, Gentry opened her mouth, but Selena spoke first. "Are the dishes done?"

"Washed, but not dried. I don't believe in drying them."

"You don't believe in washing them, either."

"Hey, rock-paper-scissors is a stupid game. If they'd taken my suggestion of a shooting competition on the side lawn, I'd've won and Jamieson would have been washing instead."

"You had one pan, a few plates, and some silverware. It didn't kill you. Besides, if I'd gotten in on the shooting competition, you wouldn't have won."

"Maybe, but *you* can't have a gun."

Selena thought of the weapons secreted in her room and shrugged.

"You expecting lover-boy back tonight?"

She shrugged again, aware of the faint heat in her cheeks, and redirected the question. "You have someone in your life?"

"If I did, he wouldn't be sticking around until this job is finished and I could see him again." Gentry smiled ruefully. "The men in my life never stick around."

"If the job is so tough on your personal life, why don't you find something else to do?"

"Where else can I work long hours, deal with scum on a daily basis, get shot at, *and* make slave wages while doing it?" Gentry picked up a dry brush and drew it over the canvas. The half-finished painting showed a beach scene, but not the tropical islands Selena usually favored. This was a small man-made beach laid out along an otherwise rugged shore, and the placid water beyond was a lake, its shores heavily wooded with oaks, red cedars, sumac. It was Tony's uncle John's place at Keystone Lake, a short drive west of Tulsa, where they'd had incredible, hot, breath-stealing sex for the first time... and the second. She didn't need a tangible reminder—the memory would remain forever in her mind—but she wanted one.

"Besides"—Gentry put the brush back on the table—"you're a fine one to be talking. This job's been hell on your personal life, too, but I don't see you walking away."

"The FBI's not going to kill you for quitting. These people

I'm dealing with want me dead whether I'm in or out. At least if I'm in, I stand a chance of getting them first."

"True," Gentry agreed, fixing her gaze on Selena. "But at what cost?"

Some things never failed to surprise Tony—such as the ability to run down to the local strip center, buy a hot dog, rent a video, pay your electric bill, and visit a prostitute—but that was the case at one particular strip center off Sheridan. The hookers masqueraded as massage therapists, but everyone with half a clue knew what really went on inside.

He parked next to a shit-box Ford, then joined Simmons, who was leaning against the front fender.

"I haven't been here since the last time I busted the place," Simmons commented. "You think they'll hold a grudge?"

"Aw, Frankie, everybody holds a grudge against you."

"What're we doing?"

"Looking for anyone who knew this guy." Tony pulled a copy of both photographs from his jacket pocket and handed them over.

"Who is he?"

"Charles Hensley. Better known around here as Carl Heinz."

"The guy you think shot at Island Girl."

Tony nodded as he studied the space on the end of the shopping center. Its broad windows were blocked with blinds. A sign overhead announced KIM'S THERAPEUTIC MASSAGE, and stickers on the door displayed the hours, along with the credit cards accepted. It didn't look any different from the dentist's office at the other end, except the dentist was legit.

"Christ, Chee, don't you have enough to do without going out and investigating other people's cases?"

"He worked for Henry. That gives me an interest in him."

"And the fact that he might have tried to kill your girlfriend puts him off-limits. If the boss finds out—"

Tony looked at him sharply. "He's a principal in a freaking organized crime/dope/multiple homicide case in which I'm the lead detective. I'm just doing my job."

"Yeah, right." Simmons looked skyward. "Just doing his job. That's what he said when he went after the fuckin' chief of police. Doing his job, and taking me with him."

"Hey, you volunteered to come along. You want to go back to your own cases, feel free."

"Nah. All my people are dead. They ain't goin' anywhere." Simmons looked at the photograph, then handed it back. "What do you know about this guy?"

"Not a lot." Tony had spent a tedious day, starting with an appointment with the lawyer who'd hired the PI—who had, predictably, claimed attorney/client privilege and shown him the door. He'd tracked down Heinz's cell phone provider and gotten his phone records, done the paperwork to get his financials, and had a records clerk digging up everything she could on both names. He'd talked to a detective in Philadelphia who said they'd watch for him and to a detective in Savannah who said they'd seen no sign of him. "He averaged four deliveries a week from the same pizza place in Brookside. He had an allergist, and called him more often in spring and fall than summer and winter. He made regular calls to this massage service, every two weeks like clockwork, and charged it to his credit card."

"Yeah, that number-crunching's hard work. Lots of stress to relieve. Any personal stuff?"

"I think the massage service pretty much sums up his

personal life." Every call on the phone records was to or from a local business. Nothing personal, nothing long-distance. If he'd kept in touch with family or friends back in Philadelphia—or with anyone in Savannah—he hadn't done so with this cell phone.

But that was what pay phones were for, wasn't it?

"So we're gonna go ask the girls what they know, and you think they're gonna tell us."

"I've never had trouble getting information from prostitutes."

"Yeah, and they probably offer to do you for free," Simmons grumbled as they started across the parking lot. "How *is* Island Girl? The feebs haven't gotten her shot yet, have they?"

"They came close." Tony skimmed over the two incidents in Savannah.

"Jesus. They might as well paint a bull's-eye on her back."

"That's what I told her." But she'd ignored him and taken their deal anyway. Hard as he was trying to deal with it, that still rankled. "I can't even blame them. To do what they want her to do, she's got to be visible. She's got to meet with these people."

"Daniels never did."

He was right, of course. Henry had never met any of his employees. But Selena wasn't Henry.

"It'd be nice if this was like TV, where the police go in and the girls are sitting around in skimpy undergarments," Simmons said with a leer as he held the door open.

"Suz not letting you near her again?"

"Wait till you get married. You'll never get it as much as you did before."

Now there was a discouraging thought.

The woman behind the counter was Asian, spoke with a

heavy accent, and answered to the improbable name of Cissy. She needed two looks at Tony, but only one at Simmons, to bring suspicion into her dark eyes and a flat line to her mouth.

"We just freakin' look like cops," Simmons muttered.

He'd rather look like a cop than a man who had to pay for sex, Tony thought, no matter how little of it he had been getting lately.

Cissy didn't want to talk—didn't want to do anything besides throw them out. "We're not interested in arresting anybody," Tony said. "We don't care what you do here. We just want to know about one client—this man."

She didn't even glance at the photo. "Don't know him."

"At least one of your employees does. He was a regular."

"Don't know him," she repeated.

Simmons rested one elbow on the counter and bent so he was closer to her eye level. "You know, maybe we are interested in arresting somebody. Maybe we ought to call our buddies in Special Investigations and get them to come over. Maybe they could bring some reporters from the local TV stations, too. It's probably been—what?—three, four months since the last story on your kind of establishment aired on the news."

She scowled at him a long time, then walked over to the hall that led to the back rooms and snapped out something in her native language. A moment later, another petite, pretty Asian woman appeared. She introduced herself as Tammy without even a hint of an accent, led them into a lounge, then sat down and crossed her legs, swinging one stiletto-heeled foot in the air.

"Yeah, I know him," she said in response to the photo. "Carl. Every other Thursday, four o'clock, for two years. Liked to talk."

"About what?"

"Computers. Money. He was always telling me I should invest in this stock or that. I passed his tips along to my investment guy and got some pretty good returns."

A twenty-something prostitute with her own investment counselor. And all Tony could manage was an IRA. "Did he ever talk about his personal life? Family, where he was from, his hobbies?"

Her smile was both sweet and seductive. "I think I was his only hobby. Said he didn't have any family that he claimed. He came from somewhere back East, but he never talked about it. Colorado—that's what he talked about." Her silky black hair swung as she bobbed her head. "Said he was gonna move there someday. He had a little place already, somewhere in the mountains, and even showed me a picture of it—he carried it around in his wallet like you would a picture of your wife and kids. Talked about it like it was some kind of dream house, when it was really just a dirty old cabin in the middle of nowhere."

A cabin in Colorado. Jeez, it might as well be a needle in a haystack. "Did he ever mention the name of the town?"

"Maybe. I don't remember." Again with the smile. "Dirty old cabins in the mountains don't interest me."

Tony asked a few more questions, but she had nothing else to add. When he stood to leave, he commented, "You didn't ask what he's done." Most people he interviewed were curious as hell; *why* or *what* were the first words out of their mouths.

She stood, smoothed her snug-fitting dress an inch lower on her thighs, then shrugged. "Unless I'm getting paid, Carl Heinz doesn't interest me, either. Now, if that's all you want . . . I have things to do."

As they walked through the lobby, Simmons called a

friendly good-bye to Cissy, who responded with a scowl. He didn't speak again until they were outside in the blistering heat. "What are the odds that Carl Heinz bought that dirty old cabin under either of the names you know for him?"

"Somewhere between slim and none." Tony rubbed the ache between his eyes before sliding on his sunglasses. "I'm so damn tired of people lying about who they are and what they do."

"Then you are in the wrong line of work, son. Everyone lies, and the more sincere they are, or the more polite they are, the bigger the lie."

The observation almost made Tony smile. He didn't want to get too cynical, but he had to admit that the first time each new suspect called him "sir," he was more than ready to put the handcuffs on.

"So . . . you want me to try to track down this cabin?"

"Frankie . . . you're offering to work?" He feigned surprise. "Jeez, give me a minute. I want to remember everything about this moment."

"Fuck you, Chee. I work."

"So you say. I've just never seen it for myself."

"Do you want me to track down the damn cabin or not? 'Cause if you don't do some work on your own cases, the boss is gonna be awfully pissed."

Tony sobered as he stopped next to his car. "Yeah. I appreciate it, Frankie."

Simmons opened his car door, grimaced at the heat that rolled out, then shrugged out of his jacket. "Yeah, well, my dead folks won't miss me. And the boss doesn't expect results from me like he does from you." He shoved a pair of mirrored glasses into place, then turned a shit-eating grin Tony's way. "Besides, I figure once Island Girl's safe, you can show your gratitude by solving a few of my cases for me."

"Yeah, I'll do that." Once Selena was safe.

If she was ever safe.

"Where the hell are you going?"

Damon stopped halfway to the stairs and slowly turned to face Robinette. They'd spent a few boring hours in the ballroom, four of them tediously discussing every goddamn aspect of this deal they were going to offer Sonny, to the point that Damon had wanted to strangle them all. If he and William had done one-tenth as much talking as these fuckers did, they never would have accomplished a damn thing.

"I'm going to the john," he said sourly.

Robinette nodded toward the matching doors that opened off an alcove nearby. "Bathrooms are over there."

"I want privacy. I'm gonna be a while." Damon gestured with the magazine he'd rolled into a tube, then headed toward the stairs again. Robinette, the prick, was so damn antsy, like he was afraid of what Damon might do if he was out of their sight for five minutes.

He should be afraid.

Damon took the stairs two at a time to the second floor and went into the master suite at the north end of the hall. He locked the door behind him, went into the bathroom, and locked that door, too. The toilet sat in its own private room between a Jacuzzi tub and a shower big enough for four. Once he'd secured that lock, he dug the cell phone from his pocket and sat down.

He'd spent part of the day figuring out who to trust with his information, and the rest waiting for a chance to act. He'd settled on the one person whose loyalty to William was beyond reproach. "J.T. This is Damon. I need some information."

"Damon Long. I heard the new boss is leading you around like a puppy on a leash—that she's got you wearing one of those electronic collars like you use to keep a dog in the yard."

The fucker thought it was funny. Well, hell, so what? Damon didn't give a damn what anyone thought. "Yeah, yeah. Listen, this guy who's working for her—Adam Robinette. Says he used to work for Hector Gonzalez down in Miami. You know if that's true?"

"Mr. Gonzalez and I weren't exactly friends."

"Can you find out?"

"Why do you want to know?"

"I just want to know if he is who he says he is."

"You think he isn't?"

"The guy's been making calls to the FBI. He could be an agent working undercover, or he could really be Gonzalez's man who's sold out to the feds. I don't know. But I want to."

The humor was gone from J.T.'s voice. "I'll look into it. You want me to call you back?"

"No." That was all he needed, for the phone to ring when he wasn't supposed to even have the damn thing. "I'll call you."

He hung up, stuck the cell back in his pocket, then leaned back and opened the magazine.

Selena checked her appearance in the dresser mirror. Her dress was linen in a deep salmon hue, simple, sleeveless, and her hair was loose around her shoulders. She wore a choker of coral beads and matching earrings, and smelled of jasmine and passionflower, and wished she could give it all up for one of Tony's old T-shirts and a few hours alone with William's journal . . . or a few hours alone with Tony.

She put the journal away, stepped into a pair of sandals, then left her room for the gentlemen's parlor downstairs. They would have drinks there, it had been decided, and dispense with the social pleasantries before moving to the sunroom for dinner. Long would join them for the meal. Robinette wouldn't, though he would remain nearby. Jamieson was likely shut away with his computer somewhere, and Gentry was upstairs in one of the guest rooms, all set up to monitor their conversation.

Like the second-floor study, the parlor held bad memories for Selena, and the coming evening wasn't likely to improve them. Frank Simmons had brought her there after the shootings that Sunday. He'd read her her rights, questioned her about William, Tony, and Damon Long, and treated her like the suspect she'd been. Left to him, she would have gone from there straight to jail . . . but Tony hadn't left it to him.

Pushing the numbness that had encased her that day to the back of her mind, she crossed the room to stand near Robinette, meticulously rearranging William's exquisite antique decanters on the ancient cherry table that stood duty as a bar. "Charlize Pawley came with him," he murmured, his voice pitched low so that Long, across the room, couldn't hear.

He'd probably known that from the moment Yates had left Savannah. It reassured her that they were keeping the enemy under close watch. "She said she would like to visit Oklahoma sometime."

"Yeah, it's such a popular tourist destination."

"I don't know. I came for a short visit, and I'm still here."

"You came to kill someone. Let's hope she doesn't have the same intent."

She gave him a dry look. "What should I tell Mr. Yates about our partnership?"

He set a glass of wine in front of her. "The truth. The accounting for such an extensive enterprise is complicated. Jamieson needs a little more time."

She nodded once, then picked up the glass. It trembled sharply as the doorbell echoed through the foyer. With a smile lacking in warmth, Robinette circled the bar and headed for the door. She watched him go, then became aware of Long watching her.

"How much do you know about that guy?" he asked with a gesture toward the door.

"Mr. Robinette? I told you, he used to work for Hector Gonzalez."

"Yeah. How'd he come to work for you?"

"He was looking for a job, and I was looking for help. He came very highly recommended."

"By who?"

She stiffened her spine. "By someone I trust. Why the questions?"

Shoving his hands into his pants pockets, he lifted both shoulders in a shrug that was as relaxed as she was rigid. "Just curious. You bring strangers into my life, I wonder about them. I wonder about him."

"If it makes you feel any better, the mistrust is mutual." She studied him a moment, then quietly asked, "Is there something I should know about Mr. Robinette? Do you think he has an agenda?"

Long laughed. "Everyone's got an agenda."

"And what's yours, Mr. Long?"

"Staying alive and out of prison. What's Robinette's?"

"Meeting his employer's expectations."

Long made a rude sound, but approaching footsteps stopped him from going further. As Selena turned to the door, she wondered what was behind his questions. Had Robinette said or done something to make him more suspicious than usual? Or was it merely dislike? If *she* was sharing quarters with the man, she was certain she would like him even less than she did at the moment.

Robinette came into the room first, heading for the bar. Yates and Charlize Pawley were a few steps behind him. There was no sign of Devlin or LeRoy. Had they come along but been stopped at the gates, or had they stayed behind at the hotel? Or was this vulnerability supposed to be a sign of trust?

"Nice place, Selena," Yates said, walking straight toward her, hand extended.

Though she wished she could have avoided it, she shook his hand. "Uncle William had exquisite taste, and the money to indulge it. I'll give you a tour later if you'd like."

"I would." He reached back and drew Charlize to his side. "I hope you don't mind that I brought a guest. You intrigued her with your description of the city, so she seized the opportunity to see for herself."

"I don't mind at all. It's a pleasure seeing you again, Charlize." She'd said Oklahoma was a lovely place. That was hardly a description to intrigue—hardly a description at all.

The woman murmured something appropriate, Yates and Long exchanged greetings, and Robinette served drinks all around. Selena sat in the chair nearest the fireplace, wishing for a blaze there to chase away her chill.

After waiting for her guests to settle on the sofa, Selena crossed her legs, swirled the wine in its delicate stemmed glass, then casually asked, "What about the task I assigned you, Mr. Yates? Have you made any progress?"

In spite of his smile, she caught the twitch of a muscle in his jaw. He gave Charlize a nod, and she removed an envelope from her purse, laying it in his hand. In turn, he leaned forward and tossed it on the coffee table in front of Selena. Though she was careful not to look at Robinette, peripherally she saw him move, coming around the bar as she set down her wine, picked up the envelope, and opened it.

There were photographs inside—glossy, full-color, a man lying in the dirt. With his eyes closed, his jaw stubbled with beard, and his hair tousled, he looked like a drunk sleeping off one too many... if she managed to overlook the gaping hole where the upper right quadrant of his face should have been.

"I remember him," Long said, giving her a start. She hadn't been aware of his rising from his seat. "I figured someone would put a bullet in his brain long before this. He was always careless."

Keeping her hand steady through sheer will, she gave the photos to Robinette, then turned an icy gaze on Yates. "I assume that's Mr. Tarver."

"In the flesh... though it's rather cold at the moment."

"I told you to find him and bring him to me. I told you not to—"

"I'm not responsible for that," Yates interrupted.

She filled her lungs though her chest was so tight that breathing actually hurt. "Then who is?"

His look, his manner, his tone, were all condescendingly patient. "The logical answer is the man who sent him to Savannah in the first place. He took money to do a job. He failed at that job. That"—he gestured toward the photo—"is one of the consequences of failure."

Death *was* one of the risks of the business. Selena understood that. She shouldn't even feel any sympathy for Buddy Tarver. He was dead because *she* was alive. He didn't know anything about her, didn't have any sort of grudge against her, and yet he had intended to kill her for no reason other than greed. She had meant nothing to him. His death should mean less than nothing to her.

But it didn't. It sickened her.

"Why would Mr. Taylor—or anyone else—send a hitter who was always careless?" Robinette asked.

Long shrugged as he dropped back into his seat. "Maybe he was pressed for time. Maybe Tarver's gotten better since I knew him."

Or maybe whoever hired him had *wanted* someone less than competent. Maybe the intent had never been to kill her, but to merely make it look as if someone wanted her dead— to cast blame elsewhere and create a rift in the organization.

Robinette directed his next question to Yates. "If you weren't responsible, how did you get the photographs?"

"You know how it goes—someone knows someone who knows someone...Our particular 'someone' works in the police department lab. He knew we were interested in Tarver, so he got us copies. So...mission accomplished."

Selena forced herself to shrug carelessly. "Though not as directed. I wanted to talk to Mr. Tarver. Clearly, that's impossible now." And that, more than his failure to kill her, was probably why he was dead. Whoever had hired him hadn't wanted any loose ends that led back to him. It could have been Barnard Taylor, as the evidence suggested. Or it could have just as easily been Yates. With Tarver dead, she would likely never know.

"We can talk about the bonus you promised me later," Yates said, settling back on the sofa, his drink in hand.

"The deal wasn't to kill him."

"No, it was to identify him. I did that, and I would have turned him over to you as directed if someone hadn't killed him first. You can't blame me for that."

If she discussed rewarding him for the man's death, she

was going to be ill. As it was, she couldn't imagine doing justice to the excellent meal laid out in the sunroom. "You're right," she said coolly. "We'll discuss the bonus tomorrow. Right now, dinner awaits us. Shall we move into the sunroom?"

14

It was easy to fall into a routine, especially when a person had as much practice at it as Kathryn did. She'd had her routines in school, in college, in her marriage. Routines were comforting. They made everything seem all right— usually.

Up every morning at eight, breakfast on the patio, a drive to the hospital, a tedious morning at Henry's side. Lunch at Utica Square, more tedious time with Henry, then back to the bed-and-breakfast. Every third day she bought pastries for the nursing staff; every fourth day she stopped for fresh flowers. In the first days after the accident, as she preferred to think of it, the intensive care unit had been flooded with flowers, but as time passed, the deliveries had trickled off to nothing.

That had been her life for more than three weeks. Might be her life for much longer. Dear God, she couldn't stand it.

That morning happened to be both a pastries and flowers morning. She balanced the bakery box in one arm, the vase in the other, as she stepped off the elevator. Her heels clicked down the hall, and the staff she passed greeted her by name. They thought she was a dedicated, loving sister, and she was.

Oh, but there could be so many more facets to love than they suspected.

"Sweets for the sweet," she said, smiling as she uttered the inane words and left the pastry box on the counter at the nursing station. She was halfway to Henry's room when one of the aides called out.

"Oh, Mrs. Hamilton, you have a guest. He's waiting in the family room."

She stopped, glanced at Henry's door a few yards away, then turned back. The visitors had trickled off to nothing in the past few weeks, as well, though she didn't blame them. There was no pleasure in sitting beside a man who was dead in all the ways that counted.

She backtracked to the family waiting room, a square space with chairs, a television, a telephone, and a dreary view out the windows. The television was turned on, though the lone occupant was gazing out the window. "Excuse me. I was told—"

He turned with a smile that sent warmth tingling through her. "Jefferson! You came!" Hurrying across the room, she gathered him into her embrace.

"I told you I would."

"You also told me you'd call me back, but you didn't."

"I wanted to surprise you."

She swatted his arm affectionately. "Calling me back— now *that* would have surprised me. How long can you stay? When did you get in? Where are you staying?"

"Just a couple days. I got in this morning, and my secretary booked me at the downtown Doubletree."

"Oh, I bet there's a suite available at the bed-and-breakfast. I'll just call—"

"Thank you, Mama, but the Doubletree is fine."

Though it would be wonderful to have him under the same roof as she, she didn't push the subject. He was there, and that was the only thing that mattered.

Taking a step back, she studied him intently. His hair was on the shaggy side, gleaming like fire where the sun touched it through the window. Fine lines bracketed his lovely blue-and-green eyes, giving him a tired look, but his smile was warm, indulgent. Though he'd been full-grown half his life, she couldn't look at him even once without remembering that handsome little towhead the lawyer had delivered to her all those years ago. He'd been afraid, but had bravely tried to hide it. He'd won her heart right then and there, and still had it.

"Why are you staying at a bed-and-breakfast?" he asked. "Too many bad memories at the Davis plantation?"

"It's not a plantation," she chided. "Though the house and its grounds would look perfectly at home anywhere in the Deep South. Do you remember it?"

He shrugged. "White house, big lawn."

"I'm not surprised you remember so little." He'd been a child the last time they'd visited Henry, and intimidated by the uncle who had little interest in or patience with him. "It's a beautiful place."

"So why aren't you staying there?"

With a sigh, she hooked her arm through his and started toward the door. "Let's get a cup of coffee and we'll talk."

"More Henry gossip?" he asked with a grin. "The old man's much more interesting now than he ever was alive."

They only went as far as the nurses' station for the coffee, where a pot was always brewing. She fixed a cup for each of them, then claimed his arm again and steered him toward Henry's room. "There aren't any bad memories at the house for me," she began. Except for those conjured by the discovery of Selena McCaffrey's photo, and they were nothing new. She'd lived with them for twenty-eight years.

"It was the FBI who told me about Henry's activities. They're hoping to arrest his associates, and they wanted to use the house while they do that." She saw Jefferson's eyes widen. She hurried on before he could comment. "I didn't want to agree, but they were throwing around words like 'criminal enterprise' and 'ill-gotten gains' and 'seizure.' Our grandfather built that house; it's always been in the Daniels family. I couldn't risk losing it because Henry was stupid enough to get mixed up with a bad crowd."

Though whether it would remain in the family once Henry finally did die was anyone's guess. Kathryn wanted with all her heart to believe he'd willed the estate to her or to Jefferson, to people who belonged; but it was entirely possible, damn his soul, that he'd left it to that girl.

It would be a cold day in hell before Selena McCaffrey would inherit so much as a dime that Kathryn had a personal interest in.

She drew a breath and waited for Jefferson's response. For a time, he was quiet, his face difficult to read. Beyond "serious," she couldn't recognize any emotion.

"Good ol' Henry," he said at last, his voice flat, even bitter. He was such a good son. He always took everything that upset her so personally. "Does he have any other surprises in store?"

"Good God, I hope not."

"How can they make a case against Henry's associates? Unless . . . one of them is helping them."

She waved one hand dismissively. "I neither know nor care. It's just all so tawdry, Jefferson. Grandmama and Grandpapa must be spinning in their graves at the shock of it all. The shame Henry's brought on the family, the stain on our good name—" She realized she'd gotten a bit strident when Jefferson laid his hand on her shoulder. With a rueful smile, she patted it reassuringly. "I'm sorry, sugar. I'm just not happy with my brother right now."

"And yet you want me to go in and see him like a good

nephew." He didn't make her answer that, but slid his arm around her. "Now don't go thinking this means I give a damn about the man, okay?"

"Okay," she agreed, relieved.

He laid one elegant hand flat on the door to Henry's room, preparing to push. "Then let's go."

February 18. I found them at last—Juan and Berta Lopez, the people to whom the Acostas sold Amalia. She's no longer with them, though of course Señora Lopez assures me she was a treasured member of their family for the months she was there. They called her Maria—a new life deserves a new name—and they loved her as if she was their own.

Of course, the authorities tell a different story. They say the Lopezes taught the child to lie, steal, and cheat, that she spent her days begging and robbing to pay for her support. No money meant no food and no place to sleep. This damned third-world scum...what was I thinking when I sent her to them in the first place?

The Lopezes sent her to live with friends in Ocho Rios—so she could get a proper education, the señora said, and have a chance at a better future. Of course, she was eyeing my Rolex at the time she said it. She gave me a name, but had no address. Such a good friend.

March 14. I've hired a man in Ocho Rios to track down Dorotea and Philip VanDerBleek. Like everyone else, that's just one set of names that they use. They're the sort who never stay in one place long, else they'd wind up in a Jamaican prison—or graveyard. My man tells me they're a modern-day version of Fagin, taking in kids with nowhere else to go, teaching them the fine art of criminal life, and putting them out on the streets. It's likely that Amalia, or Maria, or whatever they're calling her now, is picking pockets and stealing or even working as a prostitute. Wouldn't that kill her father?

Selena sighed. A new life, a new name. Dorotea and her husband had chosen to call her Rosa Jimenez. When William had taken her in, he'd christened her Gabriela Sanchez, and when her life had fallen apart two summers ago, when she thought she had killed a man, she'd renamed herself Selena McCaffrey. She didn't intend to change names again.

Except, God willing, someday to Ceola.

Somewhat reluctantly, she turned her attention back to the journal. She'd thought initially that she would devour it all in one sitting, but she hadn't. It was difficult reading that raised difficult questions. Did she truly want to know that her father had been no better than the people who'd raised her—that he had, most likely, been far worse? The others had beaten her and denied her food, affection, and any sense of security; they'd forced her to steal and, toward the end, had threatened to pimp her out to anyone with money in his pocket. But as far as she knew, even they had drawn the line at dealing drugs and the murder that accompanied it.

Her father, presumably, had not.

April 2. My man in Jamaica called this morning to say he's located the VanDerBleeks and, he thinks, the child. There's a black girl living with them, about the right age, who bears a resemblance to the photos I gave him. She's an accomplished little thief—pretty of face, fleet of foot, sly and devious and cunning. Sounds promising.

He'll send me a photograph so I can see for myself. Naturally, I'd rather have a child of my own to pass the business on to, but since that's never going to happen, this child is the next best answer. After all, she's barely fourteen and has already mastered the criminal activities in which she indulges. Completing her training will be a simple matter.

Besides, if not for me, she never would have lived long enough to grow up and work the streets. One could say I owe her.

One could also say she owes me.

Selena's palms were damp, her breathing shallow. Over the years, William had taken great pleasure in reminding her that he'd saved her life. She had always thought he was referring to the night they'd met, when the man she'd just robbed had followed her into an alley, hit her, and threatened to rape her. William had killed him, taken her to his hotel, fed her, bought her clothes, and offered her a new life in the US.

But that incident had happened in November fourteen years ago. Whatever rescue he was referring to had obviously taken place long before that.

April 16. I got the photograph, and it's definitely Amalia. The resemblance is amazing. No one who knew her parents could ever miss it. Now that I have confirmation, it's time to finalize my plans. I must—

A heavy knock sounded at the bedroom door, startling her. "Come on upstairs," Gentry called. "It's time to work."

Slowly Selena closed the journal and returned it to the night table drawer before going to stand in front of the dresser mirror. Beyond the color of her eyes and hair, she looked nothing like her mother. Luisa had been a light-skinned Latina, short and round, a stereotypical *mamacita*. Selena's skin was darker, her features more exotic, and she was six inches taller and seventy pounds lighter.

Was the resemblance William wrote of to her father? And if so, why had he said *parents*?

Unless Luisa wasn't her mother.

Her chest tightened. A part of her would love to know that the uncaring woman who'd ignored her, neglected her, and looked the other way when Rodrigo beat her *wasn't* her mother. But wasn't it better to know one parent, however inadequate, than none at all? Wasn't it better to feel the absence of only one rather than both?

Unsure of the answers, she left the bedroom, turning toward the stairs as the others trooped up. Long and Jamieson were bringing up the rear. "Mr. Long," she said before she could think better of it. "Could I speak to you a moment?"

Wearing an insolent look, Long came back down the first few steps and toward her. She walked to the window at the end of the corridor and gazed out as he joined her.

He leaned against the windowsill, arms folded over his chest, ankles crossed. Wearing jeans and a black T-shirt, he looked exactly what he was—handsome, disreputable, dangerous. "Well? You want something?"

Yes. She wanted not to show him any sign of weakness. He was the sort to make the most of weaknesses. But with a deep breath, she asked anyway. "What do you know about my father?"

He didn't look surprised by the question. He didn't look as if he gave a damn in any way. "Nothing. William never mentioned him."

"Was there a black man who worked for him? Someone he was close to? Someone he would have felt an obligation to?" After all, according to the journal, William had been paying Rodrigo and Luisa to provide for her. A generous act from a man who'd never done a truly generous deed in his life.

He shook his head again. "There were a lot of black men—and Hispanic and Asian and Indian and white, and women, too. William was an equal-opportunity employer. But I was only with him twenty years. You're twenty-eight. There could have been someone before me."

"You were with him when he took me in."

He shrugged.

"What did he tell you about me?"

"That he'd taken in an orphan who was going to call him uncle."

"Did you ask him why?"

"We're talking about goddamn William here. He didn't want you to know something, you didn't know it." Then he chuckled. "Besides, do you think I gave a damn about you or why he took you in? Not as long as you stayed out of my way and my business."

Selena had no doubt he was being truthful. He'd been twenty-one when William had claimed her. He wouldn't even have noticed a fourteen-year-old girl who presented absolutely no threat to him. If only she had remained no threat to him...

It had been a long shot that he would know anything about her father, or tell it if he did, but she'd had to try. William and his damnable secrets...

She started toward the stairs before turning back. "One last thing...did you ever meet William's sister?"

"Nah. They weren't close."

Yet Kathryn Hamilton was grieving for her brother, Tony had said, and she was somehow involved in Selena's past. *I'm sure my sister would think I've sold her out,* William had written. Of course, he could have been referring to something totally separate from Selena. After all, he'd betrayed so many people in so many ways.

Once again she nodded, hesitated, then said, "Thank you."

Knowing how difficult it was for her to say those words, he gave her a wicked grin as he pushed away from the sill.

The others were working when they joined them in the ballroom—Robinette poring over files, Jamieson at the computer, Gentry studying her own stack of papers. As Long sprawled in an armchair drawn close to one west-facing window, Selena took a seat opposite Robinette.

The papers spread across the table were printouts from Yates's financial records. Databases, spreadsheets, income and expenses sorted by category and date—it was all very detailed, just like a legitimate business. That was the reason William had pushed her to get a degree in business administration, when she'd foolishly thought that the best credentials to bring to this business were a total lack of conscience, morals, and ethics.

"What has Mr. Yates been up to today?" she asked, her voice too low to reach Long.

Color seeped into Robinette's cheeks. "He left the hotel alone this morning. We, uh, lost him in midtown traffic."

She looked up, one brow raised, though she wasn't surprised. Having driven in Tulsa, she could easily imagine getting cut off from your target. Though she would be happier to know that the FBI knew exactly where Yates was, she wasn't particularly frightened, either. The estate was as secure as she was going to get, except for the snake they'd already brought in, and Long was kept under close scrutiny. "Midtown," she murmured. "He could have gone anywhere from there."

"They'll find him again."

"If nothing else, he'll be over here after lunch. What about our partnership?"

He shuffled through the papers before coming up with one covered in his compulsively neat, small writing. "Currently, thirty-five percent of the profits from the Southeast region go back into Yates's pocket. We're going to increase that to fifty percent, with the promise of more to come. As for his bonus, you're going to give him this." He lifted a manila envelope from his briefcase just enough for her to see, then returned it. "Twenty thousand. Long says that's a good compromise, considering things didn't work out the way you wanted."

"And you believe him?"

"No. But Jamieson says it's in keeping with the entries he's found in Davis's books. He should be satisfied. Hell, *I'd* take twenty grand for not doing a damn thing."

He was talking about a man's death. Every time Selena had closed her eyes the night before, she'd seen Buddy Tarver's face, or what was left of it. And yet she was going to reward Yates for whatever role he'd played, if any, in Tarver's death.

Dear God, she hated this!

"We're looking into all the unsolved homicides of police officers in the South," Robinette went on. "We may not be able to tie any of them to Yates, but we'll try. And your boyfriend connected Carl Heinz to Colorado, for whatever it's worth. You know, he could just mind his own business. We don't need any help from the local police."

"The Daniels case *is* his business," she pointed out, her tone just as snide. "So is Carl Heinz. *You* don't have jurisdiction there." She ignored the sarcastic smirk he directed to her, glanced at Long, then lowered her voice even more. "Are you having any problems with Long?"

"No. Why?"

"He was asking about you last night—what I knew about you, how you came to work for me. He seemed more suspicious than usual."

Becoming very still, Robinette looked at Long for a moment, then shook his head. "That's just him. There's nothing here to suggest that I'm anything other than what we've said."

She didn't question him, but trusted that he was experienced enough to leave anything with his real identity, and particularly anything that might connect him to the FBI, at home. Still, *something* had roused Long's wariness. "Just... be careful."

For an instant, he looked surprised, then he responded quietly, confidently. "Always."

"Where have you been?"

Sonny lay across the bed, resting his weight on his elbows, and brushed a kiss over Charlize's shoulder as she sleepily shifted to face him. "What makes you think I've been anywhere?"

Her look was dry. "What makes you think I've been in this bed all morning? I've showered, dressed, ordered room service, eaten, undressed, and"—she covered a delicate yawn with delicate fingers—"taken a nap. All without you."

"I had some errands to run."

"What kind of errands?"

"Business errands." He rolled over and sat up, aware that she saw the pistol holstered on his belt. Airport security had required him to travel unarmed, something he generally tried to avoid. Picking up a weapon had been among his priorities.

"It took you only a few hours to purchase an illegal firearm in a city where you're a total stranger? I'm impressed." Of course, she neither looked nor sounded it. She didn't care about his career choice, didn't care whether he made money to spend on her or was poor as a pauper. In fact, he wasn't sure exactly what it was about him that she did care about. That he loved her? Didn't make demands on her? Didn't snoop into her past?

"Why don't you get dressed again, and we'll get some lunch?" he suggested, settling on his side of the bed and turning on the television as she sat up. Nothing on the tube, though, could be as enticing as that long stretch of flawless pale skin, broken only by the pale blue scraps of her bra and panties. She looked so fragile, as if one tight embrace might shatter her, but she was the strongest woman he knew.

"On second thought..." He traced one fingertip down her spine, past the narrow span of her waist, over the flare of her hip.

With a throaty chuckle, she brushed his hand away and stood. "Not without lunch. Watch the news. It won't take me long." Without false modesty, she strolled to the closet, took out a sleeveless dress in silvery blue, and pulled it over her head. She managed the back zip without any problem, though he would have been happy to offer his help. After stepping into sandals with killer heels, she went into the bathroom, leaving the door partly open.

The leading stories had been covered and the weather updated—hotter and muggier—by the time Charlize returned. She'd twisted her hair up in a knot that left her elegant neck bare and touched up her makeup, coloring her lips a soft, kissable pink. She'd refreshed her perfume, as well, its sweet, exotic scent drifting on the air between them. For a time she stood near the doorway, just looking at him.

"What?" he asked at last.

"You're not planning to kill her, are you?" For all the emotion in her voice, she might have been asking if he was planning to go out dressed the way he was. He wasn't fooled, though. She didn't indulge in small talk, didn't ask unimportant questions.

"Jesus, hon." He rose from the bed and crossed to her in three strides, taking both of her hands in his. "Look, I may not like working for Selena, and I'm probably not gonna do it too much longer, but that doesn't mean I want her dead. Charlize, you know me. I don't kill people without a reason, and not liking her isn't a good reason."

She gazed at him another moment, then smiled. "No, of course it isn't. Come on. Let's find someplace exquisite to eat."

But taking over Selena's business *was* a good reason to kill her, a sly voice whispered in his head as he followed her from the room. And that was exactly what he was intending. The idea had been in his mind for a while, just a possibility, odds for not doing it as good as they were for doing it, but this morning, when he'd laid out a wad of cash for the pistol, it had become a decision. He didn't want to work for her. He didn't want to be her goddamn partner. And so he had to kill her.

Not that Charlize needed to know that. She liked Selena—maybe because they were both cool and aloof. Maybe because neither made friends easily. Hell, maybe it was because of the paintings that had hung in Charlize's bedroom for years.

Whatever the reason, this was one decision he would keep

to himself. The less Charlize knew about it, the safer they would all be.

Damon sauntered into the ballroom after lunch, a bottle of water in one hand. Selena and Robinette were downstairs, waiting on Sonny, Gentry was a few yards behind him, and Jamieson was already at work on the computer near a side window. As the redhead plopped into a chair at one end of the table, Damon grabbed another chair and dragged it over to Jamieson's table, swinging it around so he could straddle it and rest his arms on the back.

Giving him a wary look, Jamieson closed the laptop, though not with the panic he'd shown a couple of nights before. "Do you want something?"

"I'm just curious about what you're doing."

Jamieson glanced over his shoulder at Gentry, then at the stairs. "That's not really any of your business."

"Oh, son, in this job *everything* is my business."

"I report to Mr. Robinette and to Ms. McCaffrey. Not you."

"Wrong answer. What are you up to?" Damon reached out to lift the laptop screen, but Jamieson laid his hand over it. Damon didn't force it, but settled his arms on the chair back again. "You know and I know that wasn't any kind of chat room or instant message thing that you were in the other night. All those numbers, all that data—looked to me more like . . . oh, I don't know"—he raised the bottle to his mouth and took a long drink before tossing out a bluff—"financial information."

The guy was a piss-poor actor. His Adam's apple bobbed when he swallowed, and a thin line of sweat broke out across his forehead. "You're wrong. I was just talking. It was a private conversation. That's why I reacted the way I did."

"Well, you got the 'private' part right." Book-smart, soft, and harmless—that had been Damon's first assessment of Jamieson. Though he didn't like being wrong, he did like having leverage over people. If he dug up some dirt on Gentry, he'd be three for three on Selena's private hires. "How hard do you think it will be to prove that you're stealing the boss's money?"

Jamieson's shrug did nothing to counter the fear in his eyes. "It'd be impossible because I haven't taken a dime. I was going over Yates's financial records and instant-messaging someone I know. You just happened to come in between messages. So you go ahead and tell the boss you caught me doing my job. See what she says."

It was a decent bluff, but it was too little, too late. Damon trusted his gut, and it said Jamieson was a lying weasel.

Footsteps and voices came from the stairwell an instant before Selena and Robinette—lying weasel number two—appeared. Sonny Yates was with them.

Damon got to his feet, then leaned close to Jamieson. "A word of advice—you're about the worst liar I've ever seen. Work on it before it gets you killed." He picked up the chair, then grinned. "We'll talk again. Soon."

Damon sat at the table across from Sonny and listened with half a mind while Selena outlined her offer. She looked so cool and capable—trained by the old bastard himself. What would Sonny think if he knew her computer wiz was tampering with the records and her chief advisor was in cahoots with the FBI? He'd probably kill her where she sat.

Then he'd probably kill Damon, too.

That wasn't going to happen. Damon would be walking out of this alive and wealthier than he'd ever been.

"Fifty percent." Sonny leaned back in his chair, a look of interest—and greed—on his face as he considered the offer. "Equal shares."

Damon slumped back in his own chair, watching him. Like everybody in this business, the prospect of more money tempted him. Everybody except Selena. Here she was fucking giving it away, in the hopes that it would make Yates a good and loyal partner. Hell, any idiot could tell her that wasn't the way it worked. It wasn't loyalty that had kept William's empire under control all these years. Fear, intimidation, threats, and the willingness to carry them out—that was what kept it on track. More money might persuade Yates to set aside any plans to kill her for a while, but he wouldn't forget them. Once he knew she was willing to pay him off, he would be coming back in no time asking for sixty percent, then seventy, eighty, ninety.

And when there was no more for her to give, he would kill her and take the whole business for himself. If she lived that long.

"Not exactly equal," Selena said. "That's half again as much as you're making now, without a corresponding increase in responsibilities."

"And in exchange, I won't have you killed." Sonny grinned. "And since I haven't tried yet, I'm happy to take money to continue not doing something I'm already not doing."

Damon didn't have a clue whether there was any truth to that. The logical choice for the man behind the hits in Savannah was Barnard Taylor. Selena had insulted him by meeting with Sonny first; he was from Philly; Buddy Tarver was from

Philly and used to work for Barnard—maybe still did, at least until someone blew off his face.

But Carl Heinz was from Philly, too. He'd already tried to kill her once under Damon's direction—incompetent asshole—and he had the knowledge necessary to hook up with the likes of Tarver. When he disappeared from Tulsa, maybe he hadn't gone into hiding from the law—or, just as likely, from Damon—but had headed east. Maybe he had more of a backbone, or was more afraid, than Damon had believed.

And Sonny was smart enough to make it look as if Barnard was guilty. So was Vernell. So were half the fucks who worked for them.

Bottom line, Damon didn't give a shit who was trying to kill her. As he'd said before, dead was dead.

"Do we have a deal?" Selena asked.

"Sure," Sonny replied. "We have a deal. You're safe with me."

Now, that was a lie. No one but William had ever been safe with Sonny boy, and that was only because of his anonymity. Sonny couldn't kill a ghost, and that was exactly what William had been, hidden by distance, lies, and a false identity, and protected by Damon.

Before Selena could respond to that, her cell phone rang. She excused herself from the table and went to the far end of the ballroom to answer. Jamieson returned to his computer, but Robinette remained where he was, seated at the end of the table watching them. Damon didn't have a clue where the hell Gentry was, and cared less.

"Where're Devlin and LeRoy?" he asked idly.

"They stayed behind to take care of things in Savannah." Sonny toyed with the only thing left on the table—the keys to his own rental—as he casually asked, "What's it like working for her instead of the old man?"

"Not much different. He taught her everything she knows." Those damn frigid smiles, the smugness that made him want to choke the life out of her, the way of looking at him as if he was nothing more than a bug she'd generously decided not to squish.

"When's your court date?"

Damon shrugged. "Don't know. Don't care."

"Don't intend to be there?" Sonny asked sardonically.

Damon shrugged again.

"I'm impressed—her being able to get you out of jail on such serious charges."

"It's nothing you wouldn't have done for Devlin or LeRoy, is it?" Damon paused, then grinned. "Or is it something you *couldn't* have done?"

As he'd expected, Sonny boy stiffened and puffed up. "I've never had any problem taking care of my people. Besides, I wouldn't have given such important jobs to a flunky. J.T. would have handled them, and the cops never would have had a damn clue."

"The cops were *supposed* to have a clue. That's the way William wanted it." He'd enjoyed the games, proving he was smarter, leaving clues but staying three steps ahead. But Joe Ceola had thrown a wrench in the old bastard's plans and everything had changed.

"Flunky?" he continued mildly. "Is that supposed to piss me off?" He'd been called worse names. It didn't bother him in the least. He knew he'd been the real reason for the success of William's business. Anyone who had doubts would see for themselves somewhere down the line. He would have a new base of operations, of course, and a new identity, but he would find a way to make sure the important people knew what he was doing.

"Mr. Robinette."

Everyone turned to look at Selena, holding the phone at her side, gesturing for her own flunky to join her. Looking disgruntled, he left the table, and Damon turned back to Sonny. "I can do better than her offer."

"You?" Sonny looked amused.

"You don't want to be her fuckin' partner any more than I do. William gave her a profitable business on a silver platter, and she's cuttin' it up into so damn many pieces that no one's gonna have much of anything when she's done."

"She *increased* my share."

"Yeah. Mine, too. And she's gonna increase a lot of other people's shares. Where's that money gonna come from? By the time she's through handing out all her raises and partnerships, expenses are gonna go way the fuck up, which means profits are gonna go way the fuck down. Your fifty percent's gonna be worth less than the thirty-five percent you're already getting."

Sonny boy sat looking at him as if he'd never thought of that. Of course, he hadn't known she was planning to hand out money all around. Damon leaned closer and lowered his voice. "I'll tell you something else—there's something not right here. I don't know if it's Selena or that guy, Robinette, but—"

Sonny cleared his throat, and Damon broke off an instant before Robinette appeared in his peripheral vision. Grinding his teeth, he forced a grin. "There used to be this little redhead by the name of Ginger—worked at Tommy Beaudry's place on the way to Beaufort. Holy shit, that girl was something."

"Yeah, I know Ginger," Sonny said. "I haven't seen her in a long time, but then, I don't frequent Beaudry's place."

Sitting back in his chair again, Damon glanced at Selena, then Robinette. "She gonna get off the phone and join us again, or are we supposed to sit here and twiddle our thumbs?"

"Don't complain, Long," the asshole replied. "You could be twiddling yours in jail."

"Yeah, like this is so damn much better."

But it was going to get better. He was going to get rid of Selena, and the bracelet, and Robinette and that thieving Jamieson. He was going to inherit the business that had been rightfully his all along, and he was going to stay hell and gone from prison. With a little luck.

And Damon had always had a little luck.

They sealed the deal with a handshake that made Selena wish for hot water and industrial-strength disinfectant. She resisted the urge to scrub her hand on her skirt and, instead, smiled coolly. "I'll see you to the door. I'm sure you're anxious to get home."

"Yeah. Charlize and I are catching a flight back this evening."

They were booked on an evening flight—Robinette had checked that earlier. She was looking forward to hearing the agent say they'd made the flight and were on their way back to Savannah. She would feel marginally safer with Yates halfway across the country.

They chatted about nothing down two flights of stairs, Robinette directly behind them, and across the foyer. At the door, Yates paused, then offered his hand again. "To a long and mutually profitable partnership."

She clasped his hand loosely, then let go as soon as she could. "Have a safe trip. And give my best to Charlize."

"I will." He acknowledged Robinette with a nod, then walked out the door.

Selena shifted so she could watch through the living room windows as he strolled past. A moment later came the distant sound of an engine, then a glimpse of the car as he drove toward the gate. Immediately she turned to Robinette, ready to finish the conversation spurred by the phone call she'd received a short time earlier. It had been Tony, asking once again on Kathryn Hamilton's behalf if Selena would talk with the woman. Selena wanted to say yes. Robinette insisted on no.

He raised his hand before she could open her mouth. "Kathryn Hamilton can't help with this case."

"It isn't about the case."

"The case is our only interest."

"It's not *my* only interest, and it's certainly not Mrs. Hamilton's. She wants to ask about Henry—"

"William."

"—and I have a few questions myself. It doesn't relate to the investigation at all, so there can't possibly be any harm."

"William *is* the fucking investigation—" His face tinged pink. He drew a breath, then, giving the pretense of calm except for the rigid muscles in his jaw, he said, "You don't need to be discussing him with anybody, especially his sister."

"Why not? She knew nothing about his business. You said yourself that his family was cleared from the start. All she wants is to know more about her brother. All I want is to know more about myself. You can sit in on the conversation if you'd like. You can even stop us if we venture into forbidden territory, but we *are* going to talk."

"Aren't you a little old to be pining for Daddy?"

She lifted her chin and gave him her haughtiest look. "I'm not pining for anyone."

She wanted to know who she was, where she came from, what her personal history was, whether anything she'd been told was even remotely true. She wanted to know how William had betrayed Kathryn, if she knew anything about Selena's parents, why he'd made the choices he had. She wanted to know everything Kathryn could tell her about him...though she *didn't* want to tell everything she knew about him. It was one thing to discuss William the murdering drug dealer with people who already knew that side of him, but another entirely with the sister who'd wholeheartedly believed in his honorable, respectable, law-abiding facade.

Robinette impatiently dragged his fingers through his hair. "You want to bring her here, to her brother's house where you're pretending to a bunch of dangerous people that you're a drug dealer."

"It *is* her brother's house, and will probably be her house once he dies. I don't believe anyone would be surprised at seeing her here. Besides, drug dealers don't live in isolation behind their tall fences. Yates has a social life. William had a very active social life. It wouldn't shock anyone who happens to be watching if I at least have a guest from time to time." She folded her arms across her middle. "If it concerns you so much, though, I'd be perfectly happy to meet Mrs. Hamilton someplace else."

"We don't have another secure location handy."

"Tony's house is as secure as any, more so than most. My house is safe, as well."

"Oh, yeah, let's go jump in the car and take a leisurely drive over to Princeton Court, which we *know* the PI found out about and God only knows who he told."

She allowed a small smile. "Then it appears Mrs. Hamilton will have to come here."

"She knows the house is being used for this operation—we got her permission to avoid having to get a court order. But she *doesn't* know that you're part of it. You'd be willing to risk compromising your safety just to get some answers about your past?" he asked scornfully, studying her with his cold blue gaze.

She laughed, truly amused for the first time in days. "Mr. Robinette, everything I've done with you people has been just to get some answers about my past." She paused, and the mirth disappeared. "I want to meet with Mrs. Hamilton."

"Fine. Have your boyfriend bring her here. Risk everything." He made an impatient gesture as he started for the stairs. "You know, you're not the most cooperative cooperating witness I've ever worked with."

"I'm not the least, either," she said with a faint smile as she fished her cell phone from her pocket.

Tony answered on the first ring. Just the sound of his simple hello went a long way toward easing the tension humming through her. "My guest is gone," she said in place of a greeting. "You can deliver Mrs. Hamilton whenever you're ready."

"You sound anxious to see her."

"Nah." Her voice softened as she smiled. "I'm anxious to see *you*."

"Me, too, babe. Where are we going to meet?"

"Here at the estate."

There was a long silence. "The FBI agreed to that?"

"Not happily, but yes."

"Okay. We'll be there soon, babe. Love you."

"I love you, too," she murmured.

After returning the phone to her pocket, she went to her

room to touch up her makeup, then refresh her cologne. She *was* anxious, she realized as she studied herself in the mirror. Mrs. Hamilton was William's closest relative. She could have been as much an aunt to Selena as he'd been an uncle; she could have been family . . . if he'd given them the chance. If he hadn't kept Selena secret.

Now, because of that secrecy, the woman probably resented Selena for being a part of her brother's life that he'd kept from her. She probably blamed Selena.

Her smile was faint, her eyes too shadowed and wide for it to be convincing. If Kathryn Hamilton resented and blamed her, she wouldn't be the first. If she wanted nothing further to do with her, that wouldn't be anything new, either. She was used to that.

Sick of it, but used to it.

15

The grandfather clock in the foyer chimed four times, quiet bongs that reverberated through the cavernous space. Jamieson, still in the ballroom, paused in his work to listen to its faint echoes, remembering an ugly old clock his mother had once had. Shaped like a birdhouse, it had chimed the hours, too, as a tiny bluebird popped out of its hole. It had sounded tinny and cheap, because it *was* tinny and cheap, but it had been one of her treasures.

How far he'd come from that shabby house and that shabby life...and how far he had to fall. That was one of the advantages of being dirt-poor. You didn't know anything better, and if things got worse, hell, you couldn't get much poorer. But now he had so much to lose—his wife, his kids, his house, his pride, his dignity.

He *couldn't* lose.

But he was so damn close to total defeat. Damon Long knew what he'd done. All he had to do was tell Selena, and Robinette would have the Bureau's top financial crimes people going through Davis's and Yates's records with a fine-tooth comb. A damned murderer was walking around free, and Jamieson, who'd done nothing more than try to take care of his family, would be locked away for years.

His hand trembled, making the cursor move jerkily across the computer screen. He was having trouble breathing. His chest hurt and his gut knotted. If he was a lucky man, he would have a heart attack and die. Jen would still find out what a failure he was, what a disappointment, but she would get over it. And the kids—

He tried to take a breath, but wheezed instead. When a hand thumped him on the back, he jerked away, first startled, then sickened to see Long.

"You ought to see a doctor about that," Long said as he pulled a chair closer and sat down. "It doesn't sound good."

"What do you want?" Jamieson's voice came out soft, quavery, even though there was no one around to hear. Robinette intended to stay downstairs until Selena's meeting with Mrs. Hamilton and Detective Ceola was over, and Gentry was fiddling with her surveillance equipment in a second-floor bedroom. That left him to watch over Long.

"Oh . . . a million would be a good start."

Jamieson stared at him, uncomprehending. "A million . . . dollars?" Now his voice was squeaky. "You want a million dollars? Where am I supposed to get that?"

"The magic world of online banking." Long tapped the computer with one knuckle. "Take half of it from William's accounts and half from Sonny's. Might as well screw 'em both."

"But—you've got to be—I can't—"

"Afford to piss me off." All humor was gone from Long's voice, and the look in his eyes . . . This was the real Damon Long, the one who had committed so many murders that even he couldn't put a number to them. The psychopath who didn't give a damn about any life but his own. "You've got the computer. You've got the access. Transfer a million dollars into this account." Picking up a pen, he scrawled the information on the legal pad next to the computer, then sat back, one ankle crossed over the other knee, looking relaxed and *normal*.

Jamieson sat there. He was scared spitless. He couldn't even move. Dear God, if he stole a million dollars for this killer, he'd be no better than a common criminal.

He risked a look at Long. And if he didn't, he'd be better off dead.

"You got a wife? Kids?"

He couldn't answer.

"Women like expensive things, don't they? And kids... gotta wear the right clothes, hang out at the right places, own all the latest technology. Costly little fuckers."

Jen and the kids weren't the problem. *He* was. He wasn't smart enough, successful enough, savvy enough. All he needed was a hand, a little help to get out of this hole he'd found himself in, then he could make it on his own.

Could he trust Damon Long to offer that hand? Maybe. Maybe not. But he *could* trust Long to destroy him if he refused.

"Come on, man. Get moving before one of your bosses comes back and you have to explain what you're doing." Long's voice turned steely. "Transfer the money. While you're at it, take a hundred grand for yourself."

A hundred thousand dollars. That would be enough to get him out of that hole. He'd planned to take that, plus another fifty thousand for a safety net, and not one penny more. And all he had to do to get it was fulfill Long's request. A onetime transfer.

It would save his life.

He took a breath, curled his fingers around the mouse, and began clicking.

Long opened one of those damned motorcycle magazines he was never without and began flipping through the pages. "By the way," he said idly, "while you're at it... leave a trail that leads back to Selena."

• • •

Confused, Kathryn parked near the end of the steps, then joined Tony. "I don't understand...why are we here?" *Here* was home, the family mansion where she'd grown up, where apparently Henry had grown away.

She'd told Jefferson that there weren't any bad memories for her there, but as she gazed at Tony, all she could see was the I-love-me wall in Henry's bedroom, with that photograph of his "niece." All she could think was how he'd betrayed her. Lied to her. How he continued to threaten her.

Tony took her arm and politely urged her to climb the steps with him. "Selena is staying here temporarily."

"But...how can that be? I knew nothing about this. I didn't give permission to her, only to the FBI—" Her breath caught. "She's part of Henry's drug business. She's the associate who's working with the FBI to destroy it."

"Not in the way you think."

She shook her head, dismissing him. Obviously, the girl had influenced Henry, had brought him to his terrible end. Hadn't he predicted that she would be nothing but trouble before she was even born? How ironic—how fitting—that the girl had brought the trouble Henry had predicted to *him* instead of Kathryn.

Though Kathryn was getting her share of it—along with her share of reassurance. *She* wasn't responsible for what had happened to Henry. *She* bore no blame. It was all his fault, and the girl's. Selena's.

Tony stopped at the door and reached for the bell, but hesitated. "Selena is helping the FBI, but she's not involved in the way you think. She was never a part of the business, though Henry had always intended for her to be. He'd made no secret of the fact that he wanted her to take over when he retired. That's why she's been able to step in now and work with the FBI. But she's not a drug dealer. She's not a criminal at all."

She had wormed her way into Henry's life, then she'd helped destroy him. In Kathryn's opinion, that was as criminal as behavior could get.

"Are you ready?"

She looked at Tony, then the door. Would she ever be truly ready to come face-to-face with the girl who'd haunted her for twenty-eight years? The answer was a swift and vehement no. But she had to know what Selena knew. Her future, her peace of mind, her very life, depended on it.

Not trusting her voice to work, she nodded, and he rang the bell. She concentrated on breathing, forcing thick, damp air into her lungs, letting it out slowly. She was a Daniels by birth, a Hamilton by marriage. She could stand up to Selena McCaffrey.

She expected a servant to answer the bell—servants had *always* answered the bell in this house—so she wasn't prepared to see the girl standing there when the door opened. Wasn't prepared for the renewed shock of seeing her familiar features. For the rush of panic and fear and loathing. Pure, icy loathing for this bastard black girl who dared to take up residence in the Daniels family home, to destroy Henry's life. Who dared even to exist.

"Kathryn Hamilton, Selena McCaffrey," Tony said, then stepped aside so Kathryn could enter her own family home the way a mere guest would.

"Mrs. Hamilton," Selena said, her voice quiet, her accent faint and exotic. She'd been raised in Puerto Rico and Jamaica, according to Tony, though how she'd gotten there was anybody's guess. No, not a guess, Kathryn amended. Henry knew. She really was very lovely, naturally. She was elegant and poised, qualities paid for by Daniels family money. She was exquisite. And Kathryn loathed her.

Selena didn't offer her hand. Bad manners? Or instinctive understanding that Kathryn didn't want to touch her? "Come in, please, and we'll talk."

Nudged by Tony, Kathryn forced her feet to move, to cross the threshold and follow Selena through the double doorway across from the library. The room was a deliberate choice; the girl was well aware that white-on-white wasn't the best backdrop for Kathryn's pale blond hair, fair skin, or ice-blue suit. With her own black hair, café-au-lait skin, and vividly colored clothing, though, it was the perfect stage for *her*.

"Can I get you something to drink?"

Playing hostess in Kathryn's own home, as if she belonged there. As if she could *ever* belong there. But Kathryn tamped down her outrage and fixed a polite smile on her face. "No, thank you." She took a seat on a white sofa, then smoothed her hand over a gold brocade pillow.

Tony chose a position near the fireplace, while Selena sat on the opposite sofa, a tropical creature in full Technicolor glory. It was so very easy to see what had attracted Henry to her—such beauty, such potential, such familiarity. Had he given even one thought to his sister before he'd taken the girl in? Had he cared one bit what Kathryn would think, how she would feel, if she found out? Of course, he'd never intended her to find out...but the answer was still no. Henry had cared for Henry, and the hell with everyone else.

Seconds ticked past, each one urging Kathryn to speak, say something, ask something, though the one thing that came immediately to mind—*Why aren't you dead?*—was hardly appropriate. Remember who you are, she exhorted herself. *Remember what she is.*

"I appreciate your seeing me." Good. She sounded calm, rational, polite. "I confess to being totally surprised when I was told about you. I had no idea..."

"Most people didn't. William liked to keep his secrets."

"William—is that what you called him?"

Selena nodded. "I didn't know his real name until a few weeks ago."

His real name. According to the FBI, Selena McCaffrey was hardly *her* real name. Did she even know the name she'd been given at birth? Kathryn did—and she intended to take it to her grave with her.

"You're very lovely. I see why my brother was attracted to you."

"It was never like that," Selena said stiffly. "He called me his niece, and he treated me as such."

"Of course. I didn't mean... You understand, this has all been such a shock. I apologize if I implied..." Kathryn clasped, then unclasped, her hands, causing the diamonds on three fingers to flash in the sunlight coming through the west windows. "I have to admit, I'm curious about why he chose to claim you as his niece. Why not simply say he was your guardian? Wouldn't that have been easier?"

"Perhaps. There was always the inevitable curiosity about how this very white man came to have a biracial niece. Of course, Willia—Henry being Henry, people rarely voiced that curiosity to him." Selena smoothed the silk of her skirt over one thigh, the first movement she'd made since sitting down. She was very contained, very composed. "For whatever reason, claiming a familial connection suited him. Maybe it had to do with the fact that he was looking for an heir for what he called his family business."

He'd certainly had a thing about family, Kathryn thought. Blood was blood; heritage was important; legacies and fortunes stayed within the family. That was why he'd ignored Jefferson. But to take in Selena . . . "He had heirs," she pointed out, working to keep her voice calm. "His real family. Me and my son, Jefferson."

"Perhaps he didn't think either of you would be interested in inheriting certain portions of his estate."

Kathryn raised one hand to her chest and tilted her head to gaze at the painting above the fireplace, a cool, wintry scene of gray skies and snow. "You're talking about his drug business. That would have broken Grandmama and Grandpapa's hearts, and our parents . . . ! They would be so ashamed. God help me, I'm glad they're dead so they can't know what he's done."

After a moment, she closed her eyes, drew a breath, then faced Selena again. "How did you happen to meet Henry? Tony tells me he saved your life."

Selena nodded. She folded her hands together in her lap, glanced at Tony, then squared her shoulders. "I lived in Ocho Rios at the time. One night a man assaulted me. He was attempting to rape me when Henry stopped him."

"What did he do?"

Again she hesitated, again looking at Tony. "He killed the man."

Her brother had killed for this girl. That must have been when he'd developed a taste for murder, for criminal activity. The knowledge brought Kathryn relief beyond measure. That put the blame for everything he'd done since then squarely on Selena. Not Kathryn.

"So he rescued you and you . . . went to live with him? Just like that? What about—" Dragging air into her lungs, Kathryn forced her hands to lie flat, commanded the queasiness in her belly to contain itself, and focused on keeping her voice steady. "What about your parents? What were they thinking, letting their daughter go off to live with a strange man?"

Selena shrugged with a carelessness she couldn't quite pull off. "My mother—or, at least, the woman I knew as my mother—was no longer a part of my life. As for my father, I never even knew his name. In fact, I was hoping to ask you a few questions about them."

"I don't know what I could possibly tell you, but go ahead and ask, please."

"Were you familiar with any of Henry's friends?"

"In high school and college, when they spent much of their free time here. After that ... we lived different lives in different states."

"Were any of them black?"

Kathryn's answer came quickly. "Oh, no. Certainly not." Then her eyes widened, and she made an apologetic little face. "Not that I—Henry did have black friends over the years, I'm sure—It's just that ..." She gave a helpless shrug, drew a breath, and made a show of regaining her composure. "Your father was black?"

"I always thought so. The woman I thought was my mother was Puerto Rican. But Henry wrote something in his journal that suggests Luisa wasn't my mother. If that's the case, my mother could be black, and my father could be anyone. Someone Henry knew or worked with. I'm hoping to learn more from his journals."

Kathryn's smile trembled despite her best efforts. "His journals? Dear heavens, he never gave up that silly habit of keeping a diary? We had more fusses over that when we were growing up. He loved to scribble out all his thoughts, and I loved to ferret out his hiding places and read them to my girl-friends. I thought he'd stopped that when he went away to college."

Selena merely shook her head.

"Well...I won't keep you any longer. I appreciate your taking the time to see me." Kathryn stood, but raised one hand when Selena started to do the same. "Don't bother seeing me out. I know the way." With a nod for Tony, she walked from the room, out the door, and across the porch. She was in her car, seat belt buckled, and backing out of the parking space, before her fixed, tight smile started to quiver.

Damn Henry's soul. He'd always thought he was so damn superior, smarter and better than everyone else, and he'd been nothing but a damn fool. Betraying his sister hadn't been enough. Taking in Selena McCaffrey hadn't satisfied him. Turning to a life of crime and tarnishing the Daniels name forever hadn't made him happy. No, he'd also had to put his deeds in writing. He was going to be the ruin of her yet.

Unless she took drastic action.

Tony walked out of a north Tulsa house on Wednesday afternoon and took a deep breath to clear the stench from his lungs. There ought to be a law against killing people during a heat wave, Simmons often groused. After examining a scene that was at least forty-eight hours old—forty-eight hours when the temperature hadn't dropped below eighty-five— Tony agreed with him wholeheartedly.

"How's Selena?"

He glanced at Marla Johnson as she set her kit down beside him. "She's fine." His stock answer. He couldn't wait for the day when it was really true.

"You gonna marry her anytime soon?"

"Yeah." He gave Marla a sidelong look. "That doesn't bother you, does it?"

"That you had no interest in marrying me, then went off and fell in love with the first woman who tried to kill you? Of course not. Why would it bother me?" Then she batted her lashes. "Does it bother you that I just married someone else? Are you regretting letting me get away?"

Despite the grimness of the morning, he managed a chuckle. She'd been coming on to him ever since they'd met, even after they'd broken up, and he'd never known how to react. Being newly married wouldn't stop her from delivering on those come-ons, but his involvement with Selena offered him some protection. "Sorry. I think you *and* your husband got exactly what you deserved."

She gave him a pouting look before turning her attention back to the house. It sat in the middle of a tough neighborhood, so run-down that it was difficult to tell the occupied houses from the empty ones. Kids came there to drink and do drugs; occasionally transients bedded down on its floors. The body inside could be either, neither, or both. It was hard to say.

"Guess I'd better get back inside and help Flint finish up," Marla said. "Give Selena my best."

He nodded as she climbed the steps to the sagging porch. He was anticipating the next opportunity to give Selena *his* best.

He was heading for the street when Simmons, in his beat-up old Ford, slowed to a stop, rolled down the window, and held up a folder. "Hey, I ran some checks on Charles Hensley and Carl Heinz in Colorado. Didn't come up with anything, at least not on our guy. But Charles Hensley has a brother named Norman, and Norman Hensley does own a cabin in Colorado, outside a little town named Granby. He bought it about four years ago, and just had the utilities connected last week."

"So Charles might be living with his brother."

Tapping the folder on the steering wheel, Simmons shook his head. "Not unless he's crawled into the ground. Norman Hensley died about ten years ago."

"Hell, Frankie, I'm impressed. That's damn good police work." And tedious as hell—the kind Simmons, in particular, had little patience for.

"Hey, I did it for Island Girl—to say nothing of having you in my debt," Simmons said with a grin. "I called the sheriff's department up there in Grand County. They're gonna pick him up."

"Thanks. I do owe you." Tony took the folder, then extended his hand. Surprised, Simmons shook it.

He glanced around. "You gonna do some knock-and-talks?"

"I'm gonna knock. In this neighborhood, I'm not sure anyone's gonna talk."

"Ain't that the truth? I've gotta show up in court, but if you find someone you think knows something, I'll come back when I'm done and beat it out of 'em."

"Thanks." Tony stepped back and watched him drive away.

By the time he'd questioned neighbors on both sides of the street, the crime-scene unit was gone. He decided to take a break for lunch, then he would head over to the ME's office.

He hadn't driven more than a few blocks when his cell phone rang. He didn't waste time wishing it would be Selena—she rarely called—but pulled it free from his waistband and answered without looking at the caller ID display.

"Detective Ceola, this is Kevin Stark."

Tony scowled. "What do you want?"

"Actually, I think it's more along the lines of something

you need. I had an interesting phone call just now—somebody feeling me out on the best way to eliminate a problem."

"You mean to put out a hit."

"Yeah. Now, I'm not into murder-for-hire, and normally I would've just said so and hung up except..."

Except that operating as he did, it was always to his benefit to have a cop who would cut him some slack when his information was good.

"Well?" Tony prompted impatiently.

"I didn't get the target's name—just a description. A half-Hispanic, half-black woman who's currently living in that big ol' fancy house on Riverside Drive. Sound like someone you know?"

A headache started pounding right between Tony's eyes. "Did you get the caller's name?"

"Nope. Wouldn't give it. But I did say to call back tomorrow so I could ask around."

"Could you recognize his voice? Was there anything distinctive about it?"

Stark chuckled. "I didn't peg you for a sexist, Detective. You know people who hire killers aren't always guys."

"It was a woman?" That was a change. So far, everyone who wanted Selena dead was male.

"Whaddya think?" Stark chuckled. "Wanna be listening when she calls back?"

It was funny how the mind adapted. Two weeks ago, if someone had told Selena there was a contract on her life, she would have been surprised first, then frightened. Wednesday afternoon, as she sat behind closed doors in the library with Robinette and listened to Tony repeat his conversation with the private investigator, she felt neither surprise nor fear. One more person wanting her dead didn't seem that big a cause for concern.

"According to Stark, it was a woman's voice," Tony said, "and she had a Southern accent."

"Who've you dealt with lately who has a Southern accent?" Robinette asked sourly as he looked at her.

Selena shrugged. She was the only one who'd chosen to sit. Tony was absently toying with an alabaster carving on the mantel, and Robinette was pacing from one end of the room to the other. "My social life isn't exactly a whirl of activity these days."

He pivoted to face her. "Names."

She drew an impatient breath. "Charlize Pawley. Did she and Yates make their flight last night?"

Robinette nodded. "If it's her, why not ask Yates to take care of it? It wouldn't have cost her a thing. Who else?"

She glanced at Tony. "Kathryn Hamilton. William's sister."

"God—" Robinette broke off and clenched his jaw, no doubt to keep the profanity inside. "I told you you shouldn't meet with her. I told you it was a bad idea."

"If it'll make you feel any better, I'd be happy to go on record saying, yes, you did."

He shot a scowl in her direction as he paced to the far wall again. "Okay, why would Charlize want you dead? Because she could be a part of Yates's business. Or maybe she's not a part, but she's trying to look out for his best interests. Why would Kathryn Hamilton want to kill you?"

Before Selena could answer, Tony set the carving down, pushed his hands in his pockets, and said, "Gee, her brother goes head to head with Selena and winds up good as dead. I've seen weaker motives."

Robinette looked as if he wanted to argue, but shrugged instead. "And I've seen stronger ones."

"Mrs. Hamilton resents my presence in her family home and in William's life," Selena said. "She doesn't like me because I'm black, because he kept me a secret, because he chose me, because he intended to leave me his drug empire, because he treated me like family when I'm not." The woman had been polite enough, under the circumstances, but there had been an undercurrent to everything she'd said. Not evil, necessarily, or danger—just strong emotion. She'd suffered some great shocks recently, and hadn't yet dealt with them.

"Yeah. Well, we'll keep her on the list." Finally, Robinette stopped pacing and faced her, hands on hips. "So our only real suspects are Ms. Pawley and Mrs. Hamilton. Or it could be someone you've never met, making the call for someone else, like our friends in Philadelphia and Boston—or, closer to home, good ol' Damon out in the guesthouse."

"How would Long get in touch with somebody?" Tony asked, his gaze narrowed. "You're supposed to be watching him twenty-four hours a day."

"We are, and he hasn't made any phone calls yet. But who knows? Maybe he had some sort of prearranged deal." A sly look came into Robinette's eyes. "Your sister, Lucia... she doesn't have a Southern accent, does she?"

The outward changes in Tony were minimal—the slight tensing of a muscle in his jaw, his dark gaze chilling a few degrees—but the tension radiating from him was palpable. It was hard enough for him to accept that his baby sister had fallen in love with a multiple murderer. Knowing that others knew, especially the FBI, must be even harder.

But he didn't respond to Robinette's question. Locking gazes with the man, he coldly said, "Speculating on who it is, is pointless. All you can do is guess. Tomorrow we should know for sure. We've already got a wiretap order for Stark's phone, and Simmons and I—"

"Whoa, hold up there," Robinette said, one hand up-raised. "This is an FBI case."

"The FBI has no interest in Stark."

"We damn sure have an interest in the alleged victim. Anyone putting a hit out on *our* witness gives *us* jurisdiction."

Selena could tell from the clenching of Tony's jaw that Robinette was right. "Stark brought it to me."

"And you brought it to us. Now bow out."

"I didn't bring it to you. I'm keeping you informed." Tony went on even though Robinette opened his mouth to respond. "Right now Stark doesn't have a clue why anybody's interested in Selena. That'll change if I'm yanked off the case and your people come barging in. The FBI doesn't get involved in murder-for-hire cases without a reason, and it won't take a genius to figure out that reason."

"We'll trust Stark to keep what he knows to himself."

Tony snorted. "I wouldn't trust Stark as far as you could throw him."

If Robinette took the scornful words personally, he gave no sign of it. "If it's Kathryn Hamilton, she already knows Selena's working with us."

"If it's Charlize Pawley or anyone else, she doesn't. Your cover will be blown, and your case will be history." Tony allowed a faint smile. "So will your career."

He couldn't have chosen a better argument, Selena thought. All that mattered to Robinette was his job. No way was he going to put it on the line for a pissing contest with a cop.

The silence lengthened as Robinette considered Tony's words—or, at least, pretended to. She had no doubt he'd seen the wisdom immediately, but was merely waiting so his agreement would have greater impact. Finally, he shrugged.

"Fine. You guys run with it—but I want to send one of our people along." Before Tony could protest, he raised one hand. "Stark doesn't have to know who he works for. Just pretend he's another cop. But I want our interests represented."

"You mean you want part of the credit when this is done."

Robinette smiled thinly. "I want to make sure our witness is protected. Someone will be in touch with you before tomorrow."

Tony hefted the carving again as Robinette strode away. When the door closed behind the agent, he shifted his gaze to Selena as his fingers tightened around the heavy, compact piece. "Did I ever mention that I played baseball in high school? I bet I could have knocked that smug look right off his face."

"I think that smug look is the only look he has." Grateful to be alone with him, she crossed the room, removed the carving from his grip, and returned it to its place. He slid his arms around her, pulling her until they could get no closer, then he gazed down at her. He was wearing the smile that had captivated her since the first time she'd seen it—the one that made him look younger, handsomer, and free of worries.

She raised one hand to his face, gently tracing the curve of his mouth. "I've missed you."

"Then come home with me."

Disappointment stirred inside her. They had so little time together, and she didn't want to spoil it by arguing. Rising onto her toes, she pressed a kiss to his jaw. "I can't do that." Couldn't walk away from the estate, from the case, from the FBI. Couldn't put Tony's life in danger, couldn't put her own in even more danger.

"I know." He brushed his mouth across her ear, making her shiver. "But a man can hope, can't he?"

"Sure," she murmured. Sometimes hope was the only thing that kept her going.

He slid his fingers into her hair and tilted her face to his. "Just promise me this—you *will* come home when you can."

She nodded, realized that wasn't enough, and whispered, "I swear I will."

Once again he wrapped his arms around her and held her so tightly that she almost missed his own whisper.

"And I'll be waiting."

"Man, I always wanted to spend my day hanging out in some two-bit PI's office, waiting for some damn phone call that might never come," Frank Simmons groused.

Tony didn't take his gaze from the traffic passing by outside. Together with Robinette's agent, a quiet man named Wesley, they'd set up in Stark's office shortly before his regular opening time of 9:00 A.M. Now it was nearly noon, and so far there had been no call from the unknown Southern woman.

"He couldn't have told her to call at a specific time," Simmons went on. "No, that would've been too easy. We could've been outta here at 9:10 if he had."

"You know, you don't have to stick around," Tony said at last.

Simmons gave him a dry look. "You'd be here if it was Suz...though I can't imagine the fool in the world with balls big enough to put out a hit on Suz. She'd make 'im damn sorry."

Tony smiled faintly. To hear Frankie tell it, Suz wore big hair to cover her horns, breathed fire, and ate young linebackers for breakfast. Truth was, she wasn't much bigger than his ten-year-old niece, and neither looked nor acted much tougher. She did have an attitude, but he figured that was necessary, what with her being married to Frankie. She definitely made him toe the line.

"I'm gettin' hungry," Simmons announced. "Why don't you run across the street and get us some burgers?"

Before Tony could answer, the phone on Stark's desk rang. He crossed to it in three strides, put on a pair of headphones, waited while Wesley put on his own headphones, then gestured to Stark to answer.

"This is Kevin Stark," the man said, his tone curt.

"Hello, Mr. Stark. Do you have the information you promised me?" The voice was female, the accent definitely Southern. Tony was disappointed to acknowledge that it very well might be Kathryn Hamilton. He wasn't sure why, but he'd hoped . . . What? That the lust for blood was an aberration in Henry? That it didn't run in the family?

Stark nodded, signaling that it was the same woman. "I've got a name or two for you, but first I need some information."

"What kind of information?" she asked guardedly.

Tony watched as Simmons wrote down the number on the caller ID, identified as a pay phone, then went outside to place a call on his cell phone. The dispatcher would contact telephone security, find out the location of the phone, then dispatch the nearest officer in an unmarked unit to attempt to make an identification, and the crime-scene unit would collect prints from the phone. With any luck, before the day was out, they would know exactly who Selena's latest enemy was and have enough evidence to prove it.

"Like how you picked me to do business with."

"I was referred to you."

"By who?"

A hesitation, then . . . "My lawyer."

Stark was skeptical. "You called your lawyer up, and said, 'I wanna put out a hit,' and he told you to call me?"

"I told my lawyer I needed assistance in dealing with a problem. He made a few inquiries and I was referred to you."

"And who is this lawyer?"

"No one you would know," she said dismissively. "He's located out of state."

"Funny thing—I know people out of state. I just might know him. What's his name? What state is he in?" Stark pressed.

"Patrick James. New York." Lies snatched out of the air. "What does it matter, Mr. Stark? This business is between you and me, no one else. Now, do you have the information for me, or must I go to one of your competitors?"

The manner definitely fit Kathryn. Like Henry, she was used to getting what she wanted when she wanted it with a minimum of hassle.

"It matters," Stark said. "What you're asking me to do can land us both in prison for the rest of our lives. I don't know about you, but I've got other things I'd rather be doing. You don't like me being cautious, then you go find one of my competitors, but they're not gonna be any less careful. Now . . . who's this woman you want taken care of? Where is she? What does she look like?"

There was a long silence before she answered tersely. "Her name is Selena McCaffrey. She's tall, slender, black, has long curly hair and dark eyes. She's very lovely." The bitterness in the last two words was sharp, brittle. "You'll find her at this address." She rattled off the street number for Henry's house with ease.

"I know that place. Iron fence, electronic gates, armed guards. Man, that's gonna affect the price. I'm thinkin' . . . jeez, five thousand."

"That's all?"

Stark chuckled at her surprise. "You wanna pay more, I'd be happy to take it."

Tony had worked plenty of murder-for-hire cases where the payment was five hundred, eight hundred, a thousand dollars. Hell, there were people in Tulsa who would kill a stranger on the street just for fun. But Selena wasn't a stranger on the street; getting to her was a hell of a lot tougher, thank God. The extra security justified the higher price.

"All right," she agreed. "How do I pay you?"

"I take personal checks with the proper ID." Stark laughed again at her stunned silence. "Just kiddin'. Cash. Half up front, half when the job's done."

"How do I get this cash to you?"

"You gotta meet with me. Don't worry—it'll be in public. The shopping mall or grocery store or something."

"Why can't I just mail it?"

"You wanna trust the US mail with twenty-five hundred dollars in cash?"

"I could courier it to your office."

The amusement left his voice. "And leave a paper trail for the cops? Besides, I don't do business with people I haven't met. How do I know *you* aren't a cop?"

She gave a haughty sniff as if insulted by the suggestion. Kathryn took the "servant" part of "public servant" very seriously, Henry had sometimes joked. "Very well. When and where do we meet?"

Tony scrawled on a piece of paper, then slid it over in front of Stark. "Promenade Mall, in the food court, at five this afternoon. That's at Forty-first and—"

"I know where it is. How will I know you?"

"I'll be wearing a yellow-and-green-striped shirt and an

orange Cowboys ball cap. And I'll know you by the twenty-five-hundred dollars you'll be waving in my direction."

"Very well," she said tersely. "If that's all—"

"Hey," Stark interrupted. "What am I supposed to call you?"

The phone line damn near hummed with tension, then the response came in a tone so dark that it made the hairs on Tony's neck stand on end. "You can call me Amelia."

Simmons came back in as Stark hung up and Tony and Wesley removed the headphones. "The call was from a pay phone at Utica Square."

Less than a mile from Tony's and Selena's houses on Princeton Court...and right across the street from Henry's hospital room.

"Darnell Garry got there in time. He's watching her now. Said it was an older woman, blond, pretty, rich. He got pictures. Won't be any prints on the phone, though. She was holding the receiver with a Kleenex or something."

Older, blond, pretty, rich—a fair description of Kathryn Hamilton. Not wanting to touch a pay phone receiver sounded like her, too. It seemed passions ran deeper in the Daniels family than anyone had given them credit for.

"Now what?" Stark asked.

"We'll be back around four," Tony said. "We'll get you wired before you go to the meeting." They would have officers set up in and around the food court, as well. Photographs and audiotape were good evidence, but money changing hands was better. Once that happened, they would arrest her and Selena would be just a little bit safer.

Too bad the rest of her enemies couldn't be dealt with as easily.

16

Juggling shopping bags and a Frappuccino, Kathryn claimed a small round table outside Starbucks, sat down, and gave a great sigh of relief. The hard part was over. She'd located the right man, made the request, and given him the information he needed. Now all that was left was paying the money and acting shocked by the news.

Thirty-four years married to Grant had made her quite an accomplished actress.

The best part was, for the first time in their lives, she would succeed at thwarting Henry. If he ever woke up, she would take great pleasure in telling him what she'd done. And if he died without regaining consciousness? *She* would know. That would be enough.

As she sipped her frozen drink, she pulled the cell phone from her bag and dialed Jefferson's number. She hadn't seen enough of him since he'd arrived in Tulsa—just that visit Tuesday morning at the hospital and dinner the night before. He'd apologized for holing up in his hotel room and working the whole time, but some things just wouldn't wait for him to return to Florida.

He answered on the second ring. "Hey, baby, it's your mama," she said with the big smile that the sound of his voice always brought. He was the brightest light in her life—at that moment, the only light. "What are you doing?"

"Working," she chimed in at the same time he replied, then went on. "All work and no play, remember."

He chuckled. "I remember. What are you doing?"

"Enjoying an ice-cold vanilla bean creme before heading back to that dreary hospital."

"You could head back to Greenhill. Ol' Henry won't know or care."

"But I'd know. A Daniels does not treat family that way."

This time Jefferson's response was a snort. "That Daniels has ignored this one all his life."

"That was his loss, and now he's paying for it. For once, he's getting exactly what he deserves."

"Wow. I've never heard you talk like that. What happened?"

She fiddled with the straw, stirring through the whipped cream mounded on top of her drink. "I spoke with Charles Aylesworth yesterday. I don't believe you've met him. He's an old friend from my school days, and he's Henry's attorney. Naturally, I asked him about Henry's will."

"And naturally he wouldn't tell you anything."

"Not much. But he did suggest that I would be unpleasantly surprised by the bequests." He had also told her—in strictest confidence, of course—that Henry had ignored Jefferson in death as he had in life. Not so much as one dime to his only close relative besides Kathryn.

No doubt it was Selena McCaffrey's fault.

"He's leaving it all to that girl," she said, feeling her forehead wrinkle into a frown and doing her best to smooth it again. "The Daniels fortune, the Daniels treasures, the Daniels family home, and he's giving it all to that illegitimate black trash that he called niece."

All hint of amusement fled Jefferson's voice. "It's his money, Mama, and it's been his home for forty years. He can leave it to whoever he wants. You don't need the house—your home is in Alabama with Grant—and I certainly don't want it."

"It's not a goddamn matter of needing or wanting!" she snapped, then clamped her hand over her mouth. She never swore in front of Jefferson, never snapped at him. Another thing to blame Henry for. "I'm sorry, baby," she said immediately, but Jefferson cut her off.

"Don't apologize. Under the circumstances, you're entitled to be angry. All these shocks about Henry, and now finding out that he's probably let the family property pass out of family hands . . ."

"That's not going to happen."

"You intend to challenge the bastard's will when he finally kicks off? You know Henry. It will be airtight."

"You're right. It will be." Her fingers curled so tightly around the cup that slush spilled over the top. Scowling, she wiped her fingers with a napkin, then stuffed it inside the cup and sat back. "But she can't inherit if she's not . . . around."

"But she is—" Jefferson's voice dropped to little more than a whisper, and a note of urgency entered it. "Mama, what have you done?"

She pretended a carelessness she was far from feeling. "I just talked to a man who knows a man who . . ." When the private investigator had asked where she'd gotten his name, she'd told him a half-truth. It *had* come via her lawyer back home in Alabama, when she'd called him several weeks ago. She'd asked him to refer her to a lawyer in Tulsa—not for her, of course, she'd convincingly explained, but for one of Henry's nurses who was having problems and was on a limited income. That lawyer had connected her with Mr. Stark, and the rest had been surprisingly easy.

In the beginning, all she'd wanted to know was what

Henry's mysterious "niece" knew. After their visit, she'd learned that Selena already suspected too much and, thanks to Henry's goddamn journals, would soon know *everything*.

"You put out a contract on her?"

Jefferson's shock made her shift uncomfortably in the chair. To shake it off, she stood, gathered her bags in one hand, and started toward the car, talking and walking. "This isn't the time or the place to discuss this, sweetie. Why don't you come to the bed-and-breakfast tonight and—"

"No! And you can't go back there, either! What if this private detective goes to the cops?"

"Why would he do that?"

"Because you're trying to get him to commit murder, for God's sake! Did you just call him up and ask him to kill somebody and he agreed right off the bat?"

"No, of course not. He said he had to ask around. He told me to call him back today, and that's when he agreed."

"Probably because he went to the cops and was getting you on tape. You didn't give him your name, did you?"

"Of course not! I didn't identify myself, and I called from a pay phone. I'm not stupid."

"Mama, you offered money to a complete stranger to kill someone! That's not the brightest move you've ever made!"

She paused for a delivery van to pass, then crossed the street to her rental car in the Saks lot. "Well, pardon me for not knowing the best way to handle a matter like this," she said huffily as she opened the trunk and tossed the bags inside.

"Listen, I want you to go to a hotel, check in under a fake name, and pay cash. Stay away from the bed-and-breakfast and the hospital, and for God's sake, stay away from Selena. Do you understand?"

She got in the car, locked the doors, then pressed her free

hand to the ache in her temple. "No, I don't. This man doesn't know who I am. Even if he did go to the police, how could they possibly connect it to me?"

Jefferson sighed impatiently. "If he called the cops, they would have recorded the call, and they would have sent someone to the pay phone as soon as they identified it. If you were still there, they took pictures of you, and if you weren't, they dusted the phone for fingerprints. They'll play the tape for Selena, who'll recognize your voice after your visit with her, and they'll arrest you." He was silent for a moment, then sounded weary when he spoke again. "Go to a hotel, Mama. Use a fake name. Call me as soon as you get settled—but not on your cell phone. Turn that off and leave it off. Okay?"

"Okay." The panic building inside Kathryn made her voice small. She had been so proud of herself for handling a difficult task all on her own that she hadn't considered for a moment that Mr. Stark might betray her. Dear God, what if she was arrested? She would be humiliated, mortified. And Grant...

Unable to think about Grant's reaction, she forced a sorry smile. "You're a good son, Jefferson, always looking out for your mama."

"If you watched as much television as I do, you would have known better," he said, his own amusement as phony as hers.

"I love you, baby."

"I love you, too. Do what I told you, all right?"

Barnard Taylor was kicked back in his den, a cigar between his fingers, his usual whiskey on the table beside him, and a rerun of *Law & Order* on the big-screen. When the cell phone rang just as the pretty blond assistant D.A. came on the screen, he swore and muted the sound. "Yeah, what?"

"And good evening to you, too."

Mystery Man, Barnard thought, flicking the ash from the cigar. He didn't want to talk to the asshole tonight, and he damn sure didn't want to talk about Selena McCaffrey. He just wanted to smoke his cigar, drink his whiskey, and enjoy *Law & Order*. Was that too goddamned much to ask?

"What do you want?" he growled.

"She did it. Made Sonny Yates a partner."

Squeezing his eyes shut, Barnard swore silently.

"Maybe she's planning to make the same offer to you, or maybe she's not. Maybe she thinks Yates is more valuable to her than you are. What do *you* think?"

Goddamn smug punk, hiding behind anonymous phone calls and secret bank transfers. Holding out one hand for money from Selena, and the other for money to betray her. There was something about respect, honor, loyalty . . .

Loyalty. He'd been loyal to William Davis from day one. He'd had plenty of chances to fuck him over, but he hadn't, because he'd respected the man. He'd owed him.

He didn't owe Selena McCaffrey a goddamn thing.

The bitch-girl had snubbed him. Had gone and made Sonny fucking Yates a partner without taking care of business with Barnard first. What did he think?

He thought it was time to look out for number one.

"Your guys didn't have any luck before," Mystery Man said. "But this is your lucky day, Barney. For the low, low price of two hundred thousand dollars, I can get rid of the biggest headache in your life."

"I already paid you two hundred fucking thousand."

"That was for information. This time I'm offering action. Unlike those other men you paid, *I'll* succeed."

Barnard chomped down hard on his cigar. Part of him wanted to reach through the phone and choke the life out of the little weasel, while the business part was trying to stay calm. He was already out a hell of a lot of money, and what did he have to show for it? Nothing but a fucking bad case of heartburn. If he did nothing, that money was wasted, and he hated waste.

"Okay," he agreed. "But I damn well want results."

"Like I said, Mr. Taylor, I'll get it done. I want half up front, then I'll let you pay the other half when the job's done." There was a quiet determination in Mystery Man's voice, and anticipation as well. He was looking forward to killing Selena, but it was all for the money. Nothing personal, no grudge, just pure old greed. "As always, it's a pleasure doing business with you."

"Pleasure, my ass," Barnard grumbled as he hung up. He'd sooner kill the bastard than hear his voice one more time.

But if the weasel's word was good, he would have to talk to him only one more time. Any contact after that . . . he'd be paying someone else to take care of Mystery Man.

Unable to sleep, Selena slid out of bed with a glance at the clock. A few minutes to midnight—the witching hour, her third mother, Dorotea, had often said. In the years she'd lived with the woman, it had usually been prime work time. By midnight, tourists were tired and often drunk—easy marks for an accomplished little thief.

The phrase reminded her of William, and made her look at the night table drawer where the journal was stored. She could curl up and read some more, but frankly, she wasn't up to learning anything else about herself at the moment. Her head ached, and her chest, her stomach. She felt as if all the tension inside her might coalesce and grow until she exploded into a million pieces.

Instead, she changed into a swimsuit, pulled on a robe, and grabbed a towel, then walked barefooted through the house and onto the patio. The night was hot, still, with lightning arcing across the sky in the distance, promising rain and relief that wouldn't come, not yet. She dropped the robe at the edge of the pool, then dove in, slicing through the water, luxuriating in it. For as long as she could remember, water had been her refuge. As poor as Luisa and Rodrigo had been, they'd lived only yards from the kind of beautiful beach site that people paid fortunes to call their own. She'd spent countless hours on the sand or in the ocean, avoiding Rodrigo, swimming, shelling, dreaming.

She swam, fast and furious, from one end of the pool to the other and back again, until her muscles were warm and her lungs were tight. Flipping onto her back, she floated for a time, her hair drifting in tendrils about her, her attention drifting, too.

There was no doubt that Kathryn Hamilton was the latest person who wanted her dead. Tony had showed her and Robinette the photographs of the woman on the pay phone, had played the tape of the phone call. However, Kathryn hadn't shown up for the meeting with Stark. Maybe she'd had second thoughts. Maybe she'd realized the danger of what she'd started and given it up.

Or maybe she'd hired someone else.

It was a disheartening thing, knowing that a virtual stranger wanted her dead. She wasn't a bad person. She'd never hurt anyone, never taken advantage of anyone. The only thing she was guilty of was trying to survive. It wasn't fair that so damn many people had a problem with that.

She smiled thinly at the night-dark sky. Life wasn't fair,

and she'd never made the mistake of thinking it was. Not in all the times she'd gotten hit for merely existing, or all the nights she'd gone to bed hungry, or all the times fear had practically made her heart burst out of her chest. It was a lesson she'd learned young.

A lesson Kathryn Hamilton was now going to learn.

The Renaissance was one of Tulsa's finest hotels—naturally; Kathryn didn't settle for less than the best—but in her twenty-four-plus hours there, she'd hardly noticed her surroundings. Mostly she had worried . . . but not about Henry. He could die, for all she cared. He was responsible for this mess she was in; he damn well should pay for it.

She'd watched the television news, but there was nothing about her, Mr. Stark, or Selena McCaffrey. She had flipped through the pages of the *World*, and found no mention of her. For a moment, she'd felt a great sense of relief, but it had passed quickly. If the police were looking for her, it didn't seem likely they would advertise that fact in the media.

Several times she had almost succeeded in convincing herself that that was a big *if*. Mr. Stark didn't have her name, phone number, or any other identifying information. But then she remembered the previous day's phone call with Jefferson. Though she still thought it unlikely that the police would be able to connect her to the anonymous phone calls, he adamantly believed otherwise, and he'd fed her doubts.

And so she was in hiding, wearing the same clothes she'd worn the day before, having to make do with the small makeup kit she kept in her purse, feeling unclean and cranky and trapped.

Tired of pacing the room, she sat down at the table where

she'd spilled the contents of her purse looking for lip gloss and tweezers. Her cell phone sat in the midst of the pile, turned off as Jefferson had directed. She gazed at it awhile, picking it up, then laying it down again, before finally taking it in hand and turning it on, despite his warning.

The screen showed a dozen missed calls and five messages. With one manicured nail, she pressed the buttons to retrieve the messages and listened to each one in turn.

"Mrs. Hamilton, it's Tony Ceola. Call me, please, at . . ."

"It's Tony again. I'd like to talk to you when you get the chance. My number . . ."

"Kathryn, it's Grant. Where are you? Call me immediately."

Her fingers tightened around the phone as she squeezed her eyes shut. Grant *never* called when she was traveling. He hardly even noticed she was gone. Dear God, what had happened? Had Tony called him? Had Jefferson?

"Kathryn, what the hell's going on? The police are looking for you! Are you in trouble? Call me, please."

Then the final message: "I'm on my way to Tulsa, Kathryn. Call my cell phone, call Jefferson, or call the police, please. I'm sure this is all just a misunderstanding. We'll get it cleared up in no time. Barring any delays, I'll be there around eight. We'll take care of it."

The phone slipped from her hand as she bowed her head. The private investigator *had* gone to the police. The authorities *were* looking for her. They would arrest her, take her to trial, and give her a probationary sentence of some sort. After all, she was Kathryn Daniels Hamilton.

But that was the least of her problems. Grant would be in Tulsa in little more than an hour, and her entire world would fall apart.

Unless she took action to stop it.

. . .

Tony was polishing off a helping of his mother's lasagna on Friday evening when the phone rang. Caller ID came back to a local hotel.

After his "hello," there was a moment's silence, then a sudden rush of air. "Tony? It—it's Kathryn Hamilton. I—I've done a terribly foolish thing. I didn't know who to turn to, but then I thought of you. I—I know I have no right to ask this of you, not after what I almost did, but . . . can we talk? Please? Just you and me?"

She sounded weary and frightened, not at all the way Henry's sister should sound. "Sure, we can." They would talk, and then he would haul her off to jail, where she belonged. "Where are you?"

"The Renaissance. It's off Seventy-first—"

"I know where it is."

"Of course you do." She sighed heavily. "I'm so sorry. I'm just not thinking clearly. I'll be waiting in the lobby. You'll come now?"

"As soon as I hang up."

"Thank you so much, Tony."

He hung up, then dialed Darnell Garry's cell phone. Not only was he handling the case, but he was on call that night, as well. "Hey, Garry, it's Chee. You busy?"

"Yeah. I caught a drive-by in east Tulsa. Two dead, one on his way to the hospital, and a half dozen conflicting statements. What's up?"

"Kathryn Hamilton just called. She wants me to meet her at the Renaissance so we can talk. I'll take her into custody and deliver her downtown. You want me to give you a call when we get there?"

"Yeah, sure. Oh, damn, I was supposed to pick up her old man at the airport. I would've asked you to do it, but, hell, I'll call Simmons instead and listen to him whine. Then I'll head downtown when we finish up here."

"See you there." Tony hung up, then went upstairs to retrieve his handcuffs and pistol.

Traffic was light on the Broken Arrow Expressway and Highway 169. He made it to the hotel in good time, pulled up to the front entrance, and was about to shut off the engine when Kathryn came out the door. Looking around warily, she darted to the car, her movements uncoordinated, and slid into the passenger seat.

"Thank you for coming," she said in a rush. She was pale, and her hands trembled as she fastened the seat belt. "I appreciate being able to talk in private."

They would have a private interview room at the police station, he thought as he shifted into gear and drove away. "Okay. But first let me tell you . . . this can't be off the record. I'm a cop. If you've done something illegal, I'll have to report it. I'll help you if I can, but I can't keep it to myself. Do you understand?"

She nodded fearfully.

"I also need to advise you of your rights and make sure you understand that anything you tell me can be used against you. Otherwise, I can't talk to you. Okay?"

"Oh, dear God," she murmured, but after a moment she nodded.

He ran through the Miranda warning by rote, wondering in some part of his mind whether he or Kathryn had ever thought they'd be in this situation. Mirandizing Henry Daniels's ultrarespectable younger sister ranked right up there with shooting Henry. Unbelievable.

She stared out the side window, her face turned away from him, as her fingers knotted and unknotted in her lap.

They were back on Seventy-first and sitting at a stoplight when she finally spoke. "Do you know what I—I did?"

He shook his head.

"I—I contacted a private investigator about Selena McCaffrey. About t-taking her out. Putting a—a hit on her. G-getting rid of—of her." She said the words stiffly, as if they were foreign to her. In that context, clearly they were.

She waited for a response from him, but he remained silent. He'd learned early on that silence unnerved most people so they talked to fill it. The more talking they did, the more he learned.

"I—I don't know what I was thinking. I don't even know that I *was* thinking. It's just all been so stressful—the shocks about Henry. All my life he's been the best brother a woman could ask for, and then I find out it's all been lies, that his life is filled with ugly secrets—the drugs, the murders, the girl."

Tony's fingers tightened around the steering wheel as the light finally turned green. Selena might have been a secret, but at its heart, there was nothing ugly about it. Henry had helped someone who'd desperately needed it. His motives had been less than pure, but the generosity remained.

"I just . . . I guess I just snapped. I go to that hospital every day and I stay there for hours, just watching him, hoping he'll surprise all the doctors and make a miraculous recovery, or wishing that he—that he would just go ahead and die. I talk to him about all the things we used to do when we were young, all the good times we had, and the whole time I'm thinking that I don't even know him. My big brother, who looked out for me, who teased and protected me and was always there for me, is a stranger, and it just . . ." She raised both hands to cover her face as her shoulders shook and a sob escaped her.

Tony stayed quiet, untouched by her emotional display.

After a few more shakes and sobs, she dug a tissue out of her purse, dabbed at her eyes, then straightened her shoulders. "I'm sorry. It—it's just been harder than I realized. I—I was angry. I wanted to blame somebody, to strike out at somebody, and it seemed so unfair to blame Henry when he's lying there half-dead, so—so helpless and pathetic. That left the girl." Her voice dropped to a whisper on the last words.

"It—it was a moment of insanity, I suppose. I thought . . . it was all her fault, so if she was—was gone, then everything would be all right again—Henry, our family. I just wanted to—to punish her. To remove her from his life. To get him away from her influence. So I called that man and asked him to—to find someone who would . . . take care of her."

At last Tony spoke. "You mean, kill her."

Shudders rocketed through her again. When they eased, she nodded numbly. "I never intended to go through with it. When I got off the phone and realized what I'd done, I was horrified. I didn't call him back, I didn't meet with him, I didn't pay him any money. I was so ashamed, so mortified, and I—I panicked. I drove aimlessly for hours, until I was exhausted, and then I checked into the hotel. I didn't know what to do, who to tell, how to make sure that no harm comes to that girl because of me. Then I thought of you—Henry's godson. I knew you could help."

Had she really become frightened after the call to Stark? Was that why she was confiding in Tony and laying the groundwork for some kind of traumatic-stress defense? Or was she telling the truth?

The job had made Tony cynical. One of the first lessons he'd learned was that people lied. Everyone lied some of the time and some people lied all the time. Some people had good reasons for their lies, but most just wanted to avoid the consequences of their actions.

And sometimes people told the truth. At least part of what Kathryn said was true. She had received a lot of big shocks lately, she hadn't gone any further with the murder-for-hire, and she had obviously been under a lot of strain. Maybe it was all true. Maybe it had been nothing more than a moment of insanity.

Stopping at another red light, Tony glanced her way. "How exactly do you think I can help?"

She looked surprised by the question. Was she so accustomed to others doing her bidding without question? Did she think he would vouch for her, call off the investigation, and let her go about her life as usual? If so, it just proved how little she knew about him.

"Why . . ." She blinked rapidly. Searching for the right answer? "Of course, I want you to make sure nothing happens to that girl."

"You said you hadn't paid any money. No one's going to carry out a hit without at least part of the money up front. Besides, she's well-protected."

"Good." She said it with an unsteady smile and relief in her voice. "I just couldn't live with myself if I knew I had caused harm to another person. I'd be no better than Henry." She twisted the oversized diamond on her left ring finger before saying, "I also want to—to make amends. If I could see her . . ."

"No," Tony said flatly. "That's not possible."

"But it would mean so much to me! I won't be able to rest until I see for myself that she's all right."

"Mrs. Hamilton, you tried to hire someone to *kill* her. No, you can't see her."

"Not even . . ." Her gaze cast down, she glanced his way in a gesture that was purely manipulative. "Not even if I tell you what I know about Henry's business in exchange?"

Tony turned into the next parking lot, shifted into PARK, then faced her. He needed to see her face, her eyes. "I thought you didn't know anything about Henry's sideline."

The nervous twisting of the ring started again. "I—I didn't *want* to know anything. It was so shameful that I pretended it didn't exist."

"So what do you know?"

She raised her gaze to him. "Some time ago, Henry sent me a package for safekeeping, in case anything happened to him. I was curious, so I opened it. It was records—people's names, dates, incidents, finances. I told you, my brother always loved to write everything down. When I realized that it had to do with drugs and murder, I was horrified. I put it away and put it out of my mind. But I would happily give it to you if you would just let me see Selena tonight and tell her how terribly sorry I am for what I did."

Tony studied her a long time. She looked sincere, but there was a hint of something in her eyes. That innate Davis smugness? Or something more calculating?

Finally, he shut off the engine, took the keys, and got out of the car. At the rear, he leaned against the trunk and called Robinette. The man answered with all the warmth of an ice cube.

"This is Ceola. I picked up Kathryn Hamilton, and I'm taking her downtown. But she's already trying to make a deal."

"What kind of deal?"

He repeated the trade Kathryn had suggested.

"Do you believe she has anything?"

With his free hand, Tony rubbed the ache gathering between his eyes. "Damned if I know." The longer he did this job, the harder it was to tell. And the truth was, he didn't care—didn't care whether the information existed, whether it brought down more of Henry's associates or added weight to the case against Henry himself. They couldn't make him pay for his crimes, so what did it matter?

"Why don't you bring her over?"

"Uh, *no*. She tried to hire someone to kill Selena, remember?"

"And she claims to have information that might help our case and get Selena back home sooner rather than later. Come on, Ceola. The place is secure. Selena's already met people here who went way beyond *trying* to kill someone, and she's been safe. Bring Mrs. Hamilton here."

"All right," Tony agreed grudgingly. "We'll be there soon."

Friday night in Tulsa, Oklahoma. He might as well be nowhere at all.

Sonny was restless, tired of the hassle, tired of traveling, just plain tired. He and Charlize had flown back to Savannah on schedule Tuesday night, accompanied to the airport by two of Selena's thugs in a red sedan that stayed two cars behind them. Once inside the terminal, the men had tried to blend in with the other travelers, but Sonny was too experienced at picking out surveillance. He'd known they were there to make sure he and Charlize got on the plane like they were supposed to. Since that had been his plan anyway, he'd done it.

They'd made a point of being visible around town on Wednesday, then had driven to Augusta, this time without any snoops on their tail, and flown back to Tulsa. Instead of the first-class hotels he preferred, they were staying in a dump right off the interstate, where cars whizzed past all night long, where thin walls let in far too much sound from the rooms on either side.

Where Selena would never think to look for him.

If she thought to look for him at all.

Given a choice, he would have left Charlize at home this time, but she'd asked to come with him. They were a team, she'd said. Partners. He'd been so surprised by the sentiment, he'd let her tag along.

Even though he'd come to tender his resignation in the most permanent of ways.

A hazy image of Charlize appeared in the window where he stood as she stopped behind him and laid her hands on his shoulders. Her fingers dug hard into his shoulders, kneading the muscles knotted deep there, and he winced and pulled away. She moved with him, though, making him grunt with each sharp quiver of pain even as the tautness began to ease.

"You've decided to go into business for yourself, haven't you?"

He listened for approval or disapproval, for sign of anything beyond simple curiosity and the unwavering loyalty she'd always shown him, but he heard nothing. "Yeah. I don't see that I have much choice."

"She won't let go easily."

"No."

"She'll send Damon after you."

He grinned. "She has Damon. I have you. I'd put my money on you every time."

When Charlize remained silent, he twisted his head to look at her. "I do have you, don't I?"

She gave him a cool, breath-stealing smile. "Of course you do. I've always been on your side."

Always. That was all he'd ever wanted from her.

"When are you going to tell her?"

He let his eyes droop shut as her fingers continued to work miracles across his shoulders and down his spine.

There would be no telling. This wasn't a job where you could just walk away, especially when you intended to take the business with you. No, the only option was to remove Selena from the picture. Long might come after him, or, being a reasonable businessman, he might consider losing the Southern region a fair price to pay for gaining total control of the rest of the empire.

"You're planning to kill her, aren't you?" Charlize asked. There was no shock or dread in her voice. She understood what went into running a business such as this. Even people you liked could create problems that only death could resolve.

"I don't actually have a plan at the moment," he said, and she laughed.

"You don't get out of bed in the morning without a plan."

He acknowledged that with a grunt.

"You want to share it?" Charlize asked.

He caught hold of her hand and pulled her around in front of him. "Some things you're better off not knowing. It protects you as well as me."

Her expression turned distant, hurt. "There's a lot about you I don't know. Just how much protection from me do you think you need?"

"None from you, darlin'. Just the rest of the world." Raising one hand, he gently stroked her face. "One of these days, soon as this is all settled, I'll tell you everything. All the secrets."

And he prayed to God that he wouldn't have to kill her for it.

Damon sat at the table in the mansion's kitchen, absently staring out the window as he munched on a piece of pizza.

Dinners weren't exactly sociable affairs in the house, and that night's was less so than normal. Selena and Robinette had both taken plates of food elsewhere to eat. Jamieson was looking so goddamn morose and guilty that it was just a matter of time before he told someone what he'd done, and Gentry was about as friendly as an ill-tempered snake.

Such fucking fun.

Robinette came into the kitchen, cell phone in one hand, an empty plate in the other. "Get one of the guards to take him to the guesthouse, then meet me in the foyer," he said. After laying the plate in the sink, he returned the way he'd come.

When Jamieson didn't respond, Gentry went to the intercom near the door. "We need a babysitter for Long," she said.

He flipped her off, and with a sardonic smile, she returned the gesture. "Watch him," she said to Jamieson. "I'm going to go wash up."

Jamieson didn't seem to notice her leaving. He just sat there, toying with the uneaten pizza on his plate. Damon watched him a moment, then stood and smacked both hands on the table hard enough to rattle the dishes. Jamieson started, then lifted his gaze.

"Knock this shit off, asshole. Even a blind man can see there's something wrong. You keep moping around here, and you're gonna get us both killed."

Jamieson opened his mouth, but the opening of the back door stopped him. The guard came in, looking disgruntled. "Want me to take him to the guesthouse?"

Jamieson nodded blankly.

"Come on, Long."

Damon stared hard at Jamieson until the man finally looked at him, then he grinned and winked before strolling out the door ahead of the guard. Once inside the guesthouse, he motioned down the hall. "I'm going to the john."

The guard made a bored gesture, then went to sit on the sofa.

Damon locked himself in the bathroom, then pulled out the phone and checked the battery level. It was getting dangerously low, and every damn call he'd made to J.T. that week that had gone unanswered had drained more of its power. This was likely the last call he'd be able to make before it went dead. The fucker had damn well better pick up this time.

He dialed the number, then lifted the phone to his ear. The phone rang once, then went silent. Grinding his jaw, he lowered it and saw the screen had gone dark. It was dead. "Goddamn, goddamn, goddamn!" He slammed the phone against the countertop, breaking it into two pieces, then threw both into the sink.

"Hey, what are you doing in there?" the guard yelled.

Breathing deeply, Damon stuffed the pieces back into his pocket, flushed the toilet, then walked out and down the hall to the living room. "I was looking for more paper under the sink and knocked a can of sanitizing shit over."

What the hell did it matter who or what Robinette really was? he decided as he dropped into the easy chair, propped his feet on the coffee table, and used the remote to turn on the television. So he'd delayed his escape for a few days to find out information that he wasn't going to get. It hadn't been a total loss. He had an extra mil in his account. That counted for a lot.

He intended to enjoy every freakin' dollar of it.

Starting the next day.

17

November 18. *I'm going to Jamaica next week. My man down there has been watching the girl for weeks. He knows her routine as well as I know my own. My first job will be to gain her trust, and I have a plan to do just that. What better way to gain a child's loyalty and faith than by rescuing her from a fate worse than death? The private detective knows a man—a liar, a thief, a con artist who fouls the very air he breathes. He'll do anything for money, including attack a young girl. I've warned the detective that she's not to be seriously harmed, though some pain is good. It makes the experience even more frightening, the rescue even more welcome. When I save her from this filthy lech, when I offer her my protection, she'll be so grateful. When she sees that I'm willing to kill for her—a stranger! when her own parents couldn't care whether she lives or dies—she'll be mine, heart and soul.*

The journal fell from Selena's trembling hands. Leaving it on the bed, she surged to her feet and from the room. The others had gone their separate ways after dinner. She headed upstairs, turning on all the lights in the ballroom, going to her easel. She squeezed out paints on the palette, but when it came time to pick up the brush, her fingers froze. She couldn't curl them around the smooth handle, couldn't envision touching the bristles to canvas, not in her current mood.

Frustrated, she moved to the center of the floor, planted her feet wide, and bent in a long, slow stretch. Yoga was a great stress reducer, but she couldn't think about movements, postures, or breathing. All she could think about was William.

He hadn't killed her attacker in that alley to save her life.

He'd paid him to attack her in the first place, had even instructed him how badly to hurt her, then had murdered him to earn her devotion—and keep his secret.

She'd thought he was her rescuer, her savior, when he'd been nothing but a cold-blooded, calculating murderer. There had never been anything good or honorable or decent about their relationship.

Never.

Muttering a curse, she straightened and eyed the treadmill across the room. A run sounded tempting. She could run far enough, fast enough, to exhaust her mind as well as her body. She could forget, at least for a time, just how vile a man her father figure, this man she'd *loved,* had truly been.

A time wasn't long enough, though. The knowledge would come back. She would have to deal with it.

And the best way to do that was with Tony. She was on her way back to her room to call him when headlights at the gate caught her attention. She peered out the window at the end of the hall and, with a rush of gratitude, recognized his Impala. She didn't rush down the stairs to greet him, though, but went to her room, picked up the journal she was coming to hate, and stuffed it beneath the clothing in a dresser drawer, then sat down to wait for Gentry to call her or for Tony to knock at the door.

Minute after minute passed with no intercom call, no knock. Maybe, she admitted, he hadn't come to see her but had had news to share with the FBI. But the only interest he had in common with them was her, and she didn't like being left out of conversations about her.

She headed downstairs, hearing voices from the gentlemen's parlor before she reached the halfway point—Robinette's, quiet and steely, and a woman's, her soft Southern accent distorted by emotion. So Tony had found Kathryn Hamilton. Selena wasn't surprised. One of the things William had hated most about him, besides his morality, was his doggedness. He never gave up—lucky for her.

She stopped in the parlor doorway. Robinette was closest to her, frustration on his face. Gentry was leaning against a windowsill on the far side of the room, Tony was near the fireplace, and Jamieson stood in the space formed by the sofa and two wing chairs, next to Kathryn Hamilton. She looked disheveled, her clothes rumpled, her makeup smeared around the eyes, her hair flat in places where it shouldn't have been. Even so, she still managed to look elegant next to Jamieson's jeans, T-shirt, and the gun on his hip.

Gentry was the first to notice Selena. She gestured to Robinette, who stopped midsentence to scowl at her. "What are you doing down here?"

"Joining the crowd. Someone must have forgotten to invite me."

Tony wore a frown that matched Robinette's. "You don't need to be here," he said, his steely tone matching, as well.

"Are you going to tell me that this doesn't concern me? The woman tried to hire someone to kill me. It concerns me more than any of you."

Kathryn took a step forward, but stopped when Jamieson touched her arm. She settled instead for wringing her hands with their flashy diamonds. "Oh, Selena, I've been asking to speak to you, but they refused. I am so sorry. I can't even begin to tell you . . . I don't know what happened. It was just—just—"

"A moment of insanity?" Tony's dry tone suggested he'd heard the phrase more than once that evening.

"Absolutely. Surely you understand, Selena. When Henry brought you here to kill Tony, you agreed, even though you didn't intend to actually do it. I did contact that man and offer him money—because I'd snapped. But I never intended to go through with it. You, of all people, have to understand."

Selena did understand, in theory. And if it was anyone besides William's sister, she would probably believe her. But people like Kathryn Hamilton didn't just snap. She'd known what she was doing, and she'd fully intended to carry it through, until the prospect of getting caught had made her think better of her actions.

"What would killing me have accomplished? William would still be in a coma. He would still be nothing but a common criminal. Nothing would have changed." Except that Kathryn would have had the satisfaction of knowing that she'd removed Selena from William's world.

With a glance at Jamieson, daring him to touch her again, Kathryn moved, putting a few inches between them. "You're right, of course. It wouldn't have accomplished a thing. I know that now, but at the time I wasn't thinking rationally. I thought it would fix everything. I thought it would turn Henry back into the brother I've always adored and make all this ugly mess go away . . . but I was wrong. Can you ever forgive me?"

Selena glanced at Tony, who was still scowling, then at Robinette. Neither of them was buying the remorse. Truthfully, she had doubts as well. It wasn't as if she and Kathryn had any sort of friendship. They were strangers whose only connection was through William. If not for him, they never would have met; having met, odds were slim that they ever would have seen each other again. What could forgiveness possibly matter?

She moved a few steps farther into the room, in Tony's direction. "Everyone makes mistakes," she said with a casualness she was far from feeling.

"How gracious of you to understand." Kathryn's smile was bright and warm, to match the look in her eyes as she calmly pulled Jamieson's pistol from the holster on his belt, pointed it at Selena, and pulled the trigger.

Tony shoved Selena to the floor, landing on top of her an instant before the bullet splintered the fireplace marble. A second deafening shot sounded, tearing into the wall, sending plaster dust into the air, and overwhelming the sounds of a scuffle, followed an instant later by relative calm.

After a moment, Robinette's feet appeared in the few inches of space Selena could see around Tony. "Are you all right?"

Tony rolled off her, sat up, then helped her to her feet. Rubbing her shoulder where she'd hit the floor, she nodded, then made eye contact with Kathryn, who was being restrained by Jamieson and Gentry, and shivered. William had looked at her like that once, just before *he'd* tried to kill her.

"I should have killed you the first time I ever saw you," Kathryn spat out. "You were so tiny, so innocent, and I hated you then. I despised you. But, no, Henry wouldn't let me. He said *he* would do it. Goddamned liar. You brought us nothing but trouble. Do you know what you've done? Do you have any idea how much you've cost us? Henry's life, my marriage, *my* life. You're nothing, nobody. You don't even deserve to breathe the same air we do. If there's a God in heaven, he'll strike you down. He'll make you pay, he'll—"

In the hall, the front door slammed, then a man's voice

shouted, "Kathryn! My God, were those gunshots I heard? Where are you?"

Horror spread across her face and she swayed unsteadily on her feet. "Oh, dear God, no," she whispered, then her voice rose to a wail. "Noo! This isn't fair! Not now, not after all these years..." Her face screwed into a look of pure hatred as she lunged toward Selena. The two agents dragged her back, restrained her, but that didn't lessen her struggle. "This is all your fault! I'll kill you, I swear to God, I'll kill you!"

The man burst into the room with Frank Simmons on his heels, looking around frantically until his gaze locked on Kathryn. Relief washed over the stranger's face in the moment before he noticed the handcuffs Robinette was using to secure her wrists behind her back. "Kathryn, what's going on? What have you done?"

Tearfully she tried to move toward him, but couldn't. "I did it for you, Grant, for us. I just tried to make things right," she whimpered. "I love you so much, and I just wanted everything to be right between us. I just wanted..."

"What are you talking about? What have you done? Someone tell me what's going on here." His gaze swept around the room as he sought someone in authority, skimming over Selena, then abruptly jerking back. He paled and raised one hand to his chest as if in pain, and the steps he took in her direction were unsteady. When Simmons stopped him with a hand on his arm, he looked grateful for the support. "Amelia," he whispered, and Kathryn crumpled with big, heartrending sobs.

"Get her out of here," Robinette ordered, and the two agents half dragged, half carried her from the room. Her anguish grew fainter the farther they went. "Mr. Hamilton, I presume."

Had they been expecting him? Selena wondered. Tony

had picked up Kathryn, Simmons had picked up her husband, and the feds had invited them all to a nice little talk about *her*. Only she had been left out.

The man spared him a brief glance before returning his stare to Selena. "Yes, I'm Kathryn's husband," he murmured, then directed a question to Selena. "Who are you?"

She glanced at Tony, who slid his arm around her waist as she drew a breath. "Selena McCaffrey."

A look of exquisite sorrow crossed Grant's face as he shook his head. "Not Amelia. Of course. Where is she? Is she all right?"

"I—I don't know anyone named Amelia. Who is she?"

"Your mother." His voice was soft, distant, raw with hurt. "She was twenty-six when you were born. You look exactly like her."

Selena wrapped her fingers tightly around Tony's. Her knees had grown unsteady, and a knot was loosening, then tightening, in her stomach. She wet her lips, opened her mouth, but had to search to find her voice. "How—how do you know my mother?"

He took another step toward her, and Simmons let him, and he said the words she'd thought she would never hear. "Because I'm your father."

Until the past few days, Selena had long carried an image of her father—black, loving, honorable, responsible, with a large family who would welcome her into their midst. She'd never considered whether he was rich, middle-class, or poor, educated or ignorant, a professional or a janitor or a subsistence farmer. None of that had mattered.

But she'd never imagined a wealthy, white, Old South,

plantation-owning, descendant-of-slave-holders lawyer—and William's brother-in-law, to boot.

Simmons had taken Kathryn to jail, and Robinette, Jamieson, and Gentry had politely moved elsewhere in the house, leaving Selena, Tony, and Grant Hamilton alone in the parlor.

She looked at Grant—at her *father*—and her fingers clenched around Tony's. He was probably close to sixty, under six feet, and soft around the middle. His brown hair, streaked with gray, was thinning on top, and he wore glasses that gave him an owlish look. He was handsome enough, but there was a weariness, a sense of loss, ingrained in every line of his face.

She opened her mouth, couldn't think of anything to say, then closed it again. She'd always thought she would have a million questions, curiosities, pleas, if she ever met her father, but not one came to mind at the moment.

"You seem fairly certain that Selena is your daughter," Tony said. "Why?"

Grant stared at her a moment before tearing his gaze away and smiling faintly. "If you'd ever seen Amelia, you'd be certain, too."

Kathryn had been, Selena thought, certain enough to try to kill her. And Henry had been certain enough to take her in.

"The resemblance couldn't be stronger if they were identical twins," Grant went on. "I'd be happy to submit to DNA testing for you, but I don't need the proof. I know."

"Obviously you haven't seen Amelia or Selena in a long time. What happened?"

"The name we gave you was Amalia," Grant said, and Selena stiffened. "It was my idea. Amelia wanted to name you after her mother, but I wanted to name you after your own

mother. She didn't like the nicknames that came to mind—
Big Amelia and Little Amelia, Old Amelia and Young
Amelia—so we settled on Amalia. It was close enough."

"That's what the family who raised me until I was nine
called me," Selena murmured.

Again he stared at her, as if he couldn't believe she was
real. After a time, he shook his head, drew a breath, and repeated, "What happened...Kathryn happened." With a
hopeless shrug, he explained. "I'm a lawyer. I met Amelia
thirty years ago, when I handled her mother's will. No
woman had ever attracted me the way she did. She was beautiful, kind, warm, loving, generous, sweet."

In short, everything his wife wasn't.

"We tried to ignore the feelings between us. I was married, she was black, I was white, it was Alabama...but every
time I saw her, around town, in court, in the store where she
worked, it got harder and harder until...we began an affair.
We fell in love, and she got pregnant. I wanted to divorce
Kathryn and go away with Amelia, to someplace where no
one knew us, where it wouldn't be quite so hard for us or our
baby, but she was reluctant. Alabama was her home, her family was there, her roots were there."

He rose from the chair and walked to the fireplace, running his finger over the hole in the marble from the first gunshot. "She finally agreed to leave soon after you were born. I
began shutting down my practice, and I...I told Kathryn.
She wasn't surprised that I'd had an affair. She was willing to
forgive me and even to make financial arrangements for the
child. But she couldn't handle the fact that I wanted a divorce. She became hysterical, making threats—against me.
Not you or Amelia. Two days later I went to Amelia's house,
and the car was gone, your clothes were gone...you were

gone. I searched for years, but never found so much as a clue."

"Didn't you wonder if Kathryn had done something?" Tony asked quietly.

Grant flinched at the obvious implication of the question. *I should have killed you the first time I saw you,* Kathryn had said, but her brother wouldn't let her. A shiver ran through Selena. William had been involved in whatever incident had erased her and her mother from Grant's life. Had he killed her mother? Had Kathryn?

"Kathryn admitted that she'd gone to talk to Amelia," Grant went on, "to make her see reason. She said she offered her $10,000 to take the baby and leave without seeing me again, and that Amelia accepted. I didn't believe her, not even after seeing the withdrawal from the bank. Amelia wouldn't have left, not unless she was threatened, not unless she had no other choice."

Dying certainly would have left her no other choice.

Apparently, the same thought occurred to Grant, because that sorrowful look returned. "I'd always hoped she *had* taken the money, that the two of you were alive and well and happy someplace else. I could accept that she'd stopped loving me, or that she hadn't loved me enough to stand up to Kathryn, but I couldn't bear the idea that she was . . . was . . ."

Dead. The word hung between them as surely as if a thousand voices had intoned it.

"But she never would have let you go. You were her life. She loved you more than anything. The only way anyone could have taken you from her was if she was dead." His shoulders rounded.

The look on his face was so powerful that Selena had to avert her gaze. Instead she looked at Tony's hands, holding hers, so strong and gentle and steady. She leaned against him, grateful he was there, as he'd promised he always would be.

The silence was broken by the jarring ring of Tony's cell phone. He murmured an apology, let go of Selena, and moved toward the door. After speaking for only a moment, he hung up and gestured for her to join him. "Garry got a search warrant for Mrs. Hamilton's rooms. He's going to the hotel, and he wants me to check the bed-and-breakfast. Are you okay?"

She nodded.

He cupped his palm to her cheek. "Are you sure? I can catch Frankie before he gets home and send him instead."

With a faint smile, she laid her hand over his. "Suz would kill you and him both."

His grin formed, then faded. "Seriously, are you okay?"

Truthfully, she hadn't gotten past the shock to emotion yet. She had met her *father*. Her mother had loved her, wanted her, and had likely died, in part, because of her. Getting a grip on that might take a while.

"I'm fine," she said quietly. "Just a little off balance. You go do what you have to do." Then she gave him a sultry smile. "Though I wouldn't object if you come back when you're finished."

He smiled, too. "It might be late."

"That's all right."

With a glance at Grant, Tony drew her into the hall and kissed her. When he released her, he said in a fierce, low voice, "Your mother isn't the only one who's ever loved you more than anything."

"I know. I love you, too."

"I'll be back."

She held on to him until she had no choice but to let go. After watching him leave, she hugged her arms tightly over her middle. Her father waited for her in the parlor, and he wasn't a drug dealer, wasn't a heartless murderer like William. He was a good man, who'd wanted her, who'd missed her the entire time she was gone. He knew her history, her roots, her paternal family and her maternal family. He could tell her who she was and where she'd come from—questions she'd thought she would never find answers to.

And all she'd had to do to meet him was get shot at twice. Being a target wasn't always as bad as she'd thought.

The bed-and-breakfast was less than two miles from Henry's estate. Full of questions Tony couldn't answer, the owner let him into Kathryn's rooms, a luxurious suite in the south end of what had once been a detached garage. He walked through the space once, then returned to the living room to begin his search.

There was little that belonged to her there—a novel, a pair of slippers, and a couple of brochures on long-term-care facilities. Planning for the day Henry was discharged from the hospital?

The refrigerator in the small kitchen held a six-pack of bottled water and a selection of fruit, and cosmetics and toiletries spread across the marble counter in the bathroom. There were no notes, no phone numbers, no weapons, no diary documenting her activities.

He went into the bedroom, the final room. The closet was filled with expensive clothes and smelled of expensive perfume. Purses lined one shelf, and a dozen pairs of shoes filled the other two. Another novel, along with a pair of reading glasses, sat on the night table, and a jewelry box, filled with earrings, brooches, and bracelets, was on the dresser.

So was a photograph. It was an eight-by-ten in a heavy

gold frame—a family photo, taken within the past few years. The Kathryn captured on film was a far cry from the one shrieking and wailing at Henry's tonight. This one was smiling, serene, happy. Grant stood beside her, his smile distant, looking for all the world as if he wasn't really there, and behind them, with one hand on Kathryn's shoulder, was their son, Jefferson.

Still holding the photo, Tony glanced around one last time. Not a thing that qualified as evidence. Still, he'd had to be sure. He couldn't have risked putting off the search until morning and giving the housekeeping staff a chance to unwittingly remove something important.

Not that the lack of evidence there mattered. They had the tape and the photographs at the pay phone. They had Kathryn's confession earlier in the evening. Hell, she'd tried to kill Selena in front of three FBI agents and one homicide detective. The DA couldn't ask for a stronger case.

He left the suite and returned to his car. He'd told Selena he would come back, but first he would finish up with Garry downtown. No doubt, she could use the extra time with her father.

Simmons was walking out the door at the correctional center as Tony approached. "How's Island Girl?" he asked.

"In shock, I think. Is Darnell in there with Kathryn?"

"Yeah, she's been processed, and he just took her to an interview room. Listen, I'm sorry about bringing the old man to Daniels's house. When he found out his wife was in custody, he was raising hell about representing her and demanding to see her right away. Shit, I figured the feebs wouldn't let us past the gate and he could be blamin' them instead of me."

"Don't worry about it. Selena's finally getting some of the answers she's been looking for."

Simmons shook his head. "You think she's any happier knowing Henry was her real uncle—stepuncle, at least?"

"Knowing her real uncle wanted her dead?" Tony asked dryly. "I don't think she's ever gonna be happy about anything involving him . . . but at least she knows her father now. She knows her mother wanted her. That's something." He opened the door, then turned back. "Thanks."

"For what?"

Tony shrugged. "Everything."

The door swung shut, cutting off Simmons's chuckle. In the interview room, Kathryn was sitting across the table from Darnell Garry. Her tears had dried, leaving dark shadows around her eyes, and her haughty manner had returned. Sitting there, looking like hell but acting as regal as the damn First Lady, she reminded him too damn much of Henry.

He sat down across from her. "You really didn't know anything about Henry's business, did you? He didn't send you any records. But you did know your husband was on his way to Tulsa, and that you couldn't risk letting him see Selena."

She shrugged. "Where is my husband?"

"At the estate talking to his daughter."

Kathryn's eyes narrowed and her mouth twisted into an ugly slash. "His bastard, you mean. His whore's bastard."

He pulled out a chair at the end of the table. "How long have you known who she was?"

"Since the day the FBI told me about her. Henry had a photo of her in his room. I recognized her right away. The resemblance was . . . startling."

Particularly when she'd thought Selena and her mother were problems long since dealt with. "Is that when you decided she had to die?"

Scorn etched her features. "I couldn't have cared less,

except for the fact that her very existence meant Henry had lied to me all those years."

"He was supposed to kill her ... after you killed her mother."

She clamped her mouth shut and said nothing.

"He told you he did kill her, and you believed him."

Her desire to stay silent lost out to her hatred. Color flooded her face. "He said he would do it—would get rid of that whore's body and take care of the baby, too. He made it look as if she ran away and took the baby with her. That's what I told Grant. And all that time Henry lied to me! He didn't kill her—he sent her off somewhere and kept in touch with her, then brought her back into our lives, the arrogant bastard!"

She'd told worse lies to her husband and saw nothing wrong with that, but was furious because her brother had lied to her. Because he hadn't killed a tiny baby in cold blood. What kind of sickness ran in the Daniels family?

"You killed Amelia to keep your husband from leaving you."

She lifted her chin, the haughtiness returning. She was every bit as pompous as Henry, and thought herself every bit as much above the law. "That never would have happened. She was a nobody. I was a Daniels. I was his *wife*. He *couldn't* leave me. It just wasn't done." Her shrug was dismissive, unconcerned. "It was *her* fault. If she had just taken the money and gone ... That was all I wanted, all I asked. She said she was leaving, all right—with Grant. They were going up north, where one's race didn't matter so much. I *told* her that would never happen, and she just laughed. She said it wasn't my choice. So I had to prove her wrong."

"How did you do that?" Tony asked quietly.

Kathryn crossed one leg over the other, then smoothed

the fabric of her skirt. "She lived in a shack, a tiny little house. The kitchen was so small, she kept the pots and pans stacked on top of the stove. I picked up a cast-iron skillet and . . ." She broke off, gazing into the distance, reliving the memory. Had she been horrified by what she'd done? Had it frightened her, sickened her?

More likely, she'd thought it was no more than Amelia deserved for daring to take what belonged to *her*. Her only fear had been getting caught, and Henry had handled that for her. He'd taken everything he'd learned as a cop and used it to cover up a homicide. To protect his sister from the consequences of her actions. Had that been the beginning of his criminal activity? Had it appealed to his ego, his sense of gamesmanship, that he'd been able to turn a crime of passion into the perfect murder? Once he'd gotten away with that, had he been tempted to try other crimes?

When she didn't go on, Tony did. "Twenty-eight years ago Henry lived in Boston. Did you call him? Wait for him to travel to Alabama?"

She smiled faintly. "No. As luck would have it, he was in Montgomery, interviewing for a job there. I had such hopes, having him nearby, being a close family again. I called him at the hotel, and he drove out to Amelia's shack. There was a terrible rainstorm that night. It took him forever to get there, and all that brat did was cry and cry until I thought I'd start screaming myself. I should have killed her while I waited for him. It would have been so easy—just hold a pillow over her face until she stopped that damned wailing."

Her voice was soft, her tone conversational, and Tony felt cold inside. For all the emotion in her voice, she could have been talking about something totally inconsequential instead of the murder of an infant. Selena's life had meant nothing to Kathryn, while it was everything to him.

"They offered him the job, you know," she went on in that tone. "Chief of detectives or some such thing. I tried not to pay too much attention to his police work. It was something of an embarrassment to the family. Danielses donated money, but we did *not* dirty our hands."

"Killing a woman with an iron skillet sounds pretty dirty to me," Garry remarked.

Kathryn shifted her attention to him, then back to Tony. "He turned the job down, unfortunately. It was such a disappointment, and it was all because of *her*."

"You have a son," Tony said. "What is he going to think when he finds out that his mother is in jail for the attempted murder of his half sister?"

The tenderness that appeared at the mention of her son quickly disappeared beneath hatred and loathing. "She's *not* his half sister. She's nothing to him!"

"They share the same father."

Her spine stiffened. "Jefferson is adopted. Since Grant seemed to miss his little brat so much, I thought replacing her with a more suitable child would make him happy. Jefferson was perfect—sweet, obedient, loving."

"White," Garry added, but she ignored him.

"He's the light of my life, and he should have been for Grant, too. He was everything a man could have wanted in a son, but Grant didn't care. He just wanted *her*." As if suddenly remembering Tony's question, she gestured dismissively. "When I told Jefferson that the little bitch was going to inherit Henry's estate, that I was going to stop her, he said, 'Let it go, Mama. It's Henry's property. Let him give it to whoever he wants.' Of course, he doesn't know who Selena McCaffrey really is. That might change the way he thinks."

After a deep breath, the smile and affection returned. "Jefferson's a good son. He would be here in five minutes if I called him, and he wouldn't leave until I could go with him. He takes care of his mama."

Tony exchanged glances with Garry. They'd known Grant was flying in, but there had been no mention of Jefferson coming from his home in Florida. "You mean, he's here in town?"

Kathryn smiled blissfully. "Has been since Monday. He came to see his mama, to help me through this trying time with Henry."

Garry, his expression wary, gestured to Tony, and they moved to the far corner of the room. "I talked to Jefferson Hamilton a couple times in the last two days," he murmured, "and the number I dialed was in Florida. I know it's possible to route calls all around the world, but why do you think he never said a word about being in Tulsa unless he had something to hide? She just admitted he knew about her plan."

Kathryn was a master manipulator, but that didn't mean she couldn't be manipulated herself. She was the one who'd contacted Stark and set up the hit, but Jefferson could have been the guiding force. No doubt, growing up with her had infected him with the same smug arrogance, the same sense of superiority and entitlement.

"And when he finds out that she's in custody..." Tony glanced at Kathryn, so sure that everything was going to go her way, just as it always did. "He could come rushing to her rescue, or he could..." Finish the job she'd started. And through his adoptive father, who'd been completely in the dark about his wife's plans, he had a better than even chance at gaining access to Selena.

With a yawn, Grant said, "I suppose I should see about finding a hotel."

Selena glanced at the clock on the mantel. It was nearly eleven. She hadn't come close to asking all her questions, or answering all of his, but she'd waited twenty-eight years. Another few hours wouldn't hurt.

"You're welcome to stay here." The words were out before she gave them a second thought, but she wouldn't take them back if she could. She had nothing to fear from Grant. Instinct told her that. He'd been as deeply hurt by the Daniels family as she had been—more so, in fact. She'd lost the parents she didn't remember, while he'd lost the woman he loved more than his wife, more than his life, and their child.

He considered it, then shook his head. "It doesn't seem right—staying in Kathryn's family home under the circumstances."

"It can't be any less right than my staying here," she pointed out. "I'm partly responsible for William being in a coma."

"I wish he was in a grave," he said darkly, "and that Kathryn—" Abruptly, he broke off, pressing his lips together. He'd been married to her more than thirty years, and had probably thought that nothing she did could surprise him. But she had, and in trying to save her marriage, she'd destroyed it.

Selena couldn't summon even the faintest hint of sympathy for her.

Grant's hands shook as he pushed himself to his feet. "On second thought, I believe I'll take you up on that offer."

Selena rose, too. "Why don't you get your bags and I'll show you to a room. We can talk again in the morning."

He nodded. She walked to the door with him, where Simmons had left his luggage before leaving, then took him to a second-floor guest room at the opposite end of the hall from her own room. She was about to leave him there when he touched her for the first time, his fingertips light against her cheek. "Your mother would be so proud of the woman you've become," he said, his voice choked.

Emotion clogging her throat, Selena smiled unsteadily. "A woman in so much trouble that the FBI could force her to be a cooperating witness in a sting to take down a global drug empire?"

"A strong, kind, honorable woman who loves and is loved. She had dreams for you, and except for the grand-babies, you've fulfilled every one of them."

Her eyes dampened, and she blinked to clear them. "Thank you," she murmured. The temptation was strong to throw her arms around his neck for the sort of hug she'd long dreamed of, but it was too soon. She was still too unbalanced. Instead, she settled for the farewell she'd often given William over the years—a polite kiss on each cheek. "If you need anything, I'm at the other end of the hall. I'll see you in the morning."

"Good night, Selena."

She closed the door behind her and started down the dimly lit hall. Tonight would be a good night. Tony was coming back, and Grant wasn't leaving.

She went to her own room but found herself unable to settle in one spot. After wandering through the house a time or two, she ended up in the ballroom. The lights were off in the servants' quarters, where Jamieson and Gentry were staying, and across the lawn in the guesthouse. Out the front window, she could see the dim illumination in the guard shack; out the back window, the glow of a cigarette in the night showed the location of the rear gate guard.

Impatient for Tony to arrive, when the telephone rang, she snatched it up. "Tony?"

"Sorry to disappoint you, but it's Sonny. We've got trouble. Can we talk?"

"Can't it wait until morning?"

"This is serious shit. If it could wait, I wouldn't be calling."

She suppressed a sigh. "Okay. Talk."

"Tell the guards to let me in."

Alarm prickled the hairs at her nape. "You're here?"

"Goddamn right, I'm here. I told you it was serious. I just flew five hours from Savannah. We've got big trouble. I'm talking fucking-federal-indictment-type trouble. Someone's ratted us out—someone on the inside. Someone who knows enough to send all of us to prison for the rest of our fucking lives. Can I come in and talk to you, or are you gonna sit there on your hands while this whole thing blows up in our fucking faces?"

She lifted her gaze to the front window again, where headlights showed at the gate. She wished Tony was there to advise her, or Robinette, or even Long. But they weren't, and she had to act. And it wasn't as if she was alone. Jamieson and Gentry were asleep two floors down, and Robinette was an intercom call away. "Let me talk to the guard."

There was a murmur of voices, then a stiff, "This is Tompkins. We'll send him away—"

"No, let him come in. I'll get in touch with Mr. Robinette. By the way, Detective Ceola will be returning tonight also." She'd left the front door unlocked for him, as had become her habit.

"Shouldn't you ask Rob—"

Aware that Yates was likely listening, she interrupted. "I'm supposed to be the boss here, remember? Let him pass."

"Yes, ma'am," the guard said grudgingly. "I'm opening the gate now."

18

Damon was reaching for the doorknob into Robinette's bedroom when the intercom buzzed. A glowing red light showed the panel's location on the hall wall halfway between the living room and bedrooms, and a second light indicated the call was from the house, not the guard shack. It buzzed a second time, and sound came from the other side of the door—the squeak of springs, footsteps shuffling across the floor.

Damon sank back into the shadows, his breathing tautly controlled. He imagined he could see the knob slowly turn, though in truth it was too dark. Shifting lightly on the balls of his feet, he watched as the door swung open, spilling moonlight into the hall. An instant later, Robinette walked out.

He'd taken only a few steps toward the intercom when Damon struck. Swiftly, silently, he closed the distance, coming up close behind Robinette, grabbing hold of his chin with one hand, the back of his head with the other. He twisted hard, heard the surprised grunt, felt the sudden deadweight. Letting go, he stepped back. The prick fell to the floor in a heap, motionless, his head bent at an unnatural angle.

The intercom buzzed once more, longer that time. Damon chuckled at the thought of Selena or one of the others, waiting for an answer that was never going to come.

He went into Robinette's bedroom, rifled through his

belongings, and finally located his pistol, two extra clips, and a few hundred bucks. Leaving the shoulder holster behind, he tucked the pistol into his waistband, slid the rest into his pockets, and headed for the door.

After three intercom calls brought no answer, Selena left the ballroom and took the stairs two at a time to the first floor, intending to rouse Gentry and let her alert the others. She entered the kitchen and approached the corridor that led to the servants' quarters. Her eye caught movement and she became aware of a shadowy figure standing just inside the entry hall door. She stopped so abruptly that she practically stumbled, then slowly turned to face him.

"Don't bother them," Yates said quietly, stepping into the light that came from above the sink. "This is between you and me."

The ice in his voice sent shivers dancing down Selena's spine. It was in his face, as well. Coldness. Stillness. Rage.

Regretfully she thought about the pistol and the switchblade in her room. She'd made the same mistake William had—feeling too safe in the house, putting too much faith in the alarm, the fence, the guards. In the end, William had paid for it with his life. She didn't intend to follow him that far.

"Let's go back upstairs. We'll have more privacy there." Yates gestured toward the back stairs, and reluctantly she moved in that direction. Her steps were steady but slow as she climbed to the second floor. Was there anything in the second-floor hallway that she could use to defend herself? A table too bulky and heavy to move, holding a sixteenth-century Chinese vase and a collection of alabaster carvings, the largest barely enough to wrap her fingers around. Her best chance was to break away and make it to her room quickly enough to retrieve her weapons.

Her muscles tensing, she took the last two steps at once, preparing to dash down the hall the instant her foot touched the floor. But before she could do more than that, Yates took her arm in a painful grip and steered her around the corner and onto the next flight of stairs. He didn't release her until they were well inside the ballroom.

There was precious little cover in the room—tables, chairs, the exercise equipment. No place to hide, and only a few free weights to use as a weapon. Even the telephone was too flimsy to do any serious damage. If Robinette hadn't heard the intercom, or if Tony didn't return soon, she would have only her wits to protect her.

She moved to the far end of the table, then gestured toward a chair. "Have a seat."

"I'd rather stand."

So would she. It was easier to move, dive, kick. "What's the trouble?"

"You are."

For a moment, she remained blank, then as comprehension sank in, she folded her arms across her middle to contain the trembling deep inside. "You've decided you don't want to continue our association."

"And here I thought you were too stupid to be believed." He pulled a pistol from the back of his waistband and took aim on her. "Maybe it's the late hour. Maybe they got complacent, or you just can't get good help on the taxpayers' dime, but your guys out there didn't do a very thorough job of searching me. They patted me down, and they went through my car, but they missed this up in the undercarriage."

She glanced out the window toward the front gate,

wishing she would see Tony's car there, praying she wouldn't. He expected to come back and find everything quiet. He wouldn't be prepared to walk in on a murder attempt. "You're planning to kill me. In my own house. With my people all over the place."

"Aw, come on, Selena. You're about to die. Can't you be honest now? Your people are fucking feds. You know it. I know it."

...on the taxpayers' dime... The breath froze in her lungs, and her shock must have shown on her face because he chuckled. "Oh, yeah. I know everything. They're all feds, every goddamn one of 'em, except Long. Are you scamming him, too, or did he make a deal to save his own worthless hide?"

She clasped her hands to stop their trembling. Running would merely result in her getting shot sooner and pretending innocence was likely to anger him further. Stalling seemed the best choice.

"How long have you known?" She was surprised by her own calm when inside she felt nothing but panic. She'd discovered long ago that there was never a good time to die, but now, having finally found the father she'd dreamed of her entire life, was an especially bad time.

"Not long enough. You fooled me." His gaze narrowed. "I don't like being fooled."

She shrugged dismissively. "They offered me a deal, and I took it. You would have done the same under the circumstances."

"You don't have any idea what I would do under any circumstances." His smile, so at odds with the anger and menace, made her skin crawl. "You don't know a damn thing about me."

Another shrug. "I know enough. You're dangerous. You

have no regard for anyone's life but your own." Then she offered her own chilling smile. "I know you'll never get away with killing me. The feds at the gate know I was alive and well before you got here. They'll know you killed me."

"They would . . . if I was going to let them live."

Her mouth went dry, making it difficult to swallow. The guards wouldn't be expecting trouble. It would be a simple matter for him to kill all of them. "What about the surveillance system? They have you on tape coming into the estate."

"It's all hooked into the guard shack. A little C4 will take care of it."

Why was she so numb inside? It made sense that he wouldn't hesitate to kill three people to cover up the murder of a fourth. Hadn't he executed three of his own employees just days ago before torturing the fourth into a confession?

She backed a few steps away from the worktable. The weight machine was six feet behind her, sleek steel and cables, of no help whatsoever, but on the floor behind it were the ten-pound dumbbells she sometimes used. It wasn't much, but it was all she had.

"How did you find out about the feds?" she asked, keeping the nervousness from her voice by sheer will.

"I have my sources."

"What sources?" When his gaze narrowed, she shrugged as she eased a few inches closer to the weights. "You're planning to kill me. What can it hurt to answer my questions?"

He moved with her, maintaining the same distance, keeping the pistol trained center mass. "My sources are my sources. I have more secrets than you or the old man could even imagine. He thought he was so shit-hot, but he's got nothing on me. I may not have been family to him, but I'm better at this business than he ever dreamed of being."

Her gaze locked on him, she continued to circle wide . . .

until she tripped over the upturned corner of the mat underneath the equipment, stumbled, and knocked a metal chair to the floor. Yates responded with another chuckle. "Hell of a time to get clumsy, Selena. Not that it matters. Jamieson and Gentry are snoozing like babies. They're not going to hear a thing."

As if in direct contradiction to his boast, the stairs creaked and a voice called her name. "Goddamn," Yates muttered as relief swept over Selena. It died just as quickly, though, as it registered that the voice wasn't Tony's.

"I heard something fall. Are you all ri—" Grant came to an abrupt stop at the top of the stairs. Robe belted around his waist, hair standing on end, he looked at her, then at Yates, and his brow wrinkled in confusion. Confusion, not fear. He stalked across the room toward Yates. "What the hell do you think you're doing? Put that damn thing away right now."

"Grant—" Yates echoed the name with her, and she broke off, shifting her gaze to him. He was staring at Grant with the same hatred Kathryn had shown her earlier. "What the hell are you doing here?" he snarled.

"I'm here because of Kathryn. The police have been calling with details of how she tried to hire a hit man. She'd disappeared, she wasn't answering her phone...of course I came."

"Then why the hell aren't you *with* her, instead of here, in this house, with *her*?" His lip curled in a sneer, Yates jerked his head in Selena's direction. "Get out of here, old man. Go tend to your wife. This has nothing to do with you."

"My son is pointing a gun at my daughter, and it has nothing to do with me?"

Barely able to breathe, Selena staggered back a few steps until the cold steel of the gym stopped her. Sonny Yates was Grant and Kathryn Hamilton's *son*? William's nephew?

Yates's eyes opened wide with shock. "Daughter? What are you talking about, old man? You have no—" Then his gaze jerked to Selena and filled with disgust. "*Her*? She's the one? Jesus, I'd heard talk from the servants, from Mama's friends, that you'd had an affair, that you had a bastard running around somewhere, but *her*? Good God, Grant, why would you— How could you— Does Mama know?"

"She does now." Grant took a few steps toward him, stopping only when Yates swung the gun on him. He held out his hands in entreaty. "Put the gun away, Jefferson. Whatever you think you're doing—"

"I know what I'm doing. You're the one who doesn't have a fucking clue."

"Isn't it enough that your mother's in jail for trying to kill Selena? Do you—"

"In jail?" Yates interrupted. "When was she arrested?"

Selena finally found her voice. "Tonight. Here at the house."

Yates rounded on Grant. "What the hell are you doing here? Why haven't you gotten her out? Why aren't you taking care of her?"

Grant's expression turned as cold as Yates's had been earlier. "She tried to kill my daughter, and she and her precious brother likely killed Amelia. She can rot in jail for all I care."

"You cold-hearted son of a bitch! Whatever she did, she did for *you*! She loves you, you worthless—" Yates lunged toward him, the pistol raised. Grant grabbed the gun, wrenched it free, and threw it across the room, then collapsed to the floor under the force of Yates's punch. He lay there unmoving.

Selena darted toward the weapon as it skittered across the highly polished floor. Before she'd covered more than a few yards, Yates hit her from behind, knocking the wind from her lungs with a whoosh as she crashed onto the floor. Frantically, she drove her elbow straight back, earning a grunt from him and enough easing of his weight that she was able to turn over. She bucked her hips but was unable to unseat him, brought her knee up into the middle of his back, and delivered a sharp chop across his throat. When he fell back, she scrambled away, but he grabbed her ankle in a vicious grip. Cursing her bare feet, she kicked at him with her other foot but was unable to do enough damage until she connected with his chin, snapping his head back.

He loosened his hold, and she jerked free and jumped to her feet, making another frantic bid to reach the pistol. He grabbed a handful of her clothing, swung her around, then gave her a shove in the opposite direction. Unable to catch her balance, she landed on the mat, her head hitting the leg of the exercise equipment with a sickening thud. Her vision turned blurry, and bile rose from her stomach, burning her throat. Using a handful of her hair, he flipped her over and delivered a hail of blows, smashing his fist into her face, her ribs, her abdomen. Agony flashed red and black against her closed eyelids. She couldn't breathe, couldn't move, couldn't feel anything but pain.

She tried to raise her knee but couldn't. Shoving her hand between their bodies, she gave his testicles a brutal twist, bringing an outraged howl from him. "You fucking bitch," he panted. "Fuck Grant"—he wrapped his hands around her throat—"and his nigger whore"—and squeezed—"and Henry, and fuck you—"

Desperate for air, she clawed his fingers, his throat, his face. When she drew blood, he howled again and let go to punch her in the ribs again. A bone cracked as red-hot misery raced through her. He hit her again, and everything went black. She was going to pass out, and he would be free to kill her.

Her arm trembled and her fingers were having difficulty responding to her brain's woozy commands. Once again she scratched at his face before finding his eye. When she gouged one nail deep into it, he screamed obscenities as blood began oozing down his cheek. Groping blindly, he grabbed one of the dumbbells and raised it in both hands above his head. "You goddamn bitch," he whispered, his voice raw and trembling. "I'm going to kill—"

A gunshot echoed through the room, taking off a good portion of Yates's head. Blood and tissue splattered the wall, the floor, and Selena as the weight slipped from his hand and clattered harmlessly to the floor. He slumped back, dead.

She slowly eased into a sitting position, supporting herself on her elbows, trying not to gasp for breath but unable to take it in any other way. Her legs were trapped under Yates's lower body, and she couldn't find the energy, or the pain tolerance, to wiggle free.

Footsteps approached, quiet on the wood floor, then a slim figure dressed in black knelt beside her. A gloved hand tugged off the balaclava, and blond hair fell to brush the black shirt. "Let me help you," Charlize Pawley said, sliding her arm around Selena's shoulders, gently pulling her free, then helping her to the nearest seat, the bench on the weight machine.

Her vision still blurry around the edges, Selena stared at her. "Y-you . . . you . . . why?"

Charlize crouched in front of her. "I worked for William a long time," she said simply.

"You're J.T."

Another nod. "Short for John Turner. My father. He was William's hitter. When he got sick and knew he wasn't going to be around to take care of me much longer, he trained me to take over, and when he died, I did."

"You're a hit man."

Charlize's smile was brief. "I prefer hit woman. Or just plain hitter. I was seventeen when I carried out my first job. Truthfully, I prefer the restaurant business, but I owed William a lot."

"You were watching Yates?"

Picking up a towel draped over the weight machine's cross bar, Charlize gently dabbed at the blood flowing from Selena's temple. "William never trusted anyone. Someone's watching everyone. Since my official work for him was sporadic, I kept an eye on Sonny the rest of the time."

"Did William know . . ." Selena closed her eyes for a moment. Everything hurt so bad—shades of her childhood—that she was having trouble putting questions together. "Did he know Sonny was really Jefferson?"

"No. I didn't, either, until tonight. Knowing Sonny, I'd say it was enough for him to know that he was fooling his uncle. William didn't have to know, too."

Just like William—the love of secrets and the satisfaction in knowing them even if no one else did.

Somewhere in the distance, a door closed. Tony arriving from his search of Kathryn Hamilton's suite? One of the agents awakened by the gunshot?

Charlize's voice turned grim, insistent. "Listen to me, Selena. This is Sonny's gun, right? He brought two with him. You were able to relieve him of this one and you shot him with it in self-defense. Understand?"

Selena stared at the pistol Charlize pressed into her hand, her vision still unfocused, and repeated the words to fix them in her head. "Sonny's gun . . . disarmed him . . . self-defense."

With an approving nod, Charlize wrapped Selena's fingers around the grips, pointed the pistol in Sonny's direction, and squeezed off one shot into the wall a few feet above his body. The sound made her flinch.

Then the blonde smiled. "I've got to go. I'm more used to you free than locked up."

When she would have pulled away, Selena tightened her grip on her hand. "Thank you."

Charlize's only response was a nod. Noiselessly, she crossed the ballroom, pulling on the balaclava as she went. Selena didn't worry about how she would get out of the house and off the grounds; she'd done it a time or two herself without getting caught, and she was nowhere near as experienced as Charlize.

Nowhere near as cold, either, she added as her gaze skimmed over Yates's body, then quickly away. Charlize and Yates had been lovers, yet she had killed him without a qualm. Selena would die before killing Tony, and had come precariously close to proving it a few weeks ago.

Footsteps sounded on the stairs, and Selena dragged her head up enough to watch as Gentry came into view, gun drawn. The agent looked at Grant, still out cold on the floor, at Yates, then at Selena, and she smiled. "You are hell on the bad guys," she said, a hint of admiration in her voice. She crossed the room to bend over Yates for a moment. Satisfied that he was dead, she straightened. "Where's his weapon?"

Selena nodded toward the gun on the floor.

Gentry holstered her own weapon, crossed to pick up Yates's, then came back to stand beside his body, his gun in her hand.

Pointed at Selena.

Selena was too numbed to be shocked. "You're dirty, too," she said wearily.

"I prefer to think of myself as enterprising."

"It was you behind the murder attempts." Selena pressed one hand to her rib cage, easing the ache enough to make shallow breaths bearable. "You're an FBI agent, for God's sake. That's supposed to mean something to you."

"Like being chief of police meant something to William?"

"Who are you selling out to?" she asked, just to stall because she damn sure didn't care.

"Barnard Taylor. Vernell Munroe. Would it make you feel any better to know that I started out just providing information? I didn't intend to kill you myself until I found out how incompetent they were."

"But . . . you put your own life in danger. You were with me on the street in Savannah. You got injured in the car wreck."

Gentry laughed. "Honey, I'd take a whole bunch of knocks on the head for the money they're paying."

"You almost drowned. Robinette and I saved your life."

"No good deed goes unpunished." Gentry cocked the pistol. "This is so convenient. Yates came here, intending to kill you. He shot you, you shot him, you both died. How tragic. No one will ever think to look for another explanation."

"Except for one thing—I'm unarmed." Furtively Selena closed her fingers over the grip of Charlize's gun, tucked close to her thigh on the side away from Gentry.

"I'll take care of that." Gentry examined the scene, no doubt seeking the best angle to support her cover story, then stepped over Yates's body. While her attention was diverted, Selena raised the pistol, waited for the agent to look at her, then pulled the trigger.

Gentry slumped to the floor, the pistol landing without a sound on Yates's body. Gritting her teeth, Selena got to her feet, limped over, claimed the pistol, then looked at Gentry. Blood flowed from the wound, indicating that she was alive.

At the moment, Selena didn't give a damn whether she stayed that way.

Sweat broke out across her forehead as she limped to where Grant lay. She tried to lower herself carefully to the floor, but her strength gave out, and she fell instead, jarring her ribs, whimpering with pain, too done in even to lift her head as, far away, a voice called her name. Tony. He was there. He would take care of her.

As Selena started toward Grant Hamilton, Damon removed the pistol from his waistband and silently moved away from the stairs and into the ballroom. The night wasn't turning out quite as he'd planned. No guards had answered the alarm when he'd left the guesthouse, and inside the mansion, he'd found Jamieson unconscious but alive in his bed and Gentry gone from her bed. He'd wanted to get some dirt on her, and sure enough, it had been there. She was dirtier than Robinette and Jamieson combined. Selena had the worst judgment—or the worst luck—of anyone he knew.

She fell to the floor next to the old man. She thought she was safe. She wouldn't know she was about to die. He wouldn't have the satisfaction of watching the fear rise as he took aim dead center between her eyes and—

"Selena!"

Damon froze. What the fuck was Ceola doing there? Pivoting, he took the stairs three at a time and ducked into a second-floor bedroom as Ceola reached the top of the main staircase. He didn't slow on the landing, but raced up the next flight. It would take him a minute or so to check Selena, then raise the alarm. The guards would come running, followed soon after by the police, ambulances, the press. The scene would be chaos . . . a good cover for an escape.

He opened the door an inch or so, heard Ceola's voice upstairs, then slipped out. He was down the back stairs, out the door, and ducked behind the shrubbery by the time the rear-gate guards thudded toward the house. The moment they disappeared inside, he dashed across the parking court to the garage, kicked the side door open, and fumbled around in the dim light until he found a pair of heavy-duty bolt cutters.

Sirens were wailing in the distance when he came outside again. He hunkered down in the shadows and watched as the first police car skidded to a stop in the driveway, its headlights illuminating the two guards heading toward the house. Unless they were better staffed than usual, that left only the one guard, and he was occupied with opening the gate for the cop car and the ambulance waiting behind it. Too busy to be inside the shack monitoring Damon's bracelet.

He sat down, jerked his jeans leg up, and positioned the cutters. The angle was awkward, and the metal bit into his skin. He made the first cut, setting off the silent antitamper alarm he'd been warned about. It took a couple more cuts, then the bracelet fell to the grass.

A steady stream of emergency vehicles was coming onto the grounds, their lights casting multicolored shadows over the house. Damon watched for a moment, but no one was showing any interest in the rear of the property or him. That would change soon enough, when someone realized there'd been no sign of Robinette since things went to hell.

Rising to his feet, he stayed in the shadows as long as he could, then jogged across the open ground to the rear gate. Twenty feet away, he picked up his pace, hit the gate at a hard run, swung himself over the top, and dropped to the other side. He dusted himself off, then headed into the cover along the fence line. Behind the next block of houses was woods, then the jogging trail. From there, he could go anywhere.

He regretted that he hadn't had time to kill Selena, but at least he'd taken care of that fucker, Robinette. And he was in no hurry. Revenge, William had liked to quote, was a dish best served cold.

As long as he lived, there would be plenty of time to kill Selena.

Awakening from a drug-induced sleep felt like struggling up through layers of thick sludge, their heaviness trying to pull her back down, but Selena was too stubborn to give in. She fought her way to consciousness, forcing her lids open, forcing her eyes to focus.

She was lying in a bed in a room flooded with sunlight. The gown she wore was cotton, not hers, and the sheet that covered her to her waist was coarse, also not hers. An IV was running in the back of her left hand, but other than that, she couldn't see any signs of the hellacious evening she'd survived.

She could feel them, though. Every breath hurt. Flexing her fingers and toes sent painful shivers through her, and her vision was restricted by the swelling that practically closed her left eye. Even her scalp hurt when she shifted her head a fraction of an inch.

But she was alive.

Her back ached, but when she tried to turn onto her side, a groan escaped her. The sound brought Tony, dozing in a chair pulled next to the bed, instantly awake. His clothes were rumpled, beard stubbled his jaw, and his hair stood on end, but he'd never looked better.

He stood, bent over her, and, seeing that she was awake as well, grinned that endearing grin. "Hey, babe."

She managed to lift one hand enough to touch his cheek before letting it fall again. "Are you okay?"

After checking her hand for injuries, he gently twined his fingers with hers. "I'm supposed to ask you that, though all I need is one look to know the answer."

"How do I look?"

"Pretty damn scary," he teased, then sobered. "Amazingly beautiful. You scared the hell out of me last night. When I got to the ballroom after that gunshot and found you collapsed on the floor, I thought..."

His expression said it all. She smiled the best she could, considering that her lip was split. "I don't die easily. How is Grant?"

"He's fine. Just has a headache, along with a load of guilt. He says this is all his fault."

"And Gentry?"

"She'll be okay. Robinette's with her now. He's okay, too. Long tried to break his neck, but he's too damn stubborn to die. He regained consciousness not long after I got there. He'll be in here soon as he finds out you're awake, with more questions than you probably have answers for."

Selena wasn't looking forward to trying to take credit for a death that someone else had caused, but there was no way she could sell out Charlize. The woman had saved her life. That deserved some gratitude.

"Long..."

Tony's gaze darkened and a muscle in his cheek twitched. "He got away."

A chill danced through her as she squeezed his fingers. Tony had been concerned from the beginning—had insisted Long was too dangerous, getting him out of jail too big a risk—and now he'd been proven right. The cold-blooded killer he'd worked so hard to lock up was on the run, and the blame came back to her. "I'm sorry."

"Yeah. I know. If only—" Abruptly he bit off the words and clenched his jaw.

"I am sorry, Tony. I never thought—" She trailed off. She had no defense. It hadn't been necessary for her to think that Long might escape because Tony had told her he would try. She felt sick that she hadn't listened to him.

He stared into the distance for a moment, his gaze hard, then looked at her and everything about him softened. "It doesn't matter. As long as you're all right, nothing else matters. If I'd lost you . . ."

"You wouldn't have. You're why I fought so hard. You gave me a reason."

He started to kiss her, drew back, and studied her with his brow wrinkled into a frown. Finally, he brushed his lips feather light across her cheek where it met her ear. Letting her eyes close, she savored it until an impatient throat-clearing from the foot of the bed made him straighten.

Robinette stood there, looking as formidable as he could in a robe and slippers. "It's about time you woke up." The brusque tone he was aiming for was negated by the raspiness of his voice. "Has he filled you in on everything that happened while you were trying to stay alive last night?"

"Some of it," Tony responded.

"Long tried to kill me. He had more success at escaping. Before Gentry tried to kill you, she left Jamieson unconscious so he wouldn't hear anything. A search of her quarters revealed a device used to electronically alter voices, along with Barnard Taylor's and Vernell Munroe's cell phone numbers. The cell phone provider verified that she made a number of calls to both of them. And a review of Jamieson's computer records shows that he was diverting money from

Davis's and Yates's accounts into his own and Damon Long's." His face flamed red as he said the last words.

With Tony's help, Selena settled into a sitting position, the head of the bed raised to support her. He gave her an extra pillow to press against her ribs so breathing wasn't as painful, then she faced Robinette. "So one of your agents was selling information about my movements, and the other was stealing outright." And she'd never suspected a thing. She'd thought Jamieson seemed harmless, and she'd liked Gentry. She'd even begun to think of her as a friend.

"We also found records of recent bank transactions, from both Munroe's and Taylor's account to hers in the Caymans, on her laptop," Robinette went on. "A couple hundred grand from each. Who knows how much more was to come when she'd killed you?"

Selena glanced at Tony. "And Kathryn's hit man was willing to do it for five thousand."

"Kathryn's hit man was just getting rid of a minor problem in her life," Robinette explained. "Gentry was handing over control of a multimillion-dollar business."

Selena sighed. "She was going to kill me—to make it look like Yates and I took each other out. I had no choice but to shoot her."

"I figured as much." His tone was dismissive. "Did you have any idea that Sonny Yates was William's nephew?"

"I never even knew William had a nephew until a few days ago."

"Did he happen to tell you how he got involved in the family business?"

She had no answer, but Tony had a theory. "Grant said Henry never accepted Jefferson. He didn't think adoption made a stranger family, so he ignored the kid. It was a real sore point between Henry and Kathryn, and she made it a sore point for Jefferson. Presumably, working his way into an important role in Henry's business, with Henry never having a clue who he was, was Jefferson's way of thumbing his nose at his uncle."

I have more secrets than the old man could imagine, Yates had said.

"Sonny Yates is the name he was born with," Tony went on. "But Kathryn didn't think Sonny had quite the right ring for Southern aristocracy, so she changed it to Jefferson when they adopted him."

"That's why we never got any hits on Yates when we ran him through the system," Robinette mused. "He had the benefit of having two legal names. So . . ." His chilly gaze zeroed in on Selena. "Who shot Yates?"

The first of those questions she didn't have answers for— at least, not honest ones. "I did."

He rocked back on his heels. "You know, I'd like to believe that. God knows, it would be justice after the beating he gave you, and you did have gunshot residue on your hand."

Selena glanced at Tony. Clearly he knew where the agent was going with this. She had an idea herself. "But?"

"But Yates was shot from across the room. In addition to GSR, you had blood splatter and brain matter on you, which proves that you were a hell of a lot closer than forty feet. Now I know you're a fast runner, but nobody's that fast. That means you were probably only a few feet from Yates when someone else shot him."

"Who?" she asked calmly.

"That's what I'm asking you."

A stab of pain ended her shrug as soon as it started. "Check with your guards. Who was on the grounds besides the usual crew?"

"Just Yates and Grant Hamilton, and they were both negative for GSR."

"You didn't shoot him," Selena pointed out. "The guards didn't. Gentry and Jamieson didn't, and Long was busy trying to kill you. Who does that leave?"

Robinette's stare gave her that bug-under-a-microscope feeling. "You. But the evidence says you didn't shoot him, either."

"I say I did."

"But you're lying."

"I was the only one in the ballroom with Yates," she said quietly. "He tried to kill me. I shot him."

"That's your story."

"It's the truth."

He snorted at that, and Tony came close to doing the same, but stifled it. She didn't blame either of them. It was hard to tell such an obvious lie; how much harder to pretend to believe it?

For a time Robinette simply looked at her. She resisted the urge to squirm under the weight of his gaze, but looked back, wondering if her calm, serene expression was working with her battered face.

Finally, he broke off the gaze and began rocking on his heels again. "Just so you'll know, the US Attorney will probably offer Gentry a deal to testify against Taylor and Munroe. And Kathryn Hamilton freaked out so bad when she heard that Yates was dead that they had to admit her to the psych ward. She won't go to trial for a long time, if ever."

Do you have any idea how much you've cost us? Kathryn had asked the evening before. William lay in a coma. Grant had made it clear he had no further use for her. She faced spending the rest of her life locked up. She was finally having to pay for what she'd done to Selena's mother. And her son who'd meant the world to her was dead, supposedly at Selena's hand.

But none of it was Selena's fault. In the end, the blame for Kathryn's problems—as well as Selena's—led back to Kathryn herself. All she'd had to do was let Grant go. She would have gotten over him eventually, would have built a new life for herself. But no, she'd had to hold on. Love, obsession, arrogance, pride... Her selfish decision had led to such tragic consequences.

Robinette glanced at his watch. "You sure you wanna stick with the story that you killed Sonny?"

She smiled thinly. "Until you come up with proof of another shooter."

His disdain was tempered with resignation as he shook his head.

"What's next?" she asked, more to change the subject than because she cared.

"Next? You get well. You go home."

She glanced at Tony, half-afraid to believe that "home" actually meant home. "What about the case?"

"Yates is dead. Long is gone. He knows I'm involved somehow with the FBI." His scowl deepened. "We found a tape in Gentry's room of a phone call between Long and Yates's shooter. Did you have any idea that Yates's hitter was a woman?"

Keeping her expression blank, Selena shook her head. "Though I'm not surprised. William was an equal-opportunity employer."

"Huh. Anyway, we don't have a clue what information Gentry gave Taylor and Munroe. She claims it was only your movements, but she could have told them all about us. All in all, it's time to cut our losses."

"And?" she prompted. When he looked as if he had no

idea what she wanted, she said, "You can't deport me. I might have entered the country illegally, but only because I was taken from it illegally. I was born here. I belong here."

He scowled again. Maybe it was the pain affecting her, but it somehow didn't seem nearly as sincere as usual. "Yeah, yeah, welcome to America." He started to walk away, then turned and came back. "Thanks for your help."

He offered his hand, but when she laid hers in it, he didn't shake it. Instead, he gently squeezed her fingers, released her, then walked out.

When the door closed behind him, Tony lowered the bed rail and sat on the edge of the mattress, cradling her hand in both of his. Gently stroking her hand, he asked, "You want to trust me with who really killed Yates?"

"I trust you with my life." But even though he waited, she didn't offer anything else. She couldn't.

"So . . . you're a free woman. You get to go home."

She nodded. For years she'd had no home—just places she stayed before moving on. That had changed when she'd bought her house in Key West. It had become one of the most important things in her life. In the past few weeks, she'd learned a more important lesson—home wasn't necessarily a place. It could just as easily be a person. Tony was hers.

"Home," she repeated in a whisper. At the moment, she couldn't think of a lovelier word.

Leaning forward, he brushed a kiss to her cheek, another to the corner of her undamaged eye, then the tip of his tongue moistened the corner of her mouth. "I love you, babe."

She'd been wrong. Those were four lovelier words.

She curled her fingers into the fabric of his shirt and said four more lovely words. "I love you, too."

About the Author

Rachel Butler lives in Oklahoma with her husband and son, where she is at work on her next novel of romantic suspense starring Selena McCaffrey.

Don't miss

Rachel Butler's

next thrilling novel
starring Selena McCaffrey

Coming soon from Dell Books

Read on for an exclusive
sneak peek—and look for your copy
at your favorite bookseller.

Chapter One

Selena McCaffrey stood at the living room window cradling a fat black cat in her arms, her attention on the street outside. Everything was quiet. The retired couple down the block was gone in their RV, as usual. The doctor across from them never got home before six, and her lawyer-husband rarely made it before seven. Selena's own house next door was also empty. Since getting out of the hospital a month before, she'd been staying here with Tony.

His shift had ended more than an hour ago, which meant he should be home any moment. A homicide detective with the Tulsa Police Department, he still put in far more than forty hours a week, but he did much of the overtime from home these days, where he could keep an eye on her.

Her ribs twinged as the cat shifted its weight against her, reminding her that after surviving three attempts on her life in the same night, she could use an extra trained eye. Her injuries from that night had healed, or nearly so. She couldn't say the same with certainty about her relationship with Tony.

The cat stiffened an instant before a white Impala made the turn into Princeton Court. The pleasure building inside was still new enough to catch Selena's attention. When had she ever anticipated someone coming home to her? Easy answer: never.

But then, there had never been anyone like Tony Ceola in her life before.

As he turned into the driveway, she left the window for the entry hall. She punched in the code for the alarm system, opened the door, and stepped outside. The September day was hot, making the concrete beneath her bare feet toasty. The grass offered different textures but the same heat as she strolled out to meet Tony.

He was a creature of habit. His suit coat was tossed over one arm, his shirtsleeves rolled up, his tie loosened. A black attaché case, stuffed until its sides bulged, hung from one shoulder as he headed toward the mailbox at the end of the drive.

"One of these days, I'm going to get the mail before you come home," she said, digging her toes into a particularly lush patch of grass.

"And throw off my whole routine?" He glanced through the envelopes, then stuffed them inside a catalog. He'd taken a few steps toward her before changing direction. "You've got a package."

She glanced at her house and saw that there was, indeed, a box sitting on the stoop. She wasn't expecting anything, which didn't mean that Asha, who was running the art gallery during Selena's absence from Key West, hadn't sent something. "Just set it inside the door."

"Not even curious?" he asked with a grin as he climbed the steps and unlocked the door.

"Not even a—" As he opened the door, the cat leaped from her arms, landing in the grass some ten feet away, then streaking toward the house. "Kitty!" she called, but he'd already passed Tony, bumping against the box as he dashed into the house.

"Damn," Tony muttered. He left the box and ran after the cat.

The explosion shattered the afternoon, the ground shuddering, the very air vibrating with the blast. The concussion pushed against Selena, throwing her to the ground, her eyes closed, her head down against the cloud of debris following in its wake.

The tremors were dying away when she struggled to her feet, coughing, eyes watering. Most of the front central part of the house had been blown away, from the stoop all the way to the roof peak. Glass, bricks, and chunks of wood littered her driveway and yard.

"Tony...Tony!" The first came out a stunned whisper, the second a terrified scream. Ignoring the pain in her ribs, and the glass that bit into the soles of her feet, she raced across the yard. "Dear God, please..."

"Selena!" Tony's urgent cry echoed from the patio at the rear of the house. As he emerged around the side, Selena could see that a heavy layer of dust coated his hair and face and had turned the bright white of his shirt grimy. But he looked blissfully intact, as did the startled feline in his grip. "Holy shit," he muttered. "This damn cat almost got me killed."

For a moment she stared at him, then she stepped forward, cupped his face in her palms, and gave him a hard kiss. "That damn cat saved your life." She turned to look at the house. Flames were licking through the entry, dancing along the banister to the second floor and down the hall to the kitchen, sending wisps of smoke into the still-thick air. Upstairs her bedroom was tilted crazily, with much of the floor support blasted away.

Tony began brushing away the dust and a fine sprinkling of glass shards from his hair and shoulders. He handed the cat to Selena, pulled his cell phone from his belt, tried it, then tossed it aside and took out his radio. While he called in for both police and fire department assistance, one thought kept repeating in her head:

Not this. Not again.

In her game, the rules are simple:
Kill or be killed.

Find out how it all started.
Don't miss Selena McCaffrey's
explosive debut in

The Assassin

by

Rachel Butler

Available now at your
favorite bookseller

Read on for a sneak peek. . . .

THE
ASSASSIN
In her game, the rules are simple:
Kill or be killed.
“Surprise twists, fast action, and a heroine
who's positively killer with a gun!” —Lisa Gardner
RACHEL BUTLER

The Assassin

On sale now

Prologue

The attack came from behind, a muscular forearm across her throat, diminishing the oxygen supply to her lungs. Before Selena McCaffrey could react, she was lifted from her feet, then slammed to the ground. What little air she'd had left rushed out in a grunt as pain vibrated through her midsection. She pushed it out of her mind, though, and let instinct take over. As her attacker's weight came down on her, she slashed at his face with her nails and was rewarded with a sound that was half groan, half growl. He eased his hold for one instant, all she needed to arch her back and throw him off balance. With another heave, she was free of him.

As she scrambled to her feet, his fingers wrapped around her right ankle in a grip so brutal her vision turned shadowy. Clamping her jaw tight, she shifted her weight and kicked him with her left foot, a sharp jab to the ribs. He swore, yanked her leg out from under her, then rolled on top of her the instant she landed.

His face inches from hers, he laughed. "What are you gonna do, sweet pea? Huh? I'm on top. I can do whatever I want, and there's nothing you can do to stop me. You're all out of tricks, aren't you?"

Adrenaline pumped through her, along with fear and excitement. Her chest heaving, she stared at him, locking gazes. As the muscles in her right arm flexed, she eased her left hand toward the waistband of her shorts, her fingers closing around the handle of the knife tucked there. Without breaking eye contact, she raised her right hand as if to claw at his face. Laughing, he caught her wrist and forced it to the ground at her side. But before he could get out the first word about such a predictable response, she whipped the knife up in her free hand and pressed the razor-sharp blade to his throat.

He froze. Barely breathing, he murmured, "Fuck me."

"Get off me."

He hesitated. She pressed just hard enough to pierce his skin with the knife point, bringing a drop of crimson blood to the surface. His curse was vicious, but he backed away carefully.

Once he was out of her space, she easily got to her feet, folded the knife, and returned it to her waistband.

Jimmy Montoya clamped his fingers to his throat, then stared at the blood smeared across them. "You could have hurt me!"

"I *could* have killed you."

"Bitch."

"Loser." She removed the band that held back her hair— at least, what hadn't fallen loose in their struggle—then gathered the long, thick curls and corralled them with the elastic once more.

"Weapons aren't fair."

"You weigh fifty pounds more than me. I'm just evening the odds."

"What would you have done without the knife?"

She picked up a water bottle from the nearby patio table and took a long drink. "I wouldn't *be* without it."

"Humor me. Assume you were. What would you have done in that situation if you hadn't had the knife?"

Gazing out over the ocean, she considered it a moment before replying. "I suppose I would have broken your neck."

He grinned, but the amusement didn't reach his eyes. He didn't know whether she was teasing...or meant every word.

Fair enough. Neither did she.

"See you next time."

Leaning one hip against the table, Selena watched as Montoya walked inside. Through tall arched windows, she saw him stop to correct a student's posture in the ongoing yoga class, then offer encouragement to another struggling on a weight bench.

For two years she'd been coming to his gym. The word hardly did justice to the structure, or to the elaborate grounds surrounding it. Self-defense, yoga, and tai chi were taught on the lush lawn, and a jogging trail wound along the perimeter of the property. She ran five miles there every day, lifted weights three times a week, and took tae kwon do, kickboxing, and aikido classes regularly. She held a first-degree black belt in tae kwon do and could break any bone in the human body with one kick. She could have broken Montoya's ribs, and if he were an attacker, she would have.

And if that failed to get her out of the jam, well, there was always the knife.

Her own ribs ached when she pushed away from the table. She would be bruised and stiff the next day, but she'd suffered worse and survived. She was tough. She would always survive.

Instead of showering in the locker room, she grabbed her backpack and started walking the three blocks home. She should have been gone hours ago, but she'd needed one last workout with Montoya for good luck...or was it confidence?

The June sun was warm, the air heavy with the scents of the sea and the flowers that bloomed in profusion along the sidewalk—bougainvillea, jasmine, plumeria. Selena made a conscious effort not to think as she walked—to simply breathe and relax while remaining aware of her surroundings. It didn't pay to let your guard down—*ever*. That had been a painful lesson to learn.

Her house was on the ocean side of the street, though she lacked Montoya's gorgeous view except from the second floor. The structure was more than a hundred years old and had survived tropical storms, hurricane-force winds, and decades of neglect. The white paint on the boards and the dark green on the shutters had been her spring project. The new shingles on the roof, completed over the winter. The small green lawn, bordered on all sides by a cutting garden gone wild, cultivated over the past eighteen months. The picket fence that circled the lot, repaired and whitewashed last summer. The handpainted sign swinging from a post near the gate, last week's accomplishment. *Island Dreams Art Gallery.*

She had moved into the house the day she'd signed the papers, and she loved everything about it. The high ceilings, tall windows, and oversized rooms. The wide veranda wrapping around three sides, the stairs climbing straight and true to the second floor, the butler's pantry, the louvered shutters, and the dusty chandeliers. The cypress floors, the porcelain sinks, the claw-foot tub, the marble fireplaces. The age. The history. The welcome. The security.

And the fact that it was hers. The only home she'd ever had. The only thing of value she'd ever possessed. One of only two things she could *not* afford to lose. Her home. Her freedom. Everything she was, everything she might ever be, depended on those two things. Protecting them protected *her.*

An older couple, white-haired and tanned, was coming down the steps as she approached. She greeted them, then opened the screen door with a creak. What had originally been the formal living and dining rooms was now home to her gallery. The library had become the gallery office, leaving only the kitchen and pantry to their original purposes. A mere half dozen of her own paintings were currently exhibited, along with bins of signed and numbered prints. Of all the artists represented in Island Dreams, her own work was most popular with her clientele. But that stood to reason. If they didn't like Selena McCaffrey's paintings, they wouldn't shop at Selena McCaffrey's gallery.

Asha Beauregard, her only employee, was chatting with another customer. She gave Selena a wave behind the man's back. Asha liked to say that she couldn't draw a straight line to save her life, but she knew talent when she saw it. The gallery was in good hands.

Selena detoured through the kitchen to get another bottle of water, then took the back stairs to her bedroom. Originally there had been four rooms and a bath upstairs. Now there were two—a large living room at the front of the house, with enough space for a workout when Montoya's seemed too far to go, and an airy bed/bath combination. She'd lived too much of her life in cramped, dark places. Now she liked large spaces, lots of glass, a sense of openness.

After showering, she dressed in a silk outfit, the top crimson and fitted, the color repeated in the tropical print of the skirt. The hem fluttered around her ankles except on the left side, where it was slit halfway up her thigh. Her suitcases were already packed, with just one bag left. She laid it open on the plantation-style bed, unlocked the small safe in the back of the closet, then began transferring the necessary items.

A Smith & Wesson .40 caliber pistol, illegally modified to fully automatic.

A compact Beretta .22 automatic, small enough to fit in her pocket or her smallest handbag.

A dagger, sheathed to protect the double-edged blade. The switchblade she carried had been chosen as much for concealability as function. The dagger had been chosen strictly for function.

She added extra clips for each of the guns, a change of IDs, and a stash of cash. It wasn't a lot, but in an emergency, she didn't need a lot.

Not that she was planning on having any emergencies.

She closed and locked the bag, then slid it inside the suitcase she'd left half empty for just that purpose. After securing the key on the chain around her neck so that it rested out of sight between her breasts, she picked up the suitcases and started for the stairs. She probably looked like any young woman setting off on vacation.

In fact, she was going to kill a man.